'Howlingly funny ... wickedly amusing ... does for contemporary journalism what Tom Sharpe did for Oxbridge with *Porterhouse Blue*' *Literary Review*

'Savage jokes and farce ... high entertainment in this burlesque by an old Fleet Street hand' *Sunday Telegraph*

'Lively and entertaining satire' *Mail on Sunday*

'Sex scandals involving high-ranking politicians, chequebook-waving tabloid journalists, newspaper proprietors engaged in vicious circulation wars – Tim Heald's ebullient comedy about Fleet Street has them all' *The Times*

'A riotous comic novel' *UK Press Gazette*

'Very funny ... Heald succeeds in making his righteous anger at the press and proprietors he has served as entertaining as it is instructive' *International Herald Tribune*

By the same author

Fiction

Unbecoming Habits
Blue Blood Will Out
Deadline
Let Sleeping Dogs Die
Just Desserts
Murder at Moose Jaw
Caroline R
Masterstroke
Class Distinctions
Red Herrings
Brought to Book
The Rigby File (ed)
Business Unusual
A Classic English Crime (ed)
A Classic Christmas Crime (ed)

Non-fiction

It's a Dog's Life
John Steed, the Authorised Biography Vol 1
HRH The Man Who Would be King (with Mayo Mohs)
Networks
The Character of Cricket
The Newest London Spy (ed)
By Appointment – 150 Years of the Royal Warrant and Its Holders
My Lord's (ed)
The Duke – a Portrait of Prince Philip
Honourable Estates
A Life of Love – The Life of Barbara Cartland
Denis – The Authorised Biography of the Incomparable Compton
Brian Johnston – The Authorised Biography
Beating Retreat – Hong Kong Under the Last Governor

Tim Heald's first foray into journalism was in his teens when he was a founding editor of *Sixth Form Opinion*. He was on the *Sunday Times* in the sixties, the *Daily Express* in the seventies and since then has freelanced for practically everyone. He lives in Cornwall, but wrote much of this novel while Visiting Fellow at Jane Franklin Hall in the University of Tasmania. Like Fisher he is wary of marketing men, accountants, lawyers, millionaires and people who eat lunch at their desks.

STOP PRESS

Tim Heald

ORION

An Orion Paperback
First published in Great Britain by
Weidenfeld & Nicolson in 1998
This paperback edition published in 1999 by
Orion Books Ltd,
Orion House, 5 Upper St Martin's Lane,
London WC2H 9EA

Copyright © 1998 Tim Heald

The right of Tim Heald to be identified as the author of
this work has been asserted by him in accordance with the
Copyright, Designs and Patents Act 1988.

A CIP catalogue record for this book
is available from the British Library.

ISBN 0 75282 701 4

Printed and bound in Great Britain by
The Guernsey Press Co. Ltd, Guernsey, C.I.

For
Hawthornden Castle
and
Jane Franklin Hall

CONTENTS

1	Unfit to print	1
2	A legible condition	5
3	Oh why, oh why, oh why?!	13
4	Sources close to the chest	20
5	Off the record	26
6	A frank and cordial exchange	37
7	He was unmarried	43
8	No holds barred exclusive	49
9	A government spokesman said ...	56
10	Resigned to spend more time with ...	62
11	Famous last words	69
12	Inside information	76
13	Windsock error	82
14	Special report	88
15	The man in the know	94
16	Consenting adult entertainment	103
17	A brief chapter of errors	109
18	Prime suspect	111
19	Foreign body	120
20	Chinese whispers	127
21	Hidden agenda	133
22	The harlot's prerogative	141
23	Legendary lunch(eon)	149
24	Cleansing the palate	153
25	Freedom of the press	160
26	A foreign affair	168
27	An editor writes	173
28	Unbeatable value	178
29	Doing their duty-free	187
30	Pass the sick bag	199
31	Slow news day – nothing to report	212

32 Dancing in the street(s)   219
33 Not up for it   225
34 Brief encounter   231
35 Not many dead   238
36 Sick as parrots   246
37 Good friends share a joke   253
38 File soonest: copy urgently required!!   260
39 Trunk calls   266
40 Post-mortem, ad astra   275

UNFIT TO PRINT

There are many ways to be sacked: hands-on; hands-off; brutal; bathetic; the public defenestration; the private stiletto between the shoulder-blades; the smiling breakfast; the scowling, stand-up, this-hurts-me-more-than-it-hurts-you, not-even-a-plastic-mug-of-coffee; the early retirement; the compulsory redundancy; the making way for a younger man; the wanting to spend more time with the family; the sideways shove; the hoist upstairs; the hangman's drop; the cushioned pension; the week's notice and clear-your-desk; the long ostracising squeeze of neglect; the karate chop of confrontation.

Some bosses sack like snakes; others as if they were baboons. There are those who hate the act and in doing so botch the execution and make the torture worse; there are others who revel in it and enjoy the victim's screams. Some can; some can't. Some do; some don't.

In the world of newspapers the sack comes sooner or later to everyone, though such is the vainglorious nature of the inky trade that living legends believe that last lunch-times never come.

Fisher had never been a legend. Lunch, certainly. He came from a generation reared on midday meals taken at leisure. Even if soup was missed out one ate a meat and two vegetable main course and a solid pudding. After puberty, alcohol and coffee were tacked on as necessary appendages. At Fisher's preparatory school it had been customary to suck a sweet after lunch and sit down for twenty minutes or so with a good book. It was matron's belief, shared by the headmaster, that this was good for body and soul. After lunch and rest came games. *Mens sana in corpore sano*. Or words to that effect.

For the last five years Fisher had been Literary Editor of the *Conscience*. There was nothing very literary about the *Conscience* and what little there was diminished daily. It had not always been like that. One of the reasons he had originally joined the paper was that it had a bookish quality he found agreeable. In those days the paper had been owned by a Quaker family trust. The family may have been bookish but they were not commercial. There was a hostile take-over and words, let alone books, began to beat a retreat. A few weeks ago Fisher had been told that a survey demonstrated that more than three quarters of the readership thought the paper was devoting too much space to book reviews. Fisher protested to the Editor that book review space had been more than halved in the last couple of years.

"Precisely," said the Editor. "That's what they're trying to tell us. And what I'm trying to tell you." This was only part of the truth. Although William Pool was described as the Editor, he was the Editor only in name and subject to all number of forces, the greatest of which was represented by his proprietor, Kenneth Lee, better known as Chinese Ken. Chinese Ken liked to boast that he had never read a book in his life. Despite being a newspaper proprietor he seldom read more than the headlines of his products. His only real reading was balance sheets. Ken was a past master at the balance sheet.

Years earlier, when they worked together on the Diary, Fisher and the Editor used to drink together, though even then little Pool only drank because it was the done thing. He was a sipper not a slurper. And, in deference to the times and to the image required of him, he had become an esoteric mineral water man.

Nowadays Fisher tended to drink alone.

Fisher liked language. Part of his reason for entering journalism was that he adored the noise words made. He wasn't especially enamoured of the message but he loved being massaged by the medium. It was like Church. If God existed, which he very much doubted, then he was the school bully not the headmaster. On the other hand his cohorts made a good din. You couldn't beat a candle-lit "Nunc Dimittis" in a first-division cathedral at Evensong.

There was a message for him on his screen when he returned for the afternoon's labour. It was from his erstwhile friend, little Pool, requiring his presence. Fisher had only just managed to learn how to tap into his screen and read the messages. Until recently much of office life had passed him by for this reason. He was suspicious of the so-called "new technology" and he was proud of his failure to master it. There was no soul in a computer and he could make no music with a keyboard.

He was depressed, therefore, to find the Editor, staring at his screen, oblivious, apparently, of his entry.

Pool frowned. "I've got a message from the Proprietor," he said. "It says 'In order to meet the demands of flatter organisational structures in the face of increasing market imperatives we are having to reassess our strategic imperatives which means, in the interests of downsizing, that we're offering one or two privileged personnel a personal premature exit agreement.'" He looked up and smiled wanly. "Your name is at the top of the list."

"I'm sorry," said Fisher wearily. "I didn't understand a word of that."

Pool looked sheepish. "No," he said. "Weasel words, I'm afraid. It just means you're fired. I'm sorry, I really am. He wants you out by close of play. Clear your desk by six. Personnel will sort out some kind of compensation. Not a lot, I fear. It might help to have a good lawyer, but I wouldn't bank on it. Mr Lee didn't get where he is by being generous. If I were you I'd take what you're offered and leave gracefully."

"Is that it?" asked Fisher.

"I'm terribly afraid so," said the Editor, who had once seemed such a different sort of animal. "Never mind. I expect it's for the best. You haven't really seemed entirely yourself recently. I expect you'll be happier doing something different. Try to be positive about it. I envy you in many ways. I sometimes wonder where my spare time went." And he gave a croaky little laugh and frowned back into his machine.

Fisher didn't even bother to say goodbye, just went away to clear his desk and see how many remaining review copies he could take with him to flog to some second-hand dealer. "Such is life," he thought, seeming to remember that Ned Kelly, the Australian in the iron mask, had said much the same as he ascended the scaffold and contemplated the noose.

"Famous last words," he mused. Well, he was buggered if he'd had his last word yet.

2

A LEGIBLE CONDITION

The Editor of the *Daily Intelligence* was entertaining the new feature writer with a nightcap in the flat on the seventh floor. "You don't mind champagne?" he asked, pouring Clicquot into two large flutes.

"I adore champagne," said the new girl, smiling and fluttering in the prescribed manner of the best of the smoking bimbos. In fact she had graduated from Christ Church with first class honours in English and she had coxed the Oxford eight in the University Boat Race. She may have been called Fiona or Felicity and had long legs, trim waist, high cheek-bones and a generous mouth, but that didn't make her brainless and beddable. Nor was she *that* new. She had spent eighteen very boring months composing mindless paragraphs about minor celebrities for the paper's vapid gossip column. At the *Intelligence* this was still described as the "Diary". Fiona (or Felicity) supposed that this was designed to make it seem respectable. Certainly it was dinned into them that the paper's "diarists" were a cut above other papers' "gossip columnists". She did not feel this made her respectable. Only dull.

Even so, the Editor was the Editor and she was only the newish recruit. She understood the conventions.

"If ever", said the Editor, "you want to have a bit of peace and quiet, this is always here. Just tip me the wink and I'll make sure there's a corner where you can, er, curl up and concentrate." He smiled, moustaches levitating, bristling above lubricious lips.

The seventh-floor flat was one of many anachronisms in the *Intelligence* building. The whole of the rest of Fleet Street had dispersed to glass and concrete tower blocks far from London's centre where they squatted in miserable isolation, cosseted by carpet and abundant rubber plants, relying on e-mail, the Internet and CNN for information from the outside world. Proprietors such as Chinese Ken did not like their staff leaving the office. There was no need and it cost money. The *Intelligence*, on the other hand, preferred to think that it was still part of the real world.

The new newspaper offices, even those of the self-consciously vulgar *Noise*, were alcohol-free zones with vast open-plan working areas which made anything illicit or clandestine supposedly out of the question. By contrast the "quality" *Intelligence* hung on in its original Victorian Gothick building, a warren of tiny private offices and thick oak doors behind which God knows what went on. The paper itself closely resembled the voice of God, thundering out a message of decency and common sense, completely eschewing any mention of Australian soap opera stars or Californian serial divorcees and generally upholding traditional British virtues which went out with the ark – or at least with the Swinging Sixties. But in the *Intelligence* offices themselves anything went. *Intelligence* "reporters" (older members of staff still used that archaic term) regarded themselves as the descendants of the ancient legends of Fleet Street – those household bylines who swaggered across the nation's breakfast tables in battered trilbies, belted macintoshes and who carried full flasks at their hips and empty cheque-books in the inside breast pockets of their shiny grey suits.

The seventh-floor flat had been the White-Lewises' family eyrie since they acquired the paper for next to nothing in the early years of the Depression. A Mr White and a Mr Lewis had worked a neat flanker on the derelict Proprietor of what was then a floundering low-circulation rag, catering to the servants of the *nouveaux riches*. In the 1930s this was a dying circulation. White and Lewis were originally in trade – one a grocer and one an Australian draper, and they knew this. Having got hold of the *Intelligence* they remarketed it. "Marketing" was an unknown word in those simple days but this is what they did, aiming the paper unerringly at the middle and lower-middle classes, and particularly those members of it who combined pretension with stupidity and prudishness with prurience. Despite the pompous Gothick type of its title and the unsensational, not to say boring, nature of its lay-out and typography, the *Intelligence* was on occasion a jolly rude newspaper – particularly when it came to the reporting of court cases. It ran an especially juicy line in divorces and was wonderfully good at humbug, reporting sexual crimes and misdemeanours in the most lurid detail, while simultaneously denouncing them in pithy, no-nonsense editorials. Called upon to defend this double standard, the *Intelligence*'s Proprietors responded with the proud maxim of Mr Pecksniff himself: "I may be a Hypocrite, but I am not a Brute."

It came as no surprise when, in an unashamedly dynastic move, Mr White's son, Hubert, married Mr Lewis's daughter, Beatrice. Lady Beatrice's father went on to become the first Earl of Barossa, founder of the first daily newspaper in South Australia. He was said once to have employed Rupert Murdoch's father as a copy boy. Lady Beatrice's great-great-grandfather had been transported to Van Diemen's Land for stealing a cabbage in the 1830s. Or so it was put about. On the whole she mentioned this as little as possible. Certainly she had long ago shed the slightest hint of an Australian accent or indeed an Australian anything else. She was universally accepted as dyed-blue-in-the-wool British. Pure Pom. The union proved unexpectedly happy and produced three sons – Gordon, Ronald and Colin, the eldest of whom was the man now flourishing the champagne bottle in the seventh-floor flat. He was the "Editor" but although this implied that he was riding the horse it was universally recognised that his ancient mother still held the reins.

"Well, Fiona," he said, "here's to a great future with the *Intelligence*."

"Felicity," said Felicity, obediently raising her glass. She was a terrible tease. If he had called her Felicity she would have said she was Fiona.

"Felicity," agreed the Editor, apparently unfazed. He invariably got his employees' names wrong and tended to refer to them, with a wave of the hand, as "Thingy". Thus, "Has Thingy filed from Kazakhstan yet?" Or, "I thought Thingy's leader on prescription charges was first-rate."

"You're settling in OK then?" He smiled in what he hoped was an avuncular manner.

"Oh, yes thank you, sir," she said, hoping she sounded girlish and wondering how long this was going to take because she'd had a perfectly bloody day, frankly, and her boy-friend, Bob, who worked in corporate finance at one of the unpronounceable Japanese merchant banks, was always really really sulky when she got back late.

"Oh, do please forget the formality. We're out of the office now." He gave a self-deprecating little shake of the head, a gesture much imitated down below where he was known, behind his back, by any number of names, none of them nice. Officially he liked, in the style of great national institutions, to be addressed by his proper title. After all, he reasoned, Members of Parliament always said "Mr Speaker" when talking to the man in charge at the House. Staff at proper public schools (to one of which he, maddeningly, did not go) called the boss, "Headmaster" and Army officers would salute and spit out such preposterous sentences as "Permission to Fall Out, Field Marshal". He should know, since he retained the title "Major" and used it, just like his brothers. There was much merry banter in the newspaper world about what sort of regiment they had been majors in and he never talked about his military career, always making out that this was due to modesty. "Certain things a chap doesn't discuss, don't you know?" Some years earlier the paper's Military Correspondent had checked the Ministry of Defence archive at Hayes and discovered that the "Major" had failed his commission board and seen out his time as a corporal in the Education Corps. The correspondent had been fired and, ever since, the jokes had been told circumspectly and behind closed doors and the backs of hands.

"Oh, right," said Felicity, suppressing a desire to giggle or to irritate him by calling him sir. She was damned if she was going to call him "Major" let alone "Gordon". It would only encourage him.

"I thought your piece on condoms was jolly good," he said. A new shop had opened in Oxford Street called Condomania. It was said that it was to be the first in a chain of such places. Felicity had written eight hundred saucy words laced with such remarks as "What the well-dressed man is wearing" and "Not exactly calculated to tickle your fancy". It had appeared under the heading "Coming to the AIDS of the Party" and there had been some furious letters from Gordon's fellow "majors" in the world outside. The new feature writer was of the opinion that "major"

8

was not so much a rank as a state of mind. Bob,
had been so incensed that he had even proposed
would prevent her working for what he called,
fashioned scorn worthy of a retired major himself,
Gordon justified the article on the grounds that "health
is an important part of the paper's public duty".

"Thank you," she said.

"I thought the musical ones sounded jolly funny. 'She'll be coming round the mountain!' Eh?! And the one with the bells. 'Jingle bells, jingle bells, jingle all the way!' Jolly uncomfortable though, wouldn't you say? Doing it with bells on I mean."

Felicity managed a very stiff smile. Brenda, the Editor's secretary, had said not to worry, Major Gordon never pounced at the first encounter in the flat. It was something to do with his keenness on cricket. "Everyone should be allowed a dolly first ball," he apparently said. "After that a chap's duty is to bowl as many maidens over as possible. Ha! Ha! Ha!"

The Editor coughed, a stage gesture designed to convey a return to seriousness. No longer the jocund jester but the man of the world, seen it all before, Editor of national daily, knighthood imminent, important, old enough to be your father, deeply concerned for welfare of troops and all that. "So they're looking after you? Making you feel at home?"

The flat was panelled in a smoky nut-brown plastic designed to suggest nostalgia and mahogany. The drawing-room in which this sad little tryst was taking place was hung with portraits of old *Intelligence* men and even the odd woman. The sofas were leathery but cushioned, deep and comfortable in the manner of the casting couch. Lighting subdued, nothing overhead, table lamps, brackets, all very subtle in a clubland hero sort of way.

"Yes, everyone's been very kind."

This was not very true. The other women tended to be resentful. So did the men, with the complication that most of them seemed to be potential date-rapers, gropers or the sort of sexual harassers who make anatomical observations by the coffee machine.

"I'm delighted to hear it." The Major came and sat on the sofa next to her. Too close for comfort. She edged off but not before he had managed a hand on the knee. In court he would have attempted to pass it off as an asexual avuncular gesture of no significance. She, though, doubted he would get away with it. However, he backed off a little. "It's always been *Intelligence* y to seek out the brightest and the best, and to hire them as early as possible," he said. "We have high hopes of you."

This was not very true either, at least not as far as Felicity could see. The *Intelligence* appeared to be staffed by a mixture of elderly unsackable men in shiny suits and women like her who had been taken on because of some network connection involving family or school, bolstered with the tantalising whiff of possible sexual congress. She knew perfectly well that the highest hope the Editor had of her was getting her into bed. The Majors were not alone among newspaper editors and proprietors in trying to exercise droit de seigneur, but they tried harder than most. They were also not above passing their mistresses on to one another when they grew bored.

Felicity, whose job stemmed from the fact that her father belonged to the same club – the Revellers – as Major Gordon, was not at all sure she was going to succumb. The rot had to stop somewhere and she didn't see why it shouldn't be with her. "I have high hopes too," she said. At least the champagne was acceptable. She wondered how long it would be before she could go home.

The Major clearly sensed that sexual assault should be delayed. He had gone through smutty talk and hand on knee, and that was probably enough for now. He had better retrench with a display of taking her jolly seriously as a real human being and not just the latest bit of fluff. "What are you working on at the moment?" he enquired.

She frowned. The *Intelligence* was a daily paper. Journalists clocked in half-way through the morning, then waited to be given something to do by some desk-wallah. The desk men invariably had their ideas or received their information later than they should. Or communicated the idea later than they should because they'd been in the pub, or were interrupted by a telephone call, or had just plain forgotten. The *Intelligence* was produced on the basis of short-term reflex reaction under conditions of barely controlled chaos. Felicity did not know what the Editor could possibly mean. She worked through her shift and then she clocked off. End of story. "How do you mean?" she asked, trying not to sink back into the sofa which was over-accomodating.

"Long-term project. Hasn't thingy given you a long-term project to get your pretty little teeth into?" He bared his own, which were large, ugly and stained with years of nicotine. He was a cheroot man.

"No, I'm afraid not."

"Ah, well, we must remedy that. I'll have a word with him in the morning. Get you stuck into some sort of series." He set down his glass and rummaged for his notepad, which emerged eventually from his jacket pocket in elegant alligator with gold corners. In it he wrote, "Set up long-term project for new girl." "There," he said, smirking. "We'll soon sort something out. I should like to see you doing something really worthwhile. We need to make use of that brain of yours. No point in hiring graduates with first class degrees unless you bloody well use them. That's what I keep trying to drum into the senior executives. What we want from people like you is the sort of thing which makes news and doesn't just reflect it. That's one of the things we pride ourselves on at the *Intelligence*. We don't just react to the news like the rest of Fleet Street, we actually *make* it. We set the agenda, as the phrase has it."

"Good policy," said Felicity, with a hint of irony which made her Editor surprise himself with a ratty glance of suspicion. Not that he was too worried. All women were bimbos at heart, as he knew from a lifetime seeking to prove it. This one would be no exception, whatever her so-called academic pretensions.

"What sort of thing had you in mind?" Felicity realised that a display of enthusiasm was called for, however tepid it might sound.

"Er ..." The Editor was evidently caught on the hop. "Bimbos," he said, since that was the word on his mind at the moment. "That is to say" – he flushed – "the place of the modern woman in contemporary society. Someone like yourself, for instance. We need to appeal to people like yourself. That's why we hired you. I envisage a major series, maybe even five parts if it works out, on the place of the modern woman in, er, the nineties. The post-pill years; the threat of AIDS; the battle of the sexes; is there such a thing as the 'New Man'? All that sort of stuff. Written by someone like you, it could be absolutely fascinating. We'll go to town on the promotion ... hoardings, billboards ... blurb you all over the place."

Felicity sighed. Was this what she had struggled through Middle English and post-structural semiotics for? Was this why she had read *The Battle of Maldon* and *Clarissa*?

She was saved by the bell. Actually it was too sibillant for a proper bell but that was still what one called the thing that made the noise when a telephone rang. Perhaps she ought to suggest some thoughts on the inappropriateness of the word to Trotter, the man who wrote the weekly witter on the English Language, Correct Use of. Trotter could bash out five hundred words on bells and telephones in half an hour, drunk or sober. Better drunk than sober, but five hundred words either way.

"Major Gordon," said Major Gordon flicking a switch which activated what he called "some sort of loudspeaker contraption" and enabled him to carry on telephonic communication without having to pick up the receiver.

"It's Alastair Ross here, sir." The dour Scots drone of the Night News Editor filled the drawing-room, "We've just had the first edition of the *Noise* in and they've led with 'PM IN GAY SEX SCANDAL'."

"You what!?" The Editor was suddenly extremely agitated.

"Gay sex scandal, sir. The PM."

"Bugger!"

"Looks awfully like it, sir!"

Felicity tittered.

3

OH WHY, OH WHY, OH WHY?!

L ike his counterpart at the *Intelligence* the Editor of the *Noise* was also pouring champagne, but under slightly different circumstances, in slightly different surroundings and with a slightly different touch.

"Fucking bloody brilliant, my son," shouted Sir Edward White, shaking a magnum of Moët and firing the cork at a point about six inches above the naked pink scalp of his News Editor, Albert van Blanco. Wine spewed out of the bottle, showering Albert and his expensive, tight-fitting football player's suiting.

Albert had letters tattooed on the fingers of his left hand, wore a diver's wrist-watch guaranteed to keep perfect time 20,000 leagues under the sea and was believed to have done time in Wandsworth and Chelmsford prisons for Grievous Bodily Harm. "Fucking bloody brilliant, boss," he agreed, grabbing another bottle from the bar top and shaking it vigorously. Both men used the "f"word with depressing regularity, though it was never allowed to appear in even the most salacious story in the *Noise*. If it *did* appear it was bowdlerised with asterisks. No one quite knew why the word could appear in its entirety in a "serious" broadsheet but not in a "vulgar" tabloid. Not that it was a question which greatly exercised either Eddie White or Albert van Blanco. Unlike Fisher, they took no pleasure in words, regarding them simply as a necessary means to a lucrative end.

This convivial celebratory scene was taking place in the office pub. In pre-revolutionary times all the great national newspapers had had their own licensed premises nestling in the lee of the ground-floor print rooms, where the great rotary presses had pounded away producing the product – as today's generation of executives were inclined to call what in old days was known as a "newspaper". Now that they had dispersed to cheaper parts of the city, this was one of the very few traditions which had been maintained. "Management", a euphemism meaning "them", aware that the workers did not relish finding themselves in dismal reclaimed bombsites entirely devoid of civilised distractions, had created a series of brand-new hostelries in which their employees could, in the very few minutes of free time allowed them, forget themselves with a bowl of chili and a white-wine spritzer. Shades of Omar Khayyám.

The *Noise*, *Daily* and *Sunday*, shared its compound with its sister papers, the up-market *Daily* and *Sunday Conscience*, also owned, of course, by the shadowy, if not shady, Mr Lee. "Chinese Ken" claimed to be "as English as you or me", but he was short, fat, yellow and had what the Duke of Edinburgh might have called "slitty eyes". He had also accumulated a fortune in Hong Kong. This was variously supposed to have been based on drugs, prostitution, gambling, or plastic flowers. Probably all four.

Despite sharing this isolated and hideous territory on the South Bank of the Thames at what had once been the Old Pagoda Dock, all four newspapers had their own individual pubs. These were not a lot more than glorified office canteens with booze, but each one was personal to its own paper. The hacks who hung out in them always hailed from the pub's own paper and never the twain did meet.

The *Noise*'s hostelry was a converted paddle steamer christened with the fearsome winsomeness of the chain who held the concession The Barque up the Wrong Tree. It was never, naturally, known as this but was variously called the "Barqueing Mad", the "Barker Bit" or "Fred's", after its proprietor, a dapper ex-airline steward who had served in a Fleet Street wine bar when Fleet Street was Fleet Street.

"Worth every penny." Sir Edward glugged a mouthful of the fizzy stuff from the bottle and wiped his lips with the back of his hand.

The *Noise* prided itself on being the most democratic – and demotic – paper in Britain. Its favourite phrase was "The people of

Britain". In real life, however, it was ruthlessly hierarchic. The Editor and his News Editor were not visible to the rest of the staff because they were in what – predictably – was called the "Captain's Cabin". In olden days this might have been known as the directors' dining-room. Very few people had the key to it and the key was in the Editor's gift. He could bestow and he could unbestow without reference to anyone, not even to Chinese Ken. Below the Captain's Cabin there were several layers, until one got to "Steerage", also known as the "Poop Deck". This was for secretaries and messengers.

"Twenty five thou." Van Blanco swigged from his bottle in slavish imitation of his boss. "Little rent boy never saw so much dosh in his life".

"You know" – Sir Edward placed a hand on his subordinate's champagne-damp shoulder – "it's moments like this that make the whole fucking thing worthwhile. Know what I mean? All those years of doorstepping in the wet and the cold, all those years sitting and waiting for something to bloody well happen, all those years of telephoning deadbeat rock stars and back-bench MPs and brown-nosing the bastards just to get them to utter one single lousy boring little sentence so that you can write out 'Madonna told the *Noise* late last night' or 'Sir Gerald Nabarro said . . .'. All that crap is justified by a moment like this. I mean how many people do you know, other than Fidel Castro or Yeltsin, who have actually overthrown a government. Come on? Eh? How many? Be honest."

"You reckon we *have* overthrown a government?"

"Yup. They'll never survive this. The Prime Minister *and* his Parliamentary Private Secretary. And we've got letters, photographs and a signed and witnessed affidavit. He can't get out of this one. Creep."

Sir Edward had received his knighthood as the result of favours rendered to one of the present Premier's predecessors. Despite frantic efforts to ingratiate himself with the new man Sir Edward did not seem to have made much impression. The old days of popping into Number Ten for an intimate little chat, of taking the Roller down to Chequers for cosy country weekends and running long exclusive prime ministerial interviews conducted by yours truly had gone. Or gone, at least, until the new Premier was got rid of.

So Editor Eddie had a motive for shafting the PM and when this exceedingly nasty piece of work came in off the street with his grubby bundle of incriminating evidence he had jumped at the opportunity. The nasty piece of work had been taken away for a very thorough piece of debriefing by Sharon and Stan, referred to as "My two best men" by Sir Edward. Then the Probe Team had swung into action. The Probe Team of the *Noise* was feared and envied by hard-nosed tabloid-type hacks throughout the world. A more ruthless collection of dustbin scavengers, long-lens paparazzi, bribers and fixers did not exist outside government intelligence agencies and the ranks of organised crime. That, at least, was the myth. No one had the confidence or the resources to doubt it. Within a fortnight the Probe Team had taken the information from the informer, added it to the extra stuff gleaned by Sharon and Stan, and put together a detailed dossier of the Prime Minister's misdemeanours.

It had not, to be honest, been difficult. Either the PM believed himself to be above the law and immune from public scandal, or he actually wanted to be caught out. Or that's how it seemed.

His PPS, Kim Sanderson-Wright, was a limp individual generally regarded as being wet enough to shoot snipe off. Divorced from his first wife, he would never have rated in the top hundred sexiest members at Westminster, no matter which proclivity was under discussion. Not interested, would have been the general assessment. He was a useful spare man for dinner parties in the constituency and liked to give the impression – albeit half-heartedly – that he had an occasional fling with a researcher or secretary. But he was not thought of as sex-driven.

The PM, Bryan Sutton, the Rt. Hon. Member for Sheen, was a different proposition. Like so many modern politicians he had built much of his career on the most sanctimonious flaunting of his supposedly text-book happy heterosexual family life. Wife, son, both daughters and even the labrador were on permanent parade. They appeared in all his campaign literature. References to them splattered his public utterances and they accompanied him on platforms and in magazine articles, always clean, smiling, wholesome and above all together. They were *"The Family"* made flesh, writ large, vote winners for the silent majority.

For a man such as Sir Edward White, they were a permanent provocation. "Smug bastard," he said to van Blanco. "We're well shot of him."

There had been several different addresses. One was Sanderson-

Wright's own London apartment. Another was the country house of a minor peer well known for his contribution to party funds. Others were service flats taken on short lets, sometimes by foreigners. Comings and goings at several of these places had been scrupulously logged by the Probe Team, but the clincher was that the nasty piece of work, now safely hidden abroad out of harm's way, had provided recognisable photographs of recognisable people, including Sanderson-Wright and his boss without a lot of clothes on, doing the sort of things to each other which could not be much more than hinted at even in a paper as shrill as the *Noise*.

The letters were the final straw. The Editor had caused them to be checked with the country's leading handwriting experts and after comparing them with independent examples of the two men's script they were unanimous. The Prime Minister was Piglet and Sanderson-Wright was Pooh and it was all deeply embarrassing.

"My darling Pooh, Never mind about the horrid man. Let us forget all about him for tonight we frolic. Ever thine, Piglet."

"Dearest Piglet, Let's get away even if only for a few sweet hours. Eeyore has invited us and we can plead pressure of work! Hugs and kisses from your Pooh."

Van Blanco burped. "Did you tell Chinese Ken you were running it tomorrow?"

"There are times, Albert, when it's better not to tell one's Proprietor anything at all. Ken's an excellent boss, but this could embarrass him in public. He'll love it in private. But in public he's got to wring his hands. He'll do it with a damn sight more conviction if it all comes as a bit of a shock. He's got to be able to look poor old Bryan baby straight in the eye and say, 'Honest guv, nothing to do with me. I have no control over my editors. I never interfere with my papers. So help me God.' "

"Got to live with his conscience too."

"There is that as well." Sir Eddie smirked. Van Blanco didn't mean conscience with a small "c" since this, as they both knew perfectly well, was something Chinese Ken would barely recognise even when confronted with Mother Teresa. Instead he meant the *Conscience* Editor-in-Chief, William Pool, the most sanctimonious, self-satisfied man in a world where the last of these qualities at least had long ago reached plague proportions. All newspaper editors believed that in some mystic way they spoke for the British people but the Editor of the *Conscience* did not just speak for what the people thought but also for what they *ought* to think. William

Pool was more pleased with himself than anyone had a right to be. He was also a lay reader, prompting van Blanco to remark, predictably, that he was "the lousiest lay in London". He was the last editor in Britain to kill stories on grounds of what, with a quaint, anachronistic, superior smile, he liked to call "taste". His favourite line on these occasions was, "I hardly think this will quite do." This particular sentence did, however, have Maginot qualities when confronted with an opposing view from his boss. "Ah yes, Proprietor," he would say, wringing his hands, "I hadn't thought of that. How wise, how very wise."

"I'm looking forward to Just William's leader," said Sir Eddie. "Bet you a tenner he'll manage to 'utterly and totally condemn slur and innuendo and intrusion into the private lives of bla bla . . .' without ever telling his poor bloody readers what the 'slur and innuendo and intrusion' actually is. Which means that tens of thousands of *Conscience* readers are going to be steaming in to Mr Patel's and asking for the *Noise*."

" 'Swottitsallabht, innit?' " said van Blanco rhetorically.

The two men nodded and drank to the unquestioned wisdom of this verdict when there was a sharpish knocking at the door of the Captain's Cabin.

"Yup," said Sir Eddie in his best, decisive, senior-executive, hold-the-front-page, I'm-in-charge voice.

"It's Stan and Sharon," said the *Noise*'s best man. (Stan had once, for a few brief weeks, written a column headed "The Voice of the *Noise*" but even Eddie White recognised this was going too far.)

The two star reporters entered, looking flushed and dishevelled. They were a sexual as well as a professional item and it looked to the experienced eyes of their superiors as if they had been celebrating the night's great scoop with what Albert in his old-fashioned way still referred to as "a bit of nookie". He had even installed a regular spot in the Diary headed "A bit of Nookie" and subtitled "Who's bonking who?" but since the entire Diary column, and up to a point the entire paper, was devoted to this single evidently irresistible theme the bonk slot died along with the "Voice of the *Noise*".

"You have to fly by the seat of your pants in this game," Sir Eddie always told him. "Keep surprising the reader. Always try for something new." He offered the newcomers a bottle of champagne. "Have a snort of bubbly," he said. "You deserve it."

"Don't mind if I do, darling," said Sharon. "We thought you'd be in here so we came right over to tell you about the new development."

"New development?"

"We've just had 'Boy' Perryman on the blower. Incanbloody-descent." Stan liked to boast of his English degree and was expert with long words extended – in an old *Noise* tradition – by breaking them up with expletives. Boy Perryman was the PM's Press Secretary, a smooth Whitehall and Advertising Agency amalgam with a plausible manner and a silky way of knifing his enemies in the press.

"I'd hardly expect him to be over the moon," said the Editor, "What's his line, then? I should have thought he'd be better off drafting a clever statement or buttering up the Privacy Committee. No point coming to see us. The horses have bolted. I'm not going to close any stable doors now."

Stan grinned uneasily. "What he actually said was that two can play at this game. He says that he's got stuff that'll blow the bows off our sneakers and if we don't retract like right now it'll be all over Breakfast TV, every channel. Et cetera et cetera."

"Bluff," said Sir Eddie. But he was looking shifty. "He can't have got anything ... Can he?"

"We'll soon see," said Stan. "He'll be here in half an hour. If you ask me he's got something on Chinese Ken."

"Shit!" said Sir Eddie. "That's all we need."

A sudden gust of wind whistled through the rigging up above and made the barque shudder as a wave slapped against her side, reminding the four of them that, if not exactly at sea, they were still on deep water.

"Storm brewing," said Sharon, fluttering her extravagant eye-lashes.

"Every man for himself in a storm," said van Blanco. "Perryman's just coming here to save his own skin. He's not interested in saving anybody else's. None of them ever is."

4

SOURCES CLOSE TO THE CHEST

"It would be an exaggeration to suggest that every single person in Fleet Street was mad or bad," he wrote, "though it would probably be correct to think that nearly all of them were dangerous to know." He sucked his pencil and wondered if it was true. Well, it would have to do for now. It was near enough and he could always polish it up later. He continued: "After the revolution when 'Fleet Street' had become the 'Communications Industry' or the 'Media' the workers within the trade were still dangerous to know but the incidence of conventional badness and madness declined. Whereas once they had been raffish figures with a tendency to braces and beer bellies, journalists tended to become trimmer and more clean-living. They looked as if they worked in banks or estate agents' offices and on the whole that's the sort of men and women they were."

He frowned. There was no point in keeping a diary if it did not have context. A mere record of events was meaningless if they occurred without a framework. A good diary needed a point of view. Also, if he eventually decided not to publish these jottings in their present form but to make them the basis for a memoir or an autobiography, such mandarin reflections would be essential.

"Modernisation did not make journalists nicer," he continued. "The hacks of the *ancien régime* were often immoral, frequently drunk, louche and chaotic, but they were naughty rather than nasty and they had what nowadays seems a quaint belief in 'the truth'. They did their job because they enjoyed telling people what was going on in the world and telling it as it was.'

He smiled. He believe this. It was his *credo*. "An interviewer, for instance, would not decide what he was going to write before listening to what his or her interviewee had to say. If such an article turned into a hatchet job it was for a good reason, not simply malice. The interviewer took down words in shorthand or using a tape-recorder and took pains to see that the words that appeared on the printed page were the same as the words actually spoken during the interview."

He grimaced. What an innocent world that had been. Yet it seemed only yesterday. He must be getting old. Or was the world of communications really in an irreversible downward spiral – a sort of reverse Tennysonian corkscrew.

Forward, forward let us range,
Let the great world spin for ever down the ringing grooves of change.

Only it wasn't going forward any longer.

It was, he mused, a sign of how far standards had declined and of how one looked at the world that interviewing someone without a foregone conclusion in view was now regarded as rather prissy and Boy Scoutish. To talk of "standards" and "integrity" was to invite derision, contempt, incomprehension and titters.

He accepted that such generalisations were dodgy. Even someone looking at the golden age through the rosiest spectacles would admit that there were some rotten apples in the ancient barrel. And conversely there were, in the computer and carpet era, still one or two good eggs who managed to believe in something approaching standards and morality, while actually making quite a decent fist of appearing to be a real live human being.

Such a one, after all, was Christopher Jones himself, or so he liked to believe. His enemies thought him smug but that, as far as he was concerned was their problem not his.

Jones was a dinosaur but such were his skills and his wisdom and, above all, his reputation that he was a very succesful one at a time when many of his fellow beasts, prematurely pensioned off, spent their waking hours crying into their alcohol and slagging off everyone they could think of, most of all that shadowy beast called "Management".

Jones, however, was a survivor.

He had started out in the sixties after the expected Oxford first in Modern History. His mother was French and Jones was therefore bilingual, as well as having better than average Spanish and German. Along the way he had picked up a smattering of Mandarin and Arabic, though he always protested that these were little more than enough to get him through Customs and order a basic meal. Not, in fact, true, but, like many Englishmen of his age and background, he was inclined to understatement and self-deprecation. Not that he was modest. He had a knack of looking as if he knew more than anyone else. This made him enemies, especially among those naturally given to chippiness. Worse still, he had a habit of appearing amused by what he knew, which made the same people seethe.

His first job had been with Reuters, where he stayed five years. He had really come of age in 1968, when he seemed to crop up everywhere in Europe from the barricades of Paris to Wenceslas Square in Dubček's Prague. He was the only Western correspondent to get a proper interview with de Gaulle when he went calling in Ceauşescu's Romania. This was when the student riots were at their height back in France. Jones constantly stole a march on his more experienced colleagues. He was always a step or more ahead of the game. His network of contacts was unparalleled and his use of it second to none.

At the end of that year Lady Beatrice made him an offer he felt he could not refuse. In her prime, her ladyship was a prodigious talent spotter. She occasionally indulged herself with huge interviews with world leaders. Several times she found herself kept waiting in the world's anterooms only to discover that the VIP who had already penetrated the inner sanctum was this pipsqueak Jones. So, being a wise old bird with much less vanity than her enemies believed, she hired him. The new job allowed him his freedom, limitless expenses, a considerable retainer and extra money for whatever the paper published. In return he gave the *Intelligence* his exclusive services as far as journalism went. He was free to broadcast whenever he wished and there was no restriction on his book-writing. His title was "Chief Special Correspondent" but Jones was not bothered with titles of any kind. Not his style.

He had married a girl from Bratislava but she had been killed in a road accident in the early seventies. There was a son, brought up mainly by Jones's sister who was married to a vet in Wiltshire and had a large family of her own. Jones was a devoted but largely absent father. As far as women were concerned there had been the occasional fling but no one had come near replacing Jana. Jones, in middle age, had become a loner, solitary, enigmatic, cards close to his chest. Some of his enemies considered him a closet queen, but the consensus was that he was simply not interested in sex.

Not that he was reclusive. Rather the reverse. He was perfectly clubabble and much given to international seminars at places like Ditchley Park, Königswinter, or Chatham House, where the international Great and Good gathered for the occasional gabfest. On these occasions he did more listening than talking, but what he said was always heeded with respect, liberally tempered with resentment.

From time to time one or other of the *Intelligence*'s competitors would attempt to poach him and, if only to keep Lady Beatrice and the *Intelligence* on their toes, he would agree to lunch with a rival editor or proprietor, usually at Wilton's or the Savoy Grill. On these occasions he would say very little, but listen carefully with his head slightly cocked and his sardonic, lazy half-smile implying the usual superior knowledge and inner amusement. He would eat fastidiously and drink sparingly though well, then thank his host – seldom if ever a hostess – and tell him he would think about it.

Such was the London intelligence game that sooner or later word would get back to the *Intelligence* and Beatrice or one of the Majors would say nervously, "I understand you've been lunching with the opposition?"

And Jones would smile and murmur something reassuring but non-committal about supping with a long spoon.

This had the effect of making his employers jittery, which was, of course, half the point. It helped keep his salary on the move, though he was never so crude as actually to ask, let alone to use one of these regular approaches as leverage. It was sufficient that they were observed and absorbed. He liked the rest of the world on its toes as far as he was concerned. "Keep 'em guessing" was his password.

It was universally assumed that he had a working relationship with the British intelligence services and this was a belief that he liked to foster. His work and his travels inevitably brought him into contact with intelligence officers of many nationalities. He was scrupulously civil to all of them, but was careful in his dealings even with the British. He knew all too well that it was best to keep your distance. This was another of his maxims. Detachment, in a journalist like him, was a necessary virtue. He needed to be inside and outside at one and the same time. Difficult, yet essential.

As far as British politics and British journalism went he was as shrewd and well informed as one would expect. He had known for months that the Prime Minister was bisexual and that he was living dangerously. He knew that the *Noise* was on to the story and liable to break it at any time. He had chosen, however, not to mention it to anyone. There seemed little point. He liked to be informed of what was going on in the world, to observe; but he seldom interfered and he always knew more than he wrote. He was not interested in "scoops", which he considered meretricious. They also drew attention to one. Too many scoops, he reckoned, and people would stop talking to him.

His only real confidant was his diary. He wrote this up every day in a blank, stiff-covered notebook. He wrote in very dark artist's pencil and the handwriting, though superficially neat and tidy was, on closer inspection, virtually unintelligible to anyone except himself. In this it represented his own character. Those who did not know him well, but thought they did, were inclined to think and say that you could read Jones like a book, that what you saw was what you got and he was a regular guy. Neither it nor he was as simple as that.

In his diary that night, composed over a nightcap of the Macallan as he sat in his elegant attic flat high above Pall Mall, he wrote as follows:

> The PM is being a perfect ass. He and Sanderson-Wright are becoming more and more careless and seem not to care who knows. S-W is a regular at some gay bar in Bloomsbury and apparently makes no secret of his identity. Our people have warned him, of course, but he seems to think that his position makes him untouchable. Actually, the reverse is true. I am keeping shtum. It's not my scene.
>
> There is trouble brewing at the *Intelligence*. I admire their refusal to be stampeded by the barbarians, but they are in danger of burying their heads in the sand. Beatrice is showing her age and the offspring and their spouses are gathering like so many vultures. What a desperate institution the family can be. Those women are real harpies.
>
> I feel uneasy about practically everything. Things seem on the verge of falling apart.

He sighed. God knows, it wasn't just his age, was it? Perhaps he was just stale and old-fashioned, but he thought not. There was something rotten in the state. He wrinkled his nostrils, finished his drink, set aside his pen and book, and prepared himself for sleep.

5

OFF THE RECORD

Between them the three Majors looked as if they were in command of the *Intelligence*.

Major Gordon, as we have seen, was called the Editor. Major Ronald was the Managing Editor. This meant, more or less and up to a point, that Major Gordon was in charge of words and Major Ronald of money. Major Colin was the Literary Editor, which signified that he was not considered a lot of cop. Being Literary Editor allowed him to affect corduroy trousers and a patronising attitude to the hurly-burly mainstream of *Intelligence* life. A similar indulgence was extended to Dr Clancy, the Chief Leader Writer, and Trotter, the man who wrote about words. They were licensed jesters, peripheral to what was regarded by their colleagues as "the serious business of newspapers". These colleagues spent many of their waking hours talking about this alleged seriousness, hoping that by doing so it might become real.

But the real powerhouse, the muscle and brains of the *Intelligence*, was the Majors' mother. The fact that Lady Beatrice was said to have known Lloyd George in a full biblical sense denoted that she had to be the oldest newspaper tycoon in the country by – at a conservative estimate – more than a quarter of a century. Nevertheless, she still referred to Chinese Ken as a senile tortoise. She had been seeing off all manner of rivals ever since her husband, Les, was killed by one of the last doodlebugs of World War Two while – following a family tradition maintained by his sons – enjoying the favours of one of his junior reporters at her flat in Bayswater.

Like many autocrats she was a considerable aphorist and grinder out of ill-considered clichés. Her favourite was a wheezy "Life goes on, life goes on". Over the years, as her mortality became increasingly doubtful, this assumed an ever stronger personal significance, but this was not her intent. What she meant was that whenever some earth-shattering event, some cosmic cataclysm, some Armageddon or Holocaust caused her to shriek to her minions that most arresting of all famous journalistic commands "Hold the Front Page", there was always a host of lesser stories about vicars and knickers and cats up telegraph poles. These everyday stories of everyday folk were the woof and the warp, the grist to the mill. And so on. "There is more to the *Intelligence* than the headlines" was another of her much repeated lines. This was the way Lady Beatrice liked to talk and it was her credo. No matter how dramatic the front-page splash, the down-page par on page seven creeps on its petty pace. There *are* people who read the results of the Sussex County FA Senior Cup and who care about the temperature in Funchal. This she profoundly believed, for she was such a newspaper reader herself. She approached newspapers from the back to the front, from the bottom to the top.

It was therefore predictable that she would use this latest national scandal as an opportunity to remind everyone that despite the "Prime Minister's Mister Poofter peccadilloes" (her own phrase – she was much given to alliteration) "life goes on".

Or not.

Even the redoubtable Proprietor and Editor-in-Chief of the *Intelligence* could not go on living for ever and the signs were that although there *was* life in the old girl yet, it was not in inexhaustible supply. She was slowing down, losing short-term memory and temper. Besides, the Majors were not getting any younger and every generation must have its chance and take its turn. It is neither just nor sensible to keep young men kicking their heels while waiting for their aged mothers to kick the bucket and as the years passed this sentiment became increasingly prevalent. Even those who could not stand the Majors began to feel sorry for them. The Majors themselves became fretful and ratty, and indisputably middle-aged.

As the years passed, talk of the succession increased. No one except Lady Beatrice actually knew anything because the *Intelligence* was in all essential respects a private dictatorship. There was a whole paraphernalia of directors and boards and department heads and even ombudspeople, but these were mere flummery designed to imply fair play and democracy where none existed. Ignorance of the future did not, however, stifle debate. The less they knew the more they gossiped and, as always happens, those who possessed the least shrewd intuition invariably expressed themselves with the greatest certainty. Dr Clancy said an outsider would be appointed, since it would be impossible to choose between the three sons. Graham Parkinson-Woodruff, the Chess Correspondent, believed there would be a triumvirate. Stomper-Watson, the Obituaries Editor, believed that the Editor-in-Chief was dead already and that the person purporting to be her was a Frankenstein's monster produced by an ingenious application of the new technology. This probably had something to do with the fact that he had, naturally, written Lady Beatrice's epic necrology several times already – aided and heavily censored by the subject.

Then, on the very morning of the *Noise*'s revelations about the Prime Minister having it off with his Parliamentary Private Secretary and assorted third parties, Lady Beatrice summoned her sons to a serious family conference over an early breakfast at the penthouse flat she maintained on the roof of the Carlton Hotel. "Well, children," she said, "this is it. Time for a change. I cannot compete in a world where the Prime Minister of Great Britain is found in bed with a male colleague and where it becomes the subject of a circulation war with that odious Kenneth Lee. Honourable Members indeed. For myself, I don't care what the Premier does with his members. Or member. This is the journalism of the gutter. We have had enough."

Lady Beatrice was much given to describing herself as "we", particularly in moments of stress. Today she was wearing her blue, a sure sign of trouble. She had long ago abandoned any attempt at shape and spent her days encased in a series of tents and kaftans, silk in summer, woollen in winter. These were mostly plain, but she gave them variety by adding bangles. Bangles on her fingers and wrists, bangles on her ears, bangles and brooches where her breasts had been (a middle-aged mastectomy, or so it was said). Had she been of a later generation she would have had her nose pierced, but apart from that and perhaps her ankles, which were invisible beneath the folds of her tent, she had bangles wherever she went. Out of doors she wore a hat, wide-brimmed, jaunty with ostrich feathers. Sometimes, indoors, she wore a severe black cloche with *diamanté* studs. Today she was bare-headed, her powdery scalp showing pinkish through the straggly white hair. Her facial make-up was white and caky, relieved by thickly applied plum at the lips and heavy grey-green around the eyes, which still flashed, feline and emerald green, the one part of her which seemed not yet to have wearied with age.

"In any case" – she prodded with her stick at Boyle, her Webster terrier who was nibbling tiresomely at the tassle on her shoe – "I shan't see eighty again."

The three boys shifted their bottoms nervously on the leather upholstery of the dining-room chairs. None of them would see fifty again. To them that seemed just as bad. Gordon, in particular, was feeling indescribably seedy, having had virtually no sleep. He had spent most of the night fiendishly supervising the *Intelligence*'s response to the *Noise*'s scoop. The new girl had come up with a first-rate think piece which even Thingy, the Night News Editor, had approved. However, it had left him feeling almost as old as his mother. The girl, Fiona, Felicity or whatever her name was, made him feel older yet.

"With respect," said Gordon, "the public has a right to know."

"Oh, bugger the public," said the old lady. She meant it. The one thing she had never enjoyed about newspapers was the readers. This was common among newspaper proprietors, even though they pretended otherwise. Lady Beatrice hated the very notion of "the public". To her it was just a euphemism for the mob. "The will of the people" was a pretext for fascism and dictatorship. As far as she was concerned the only way it could be expressed properly was through the ballot-box. This was emphatically unlike Chinese Ken, who genuinely appeared to believe that there was such a thing as popular opinion and that he articulated it. Lady B took the Reithian view that nearly everybody except her was exceedingly stupid; she and her papers did what *she* decided, not what *they* wanted. The idea that her readers should tell her what to print was ludicrous. And dangerous.

"They do buy the paper," said Gordon rebelliously.

His mother stared at him. "That's an extraordinarily silly remark," she said, "and a complete *non sequitur*. Anyway, even a year or so ago I thought I should have been on the bridge with the rest of you, keeping the ship on a steady course until the Good Lord toppled me off my perch. Now, frankly, I suddenly feel very tired of it all. To put it simply, we can't be bothered."

This was true. Gordon had telephoned his mother as soon as he had taken in the *Noise* front page. She had been asleep and responded badly to his call. No child enjoys being told to impale himself on his spike by his mother, not even when he's over fifty. The old bag really is past her sell-by date now, had been Gordon's thought, but now at breakfast he expressed himself a little differently. "Oh, I say, Mother." He assumed an expression of pain bordering on anguish, his brown spaniel's eyes on the point of overflowing. "I'm sure I speak for the family when I say that the only thing, absolutely the *only* thing in all the world that we are concerned about at this moment in time is your personal happiness. I really do mean that, Mother, most sincerely."

"I concur." Ronald smiled caringly at his mother. "I know we aren't always perhaps the most demonstrative chaps, Mummy, but I'm sure you know that we all care desperately about you and your well-being. You've done such a tremendous amount for us and the *Intelligence*, given us all so much of yourself. I do hope you appreciate how terribly, terribly grateful we all are and how very very anxious that you should be happy."

"Yes, well I'm not happy," said his mother helpfully but not unkindly. She even allowed herself an uncharacteristic dab of the eye to indicate that she was moved by these affirmations of filial piety. Astonishing how even the most cynical old battle-axe will believe the most arrant hypocrisy when it comes from her own flesh and blood, thought Ronald. He blushed.

"Colin," she said, looking down the broad mahogany table to her youngest son, tousle-haired in his tweed jacket and black silk roll-neck. She felt he was too old for this sort of left-bank Bohemian look. Nobody thought for a moment that he was given to hanging around the Deux Magots discussing existentialism. He looked ridiculous. Nevertheless, he was her youngest and she loved him most of all.

"Yes, Mummy." He had been staring at the table top, rolling a yellow pencil up and down on his blotter, apparently abstracted.

"Do you have anything to say?"

"To say?"

"To say. Yes." Lady Beatrice gripped hard on the ivory handle of her stick. She wondered sometimes about Colin. So like his father, God rest his soul. Perhaps it would have been better if Colin too had been struck down by a doodlebug.

"No," said Colin, "I think Gordon and Ronald have summed it all up very competently." He lowered his voice a fraction. "As usual."

A moment of family electricity, apparent to all, but not something to be articulated. Gordon and Ronald were always exasperated by their little brother but they seldom said so out loud. He was a proper little Benjamin and mother's pet. In her heart of hearts Lady Beatrice had few illusions about her youngest, which was why he had been shunted off into the footling world of books. But she still indulged him. "Your mother spoils that brat rotten," Gordon frequently observed to Ronald.

"Very well," said the Editor-in-Chief.

The ensuing pause was interrupted by her secretary/house-keeper/dresser and all-round factotum, Mrs Kent, with a refill of coffee. In the ensuing clatter, mother and the two elder brothers riffled papers and files, frowning with efficient self-importance, while Colin continued to roll his yellow pencil. Eventually the coffee was served and Mrs Kent withdrew.

"So." Lady Beatrice bared her teeth, still her own though jagged, ill-angled and gapped. "I had assumed that by now I would be dead and the three of you would have inherited the *Intelligence* according to the terms of my will. However, I seem to be taking an unexpectedly long time to die. So I have decided to take the matter into my own hands. If the Good Lord is unable to order things rather better than he has I have no alternative but to take over. We've had a good innings and one should know when to retire hurt. I knew this Bryan creature was a common little thing but allowing himself to be interfered with by Sanderson-Wright *and* exposed in the *Noise* is more than I can cope with. Indecency compounded by incompetence. He's got a perfectly nice wife. And if she's not satisfactory there are lots of sensible girls in the office who'd be only too happy to oblige the Prime Minister. Can you imagine what dear Winston would have said? Having it off with one's PPS. I mean, not even Major Attlee would stoop to such a thing."

Logic had never been Beatrice's strong suit. Indeed, it was her erratic illogic that helped make her so formidable.

"You don't mean ..." said Ronald.

Lady Beatrice glanced at her middle son, seeing immediately

what he thought she meant. "No, Ronald, I am not going to take pills, nor shut myself in the garage with the garden hose and the engine running. There will be no scandal and no drama. I am simply announcing my intention to take early retirement – a rather late early retirement, I agree, and I apologise. I had hoped to be retired by act of God but since God is so slow in coming forward I am about to do what I would infinitely prefer not to have done, which is to retire. I am at odds with life."

There was no denying the look of satisfaction on the faces of the two older boys, even though they were at pains to disguise it. Colin seemed hardly to be aware of what was being said.

"Pay attention, Colin," said his mother, bringing her stick down on the table top with a sharp rap which spilled coffee from all four cups.

"With respect, Mummy, I *am* paying attention."

"Colin's upset," said Gordon. "I suppose this had to happen sooner or later, but frankly it's a blow. The *Intelligence* won't be the same without you, Mother; life won't be the same without you; the world won't be the same without you."

"Thank you, darling, though let's not get too carried away. I intend taking the title 'Proprietor for Life' and 'Editor-in-Chief Emeritus' so even though I'm standing down I shall still be very much a part of the fabric of the place."

"Oh, quite, quite," Gordon managed to seem brisk and emollient at the same time. "Nevertheless it *is* the end of an era. A sad, sad day for all of us."

"What exactly do you propose?" asked Ronald.

His mother sighed. "We have always been a very close family unit," she said, "and we have always taken decisions together, in unison and with proper consultations between all four of us, as well as, where necessary, with Ann and Carol." She was referring here to her daughters-in-law, Mrs Gordon White-Lewis and Mrs Ronald White-Lewis respectively. These two women did not like her, nor did they like each other; nor indeed, their brothers-in-law. What Lady Beatrice said was quite untrue. Ann and Carol White-Lewis had never been consulted about anything since their husbands asked them to be their wives. Even that had been in the nature of a command or at the very least one of those Latin questions to which only the answer "yes" is acceptable. Nor had the other members of the family ever been consulted except for form's sake. For more than forty years Lady Beatrice had commanded and the rest of the world, family included, had simply liked it or lumped it. The White-Lewises were not a listening family. Even when they seemed to be listening to each other they were merely waiting for a gap in the conversation into which they could barge.

All three sons therefore knew that their mother was being less than honest with them.

"I have always intended to divide up the *Intelligence* between the three of you," she said, "but before I finally, finally decide how to do that I'd like to hear what you have to say ... Gordon, as the eldest, perhaps you'd like to go first."

Gordon coughed, then pulled a white silk spotted handkerchief from the breast pocket of his pin-striped, Savile Row, man-of-the-world jacket and blew his nose long and loud. After refolding the handkerchief and replacing it, he began to speak. "I must say", he said, choking with what could have been phlegm but was obviously intended to represent emotion, "that I find myself at a point where my love for you renders me virtually incapable of speech. I am very very sad. And shocked. Sad and shocked. Shocked and sad. Very. But life must go on and I shall do my level best to ensure that it does. I shall always be mindful of your example and of your wishes in all things."

The old lady appeared pleased. "Bravely spoken," she said, seeming to believe every word of a speech Gordon had been rehearsing since he was twenty-one. "Broadly speaking, the plot is that the holding company remains intact but that you are assigned the daily paper, together with syndication, books and various other items we can deal with in the fine print. How does that strike you?"

The handkerchief was out once more and amid the choking Gordon was understood to say that he was quite overcome and would do his absolute level best to continue to strive to do honour and justice to his mother's lifelong labour, affection and trust.

This seemed to go down quite well. At least their mother did not demur.

"What about you, Ronnie?"

Ronnie was polishing his glasses and blinking back what were obviously meant to be tears. Either that or he was squeezing up his eyes in a painful and unsuccessful attempt to conjure water out of them. "What more can one say?" He leant forward and squeezed his brother's well-tailored elbow. "Gordon's said it all, really, except that, to be absolutely honest and speaking entirely for myself I'm bound to say that if anything he actually underestimates the total and unrepayable debt I personally owe to you. I know that it's very un-British and unlike us as a family to be sentimental. Nevertheless, there *is* a time and a place for everything including, let's not beat about the bush, tears and emotion. I can only say that I owe everything to you, Mummy, and I find it very hard and distressing to contemplate life at the *Intelligence* without you. But naturally I'll be more than happy to go along with whatever you decide. If you feel you have to go then go you must." Ronald could hardly finish the last sentence. His lip quivered and he shook, visibly and audibly.

His mother gave him a sharp almost sceptical look which suggested a possible disbelief in this triumph of sycophancy over cynicism and sincerity. However, like so many of her ilk, Lady Beatrice was passionate for truth but lukewarm about home truths. "I've marked you down for the *Sunday*," she said, "and I'll leave you merchandising and subsidiary rights. The bits and bobs, as I've already said, we'll save for the fine print."

Major Ronald said "Great, terrific, wonderful" and endorsed the adjectives with suitably adorational body language.

Finally their mother turned to Colin, still moodily rolling his yellow pencil up and down his blotter. "Well, darling?"

"Well, what, Mother?" The Literary Editor's body language was not as good as Major Ron's. He sat slumped, absorbed in his pencil rolling, avoiding all eye contact.

"What about you? Your brothers have spoken most eloquently and movingly about their love for me on this really rather important day in all our lives. Now what have you got to say for yourself?"

"Nothing, really."

"Nothing?"

"Look, Mother, it's all very well but I can't put on a display like Ronnie's and Gordon's. Of course I love you. You know that. I'm terribly grateful for everything you've done for me and for the *Intelligence*. Fine. Great. Wonderful. But I really don't feel up to banging on about it."

"Banging on about it?! Is that the best you can manage?"

Colin at last looked up from the table. "Look," he said, "I don't mean any disrespect and I certainly don't intend to imply any lack of devotion. In fact, if I may say so I think I'm a very much more devoted son than either of these two here. As you know full well, I have always been a dutiful and loving son to you and I trust I always will be. End of story."

Beneath the pallor of the chalk-white make-up on the face of the great tycoon for life there burned an unhealthy pink glow. "Is that your final word, Colin?"

"Yes."

"After all I've done for you," said his mother, "how can you be so ungrateful?" Colin was on his feet. "I am *not* being ungrateful; I am merely telling it how it is."

Lady Beatrice was also on her feet. The other two brothers were trying not to look smug. "I should have known it would come to this," said the old woman. "All your life you have been the one who's been indulged and pampered. You've been allowed to dabble with your concrete poetry readings and hang around with that ridiculous Brendan Clancy, while your brothers have had to get on with all the hard work, running the paper, fighting off the *Conscience*, disciplining the work-force. Well, my sweet spoilt child, the game is well and truly up." She gave something more than a sigh but less than a wail. "How could you, Colin? How could you?"

"Mother," Colin looked wretched but mulish. "I refuse to be drawn into this preposterous charade simply to feed your vanity. I make no complaint about anything. You have always been a very loving, very fair mother and I for my part have always tried to be a very fair and loving son. However, I refuse to perjure myself and pretend to feelings I simply don't have and which, if I may say so, seem to be not only well over the top but positively unnatural. One might almost say incestuous."

"I say," said Major Ronald.

"Now look here," said Major Gordon.

Middle-aged though they were, none of the boys had ever before spoken like this to their mother. Gordon stared at the ceiling. Ronald at the floor.

But Colin looked his mother straight in the face. "I'm sorry," he said. "I am telling the truth. No more and no less."

"There's a time and a place for that sort of thing," said Gordon dangerously.

Lady Beatrice was not herself, even though the icy voice and the firm grip of her fist on the stick might have suggested otherwise. "Your truth is your come-uppance," she said. "You may have thought you had an inalienable right to what no doubt you would describe as a 'fair' share of the business I have spent a lifetime building up. If so, you are much mistaken. You're no son of mine, that's for sure."

Saying which, she stomped to the door, opened it and shrieked a summons to Mrs Kent, who came straight away, eyes round with alarm. She had been Lady Beatrice's secretary and right-hand woman for almost fifteen years, but she had never seen her like this, not since the council tried to close the *Intelligence* canteen on account of the cockroaches and a disputed rat-dropping.

"Take a letter please, Mrs Kent," said her boss. "To Stephen Jennings of Jennings, Jennings, Muncaster and Jennings ... My dear Jennings, This is to advise you that I wish to change my will in order to disinherit completely my son Major Colin White-Lewis, his portion of my inheritance to be divided equally between my two elder sons ..."

Mrs Kent stood with her pencil hovering above her shorthand pad. "But Lady Beatrice ..."

"Don't 'Lady Beatrice' me," said Lady Beatrice. "Just take down the letter."

6

A FRANK AND CORDIAL EXCHANGE

L ady Beatrice was not the only newspaper proprietor to react badly to the revelations about the Prime Minister's sex life.

Chinese Ken was not amused.

In the event, Boy Perryman, the PM's Press Secretary, thought better of bearding the top brass of the *Noise* in their bunker at the Barque. White and van Blanco, Sharon and Stan waited and waited, slurping champagne beyond the small hours until it was not only obvious that Perryman was a no-show but that had he appeared he would have got nothing even approaching sense from any one of the quartet. They all prided themselves on being able to hold their drink but their alcoholic ambitions proved unrealistic.

And so, unsteadily, to bed . . .

"Mr Lee wants a word." Thus Sir Eddie's secretary the second he stepped into his office fresh(ish) from the ten-minute journey in the silver Merc driven by the ex-night-club bouncer in the peaked hat who went with the job.

"Shit. Give me a double Alka-Seltzer and five minutes." The Editor had been weaned on B movies with Bogart look-alikes in braces and green eye-shades. It was the main reason he took up journalism in the first place.

He loved being at the centre of a story such as this one because it made him feel as if he were in that sort of movie. Good stories were what made newspapers worthwhile. And this was one of the best. What was the point in playing safe? Some of his peers, a dying breed, thank God, boasted about producing "papers of record". Eddie didn't see the point. If that was all there was to newspapers you might as well be a stenographer. "Take a note, White." Nothing more than dictation. He was told by his enemies that there were armies of people out there who still believed that the press existed simply to take down what other people wanted taken down. And, as van Blanco was always saying, they didn't mean trousers. Men like Boy Perryman issued statements and press releases and expected you to carry them verbatim without so much as a sniff of scepticism. Not Eddie's style. He didn't allow anything or anybody to get in the way of a good story.

"Terrif," he said, knocking back the still dissolving fizzy pills. Bit of an anticlimax after the champagne of a few hours earlier, but he needed it. He had always vaguely supposed that hangovers were something you grew out of in later life but his were getting worse. At least he still got hangovers. In the old days when he was a stripling on Fleet Street chasing ambulances there were plenty of hacks, including editors, who never dried out enough to experience one. They must have slept with intravenous drips. "Shan't be long," he said to his secretary though she was officially described as his "assistant" just as those who used to be called "correspondents" had all been mysteriously elevated to the rank of "editor" as in "Angling Editor," "East Anglian Editor" or, most mysteriously "Style Editor".

Eddie had used these elevations shamelessly to save money. "You can't have a pay rise but from now on you can call yourself 'editor'." White never ceased to be amazed by other people's vanity. He tightened his tie and squirted a splash of oral deodorant in the direction of his tonsils. Ken Lee was not a bad proprietor as proprietors went but he shared the prevailing puritanism of the modern generation of superbosses. He objected to hangover halitosis, not merely on aesthetic grounds but because he disapproved of booze.

When he arrived in the chromy ante-room outside Ken's office, White found William Pool already sitting on the edge of one of the airport lounge-style sofas. He was holding the inevitable clipboard and scribbling on it with a propelling pencil, while addressing himself to the late editions of the morning's papers. All of these, save the *Conscience* itself, had led with some version or other of the *Noise*'s story about the Prime Minister. Unlike Eddie White, Pool looked quite well in a pallid way. He gave the impression of having been up for several hours, having started with a good grapefruit-and-dry-toast breakfast. "Good Morning, White."

Eddie hated being called "White". "Morning Bill."

Pool loathed being addressed as "Bill". "You seem to have created quite a stir."

"Yeah. Great story."

"I'm afraid we didn't take that view at the *Conscience*." Pool allowed his fellow Editor one of his frequent smirks, a thin-lipped flicker of condescension. "Our feeling was that a sexual peccadillo was just that. No more, no less. And we at the *Conscience* believe that even a prime minister is entitled to some privacy. Not to mention respect."

Eddie returned the smile with a well-practised glare. "That's your privilege," he said. "My job's selling newspapers. I can't afford scruples."

"I know your views on newspapers," said Pool. He had been at a minor public school and a dim Cambridge college. Now he believed himself to be a pillar of the British Establishment, a fully paid-up member of the Great and the Good. Once upon a time the *Conscience* had indeed been a great British newspaper, caused cabinet ministers to tremble, made Trade Union leaders think twice and had been required reading in such places as All Souls College, Oxford. Now, however, times had changed. What had mattered then mattered no longer and what used to matter not at all mattered quite a lot. This was the view of the Editor of the *Daily Noise*. It was not shared by the Editor of the *Daily Conscience*.

"The Proprietor", said Pool, "is unamused."

"This Proprietor is amused by profits," said Eddie. "A bloody good old-fashioned scandal drives up the circulation like nobody's business. You ought to know that by now. You were on the *Intelligence* once and they're as scandalous as the rest of us."

It was true that as a very young man Pool had worked on the *Intelligence*, but he did not like being reminded of his days as a junior gossip columnist, now that he was a figure of importance and distinction with a long entry in *Who's Who*, a place on the governing body of his old school and membership of Bretts. He always wore the hideous mauve-and-fuchsia-striped tie of that club and enjoyed taking people of what he conceived to be similar status as himself to what he habitually called "luncheon". "I fail to see what my early career has to do with today's newspapers," he said, huffily.

Chippy little bugger, thought Eddie.

Before he could say so they were interrupted by the incursion of Chinese Ken's PA, power-dressed to kill and saying, "Mr Lee will see you now, gentlemen."

Since Chinese Ken paid their salaries both men, powerful, adult and self-sufficient though they considered themselves, rose as one and walked, silent and sheepish, to the Proprietor's office like eight-year-old new boys summoned to the headmaster's study.

"Good morning, Chairman," said Pool, unctuous before his boss's football pitch of a desk.

Sir Edward's greeting was a perfunctory grunt of "Boss".

Chinese Ken did not reply, did not look up, did not invite them to sit and himself remained slumped in a high-backed, custom-built, alligator-skin, revolving black chair from the absolute ultimo numero uno designer of such things, who operated from a small village just outside Milan.

"Well," he said, finally disengaging himself from his blotter, "perhaps you'd like to explain, Edward." Ken only used the formal Edward when he was trying to show him who was in charge.

"Explain what, exactly?"

"Don't get smart with me." Ken's voice, never deep, tended to shoot up to querulously near falsetto when he was angry. He was livid now and squeaking like a bicycle chain without oil. White wished the throbbing in his head would go away. He tried to focus on the top of the tower at Chelsea harbour on the other side of the Thames, framed by the proprietor's cinemascope plate-glass window. Unfortunately it had a pulsating aircraft warning light on top, which blinked in perfect pace with the metronome between his temples.

"We received information indicating that the Prime Minister had been conducting a homosexual liaison with his Parliamentary Private Secretary and that this relationship was part of a large homosexual network involving a number of prominent people. I considered that if this information turned out to be accurate I had a duty to publish. In the public interest."

If this was the sort of game Ken was going to play then Eddie could play it as well. He'd stop short of calling the little man "sir" but otherwise he could slip into the clinical dispassion of a policeman giving evidence in court with little difficulty.

"Why wasn't I told?"

"This was a highly sensitive operation and I judged it sensible to operate a security policy based on 'need to know'. In my judgement there was no need for you to know."

Ken was not amused. Very little amused Ken and quite a lot made him cross. The Editor of the *Noise* was visibly shortening a fuse which was not long at the best of times. "Then your judgement stinks," he shrilled. "You do your level best to unseat the Prime Minister of Great Britain and you don't tell your Proprietor. What sort of judgement is that, for fuck's sake?"

"Editors edit," said Eddie, "and proprietors propriet. You know that, you've always said it and you've nearly always acted on it. For which I'm duly grateful."

Now Ken went very quiet. This was an even worse sign than high pitch. "You don't know anything about what it means to be a proprietor, do you, Edward?"

"I've always been perfectly happy to get on with doing my job while you do yours, if that's what you mean."

"As a proprietor," said Ken, in a squeaky stage whisper, "I am acquisitive. I seek to grow. I do not stand still. Understand?"

Eddie nodded.

"I don't think you do," said Ken, "but I'll try to explain in simple language that even a *Noise* reader would understand. For some months I and my colleagues on the International Board have been seeking to acquire a major television company. I'm certainly not about to favour you with any business secrets but I can say that following the privatisation of the nationalised parts of the British broadcasting industry I had been confidently expecting to make a significant expansion TV-wise."

He paused, partly for effect and partly to catch his breath. Eddie was aware that Pool was wearing his most priggish smirk. *Schadenfreude* affected him like that.

The Proprietor banged his fist on the desk top. "I have been cultivating Bryan Sutton like a prize bloody camellia," he said. "I need the government on my side if I'm to have a prayer of taking over the BBC. You wouldn't think of that, would you. Sutton has been to the apartment. I said he and Thelma could use the yacht. I contributed to party funds. And now look what you've done."

"It's a cracking story," said Eddie.

This remark really did silence the Proprietor. To anyone who did not know him it might have seemed as if he were having some sort of stroke or fit, but it was nothing as life-threatening as that. Just rage.

"What the chairman is trying to tell you is that the Prime Minister's goodwill was essential to the prosperity and expansion of the company," said Pool.

"And what I'm trying to tell him – and you – is that a story is a story. As Editor of the *Noise* I had a duty to publish. You don't have a monopoly of integrity, you know."

"Oh, really!" Pool sighed, with a smile of oleaginous contempt.

Ken regained the power of speech. "I would like", he said, "to have the pleasure of saying 'You're fired'. But I wasn't born yesterday and I know bloody well you'd be expensive and difficult, and this probably isn't the moment." He stabbed a stubby finger at Eddie. "I'm announcing a new appointment, Edward," he said, "to take effect as of now, which is to say immediately, at once and without any bullshit. Mister William Pool to be Group Editor-in-Chief. Which, being translated, means that you report to William at all times, you answer any question he may choose to ask, you drop any story he does not like, you are at his beck and call at all times and you lick his bloody arse whenever he wants you to."

"Thank you, Chairman," said Pool, managing to convey fawning satisfaction with veiled distaste at such vulgarity.

"Great," said Eddie, "brilliant. If you think that one's going to work you know nothing about newspapers, you know nothing about the *Noise* and you know nothing about me."

And he saw himself out.

7

HE WAS UNMARRIED

Dr Brendan Clancy Ph.D. (Galway) still wrote in fountain pen, not cross-hatched and on the backs of envelopes like proper old journalists, but still in real ink with crossings-out and insertions, blotches and grubby fingerprints. This would not have been tolerated on any paper but the *Intelligence*, nor from any other journalist but Clancy. The new breed of journo didn't believe in paper and ink but was only happy with the gentle clickety-click of the keyboard and the winking lights of the screen. Clancy insisted that time spent staring at what he refused to call a VDU – "Visual Display Unit, my arse!" – led to serious disease if not actual insanity, just like masturbation before about 1960. In this, as so many things, he was eventually proved maddeningly right.

Clancy had been with the paper almost for ever and, it was alleged, had once upon a distant time been intimate with Lady Beatrice: not an entirely sober encounter and said to have been conducted standing up at the Chelsea Arts Club, possibly during dinner. There were those who even suggested that Major Colin was Clancy's natural son. It would account for the youngest Major's own mild eccentricity and love of language and literature. The Chief Leader Writer and the Literary Editor were not dissimilar – louche but literate.

Dr Clancy was the author of *The Celtic Muse in County Galway*, 1893–1894. It was his only complete work, published by a long defunct academic press of Republican inclination, and had long been out of print. Over the years, Clancy's ginger beard had turned silver and he had assumed the patina of age and mildly spurious distinction. Without ever having written anything very memorable he had become, if not the "Father of the Modern Leader", at least the "Grand Old Man of Leader Writing". In his more lucid and realistic moments he used to say to young colleagues or students on work experience: "Publish and be damned. But publish too much and be damned with faint praise." Then he would chuckle into his whiskers as if he had said something incredibly profound.

While the young and impressionable were wondering what to make of this he would follow up swiftly with the story of Jones of Monte Carlo. Because he was old and his memory was wandering and inventive, it was not always Jones of Monte Carlo but could be Smith of Buenos Aires or White of Macau or even Green of Grantham. Basically, the story was a hoary old chestnut about a moribund foreign correspondent who had become excited when the paper which employed him changed hands. Having done nothing for years, he suddenly filed a story, whose only effect was to make the new owners aware that he existed and was costing them money. Consequently he was fired.

Clancy loved telling this story to the young men and women who came to him wet behind the ears and left after a year or so, armed with enough Clancyisms to outbore any lunch-time companion on earth. The moral was plain. Never volunteer. Never do any work unless you have to. Sit tight, don't move, only speak when you're spoken to and you'll end up like Dr Brendan Clancy, Grand Old Man of Leader Writing, universally revered and respected.

So, at morning conference, Dr Clancy made no comment about the Prime Minister shock-horror. Privately his view was that he had been here before. He had written leaders about practically every one of the sexual-political scandals which had afflicted Britain since the war, most notably, of course, the Profumo affair of 1963 with its entertaining cast of society osteopaths, night-club hostesses, Soviet diplomats, Rastafarians and rent racketeers. Clancy had very much enjoyed taking a high moral tone over Profumo but this latest business struck him as just grubby. He had an old-fashioned distaste for "homosexualists", which younger colleagues viewed with suspicion. Some of them thought he was

44

not as much of a randy old goat as he made out. He protested too much. As the Editor Major put it, "If you ask me, old Thingy in leaders is a damn sight more left-handed than he'd like to admit."

"I asked Felicity to sit in on conference since it was she who did so much to get us out of a fix last night."

Major Gordon smiled wolfishly and Felicity dimpled demurely. She had, in fact, excelled last night, though Clancy, privately and not for publication, was none too pleased. Major Gordon's response to the *Noise*'s exclusive had been to run a short though prominent news story based on the *Noise* report and to accompany this with an anonymous, boxed editorial written by Felicity and tarted up with a few well-worn phrases of his own along the lines of there being "no spectacle so ridiculous as the British public in one of its periodical fits of morality". Major Gordon had a short, sharp list of all-purpose quotations which he liked to insert into his staff's copy when the mood took him. Many of them, like this, were from Macaulay, though Johnson was also a favourite source. He often muddled them up and got them wrong, leaving Clancy to make corrections and apologies, and to field readers' nit-picking letters of complaint.

"Righty-ho," he said. There were about twenty odds and sods gathered for the morning conference. They were mostly so-called "Heads of department". After their meeting was finished there would be another for the leader writers only. This would be a more cerebral, that is to say pretentious, affair. The main conference was a more pragmatic, nuts-and-bolts business. The Editor delivered a brief post-mortem on the efforts of the previous twenty-four hours, picked out one or two aspects for praise and condemnation, then highlighted stories in rival organs which he would like to have seen in his own or, as often as not, which he was mightily relieved not to have done. He always began by saying "Righty-ho" and after the post-mortems he would invariably ask, "What have you got for us today then, Sonya?" Sonya Waterston was the News Editor, a boot-faced lesbian who had previously been Chief Crime Correspondent. She rode to hounds with the Pytchley and the Whaddon Chase and was universally regarded as a hard case. She was some kind of White-Lewis cousin.

"I'm sorry we missed out on the Prime Minister story in the first edition," said the Major. "But we caught up well. I've had words with Boy Perryman and between you and me I think there's a great deal more and at the same time a great deal less to this story than meets the eye."

He looked round the room with a knowing expression. These oracular, orotund utterances were an integral part of his editorial style. Ambiguity could always be justified later on. Not like certainty. Gordon mistrusted certainty. He liked to be able to say, after the event, "As you will recall, I always had certain misgivings about ..." or "I always said I wasn't at all sure whether ..."

"How do you mean exactly?"

This was Stomper-Watson, Head of Obituaries and an old sparring partner. He and the Major had once locked horns in a famous but mutually forlorn pursuit of one of the country's most desirable theatrical Dames. Stomper-Watson had turned the naïve question into a maliciously effective conversational weapon. At conference he tormented the Editor with a torrent of meek, nobody-told-me interrogatives. They were loaded with the same apparent doubt and ambiguity as the Major's diktats.

And they were just as deadly.

"I mean", said Gordon, "that I have a hunch that there's very little in the sexual impropriety side of this affair but quite a lot in why it's a front-page exclusive in the *Noise*. I don't much care what the PM does with his spare time, but I do want to know who told the *Noise* about it."

"Ken Lee's very thick with the PM," said Sonya. "It doesn't seem in character for Lee to have shopped him."

"But White hates his guts." This from Trotter, the man with the way with words.

"Did *we* have the story?" Another of Stomper-Watson's apparently guileless under-arm lobs.

"Of course we didn't have the bloody story." Gordon allowed his lack of sleep to surface in an ill-tempered snarl. "If we had we'd have gone with it."

"Would you?" Stomper-Watson was chancing his arm and knew it.

So did everyone else, including the Editor who defused the situation with an altogether more ingratiating – though not entirely convincing – stretch of the lower facial muscles. "Fair question, perfectly fair question er, um." He was obviously groping for Stomper-Watson's name but gave up, simply repeating, "perfectly fair." Then, seeking to give an impression of furious concentration, he continued, "Between you and me – and I don't want a word of this appearing in some mucky little Soho scandal sheet, Boy Perryman is of the opinion that this is a cheap smear set up by the security services. We certainly didn't have wind of it, did we?"

He covered the room with a questioning sweep of his red-rimmed eyes and got a universal shake of the head.

"Why should the security services set up the Prime Minister?" Stomper-Watson wanted to know. "He's well to the right of Attila the Hun. Exactly their cup of tea. It's the sort of thing Boy Perryman *would* say."

"Who knows?!" said the Editor rhetorically. "The security services are a mystery wrapped in an enigma as Churchill so succinctly put it, though he was talking about something else at the time."

"Actually he said it was a riddle wrapped in a mystery inside an enigma. And he was talking about Russia." This, of course, from Trotter, who looked pleased with himself. He was wearing the usual carnation in his button hole, a sartorial flamboyance which, for some reason, invariably got up Major Gordon's nose. Figuratively speaking.

"Yes, yes," the Editor said testily, aware that this conference was beginning to lose momentum. "I think that's the sort of observation best kept for your column, Mr Trotter, if you don't mind. Some of us have a paper to bring out."

Trotter went the colour of his boutonnière and stared at the floor. He did not enjoy public rebukes even though he was good at handing them out himself. He had a reputation around the office for being a sarky little bugger.

"Righty-ho, then," said the Editor, "just to recap. We missed out on the first editions because the *Noise* had an exclusive, which we think has some very dodgy elements in it. We caught up well and I'm sure Sonya and the political chappies will keep us well abreast of the situation. I certainly think we should have a hard look at the security side of things. So, what else have you got for us, Sonya?"

Not a lot, as it happened. She seldom did at morning conference and one knew that most of the "stories" she recited in her gravelly hunting-field shout would bite the dust by early evening. The Queen was doing a walkabout in some Scottish housing development and other Royals were walking about elsewhere. Sonya invariably opened with the royal stories in deference to a long-established *Intelligence* tradition. The paper always wrote about royalty but did so, even when their rivals were at their most intrusive and sensational, with deference and circumspection. There had also been a bomb scare on the London Underground; a professor from the University of East Anglia claimed to have discovered a species of previously unknown frog; the short-list for a new literary prize had been announced; a right-wing back-bencher had said that as far as he was concerned "Wogs began at Calais"; and a "survey" revealed that one in three six-year-olds knew where babies came from.

"Oh dear," said the Editor when Sonya had finished. "How about a vox-pop questionnaire asking a cross-section of people in the street where *they* think babies come from? Might yield some interesting copy."

Trotter and Stomper-Watson exchanged raised eyebrows and Dr Clancy kept his head down.

"I'll see what I can do," barked Sonya and the Editor reflected that it was all those years of gin and Old Shag tobacco that had given her a voice like that and, before long, he wouldn't be surprised, lung cancer as well. She smoked her horrible tobacco in a curvy Meerschaum pipe purchased in Interlaken during a walking trip in the days of her long-distant youth. Out loud he said, "Good."

Then his buzzer sounded. It was his personal assistant. "I'm sorry, sir, but I have Mr Perryman on the line. He says it's urgent. Something to do with the Prime Minister and Mr Sanderson-Wright."

"Ah." The editor was disconcerted yet flattered. It was reassuring to be yanked out of one's conference by the Great and, well, perhaps not so Good. "Clancy," he said, because this was the first name that came into his head. "Would you be so good as to take over pro tem?" He rose and coughed a theatrical phlegm removal. "I'm sorry about this." He smiled the smile of absolute self-importance. "It's Number Ten. Something seems to have cropped up."

8

NO HOLDS BARRED EXCLUSIVE

S tan and Sharon had been given the day in bed.

This was not the same as being given the day off, even though they both felt they deserved it.

"Oh Christ!" said Sharon as the alarm trilled at 8.30, "can't we take the morning off?"

"You know we can't, sweetie." Stan was levering himself out of bed, heading for the electric kettle and the cafetière. "Nice hot mug of Kenyan caffeine and there'll be no holding you."

"I've got a headache." Sharon giggled. "Can't we fake it?"

"You may fool me," Stan called from the kitchen, "but you know bloody well you won't fool the Editor."

This was true.

The success of the *Noise* was based on a brilliantly sophisticated formula of Lowest Common Denominators devised almost single-handedly by Sir Edward White. Personal abuse, scandal about television stars and members of the Royal Family, female nudity, if possible featuring disproportionately large mammaries, competitions for the simple-minded with Costa holidays as the prizes, very few words in very large print – these were the *Noise* staples. The pervading themes were vulgarity and repetitive name-dropping, but above all sex. The *Noise* oozed sex. It titillated and nudged, it sniggered and it informed. Sharon and Stan had an agony column apiece: "Sharon Says" on Tuesdays and "Stan Says" on Thursdays. They also ran regular consumer guide series with such titles as "A Hundred and One Ways to Satisfy Your Man", "Eating Your Way to Climax – the Oral Guide to Pleasure", and "Have Sex and Stay Slim". Occasionally they did "in-depth" investigations. Their most celebrated was a probe into sex and the Church called "Orgasm Gaiters".

The series they were working on at the moment was about politically correct postures for sexual intercourse in post-feminist society. "Holy Father! – Nun too good for the Missionary Position", and "How to be top – women in the saddle" were two of the headlines they were playing with, though the secret of this sort of series was not to be too raunchy but to present the material in a sort of pseudo-psychotherapeutic style so that it resembled a guide to "How to make a million pounds in a fortnight" or "Motor cycle maintenance made easy." It was a bizarre formula but, as the circulation proved, it worked wonders.

Stan and Sharon not only wrote these things, they also did most of their own research. They were the Torvill and Dean of sex. In different circumstances they would have been King and Queen of the light-blue video circuit but they had their journalistic integrity to preserve. They were professional reporters: members of the National Union of Journalists – not Equity. However, there was nothing amateur about their performances together. In their case practice had made just about perfect and from foreplay to climax they were able to go through the most complicated manoeuvres with absolute precision and brilliant team-work, understanding each other perfectly with never any need to issue verbal instructions of the sort usually associated with such activity. Never a whispered "Not so hard" or "Just there ... mmmm" when Stan and Sharon were in bed together.

Radio Four was into the weather forecast by the time Stan came back with the coffee. He'd cooked toast too – a major post-feminist gesture from Stan of the *Noise*. Butter and marmalade also, though these had sexual undertones as well. "Breakfast in bed – finger-licking good!" The *Noise* aphrodisiac pages were well into the sexual properties of jam and preserves.

The series on post-feminist posturing was their most important work in progress but there were a number of other regular slots such as the weekly aphrodisiac ("What turns you and your partner on"), the weekly position (there would have to be a certain unavoidable overlap here with the current series) and a surprisingly popular once-a-week piece in which they took a piece of classic softish pornography or, as the *Noise* liked to call it, "Erotica", and acted it out. Then they reprinted a potted version and gave tasting notes to help readers adapt it to their own purpose.

Today's first task was to write the consumer's notes on this week's sex in literature.

"What are we doing then?" asked Sharon, sitting up to drink her coffee.

"I've chosen a bit of Anaïs Nin," said Stan, crunching into his toast with avid teeth.

"Oh Christ!" Sharon was so angry she spilt coffee down her front. Uncomfortable since she was unclothed. "Now look what you made me do," she said, dabbing at her painful breasts with the duvet cover. "You can't mean Anaïs Bloody Nin. I am not going to put on that ridiculous satin dress just so you can peel it off in one easy lascivious movement."

"How did you know?" Stan enquired.

"Because that's what Anaïs Nin is all about: peeling satin dresses off pliant negresses with throbbing buttocks and then taking a long time screwing. I think Anaïs Nin is a pain."

"You know perfectly well that she's Eddie White's favourite author."

"She's Eddie White's *only* effing author."

"Look." Stan sat on the bed and stroked Sharon's ruffled golden tresses, feeling himself stir as he fixed his smouldering eyes on her parted sensuous lips ... he checked himself. He wasn't supposed to start thinking like someone in an Anaïs Nin sketch until the action had begun. "You like the satin dress and we got it on expenses because Eddie thinks Nin is *le dernier mot* in porn for girlies. Now we owe it to the Editor to do one of her bits once in a while."

"But I do have to put on the satin dress?"

"No, you take it off."

"Well I'm starkers at the moment so I've got to put the bloody thing on before I can bloody take it off again, don't I? Can't we just skip the satin-dress bit?"

"No Sharon we cannot skip the satin-dress bit. We're already skipping a longish sequence in a bar where we clap eyes on each other for the first time."

"Clap being the operative word."

"Don't be childish. You know perfectly well we put in the safe-sex warning. The *Noise* says BE PREPARED – CARRY A CONDOM."

Sharon sighed and drank some coffee. "All right," she said. "What do we do?"

"I," said Stan, "having seen you in this bar, have been propositioned by a gent who explains that you are a lady who likes solely the unknown. So the only people by whom you enjoy being laid are complete strangers who you'll never see again. And such a one am I."

"Why you?"

"Oh, for God's sake." Stan had finished his toast now and was becoming seriously exasperated. "Let's just get it over with then we can move on to something more interesting."

"I just like making it up as we go along," she protested. "It's so much more creative."

"That's not the point." Stan reached down to the floor and picked up his well-thumbed paperback of "erotica". "Now," he said. "I arrive in the room which is all white fur and mirrors."

This required some licence because the prevailing tone of the Stan and Sharon boudoir was black. But they did have a lot of mirrors.

"And to start with we're both dressed. It's easier for you because you've got nothing on under your satin. I've got to wear the whole hog."

"This is silly."

"I know." Stan smiled. "But it's what we get paid for. And it beats work."

"Speak for yourself."

"Oh, come on, Sharon. You know you like it once we get going."

This was true. Sharon adored it when she got going but she disliked charades. "Oh shit," she said. "Just let me do my teeth."

Which she did, spitting venomously into the basin and dosing (just like her Editor at much the same time) on Alka-Seltzer. Then she put on the gown, which was hanging in the dressing-room, and returned to the bed where her colleague was back in the suit he had so comparatively recently relinquished and chucked, as was his custom, all over the floor. "Now what?" she asked.

"We sit and look at each other and take our time."

"Oh, for God's sake, Stan, we haven't . . ."

"Got all day!" sang Stan exultantly. "All day is exactly what we have got so let's make the most of it. Now then." He consulted his text. "You're standing with your lips slightly apart and I'm standing looking and then I pass my hands along your satin curves. *Comme ça.*" And he executed a suitably languorous finger-tip roam round her breasts and hips.

Sharon sighed. "Do get on with it," she said rattily.

"Sharon," he snapped back, "the whole point is that we've got to convey to the reader what it's like to spend all this time with you just watching while I caress your whatsits. And you're supposed to be bewitchingly silent with your lips parted for kissing, not for making bloody silly remarks. Now sit down and take off your slippers so I can hold your feet."

She giggled. "I'm not wearing slippers," she said.

This he ignored. Instead he started to run his hands up and down her legs under the dress. She seemed to enjoy this, which was not what the book stipulated.

"Keep your thighs together," he commanded. "I'm supposed to kindle you into a state of uncontrollable desire. But not just yet."

"Oh God!" she said, allowing him to kiss her as nearly as possible all over with mechanical passion, one eye on his text, which he had to keep smoothing down with his left hand. This detracted still further from the spontaneity of his seduction.

"Can't you make your hair a bit more dishevelled?" Stan asked. "And why hasn't your dress fallen off your shoulders? I'm supposed to push it off altogether with my mouth, revealing the rosy tips of your breasts and no, you are *not* supposed to help. Your sex is supposed to be cool and soft to my finger et cetera et cetera. You're meant just to lie there while I have my way. At least for the time being. You can help me get the dress off a bit later. Then you quiver and ask me to get mine off."

"Quiver!?" said Sharon incredulously. "What the hell do you mean 'quiver'. For God's sake, just get'em off and let's get on with it."

They were silent for a moment while with a little assistance he peeled off her satin, did some slightly half-hearted writhing and ran his tongue up and down her inside leg. Then he undressed speedily, revealing an acceptable erection.

"I wish I felt as excited as you do, Stanley," said Sharon.

"You're supposed to kiss and fondle it," said Stan. "Eagerly, if you don't mind. And no faking. Then you turn over so I can fondle your bum and explore ... hang on ..." He paused to scrutinise the page. Not that easy in his aroused state, especially as he really needed reading glasses. "I'm supposed to explore and touch every nook of your body, open your sex with two fingers and feast my eyes on your glowing skin. OK. How are you doing?"

"To be honest, Stanley, I've got a bit of a hangover. Do you think you could get on with it? It may feel better when you're properly inside."

"But it's supposed to be protracted. Remember we're complete strangers. This is our only time together. Just a sec." Again he paused to read. "After a bit you open your vulva with your lovely fingers and then we suspend our pleasure for a bit until you can't stand it any longer and you suddenly gyrate round my erect penis and cry out and I experience a lightning flash of ecstasy."

"Jesus!" said Sharon. "Did that silly bitch really write that crap?" She sighed deeply and turned on to her stomach so that he could move on to the next stage of sex by numbers.

Even as she did there was a shrill high-pitched squeak, which made her cry out. It was not, however, her colleague Stan coming to an early and unscripted climax, and what she cried out was not "Yes, yes, more, more, oh my darling come come" and all the other stuff Nin girls were supposed to shriek at such moments but, "Oh, Christ, it's the fucking phone!"

She picked up the receiver just as he bit into her flesh in the hope of inducing a quiver, but actually causing her to let out a yelp of pain. "Stan!" she hissed. "Cut that right out. It's for you. Bad line. Stage Irishman. Someone at the office having a joke I guess."

Stan sighed and took the receiver, listened a moment, went a sickly green colour, asked weakly "Who is this?" and replaced the receiver. He had gone suddenly and pathetically limp.

"What's the matter darling?" Now that he was detumescent Sharon was solicitous.

"He said it was the Red Hand of Ulster," said Stan, "and he was going to get me by the end of the week."

"Oh, Stan!" Sharon took his fading penis in her hand and smiled in a pathetic attempt at reassurance. "Oh, Stan! I knew you'd come on too strong with that Irish piece. They've got no sense of humour in Ulster." She gave his organ an encouraging squeeze. "Never mind, though. They don't shoot journalists."

Either the Alka-Seltzer, or the murder threat, or Stan's sudden lack of enthusiasm seemed to have perked Sharon up no end.

"Let's forget the sexy book bit," she said. "I've got a better idea. That mail order stuff arrived yesterday and I'm dying to try out some of the musical condoms."

9

A GOVERNMENT SPOKESMAN SAID . . .

B oy Perryman, formerly Savile Row but now Italian-couturier suited with blue-and-magenta Guards tie – National Service with the Welsh – sat in his scarlet Jaguar E-type alongside a stout red-faced man in standard blue chauffeur's worsted and matching cap. It was too cramped and sporty to be a chauffeur-friendly car but, like Perryman, it had a certain suave raffishness about it. There was a dated quality to this style but Perryman also had that faintly "left over from the previous reign" air about him, a whiff of luncheon and cigars not often encountered in the new age of designer mineral water and politically correct smoke-free everything. His hair shone with a lustre imparted by a sticky pomade from the court hairdresser and he bought his shoes at Lobb's.

Yet despite appearances he was very far from being yesterday's man. Indeed, he was sometimes thought to be the most powerful figure in government, a tricksy Vicar of Bray who had survived three premierships and had a penchant for back-stabbing unexcelled in public life. Smiled a lot, bit of a lady's man, unmarried, useful bridge player, premier-league shit. The younger breed of ascetic polytechnic-trained spin-doctors loathed him but were still circumspect. Privately, they were afraid. "This is a bit of a bore," he said, out loud but to no one in particular.

"Bore" and "boring" were his most damning words, delivered in a self-consciously languid drawl darkened by a lifelong addiction to expensive unfiltered cigarettes. Preferably Abdullahs. This particular bit of a bore was the traffic in Trafalgar Square, which was impeding his progress towards Fleet Street, the *Daily Intelligence* and Major Gordon, its Editor. Reflection on the morning papers made Perryman sense that the Major was his most likely ally. It was true that little Pool at the *Conscience* was, on the basis of his editorial coverage, the most obviously well-disposed of the Fleet Street editors, but Pool was, in Perryman's judgement "a boring little man" and not to be trusted. Perryman was suspicious of self-righteousness, was only really at home with the devious. He liked other shits and was acute enough to recognise that it took one to know one. In his old-fashioned way Major Gordon was a considerable shit, which meant that, unlike Pool, he was someone Perryman felt he could do business with. Pool, however, was someone who used the excuse of "integrity" to stab you in the back, took refuge behind such well-worn hypocrisies as "in the public interest" and "the right to know". Perryman liked to say that Pool was so wet he should have carried a flood warning but he still found him faintly fazing. Out-and-out rogues were more straightforward. The new sanctimony perplexed him.

"Seriously boring," said Perryman, gazing irritably at the back of a bus full of Japanese schoolchildren. The bus was not moving.

He forced himself to relax, tapped a cigarette from a packet of Capstan Full Strength and knocked it against the dashboard before lighting it. He breathed in deeply, enjoying the rasp of strong smoke passing through his tubes. Boy was a throwback, out of kilter with the times, but a strong enough personality for this not to matter; indeed, for it to be a positive advantage. The majority, obsessed with contemporary fashion, modishness in every shape or form, were fazed by Boy's outrageous contempt for the present. He liked blowing smoke at vegetarians. "So what's your view, Trumper?" he asked.

One's chauffeur's views were invaluable. The nearest, in Boy's case, that one ever got to the man in the street.

The man in the peeked cap responded with Jeeves-like enigma. "View, sir?" He flicked gears, snapped the accelerator, zipped past the Japanese tour bus and inserted the E-Type into a space too small. Other drivers hooted.

Boy smiled. "Today's news, Trumper old thing. You must have a view. Did he or didn't he? If he did, does it matter?"

"I'm not paid to have views, sir." This was not quite true.

Trumper was one of the most experienced drivers in government service. He knew secrets others could not imagine. Sometimes he passed them on but always carefully and for a good price, even if money was not involved.

"Of course not, Trumper. You're paid to drive this car. Which, on the whole, you do perfectly adequately. I on the other hand am paid to negotiate between Her Majesty's Government and what once used to be known as the Fourth Estate. And when the little ticks get above themselves, as *entre nous*, they appear to be doing at this very moment, then I need to be able to quote public opinion at them. They know even less than I do about what 'people' are thinking, which frankly is as near next to nothing as dammit. In order to call their bluff I need to be able to preface some of my judgements with such introductions as 'people don't like' or 'people are talking'. And I can't do that without having my ear pretty close to the ground. And in this manner of speaking you're the ground, Trumper. Do you get my drift?"

Trumper had a degree in philosophy from the London School of Economics, though he kept quiet about it. He was also keeping a diary which would one day, he hoped, eke out his pension. "I get your drift, sir."

He was a nifty driver, too. He shot a red light, just evading a black taxi-cab which hooted. The cabbie stuck up two fingers and Trumper grinned. He hated taxi-drivers.

"So what *do* you think?"

"I think a man's private life is his private life. Like private. Same as people's opinions. If you pay a man to drive a car you're entitled to expect him to drive your car, not act as your private think-tank. If you want my opinion you have to bloody well pay for it." He enjoyed winding up old farts like Perryman.

"Don't get smart with me Trumper." Boy Perryman smiled. "You know perfectly well you're the highest-paid chauffeur in Whitehall."

This was probably true, though unprovable. Besides which, most of the Whitehall chauffeurs seemed to have alternative sources of income.

"My opinion is that our man's in trouble," said Perryman. "It would be all right if it were straight sex. And at least it's not little boys ... yet. But 'people', whoever they are, still don't care for left-handed behaviour. You can screw anyone from the opposite sex any way you like and no one gives a toss. But gay lays are still out."

Perryman winced as Trumper squeezed the car into another impossible gap. "Do you really think that's true?"

"Pretty much." Trumper was driving, as always, in impenetrable dark glasses which made him look sinister as well as unreadable. "By the way," he said, "since when has the Prime Minister been gay?"

"The Prime Minister is *not* gay." Perryman's lips were tight. "The Prime Minister is not gay; the Prime Minister has never been gay; I have known the Prime Minister for the better part of my adult life and I have never had the slightest indication that the Prime Minister is anything other than a perfectly normal red-blooded heterosexual male. Do you really believe the *Noise* rather than someone like me?"

"I'm not the media, guv, and this isn't a press conference."

Perryman laughed nervously. "It actually happens to be true," he said. "Our man was set up by the tabloids and this time I'm going to get them. I really am. They think they speak for Britain. They think they run the country. Some of us think their bluff should be called. They're no better than playground bullies."

Trumper flashed a quick sideways glance at his boss from behind the shades and said nothing.

Privately Perryman was far from certain. The *Noise*, horrible though it was, had a tendency not to go for the ministerial jugular unless it had a cast-iron case provable at law. Also, he was uneasy about the Prime Minister's reaction, which seemed edgy to the point of panic. He was not, if one were to be completely honest – not something he liked to be even with himself – entirely sure about the Prime Minister, period. Admittedly the job was not up to much these days, but even allowing for the fact that the main requirements were the ownership of a dark suit, an ability to wield a rubber stamp and deliver a thirty-second "sound bite" to the TV cameras on cue, he was still not sure the present man could really deliver. Man not up to job, which itself not up to much, equalled a depressing formula.

But not as depressing as these bloody press people. In all his years of dealing with the media Perryman had never known a time like it. Only the Majors and their mother were what you might call respectable. What he found extraordinary was that as the power and the quality of the newspapers declined in the face of advancing television, the post-literate society, the Internet and life itself, so the people who worked for the things became more and more bumptious and pleased with themselves.

A case in point was an article of Pool's which had appeared a week or so earlier in the *Conscience*. Perryman disliked Pool very much. He was a counter-jumper – socially, intellectually and professionally. Perryman couldn't place him and that infuriated him. He didn't even have the guts to be himself. When Pool wanted to say something particularly dear to his heart he ventured out of the anonymous leader column and on to the editorial page, usually occupied by windbag back-bench MPs or Fellows of Oxbridge colleges with time on their hands but no cash – Oxbridge traditionally paying its members in a particularly snobby sort of luncheon voucher.

Like the sort of banana or cigarette economy dictator who immediately dons a uniform and makes himself a field marshal, Pool was never really happy without his title, preferably wielded from behind an enormous desk and in an important leather chair. On this occasion he did not sign himself "William Pool" like any normal person but "The Editor". Sure sign of insecurity. Not to mention self-importance.

This particular piece was headed "The Fourth Estate: a national debt". It began by saying that at no time in the country's history had the importance, prestige, *savoir-faire*, intelligence, breeding, appearance and general wonderfulness of the British journalist been more apparent. This, argued "The Editor", was further emphasised by the fact that all the other pillars of society were in a state of terminal decay. Government was a laughing stock in thrall to Brussels, Washington and anyone else who stood up to it (including the press); the law was just a lot of silly old men in wigs totally out of touch with what "makes society tick" – unlike the press in general, the *Conscience* in particular and "The Editor" most of all; the Church was the same in cassocks except, of course, for the "happy clappies" who were a lot of "progressive" gays and lesbians who should never have been admitted to holy orders; and as for the so called "Royal" Family, say no more – if Alfred the Great could see them he'd be turning in his grave. Pool was a great fan of Alfred the Great, having "done him" once upon a time at university.

Perryman had laughed when he first read the article, but it gradually became apparent that almost everyone else in the world took it seriously. To him this was beyond belief, but then so was practically everything else in the world today as far as he was concerned. Not least, London traffic and Trumper's driving. A lot of it was to do with this "classless society" rubbish. Perryman was all for equality of opportunity, at least in theory, but it was perfectly obvious to right-thinking people of his generation that a "classless society" was inconceivable. It was a popular mantra hypocritically parroted out by "classless" rulers like the present Prime Minister, but to Perryman it was a meaningless bromide. One could have any number of different theories about the nature of class and how many different classes there were in the world. He personally sympathised with the intricacies of the Indian caste system and could see that "sweepers" were an identifiable and well-defined group, just as were the people in London who lived in cardboard boxes and appeared to have their headquarters in the tunnels between Waterloo Station and the National Theatre.

In Britain, as far as Perryman was concerned, there were basically two classes – officers and men, gentlemen and players, us and them, "chaps" and "oiks". Perryman believed himself to be part of a ruling class and he did not like the idea of people from the other class climbing on board. There was too much of that sort of thing going on in every walk of life. Without order there was chaos. It was obvious.

He was musing thus when the E-Type came to a sudden juddering halt and he realised with a shock that they had arrived. He pulled himself together and prepared for a serious word with the Majors.

10

RESIGNED TO SPEND MORE TIME WITH . . .

Like many of the newly sacked, Fisher found inactivity fun. He woke latish and read the paper in pyjamas while Jeannie Cadogan, the girl-friend, got ready for work. She had a moderately high-powered job in advertising. After she left in a flurry of expensive scent and sensibly chic suiting, Fisher poured himself another coffee and returned to bed where he snoozed, fiddled with the crossword, listened to the remains of the *Today* programme and scoured the job vacancies in the *UK Press Gazette*. These were universally unappealing. Besides, as he was white, male and middle-aged, he knew that he hadn't a prayer of even getting an interview. The fact that he could spell, punctuate and unsplit an infinitive was of no interest to man or beast.

Presently he bathed and shaved, read a little, listened to Classic FM and went shopping. This leisurely trawl involved little more than the purchase of ingredients for supper which, now that he was unemployed and Jeannie was not, he felt prepared, if not obliged, to cook himself. The trip invariably ended in the pub where, being a creature of habit, he always had a cheese ploughman's and two pints of John Smith.

Afterwards he dozed again, re-engaged with the crossword, watched *Ready Steady Cook!* on BBC2 (hoping for inspiration for the evening meal), made a phone call or two to friends (most either in a similar situation or unhappily employed) and waited, edgily, until six o'clock when he poured himself a stiff Scotch, turned on the early evening news and the oven.

By the time Jeannie returned from the office Fisher was surrounded by culinary debris. He was also agreeably mellow, if not exactly inebriated.

As the days went by Jeannie, grappling with the demands of such clients as the Australian Emu Marketing Board and, during the day, never drinking anything stronger than a double espresso or a very weak white-wine spritzer, became increasingly unamused.

Finally, after a fortnight, she told Fisher that this simply wasn't bloody good enough and he must find himself a job or she was going to leave.

His first reaction was shock, swiftly followed by resentment, truculence, disbelief and a lot more whisky. In this last she shared, with the result that, after a while, meaningful dialogue became impossible.

It was resumed the following evening.

"I'm not prepared to work my bloody arse off every day while you act the couch-potato at home and down the Pig and Whatsit."

"Whistle."

"Don't be so pompous. You know perfectly well what I mean."

"I do supper."

"More trouble than it's worth. You're a bloody awful cook and it takes me twice as long to clear up after you as it would if I'd done the whole thing myself."

"That's not entirely fair."

"No, it most certainly is not entirely fair. I'm keeping the two of us afloat and getting sod all in return."

"There's my redundo ..."

"You know perfectly well that your wife and children will have gobbled up your redundancy money in six months at the outside."

This was true. Fisher's wife was expensive and the boys were at some dim boarding-school in Devon. It was not a smart school but its fees suggested otherwise.

"So what exactly do you suggest?"

"Get a job."

"We've been through all that. There are no jobs."

"There are millions of newspapers absolutely stuffed with words. Someone has to write them."

This was true. It was a conundrum. When he began his career as a journalist there were fewer titles and fewer words. Conversely it seemed to require many more people to produce them. In the print industry, he knew, there was a disgraceful incidence of "Old Spanish Customs" who prayed on avuncular, benevolent and financially incompetent proprietors. Then a new generation of hard-nosed Thatcherite millionaires had transformed newspapers by sweeping away the bad habits of printing history and replacing them with white-hot new technology. Having dealt with the printers this unattractive gang of, mainly foreign, parvenus had turned their attention to the hacks. It was axiomatic that whereas the old proprietors, even the parsimonious ones such as Lord Thomson of Fleet, rather liked journalists and journalism – it was one of their reasons for being in the game – the new lot loathed them, particularly when, like Fisher, they had been to a proper university and cared about correct English. Having eliminated the hated printers, they would like to have got rid of the horrible writers as well. Thanks to a policy of getting machinery to do as much of the job as possible, coupled with an apparently total indifference to the quality of the stuff that separated the advertisements from each other, the new press lords had succeeded in making gratifying depredations. There were still journalists in employment but they were a beleaguered crew of desk-bound apparatchiks unrecognisably different from the swashbuckling buccaneers of Fisher's apprenticeship.

The new wisdom was that the journalists of the *ancien régime* such as Fisher had spent all the time eating and drinking lunch. "Lunch", indeed, had become the great pejorative of the new journalistic puritanism. Modern young Turks delivered the word with a nasal sneer. To admit to taking lunch was on a par with conceding an addiction to cocaine or small boys. This was partly to do with control. If employees were out of the office eating and drinking – or indeed engaging in any other activity – nobody knew what they were doing. Editors, themselves operating in the new climate of fear, lacked the confidence of their predecessors and became apprehensive if they could not actually observe those supposedly under their orders. This was Fisher's dictum: "Out of sight, out of control".

In Fisher's early days in newspapers he had been encouraged by his bosses to get out and about. Latterly, if he was not crouched over his screen courting any number of as yet unknown diseases of the spine and/or central nervous system he was accused of skiving off.

All this and more passed through his mind as he considered Jeannie's words about work. "I'm sorry," he said, "I just don't think I'm going to get a job."

"You might if you weren't so pompous and conceited. You may have to lower your sights. What about subbing? Being a sub is a perfectly respectable profession. You've always said so."

This was true.

"There aren't any sub-editors any longer. You know that. The hacks do it themselves on their computers. That's why there are so many typos nowadays."

There was a silence during which they glared at each other. This was not what either of them had signed on for.

"Well, why not try something completely different? You've always said you wanted to do something different."

"Garlic farming I suppose?"

He had occasionally fantasised about starting a garlic farm in Provence. Or becoming a master *chevrier* with a bicycle and a beret.

"I'm actually being perfectly serious," she protested. "It's not too late to start again. What about teaching?"

"What about teaching?"

"You could do it. You've got a perfectly respectable degree. You're a very good teacher. You said so yourself. All those young journalists on the Diary ..."

"You need more qualifications than a degree to teach these days. It's all quite different. Life's moved on."

"You're being very defeatist."

He sighed. "It's not defeatism, it's realism. There is no room in the world for middle-aged, middle-rank journalists who have been made redundant."

"Sacked."

"Exactly."

"What about the *Intelligence*?"

"What about the *Intelligence*? As it happens I *have* written to them, but what of it?"

"They still employ middle-aged white Anglo-Saxon males with drink problems."

"I think that's a bit harsh on them. And me, come to that." He frowned. He didn't actually think she was being especially severe on either count, but it would be tactically unsound to admit it. "In any case," he continued, "Colin's the Literary Editor there and he's family. So I'm unlikely to succeed to that particular billet. Besides, every single hack like me in the whole of London is beating on the *Intelligence* door. It's our last refuge but they've got a serious over-population problem already."

"But darling, you're not just any old hack. You're very good. The best. Why do you think I'm here?"

"You're very sweet." He meant it. "But as I keep telling myself and anyone else who cares to listen, virtue is no reward these days. Rather the reverse. If you're any bloody good in newspapers it just emphasises the mediocrity of the herd. I acknowledge that's the lament of the superannuated throughout history. On the other hand I just happen to believe it's true. I suspect people like me have been saying that for ever, which only goes to show that true wisdom is the prerogative of the aged and the rejected. I bet Cardinal Wolsey thought the same when Thomas Cromwell got his job."

"That's hardly the same."

"Oh, I don't know."

Fisher had a highly developed sense of the historical and of the absurd. He saw no reason why he should not have been Cardinal Wolsey in an earlier life.

Or, for that matter, Thomas Cromwell.

"Oh dar*ling* ..."

Her fond frustration hung in the air like the gun-smoke of a warning fusillade across the erring bows of a Spanish trawler in Cornish waters. Then she said: "You're probably right. A job as such isn't the solution."

"What, then?"

"Self-employment. Your own business."

"Do me a favour. Every second one of the people I started out with is pretending to be a self-employed freelance. Nearly all of them are lucky if they can place 'A weekend walk in Brontë Country' with the *Auckland Advertiser*. I'd be better off drawing dole. Much."

"Your own business, then."

"You mean back to garlic farming?"

"No." She smiled indulgently. "I accept that you have to stick to what you know best."

"But I only know about journalism."

This time her smile was not so much indulgent as knowing. "I understand that, darling. You know about nothing except journalism and you're effectively unemployable. On the face of it both these sound like negatives. But we mustn't allow ourselves to think negatively. Therefore we have to stand both propositions on their heads. You are one of the world's leading experts on journalism with some twenty years' experience of the profession at the top end of the market. You are therefore brilliantly equipped to run your own private newspaper company."

Fisher was becoming bewildered. "You're not suggesting I start a newspaper," he said. "The last twenty years are littered with poor schmucks who thought they could start their own newspapers. At least if you edit an established newspaper you end up with a knighthood. If you start your own it's just bad debts, bad feeling and a lifetime of whingeing self-justification. So, thanks but no thanks."

"Of course not," she said. "I think some kind of consultancy is called for."

"Consultancy!?"

"Absolutely." She grinned. "Consultancy is the property development *de nos jours*. The great scam. I'm quite sure that with a bit of making-over; some decent stationery; an acceptable PA; a New York office and various other bits of bogus flummery you could easily make a go of it as a media consultant."

"That doesn't sound like me."

"Maybe not." She smiled. "But you're not too old to be re-invented."

He smiled too, though without as much conviction. "I'm not at all sure I have anything to say that anyone in newspapers is going to want to hear," he said.

"You know that," she stated, "and I know that. But there's no reason why *they* should know that. Believe me, there are plenty of people out there longing to pay serious money for consultancy. It saves them having to think for themselves. It prevents them having to actually do anything. Having a 'consultant' will make them feel good. You see, cripples need crutches."

"A media consultant," he said. "Me."

"Jawohl. First of all we need a resonant name. Something like Saatchi and Rothschild or Cazenove, Baring, Getty."

"What's wrong with Fisher and Fisher?" he wanted to know.

She thought for a moment. "Fisher Cadogan and Fisher," she

said, "London Hong Kong Paris and New York. And no commas. Commas are *passé.*"

FAMOUS LAST WORDS

"'Proprietor-in-Chief' and 'Editor Emeritus'," said Stomper-Watson, chewing thoughtfully on the end of his pencil. "Well, at the very least we're going to have to update the old girl's obit. Priscilla, could you find me the galley proofs of our obituary of Lady Beatrice and ask Mr Trotter if he could possibly drop by for a moment when he can spare me a second."

His secretary, an old-style twin-set-and-pearls naval officer's daughter, said "Certainly Mr Watson" and vanished in the direction of the morgue and the great wordsmith. Trotter and Stomper-Watson often pooled their talents on important obituaries; the former being a past master at embellishing – or, as he put it, "tarting-up" – the Obituary Editor's functional but pedestrian prose. You had to watch Trotter, of course, for he had a tendency, in the interests of entertainment and linguistic *joie de vivre*, to embellish the facts and generally play fast and loose with the life under review. Not a man to be uneconomical with the truth.

"But what *is* truth?" Trotter would protest, eyes rolling, whenever some literal-minded sub-editor questioned the veracity of a particularly far-fetched anecdote. When the sub came back with the correct newspaperman's response that truth was anything that would not end in a costly libel action, he liked to explode in triumph that "you cannot libel the dead". This was true, up to a point, but, as the paper had found out to its cost, dead men's relations could be extremely tiresome on behalf of their late loved ones. They also tended to be friends of Lady Beatrice or one of the Majors. From time to time there were disagreeable scenes. As Obituaries Editor, it was Stomper-Watson who had to endure these unpleasantnesses even when the malevolent fabrications had been perpetrated by Trotter.

At these interviews he would hang his head, express contrition and never pass the buck. Only afterwards would he allow his irritation to show as he remonstrated with Trotter. Thus, "But you swore that story about Lady Zeebrugge and the dormouse was true."

"Well, it is sort of true," Trotter would respond.

"Then why did none of the other papers have it? And why do the family insist that it's a complete fabrication?"

"Well they would, wouldn't they? And the opposition didn't have it because they're not as clever as us."

"Meaning not as inventive?"

At this point Trotter would squirm a little, squint at his shoes and say, "Just because it's not literally true doesn't mean to say it's not figuratively true. Which is to say that if it didn't actually happen then it should have done. It says far more about the real Lady Zeebrugge than that garbage in the *Conscience*."

"But the family *liked* the *Conscience* obit."

"We're not paid to write what the family like."

And so these post-mortems of post-mortems would wrangle on, not getting anywhere until finally an exasperated Stomper-Watson would take Trotter off to the Belt and Braces for a pint or two of Special. Sometimes it seemed that Lady Beatrice and the Majors seemed to be on the verge of losing their nerve but they never, quite, did. The obits were one of the few aspects of their paper which was genuinely admired by their rivals. Somehow they contrived to be thoroughly reactionary and yet ground-breaking at the same time.

Stomper-Watson was musing on his friend and colleague's foibles when the man himself breezed into his office, bringing with him his unmistakable aroma of cheese, onion, nicotine and last night's beer. "What ho!" he said, in his leather-brown voice. "So who's toppled off the sodding perch *aujourd'hui*, eh?"

"Lady Beatrice is pushing off upstairs," said Watson.

"Metaphorically or literally?"

"Figuratively. I think the exact terminology is 'relinquishing day-to-day control of the *Daily* and *Sunday Intelligence*.'"

"Good grief!" Trotter raised his eyes. "The Prime Minister in a gay sex scandal with his PPS and the old bird chooses this moment to give it all up. Beyond belief."

Trotter, like Stomper-Watson, was a long-serving *Intelligence* man who remembered the Majors when they were dashing young things with brilliantined hair and a penchant for nights out at Quaglino's and retained an abiding respect for what he referred to as "the sheer bloody journalistic professionalism" of Lady Beatrice.

"I can't see her letting go altogether," said the obituarist. "She'll let the Majors do all the work and interfere like fury whenever she feels like it. But, let's face it, none of us is getting any younger."

"She never ever gives her birth date," said Trotter. "As far as the obit goes I'm going to put 1 April 1912, which must be about right, give or take a decade or so either way. If she doesn't like it then too bad. If she'd wanted the right date she should have told us and not been a vain old fruit bat."

An irritable parakeet sound of disapproval greeted this last sobriquet and the two men looked up to see that the new Proprietor-in-Chief and Editor Emeritus was standing in the doorway, eyes so narrow that they were just two blobs of mascara, the vivid scarlet lips pursed into a circle of rebuke. "*Mister* Trotter!" she said, wobbling with a consuming crossness that they had all seen a thousand times before. "I'll thank you to remember who pays your mortgage."

This was a much-loved line, invariably included when any member of the *Intelligence* staff was doing his or her Lady Beatrice imitation.

The two men's already pinkish complexions intensified. Stomper-Watson stood up; Trotter, standing already, stiffened to attention.

"I assume the two of you are revising my obituary?"

Just at that moment Priscilla tip-tapped back into the office holding confirmation of Lady B's suspicion in the shape of a long, yellowing galley proof. She froze as she saw the imposing back view of her super-boss and might have tried beating a retreat, were it not for the surprisingly quick hundred and eighty degree swing of Lady Beatrice's tent-clad frame.

"Ah, child!" said Lady Beatrice, using her habitual form of address for anyone, of either sex, whom she suspected of being younger than herself. "I presume you are holding Mr Trotter's account of my life so far." She swung back to confront the two discomfited hacks. "And what, darlings, were you going to add in the light of my latest decisions? Were you going to scrawl 'finis' at the end of the last paragraph? Were you going to say that the old girl had finally given up the ghost? 'In her declining years the Proprietor eventually realised she was going completely gaga and resigned.' Something like that Mr Trotter?"

"As a matter of fact," said Trotter, "I was going to write something along the lines of 'at last Lady Beatrice shook all cares and business from her age, conferring them on younger strengths'."

"Ah Mr Trotter, Mr Trotter," said Lady Beatrice, "I suppose that's Shakespeare."

"Yes, actually. Well, sort of. Shakespeare marginally laundered. But yes, in effect, Shakespeare."

"It usually is." Lady Beatrice smiled at her triumphant guess-work. She had been playing this game for the best part of thirty years, ever since she had hired Trotter to look after vocabulary, lexicography and house style after hearing him in a BBC Third Programme debate with the word expert from the *Conscience*. Trotter had won.

"We do try to keep obits up to date once they're on file," said Stomper-Watson defensively, "and in the circumstances it seemed only proper to update your own. After all, this is the end of an era."

"One," said Lady Beatrice, "if there is any updating of my obituary to be done then I'll do it. Two, it is not the end of an era. It's not even the beginning of the end."

"But", persisted Stomper-Watson, "you *have* handed over the day-to-day running of the papers to the Majors?"

"Oh, pish-tush. The point is that at the end of the day I am still in charge. You're quite right that I no longer wish to be bothered with the mundane, the trivial, the tiresome, the signing of expense chits, the fine-tuning of leaders, the chivvying of people like you. But when it comes to matters of importance the buck stops here. So, child, if you would like to hand over your galley proof I will make the necessary additions and emendations and return it to this department after morning conference."

"We were speculating", said Trotter with the honesty which he had always regarded as the best policy as far as the ancient termagant was concerned, "about why you chose to do this in the middle of the 'Prime Minister in gay sex romp, shock-horror gasp' crisis."

Lady Beatrice smiled flintily. It was true that she had always found Trotter's plain, if sometimes convoluted, speaking a disarming ploy. She, in turn, had always enjoyed imparting little confidences to him, knowing that he was a compulsive and inveterate gossip. If you wanted the office to know your innermost but unspeakable thoughts the best course of action was to entrust them to Trotter. "With regard to the story about the Prime Minister and his wretched boy-friend I have to confess that my heart is not in it. The point about Mr Sutton is that he's not up to the job. Whether or not he's screwing his Private Secretary is neither here nor there. If you two were assessed on the basis of your bedroom behaviour you'd doubtless have been fired years ago. And I'm not being unkind. The same could probably be said of myself. We've never pretended to be angels but we have always been good at our jobs. Mr Sutton is no good at being Prime Minister. But no one seems to care about that any longer."

"Yes, but", said Trotter, "there is a point of view which thinks that private and public morality are linked. And there is Mrs Sutton to consider. Not to mention the children. Don't you think we're entitled to expect higher standards of behaviour from our rulers?"

"Oh, humbug, darling. You sound like little Mr Pool at the *Conscience*. Pooter and Pecksniff rolled into one. I do dislike that sort of adenoidal hypocrisy. He really does think he's the national conscience. *And* I understand he's been promoted and put in charge of Sir Edward White and the *Noise*. Nominally, at least. Though it's probably just cosmetic, like our little change here."

Stomper-Watson was less of a familiar, more in awe of Lady B. Nevertheless, encouraged by his colleague's relative daring, he tried a different tack. "Why bother?" he asked. "Why not just carry on as before? Or if you have to go then fade gradually rather than go up in this melodramatic puff of smoke."

"Do you have children, Mr Watson?" she asked, fluttering enormous eyelashes.

He and Mrs Stomper-Watson had tried, God knows, but to no avail. "No," he said.

"Well if you had you'd know that they get restless with one in one's old age. They think that because you have wrinkles and walk with a stick, somehow you're not up to the job and that they can do it better. All sorts of fearful nonsense of that kind. I was afraid the boys might be getting stale, so I'm letting them have more of their head. If the Queen had done the same with the Prince of Wales the Palace wouldn't have got themselves into the sort of muddle they're in now. You must always humour the young. That's why we have a popular music correspondent."

"I see," said Stomper-Watson, not altogether convinced.

"Well. I'll potter off and attend to this. And no tinkering around with it behind my back." And the old woman left, whacking a chairleg with her stick and grinning with an expression which was not entirely sane.

"What do you make of that, exactly?" asked Stomper-Watson.

"Machinations, hollowness, treachery and all ruinous disorders," said Trotter. He smiled. "She's playing a jolly dangerous game if you ask me. Abdicating and yet not abdicating. Even for a Lucrezia Borgia like Lady B that's a dangerous tactic. The Majors aren't stupid and once their hands are really on the levers of power they won't hesitate."

"Major Colin's never going to get his hands on the levers of power."

"Of course not, but Gordon and Ronald can be seriously ruthless given half a chance and if you ask me Lady B's giving them half a chance. And then there are the wives to consider." At the thought of Lady Beatrice's daughters-in-law Trotter could not suppress a shudder.

"Hmm. And why's she doing it at a time like this when we're in the middle of the biggest bloody story in yonks?"

Trotter frowned. "She's never enjoyed sex scandals. Not like her sons, who've always salivated over them. I have an instinct she's happy to stay out of this, partly because there's an element of the prude in her make-up and partly because she doesn't think politicians should be judged on how they perform in bed. But also it's the perfect smoke-screen. Most people are going to be far too preoccupied with Sutton and Kim Sanderson-Wright to bother with a Palace Revolution at the *Intelligence*. Classic ploy."

"I wonder what she said to the Majors?" said Stomper-Watson. "She obviously didn't say the same as she said to us. We think she's told the truth to us and they presumably think they've been told it too. So which is right? And what *is* she up to?"

"Too much speculation is bad for the digestion," said Trotter. "And talking of Sutton and Sanderson-Wright, I suppose you're going to dust their pieces off? Only I've got to do a leader pager on the lexicography of political correctness. Major Gordon wants it for the Saturday Arts page and frankly it's proving a bit of a bugger. I'm not sure I've got time to update any more corpse careers. In any case too much cerebral ambulance chasing gets me down after a while."

Stomper-Watson laughed sympathetically. " 'There was a time when we were not', " he said, " 'this gives us no concern – why then should it trouble us that a time will come when we shall cease to be?' "

"Hmm," said Trotter. "Hazlitt?"

"Yes," said Stomper-Watson, mildly irritated. He had come across the lines only the other day and had been saving them up for just such a moment in the hope of catching Trotter out. But this, as he had discovered over the years, was a difficult thing to do.

12

INSIDE INFORMATION

"Sharon, don't get me wrong. Musical condoms will make a great piece and you'll do it fucking brilliant, but it's going to have to wait." Albert van Blanco was in the newsroom at the *Noise*, in shirt-sleeves and a pair of scarlet braces from Chicken, Alaska. He had once been to Chicken, Alaska on a press trip and had returned home with the braces and a packet of condoms labelled "I got laid in Chicken, Alaska". Albert thought this pretty bloody funny and often included it in his night-club chat-up routine. He was of the opinion that it turned some ladies on.

"Sharon, I'm sorry. I'm sure the research is going really really well but I'm going to have to take you off the job for today. And Stan too. Any case you don't *need* all the research you do. Use your imagination. Like everyone else. Real sex is out the window anyway. No one's actually *doing* it any longer. It's all 'virtual'. Naked ladies dancing on table tops but no touchy. Copulating on the Internet. Doing it to each other the way you do is like, well, yuk."

The News Editor was talking into a telephone, which he cradled between his chin and his shoulder just as he had seen it done on the movies in his childhood. He was also talking round a large cigar, unlit, which was held between his teeth with a matchstick. Many years before there had been a senior journalist on the *Daily Express* who used a cigar as just such a prop, together with braces and carpet slippers. As a teenage tea boy van Blanco had been hugely impressed by this and now unashamedly tried to recreate in himself what he thought of as "the Raybould effect".

Sharon and Stanley were at home in bed researching the musical condoms when the phone went. As they were between orgasms Sharon answered it on the grounds that it might be someone interesting. The minute she heard the News Editor's voice she naturally regretted the decision. On the other hand, she reasoned, the bastard paid the rent and if you spend too much time not answering the phone to bastards who pay the rent you're liable to come badly unstuck. "You bastard, Bert," she shrilled.

"I know, luvvy, but this is a big big story and I need Stan on his bike to get a big big interview with the PM, or with his lover, or the wife, or someone. Only big. And I need you to do one of your cod 'A Doctor Writes' pieces about 'Bisexuality'."

"I'm not into bisexuality Bert." Sharon pushed Stan away from her quite roughly, causing his condom to play the first few bars of "Little Bo Peep" in an unexpected falsetto.

"Darling, I *know* that, but for me and for the *Noise* you can do it. You're the most heterosexual lay I know but for once in your life think lezzy."

As a matter of fact Albert van Blanco had never had the pleasure of Sharon, which for him was a matter of some regret. It was not for want of trying.

"We're not talking lezzies here, Bert, we're talking pooftahs. I don't know anything about gay blokes."

"That's got nothing to do with anything. Make it up. Use your imagination. Think bum."

"You what?" Sharon was not familiar with this phrase.

"Think bum. It's what being gay's all about – rum, bum and concertina – old navy tradition. The Prime Minister's got a thing about men's bums. Let's hear it from you, Sharon. I want five hundred words by an expert on why a happily married prime minister of Great Britain jeopardises his entire life's work, wife and kiddies, all for another man's bum. Get something about Freud into it. And public schools. Public schools are what it's all about. You put these teenage kids into dormitories with lots of other teenage kids and no girls and wham bam, they're all hard at it. And don't forget the beating. They all get beaten on the bum. It all comes back to bums in the end. Don't forget the Prince of Wales and Gordonstoun. Cold baths. Cherry brandy. Great stuff."

77

"But ..." Sharon sighed. "The Prime Minister didn't go to public school. He went to some sodding grammar school in South Wales."

"For Christ's sake, Sharon, it doesn't bloody matter. Just write the effing piece. You don't have to come in to the office. Just write it from home and put it over. What do you think your lap-top's for? Lap-top, eh? Get it? Good, meaty stuff. Lotsa sex but written like you know what you're on about. We'll put some high-class-sounding byline on it. And don't forget Freud. Now, can I have a word with Stan?"

Sharon grunted a grudging affirmative and passed the phone to her partner.

"Mornin', boss," said Stan, sounding chirpier than he felt.

"Morning, Stanley. We need a really strong follow-up to the PM story for tomorrow. Got to keep ahead of the pack."

Inwardly Stan sighed. This did not sound like good news. In any event it was the end of an exciting and innovative day in bed. "Sure thing, boss. What did you have in mind?"

Van Blanco scratched his pate. "Some seriously good quotes would be best," he said.

"Meaning Prime Minister quotes and lover-boy quotes and wronged-wife quotes?"

"Yeah, right." Van Blanco spun the cigar round his mouth. "So far we've just got second-rate back-bencher quotes and mother-in-law quotes. The mother-in-law quotes will be OK with a bit of work, but we need something juicy from one of the key players. Know what I mean?"

Stan knew what he meant all too well. Some second-rate minor politicians who had been snubbed, insulted, or ignored by the Prime Minister had come out of the woodwork and been induced to utter remarks along the lines of "I always thought there was something peculiar about those two" or, "I remember seeing them dealing with the boxes and files together and thinking how closely they worked." These would be translated into *Noise*-speak as "What a pair of queers!" and "He couldn't keep his hands off his box" or "out of his files". Amusing enough on the inside pages of the paper but not the stuff of a loud *Noise* front page.

"Where is everyone?" asked Stan.

"The wife's gone back to Mum down in Frinton," said van Blanco. "Freddie Baker's doorstepping her along with a million and one others. They've drawn the curtains and they're sitting tight. Local Bill are a nightmare as you can imagine in bloody Frinton. Downing Street's sealed off and no one's saying a dicky-bird. Even Boy Perryman's gone shtum. He was coming here to have a go at Ken but our info is that he's thought better of it and gone to chew things over with the Majors at the *Intelligence*. His sort of people, don't you know, eh, what?!" Van Blanco did a curious imitation of what he imagined to be an old Etonian accent. It sounded even funnier for being funnelled round his cigar.

"So where's the PM?" Stan wanted to know.

"Dunno." Van Blanco sighed. "My guess is Chequers. It's most other people's guess too."

"So you want me to go down there?"

"Yeah. Sid's going with you for pix. He'll come by the flat in about twenty minutes and pick you up."

"Shit!" said Stan. "I'll never get in." He had done Chequers many times in the past. It would be sealed off by police and security, and quite impenetrable. The grounds were enormous and even if one was able to get over the perimeter wall the approaches to the house were scoured by radar and closed-circuit TV, as well as being patrolled by police dog handlers with killer Alsatians, or German Shepherds as they were supposed to be called nowadays.

"We've got a chance," said the News Editor, putting on his best "hold-the-front-page" voice. "The local stringer, bloke called Bill Harper, he's got a contact with the laundry in Great Missenden which is due in today. If you can hitch a ride in one of his hampers you can go as high as you like with the old cheque-book, know what I mean?"

"You want me and Sid Green to go in to Chequers in a couple of laundry baskets? Give over!" He leaned across and gently caressed Sharon's left nipple with his spare hand. What a sod life was, having to play peeping tom on a gay PM when you could be at home conducting well-paid research with the love of your life. Well, if not the love of your life, the light of your loins. Thinking of which he realised that he was still wearing his musical condom, shrivelled now, thanks to the cold-shower-like quality of this telephone conversation. It was a tasteful but unerotic shade of lime green. Almost Irish.

"Do you have a better idea?" van Blanco wanted to know.

"Other than staying here, I suppose not."

"You know bloody well you and Sharon can screw on company

time whenever you want. Except when there's a story like bloody this."

Van Blanco certainly had an interesting way with the English language. But then his surname did suggest that it was not his mother tongue.

"Oh, OK. Tell Sid I'll be outside in twenty minutes all ready for going in with the dirty linen."

"Clean linen, you nerd, Stanley. The laundry will be taking clean linen *in*. That's what laundries do in case you hadn't noticed. They collect the dirties and they do what's called laundering which means taking the muck out of everything and making it all shiny white. A good laundry does it in private. Our job is to make them go public. Make sure all the dirty washing hangs out. Eh, Stanley? Joke. Geddit? You'll be going *out* with the dirty linen."

"That's a point," said Stan. "We may be able to get *into* the place in laundry baskets but how the shit do we get out again?"

But the great News Editor had hung up. All Stan got was a metallic dialling tone.

"Did you hear that?" he asked his partner who was lying flat on her back staring at the ceiling, starkers.

"What?"

"What Bert wants me to do?"

"No, sorry. I was thinking about men's bums."

"He wants me to smuggle myself and Sid Green into the Prime Minister's country house with the laundry."

"Sounds fun," said Sharon. "Do you have to keep that condom on? It's a terrible colour and it's played its tune."

"Oh. Sorry." He rolled it off, wrapped it in a tissue and laid it gently on the bedside table.

"I dunno," he said. "Is this a sensible job for grown-up people?"

"Don't ask me." Sharon sighed and scratched her inside left thigh in an absent-minded way, which quickened Stan's pulse more than somewhat. "Who said anything about either of us being grown-up?"

Stan was poised for a lascivious lunge but thought better of it. Sid, the photographer, would be ringing the doorbell in not much more than quarter of an hour and Sid was a hard man with a streak of sneak in him. You had to be very professional working with Sid otherwise Albert or Sir Eddie would get to hear of it and trouble ensued. Sid was not to be trusted. If you played ball with him there was a fifty-fifty chance he might play ball with you. If you didn't play ball with him then forget it.

"What's he want from you then?" Stan asked, sitting up and contemplating Sharon's full frontal. She was a cracking piece of symmetrical, gym-conditioned, nutritionally balanced, sexually voracious woman. He could kill van Blanco and the Prime Minister.

"He wants a piece on Freud and the male bum," said Sharon, sizing him up. "Here. Stand up. Turn round. Bend over. Straighten up. Hmm. Do you see anything in other men's bums?"

"Don't be disgusting." Stan was genuinely shocked.

"Well the Prime Minister does. He's risked everything for it. That's what Bert van Blanco thinks. And when you think about it he's sort of right. Does seem a shame. Anyway he wants me to write a piece of deep Freudian analysis only made so the average *Noise* reader can understand it. You know, if I were a bloke I can't say I'd be turned on by your arse."

"What's wrong with it?" Stan was, privately, proud of his bottom which had very little sag and might almost be considered, well, pert.

"Bit spotty; bit hairy. Not like a Greek-statue bum."

"Sharon," he said, "that tends to be the way with the male bum, especially when British. And in any case, if I were you I wouldn't be too physical. I mean plenty of *Noise* readers are going to be gays and bisexuals, and for many of them their way of life is going to be, like, a state of mind. Gays and bisexuals have finer feelings too, you know. I mean the PM wasn't just lusting after his PPS's body, he was in love with his mind. Or words to that effect, if you know what I mean. There's a whole emotional, mental dimension to this business, doesn't matter if its gay, bi or hetero. We're not just animals, Sharon. There's more to sex than flesh and blood."

"Speak for yourself, sweetie," said Sharon.

And then the doorbell shrilled. Sid Green was early.

13

WINDSOCK ERROR

B oy Perryman had expected Lady Beatrice to be of the party, but instead he found only Gordon and Ronald in the oak-panelled *Intelligence* number one dining-room. Other newspapers far out in the sticks beyond Wapping or Hammersmith had invested in large numbers of dining-rooms, partly because the new offices were in gastronomic wildernesses but also because the latest generation of proprietors preferred their employees to be manacled to their desks. The last thing they wanted was a whole load of hacks to be lurching in and out of high-class eateries chalking up huge expenses. That was "sixties journalism" – the most savage insult a man like Chinese Ken could hurl.

The *Intelligence* had just the two rooms for entertaining people to lunch or dinner. One was the very grand panelled room in which Boy and the Majors found themselves and which was reserved entirely for the use of the Majors. The other was a rather down-market affair for the benefit of senior executives. It was little used.

Boy accepted a glass of champagne in a crystal flute and squinted at the flattering Bryan Organ portrait of Lady Beatrice which hung above the enormous Balmoral-style sideboard. Her ladyship appeared to squint back at him, her expression almost conspiratorial.

"Lady B not with us?" he asked in his most breezy voice, the one which said, only not exactly in so many words: "how pleasant to be among civilised human beings and not those yobbish barbarians from the tabloids."

"Er, no.' Gordon went a little pink and shifty. "There have been one or two changes here. Ronald and I are now at the helm."

"Oh." Boy frowned, though more from intrigue than irritation.

"Mother's not getting any younger," said Ronald, also glancing at her portrait, though with an apprehensive expression rather as if the old girl might leap off the wall and handbag him, "and in fact she was the one who suggested a sort of shuffle upstairs. I think some peace and quiet will do her good."

Boy raised an eyebrow. Peace and quiet were not words he associated readily with Lady Beatrice but he was not here to get into an argument about that. This was a family affair and he knew enough about families to stay well clear. All the same, he would be surprised if this particular change were to go smoothly. It was not in Lady Beatrice's nature.

"It really was Mother's idea," said Gordon, his back to the leaded window looking out towards St Bride's church. "She's taken on a couple of fancy titles but of course they don't actually mean anything. From now on I shall edit and Gordon will manage. It's a very sensible way of dividing responsibilities. And she's certainly earned retirement. Nobody could have worked harder. Now she's ready for a break."

They sat down. The butler introduced a tureen from which he ladled beef consommé tricked out with some shredded carrot. Then he poured Sancerre. Then fizzy Malvern water. Then he left.

"I do hope", said Perryman, "that we can rely on your support."

"How do you mean exactly?" Gordon was deliberately disingenuous.

"Over this ridiculous story. We've simply got to stand up to filthmongers like White. That sanctimonious Pool's no better. In some ways he's even worse. At least White's an out-and-out shit and doesn't make any bones about it. Pool pretends to be properly behaved but in all honesty he's saying almost exactly the same as the *Noise*. Just using longer words. He's a tabloid in quality clothing."

"I have to say that it's not looking good." Gordon slurped soup and avoided eye contact with the man from Number Ten.

"You don't honestly mean you believe this drivel?" Perryman spoke with heat.

"I didn't say I did and I didn't say I didn't. I just don't think it looks good. What do you think Ron?"

Ronald didn't enormously enjoy being called Ron, even by his elder brother. He would have preferred not to have committed himself but after a few seconds of deferring comment on the grounds of soup in mouth he said, "I agree."

"With who?" asked Gordon. "Thingy here says the story is ridiculous and I say it doesn't look good. What do *you* think?"

Another pause. Then, thoughtfully, "It may be ridiculous but it still doesn't look good."

The other two men eyed him reproachfully.

"With respect," said Perryman, "that's the sort of remark I'd expect from little Pool."

"Sorry," said Ronald, "but the two points of view are entirely consistent. If you say that you know the story is ridiculous then obviously I'll take your word for it. On the other hand the *Noise* stuff was horribly plausible. Photographs, letters and, also, where *is* the Prime Minister? I don't understand why he hasn't been on the doorstep of Number Ten frothing into camera, threatening writs and retribution."

There was a silence broken only be the sounds of soup, wine and bread rolls being consumed by an all-male public-school-educated company.

"Ronald has a point," said Gordon. "Where is he? He really ought to be issuing writs. Or even getting on with business as usual. He should be seen shaking hands with someone. Surely you can wheel out some visiting head of state, preferably with an imperfect command of English so you just get smiling. We'd run that on the front page. Given the circumstances. But we can't do that if we don't know where he is."

"We think he's at Chequers."

This time the pause could properly be called pregnant. It was interrupted by more butling. The soup was replaced by steak and kidney pie with creamed potatoes and cabbage. There would be steamed treacle pudding later. The wine was club claret from the Revellers.

"You *think* he's at Chequers?" repeated Gordon, dabbing mash on top of a slice of kidney, then putting it down while he reached across the table for mustard. "You THINK he's at Chequers?"

Boy Perryman made the most of his mouthful, then washed it down with wine. "First-rate claret," he said. "Can't beat a decent club claret. Yes, I'm pretty certain that's where he is. Chequers. He's grown very attached to the place. Gives him time and space to think. Very attractive in a crisis. Downing Street's so ... well so exposed. It was Clarissa Eden, wasn't it, who said, in 1956, that the Suez Canal seemed to run through the drawing-room. She was talking about Number Ten. You'd never get the Suez Canal running through the drawing-room at Chequers. Country residence and all that. Place of tranquillity and serenity where a prime minister really can get away from it all, recharge the batteries, think things through and get away from the gutter press."

"Boy, you're wittering," said Major Ronald with unusual directness. "Is the Prime Minister at Chequers or isn't he?"

Perryman had not, if he was completely frank with himself, expected to be asked this question in quite so brutal and unequivocal a form. Like him, the Majors normally favoured an elliptical form of speech and seldom came to the point. Conversation with them was English in a very traditional manner with an enormous amount of nodding and winking. The sub-text was more important than the text. What was left unsaid was more significant than what was said. The inflection, the emphasis, the sound of the words were more revealing than the words themselves. This style was reflected in the paper itself. The leaders, in particular, sometimes seemed to be written in a code or dialect which only a regular reader could crack. "Er," he said, attempting to cover his confusion with another gulp from his goblet.

The two Majors regarded him beadily.

"Look," said Boy, "this is absolutely *entre nous* and off the record."

Gordon looked at Ronald. Ronald looked at Gordon.

"You're perfectly well aware we can't give that sort of undertaking when it's a matter of vital public interest," said Gordon, "but you can trust us. You know that."

"Absolutely," said Ronald. "Mutual trust between Downing Street and Fleet Street. Essential in a free society."

Gordon gave Ronald another look, this one distinctly unfraternal.

"This Prime Minister", said Boy unhappily, "does like to operate on an unusually loose rein."

"Meaning ...?" said Gordon, who clearly smelt something ratty.

"Meaning that he likes to have time to himself."

"I'm not entirely with you," said Gordon. "When you say 'time to himself' what exactly are you driving at?"

"He likes to be by himself," said Perryman, pushing his knife and fork together with his food half finished. He no longer felt hungry.

"By himself?" said Ronald.

"Do stop repeating everything Boy says." Gordon did sometimes allow his irritation to show in moments of stress and he was definitely stressed at the moment. He needed a serious session in bed with someone sympathetic, preferably the new feature writer whose name at the moment escaped him. The thought of her naked body crossed his mind even as he snapped at his brother. There was some statistic he had read somewhere, perhaps in his own paper, about the average Englishman thinking of sex once every three and a half minutes. If so, then he supposed he was your average Englishman, though it was maddening when naked ladies leapt into your mind when you were attempting to have a serious conversation about a prime minister who appeared to have got himself into bad trouble. Particularly when your idiot brother was cocking things up by being, well, idiotic.

"Am I right in inferring", continued Gordon, trying vainly to get rid of his mental image of the naked feature writer, "that you've lost the Prime Minister?"

Boy stared morosely at his wineglass. "Not exactly lost," he said, pronouncing the word "lorst", in the old-fashioned way, "more like 'mislaid'."

"But hang on." Gordon was interrupted by the butler who removed the remains of the main course and brought on pudding plates with a treacle sponge and custard. When he had removed himself again Gordon continued, "Frankly, Boy, what you're saying is simply outrageous. Here is the Prime Minister of Great Britain accused of an adulterous homosexual affair and you say he's gone AWOL. I mean it won't do, it really won't. What do they say at Chequers?"

"They're not sure."

"What about the security people? The police, I mean."

"This is excellent sponge," said Perryman, who tried never to let anything interfere with good manners. "As you know, an element of the security operation has been privatised in line with the party's political philosophy. And, between you and me, like a lot of privatisations the thing hasn't worked out awfully well. In fact, not to mince matters, it's been a balls-up."

"You can't mean the whole thing's been privatised. What about the police? You're not telling me the police have been laid off?" Gordon's moustache, now flecked with custard, was quivering.

"Not exactly, no." Perryman was obviously disconcerted. "It's a sort of shared responsibility. The goons on the gates are private security men and the PM's personal detectives are from the Met. But there has been an element of confusion. Under the new arrangement no one seems to know quite who's in charge. So there have been times when the police assume something's being taken care of by the private boys while the private people assume it's a police responsibility."

"So that in the end no one's taking care of it?"

"Up to a point."

"Bloody hell." Gordon was shocked. So was his brother.

"And this is what's happened today?"

Perryman seemed on the point of prevarication but then thought better of it. "When we checked earlier the security firm – they're called Trans Global Lifeguard Services – said the police were responsible for him. When we rang DI Manners he said he understood that TGLS were in charge."

"But the upshot is that no one knows where he is."

"He slept there last night," said Perryman, "and he had breakfast. Quite a hearty one."

"Privilege of the condemned man," said Gordon sardonically. "Prime Minister goes missing. Not a bad headline, eh?"

14

SPECIAL REPORT

At least, reasoned Stan, he was better off going in than coming out. The smell of boiled and starched linens and other newly laundered fabrics was a great deal more agreeable than the stench of the same stuff soiled. Curled up in the back of the laundry van, cushioned and buttressed by softness and sweetness, Stan felt ridiculously secure and safe. The fact that he and his lensman were smuggling themselves into the Prime Minister's country retreat just when the man was at the eye of a climactic sexual scandal receded. For a few moments he was lost in a gently jolting womb.

Stan snoozed.

The van was passing through a highly traditional English countryside. Neat hedges and fences enclosed neat fields of grass, corn and gleaming yellow rape-seed. Neat cottages of newly pointed red brick with newly neatly bottle-bottomed windows and lantern lamps and wrought-iron names like "The Nook" and "Ingleside" were discreetly covered in the neatest of wistaria and clematis and clambering roses. Here and there a television dish disturbed the precision of the gabled rooftops but even this evidence of the communications revolution seemed domesticated and safe. You would never assume that they were bringing soft porn and international violence into these idyllic commuter residences.

Herein, of course, lay the paradox, widely recognised even by

Stan, who had made only the briefest study of crime and murder and general unpleasantness. This smiling English façade grinning at his laundry van was a conman's face, a benign expression of goodwill behind which there lurked deception and betrayal, and sometimes sudden death.

Stan and Sid Green knew this but somehow the starched clean linen and the comfy Englishness of their surroundings lullabied them into a siesta of smugness.

For a time this was justified. Lolling amid lavender-scented laundry, Stan and Sid penetrated the Chequers cordon with ease. The ring of steel surrounding the Prime Minister's country residence was, in truth, little more than a Maginot line. It looked impenetrable and the government's security advisers believed it to be so. But their belief in its impenetrability was what made it vulnerable.

The laundry van was a regular visitor; the driver the same driver as usual. The number-plate was the correct number-plate. The laundry itself had phoned, as always, to say that the clean goods would be delivered at the regular time and in the regular way. It would have been correct, naturally, to have opened the van and taken out the laundry bags one by one and searched the lot with the assistance of sniffer dogs.

This, however, was the real world. No need for conspiracy when cock-up was so pervasive. The laundry van passed through the two sets of electronic gates, under the barbed wire and the cameras, over the cattle grid and into the park, with little more than a cheery wave from the guys on guard. Experts would say it "couldn't" have happened. "Sod's law", "bad luck", "a chance in a million", call it what you will. Stan and his laundry van bucked the system because of human fallibility, the lesson of history no contemporary analyst ever learns. Later, in the aftermath of this affair, conspiracy theorists would rise up in droves, alleging that Stan and Sid were deliberately allowed into the Chequers area and that the security forces and intelligence organisations knew exactly what the two *Noise* men were doing long before they knew themselves. Such stories were plausible but not to be believed.

Up to this point Stan and Sid were lucky. All had gone according to plan. Once through the perimeter, their driver banged twice on the partition and they emerged, ready to leap out at a bend in the drive where there was shrubbery thick enough for them to hide and take stock.

Over the years both men had survived sticky situations. They had done little wars all over the globe; they had come under IRA mortar attack near Crossmaglen; they had been "arrested" by drunken Bosnian Serbs; threatened with rape in Rwanda; evaded Syrian rockets in the Golan Heights and Zulu machetes in Natal. They had floundered down the ski-slopes of Klosters in pursuit of princes and princesses, and smoked dope with Colombian drug barons.

In doing all this they had run risks and taken chances, but they had nearly always got the stories and evaded their enemies. This they had done by displaying "rat-like cunning" (Nick Tomalin's famous prerequisite for journalistic success) at all times, by being adaptable and fast on their feet, capable of acceptable bluff or what Tomalin in the same essay on journalism had described as having "a plausible manner". They had flown, always, by the seats of their pants. When they made plans they were loose, because experience had taught them that plans always had to be changed to match circumstances and situations. Too rigid an agenda was fatal. Basically you made life up as you went along, took it second by second, minute by minute, hour by hour, day by day. You reacted, and reacted fast, but that was the nature of the journalistic game. You were, in the last analysis, a reporter of what others were up to. It was not up to you to call the shots. You had to be there when the shots rang out. You had to be in poll position. You had to file fast. You were a fly on the wall and the game was staying on the wall and out of the web. Other people were always the spider. That, too, was a fact of life. Or it was in Stan's book. That, anyway, was his way of looking at things.

It was 3.15 p.m. when the van slowed to little more than walking pace and the driver banged again on the partition. They had three hours before he picked them up again in the same spot. The second visit of the day was unorthodox but the excuse seemed perfectly respectable. A particular damask table-cloth, a gift from the government of one of the Baltic states to Mrs Thatcher during her premiership, had been "overlooked". The laundry, which prided itself on rectifying such errors with the greatest possible expedition, was therefore going to send it out later this afternoon. The deal was that between six and a quarter past the van would slow again by the same bushes and Stan and Sid would leap aboard, making a safe exit with plenty of time to catch the first edition with whatever scoop they had come up with.

Three hours. For hard and seasoned operatives such as these two, three hours should have been more than enough time for them to "take a bit of a fuckin' looksee" as van Blanco had put it. Of course, they might not find out anything at all, but that was always a hazard of investigative journalism. On the other hand, with the passing years "investigative" journalism had become significantly more "inventive". In other words, if in doubt make it up. The point was that you could slap Stan's byline on the story with the words: "Chequers, Friday" underneath it and you were half-way there. Bit of purple prose, bit of conjecture, paragraph or two of pure fabrication. All this leavened with the occasional true "fact" and you had the sort of story which made the *Noise* the *Noise*.

They were about a hundred yards from the house, but with a clear view of the terrace which ran along the front. Most of the windows along this side of the house seemed heavily draped and curtained. The place had a desolate air and a chilly one as well. It wasn't too fanciful to imagine a dead body in the library, for the house had much of crime fiction's golden age about it. It would have done nicely as a setting for a TV Agatha Christie.

"What now, boss?" asked Sid. Sid's camera lens was as ferocious – and as conspicuous – as a bazooka.

"Sit tight for a few minutes," said Stan. "See if you can make anything out."

This was Stanspeak for "Haven't a clue, mate". But it made sense for Sid to peer through the old telescopic and see if he could pick anything up. Then they could consider whether it was safe to move nearer the house. Or desirable. It might seem feeble to spend three hours here in the shrubbery but on the other hand it could be the safest option and they had a perfectly good view. They watched the laundry van pull up at the tradesman's entrance and effect its delivery, take on board a consignment of new dirties, then scrunch round on the gravel and head back home. Stan had half a mind to flag him down as he passed by, but thought better of it. Van Blanco would have been unamused by such feebleness.

"Dead as a bleeding dodo," said Sid, after a few minutes. He had cased every window in turn and found nothing.

"I suppose", said Stan a touch morosely, "we'd better get round the other side and see if there's anything there." In his head he was already composing his opening paragraph. "An eerie silence surrounded the missing Prime Minister's country seat last night.

As I walked through the beautiful gardens enjoyed by generations of British prime ministers I was alone with the ghosts of our Imperial past." It was turning into that sort of piece: a sidebar to the hard news story which would lead the front page, or possibly even an inside-page job with a muzzy Sidpic of the deserted house.

"Yeah," said Sid.

Stan gestured towards a thicket of rhododendron about fifty yards to their left. "That looks like an OK OP," he said, showing off his knowledge of military slang gleaned from his time as a war correspondent.

"Observation Post," he explained.

Sid nodded. "Sure," he agreed.

There was open ground between the two clumps of bush. No cover.

"How do we get there?" asked Sid.

"Stroll," said Stan. "There's no one around. And if we do get spotted you know the drill – righteous indignation, press cards, freedom of information, all that crap. No one's going to mess around with the *Noise*. The worst that can happen is we get slung out and van Blanco throws a wobbly."

Actually that was pretty bad, as van Blanco was inclined to get physical when he threw one of his wobblies. On one occasion he'd broken the Chief Crime Reporter's nose for him when he'd got pissed in the lunch-break during a particularly juicy Old Bailey trial and failed to sign up the murderer's mistress.

"You're the boss," said Sid. He didn't seem altogether comfortable.

"Yeah," said Stan, suddenly seeming a touch unsure himself. "Are you sure there's no one around?"

"Pretty much," said Sid. He scanned the gardens again, traversing the view from left to right with a measured stare. There was no one to be seen. "Coast looks pretty clear to me," he said, rising from the ground and brushing off earth and dead leaves.

Stan did the same.

They walked slowly towards their next hiding place almost as if they were day trippers with National Trust membership passes. They had almost reached the bushes when there was a shout. It was delivered in unmistakably British Army officer-class tones and with equally unmistakable authority. Parade-ground stuff. What it actually said was not altogether clear. It sounded like "Oi, you!" but any dog would have recognised it. It was the master calling the cur to heel. Down boy! Stop! Don't move!

"Yes, you," called the officer voice, as if there might have been hundreds of others in the park. And Stan and Sid, who had been in similar sorts of situation all over the world froze to the spot and stood very very still, knowing that the one thing you didn't do was move at all because even trained British Army soldiers could be trigger-happy when confronted with the unexpected and the unknown, and there was no telling whether or not there might be a booby-trap or other men hidden, with arms perhaps, and the average squaddie was, after all, still in his teens. Still, Army discipline was strong and, although there was obviously going to be trouble and van Blanco and Eddie White and Chinese Ken would have their guts for garters there was no cause for panic or, really, undue concern. It was a bitch and a bugger, and they had fucked up but there'd always be another day.

These were the thoughts going through Stan's mind in the afternoon sunlight in the Prime Minister's garden. So it came as a surprise when there was a muffled shot and something caught him square in the back and flung him several yards ahead flat on the grass. Or it would have come as a surprise to Stan if he had had time to realise what was happening. In the event death came, as it does so often, with complete unexpectedness and extreme speed. Had he not been so dead, Stan would have been quite peeved at being caught out like that. It made him look so unprofessional.

15

THE MAN IN
THE KNOW

Christopher Jones never revealed his sources. It was a journalistic axiom of his youth. In those days it was accepted that journalists always had sources for their stories even when, as in the Watergate affair, the source was given such a dubious-sounding identity as "Deep Throat". Jones had been a key, though for the most unidentified, player in Watergate and he knew all about Deep Throat, though he never talked about it.

Like many old-fashioned journalists Jones not only had immaculate sources, he was also strong on intuition. Information came to him almost as much by osmosis as hard specific individual facts purveyed by an identifiable informant. Thus, in the case of Stan's death he was reliably informed by two different men, one of whom worked for the military and the other the civilian power. In addition Jones made a number of corroborative enquiries, then deployed his brain.

After this he wrote in his diary – but not for publication:

Our people have shot a *Daily Noise* reporter called Stanley Morris. Seems to have been an all-round cock-up. Morris and a photographer infiltrated the Chequers grounds in a laundry van (bribery, I guess, though I'm not entirely clear about that). One of our patrols picked them up while they were playing Grandmother's Footsteps in the garden and Morris got shot. He shouldn't have done and the man who did it loses privileges or gets a short spell in jankers. Not entirely his fault, though. If you do come across some unauthorised interloper in the PM's backyard it's not altogether unreasonable to pull the trigger and ask questions later.

In any event the man's dead. Our people took him away and dumped him in a lay-by somewhere up north and are going to lay the blame on one of the Proddie freedom-fighting gangs. Not unreasonable, since the man Morris seems to have fallen foul of them in the past. About the only good thing you can say about him apparently.

As for the lensman, he's been given a serious talking-to and advised that if he spills anything approaching the real beans the Prods will have him too. So he should stay pretty well shut up.

Jones paused and tapped the end of his pencil against his teeth. As far as home affairs were concerned he remained resolutely unjournalistic. That way, in his experience, lay only embarrassment. From time to time he was locked up in or expelled from some foreign part, but that didn't bother him. Regimes came and went, and sooner or later another dictator came along who was prepared to waive any previous embargoes or restrictions. But he wasn't keen to run foul of the British authorities, secret or not. So this particular matter would remain confined to his diary. He very much doubted whether any other journalist would manage to establish the truth. The powers that be at the *Noise* would presumably put two and two together, but he guessed they would be too embarrassed to go public. Laundry van indeed! He snorted.

He didn't like it though.

Every so often when he finished a few volumes of diary he put them in a sealed box and took them down to his old college library. He had toyed with the idea of putting a fifty-year rule on them but had decided in the end that they could be opened immediately after his death. They would have more news value then. He liked to think of his jottings as a sort of literary time bomb, a booby-trap tied to his obituary. And with this in mind he continued to write.

Thoroughly irresponsible of the *Noise* people to mount such an operation. They must have known the risk to their man. I suppose they think that having got away with it so often at Sandringham and Balmoral they could chance their arm. They should have realised that snooping around the Royals is a risk-free enterprise, even post-Diana, in a way that snooping round the PM just isn't.

Having said which, Sutton's behaviour is bizarre. My information is that he and his paramour are holed up somewhere working out their next move. Possibly at Chequers. Possibly elsewhere. Most likely in a cottage on the estate which would explain why our people were so trigger-happy. No one is saying much and I suspect that part of the reason for that is that they simply don't know.

Sanderson-Wright's proclivities have always been well known – which made the appointment all the odder. Everyone in the gay community knew. He frequented all the usual clubs. Hung around with all the usual people. There's been talk about the PM, too, but even I wouldn't have assumed he would be quite so silly. Up until now he'd been careful. Very. I don't know about power corrupting but I do know it makes some people feel they're beyond the reach of the law, the press, the public ... God even, if they believe in one. Sutton was an arrogant sod, especially when he started to get promoted. He believed his jobs and his status made him special. His high-blown pride always looked as if it was about to break under him.

Jones smiled to himself, then frowned. It was Shakespeare but one of the less good plays. *Henry VIII*, he thought. Still, he mustn't clutter up the diaries with two many literary allusions. That would kill off any chance of a decent serialisation. He must remember the shining example of Alan Clark and keep himself accessible to the common man, even though the common man was absolutely what he was not. At least not in his own estimation. He wondered sometimes if he might consider publishing during his lifetime but thought, on the whole, not. He couldn't bear being exposed to the hostile opinions of those he despised.

"Interesting", he wrote, "how the public seem to have reacted to this entire wretched business. Whole notion of popular opinion; public outrage; what people think; man-in-street etc. etc. turned upside down ever since Diana death. Mass hysteria? Life = soap opera ... discuss."

He paused and stared at the chewed tip of his pencil. One day he *would* do something with these diaries but he was damned if he knew quite what. They contained some revelations calculated to make most people eat more than their hats. He had made it his business to lunch with the Director of Six at his club immediately after the affair blew up. The Director was an almost exact university contemporary ("*O tempora! O mores!*" Jones wrote sententiously – a phrase which cropped up with disturbing and increasing regularity in his columns and which would have to be ruthlessly edited before publication could be considered).

The view at Six [he noted] after lunch is as cynical as I can remember. The boss believes we are all in the hands of the mass media; that "dumbing down" has effectively lobotomised the nation. New teaching methods, the Internet, Chinese Ken and the *Noise*, market forces, ineffectiveness of dithering Church leaders, legacy of Thatcher, cowardice of judiciary, penury and constant vilification of so-called intelligentsia, collapse of chattering classes. He was seriously muttering about appealing to the generals. I told him this wasn't the Balkans.

Of course we all know that the PM was set up – though precisely how and by whom remains unclear. Boss's relations with Yard strained. Likewise with Five. But the guts of the story not in dispute. He said that half the trouble is that people so sated by scandal that nothing surprises or shocks any longer. Everyone expects and assumes national leaders hand in till, trousers permanently round ankles and so on.

He sighed. It *had* been a dispiriting lunch. He didn't think the Director was looking at all well. It was partly, he supposed, the burden of office but he wondered if there wasn't something physical as well. Very nasty cough. And he'd lost weight. One had to remember that Sutton was the boss's boss. The Director was answerable only to the PM – direct line, instant access and all that stuff. It must be a bit of a shock to find one's supposedly whiter-than-white superior going off the rails in quite such a spectacular fashion. He began writing again.

I also took the precaution of having a drink with Boris to see what the thinking was on the other side of the curtain. [Boris was the London correspondent of an influential Russian weekly, a former KGB man, still well in with the new regime, one of the great survivors, not a fibre of integrity in his entire being.] Boris also takes the dim view. In fact he seems to be of the opinion that we're on the verge of mob rule. I said that on the contrary the apparent public apathy over the Sutton affair suggested the reverse and that the great British public had lost its soul and become a sheep at the mercy of the tabloid wolves – even if said wolves really sheep in wolves' clothing, velvet fists in iron gloves. [He paused and nibbled the pencil. That wasn't quite right. Never mind, better get the words down while they were fresh in his mind, he could always edit later.] No, no, said Boris. This is lull before storm.

He detects a great seethe underneath this apparently massive popular indifference. Cake and circuses only last so long. Football and freebies only appease for so long. Today's silent majority is tomorrow's howling mob. Old Russian proverb. Something like that. He says the British have lost the capacity for rational collective thought which may sound a touch apocalyptic but isn't in fact so far off what the Director was saying at the club. If the tribe has lost its head then there's no telling what may happen.

Jones put down the diary and went and poured himself a Talisker. What an extraordinary thing testosterone was. Two less sexually appealing specimens than Bryan Sutton and Kim Sanderson-Wright were hard to imagine. And yet one could hardly suggest they were in love with each other's minds. It was deeply perplexing. To throw away so much for so . . . He shook his head and took a controlled sip of the amber hooch. Control. That was the word. He shook his head again. No control nowadays. Very worrying. Or in so far as there was control it was being exercised by some dangerously uncontrolled and uncontrollable people. Not good, not good at all. He wondered if his diaries would sell in the States. Some impenetrably British memoirs had crossed the Atlantic with success. Take Alan Clark again. He pursed his lips. He really must try to make his entries a bit shittier. More sex. More Royal Family. But no. He caught himself just in time and smiled. "To thine own self be true," he murmured.

He set down his pencil, snapped shut his book and turned on his wireless just in time for the shipping forecast. Thank God for something of permanence and worth in this meretricious tinsel world, he thought, as he listened to tales of storms in Lundy and Finisterre. You couldn't help feeling sorry for that reporter from the *Noise*. Stanley whatever-his-name-was. Only obeying orders, then blown away by a squaddie who'd taken the safety catch off his Armalite. There was a force eight blowing up off Portland Bill. Jones shuddered.

Next morning he was still musing on the mysteries of sudden death, which was now much nearer to hand for he was at the back of the church and Stanley Morris, late of the *Noise*, was up at the front. Stan was in a shiny oak box with brass handles and two wreaths, one from Sharon and the other from "Editor Eddie and all at the *Noise*". Behind his pillar Jones watched and scribbled. "Classic Fleet Street funeral," he wrote, "St Bride's ... Wren church wedding cake spire, also last resting place of Wykeham the Worde. G. Chaucer worshipped here and S. Pepys baptised. Original church destroyed by Great Fire of London and Wren church by German bombers in World War Two. Modern building erected in 1950s according to Wren's original plans so present edifice half-way between real thing and fake. Rectors prone to showmanship, good causes and BBC radio."

He leaned back in his pew and gazed round, comforted by the church's beauty and familiarity. In the days when the whole of the newspaper industry – "industry" being perhaps a euphemism for such a disorganised apparatus – was concentrated in a tight geographical circle which stretched no further from Fleet Street itself than the Gray's Inn Road or Tudor Street on the approach to St Paul's Cathedral, St Bride's really was the parish church. British journalism was, if "industry" really was a remotely apposite description, a "cottage industry", not a heavy one. The peasants toiled in the word factories up and down Fleet Street, drank in the pubs, fought and collapsed on the pavements and in the gutters, and worshipped at St Bride's.

Actually very few of the old hacks and hackettes were practising Christians, though a quorum could be found in the church on high days and holy days. However, it was when one of Fleet Street's finest toppled off the perch that the church truly came into its own. Jones had been attending St Bride's on occasions such as this for longer than he cared to remember.

Compared with the places where the seriously Great and Good are commemorated St Bride's was quite cosy. Two or three hundred mourners in Westminster Abbey rattled around like peas in a pod, but a hundred and fifty at St Bride's seemed like a full house. A hundred and fifty was, Jones reckoned, just about the number gathered here to celebrate the life of their dearly beloved Stan.

"Goodish crowd," wrote Jones, "but not because he was Stan. Not really, even though the *Noise* has made great efforts to turn him into the heroic phrase-maker that he had never really seemed in life. Most people here because of what Stan and his death stood for, i.e. freedom of speech, the liberty of the individual, the power of the printed word, pen mightier than sword."

"All things bright and beautiful" was an odd choice of hymn, he thought. Nor was "Let us now praise famous men" the lesson he would have chosen. Then they sang the twenty-third psalm. And Bunyan's pilgrim hymn. And the reading he personally loathed about how the deceased wasn't actually dead meat in a wooden box but had simply nipped next door where presumably, being Stan, he was having a fag and a pint, and watching *Match of the Day*. And now it was the turn of the *Noise*'s editor. Jones winced.

"Death is only a horizon," intoned Eddie White, a far cry from the sozzled euphoric in the editorial bar, "and a horizon is nothing but the limit of our sight. Truly, as Henry Scott Holland tells us, in the reading you have just heard, Stan, our Stan, has only slipped away into the next room ... he is he and we are we ... let his name be ever the household word that it always was ..." And so on.

> Modern journalism brilliant at filling maximum space with minimum cost and effort. Genius of modern newspapers lies in ability to rabbit on about nothing. Thus columns by the Norrises, Horaces and Borises of the world, blonde bimbo weather girls and pompous elder would-be statesmen and not-quite-ever-wases. Thus White from the pulpit. It doesn't matter that as soon as he sat down no one would be able to remember a word of what he had said. Point is that it sounded good. Triumph of style over content. Business of newspapers to be ephemeral and same with the memorial address in St Bride's. In old days today's newspapers wrapped tomorrow's fish and chips. Few fish and chips left and anyway wrapped greaseproof paper but principle same: here today, gone tomorrow. Like Stan. Like White's sermon. Like morning paper. Like all of us. Like life.

He snapped his diary shut, feeling smug, and joined in as they sang "The Battle Hymn of the Republic" with gusto and "The King of Love my Shepherd is" with feeling. The choir performed an exemplary "Nunc Dimittis" and Chinese Ken read the first fourteen verses of the third chapter of Ecclesiastes, the section which included the stuff about there being "a time to be born, and a time to die". All this was the woof and warp of the Fleet Street funeral. Very few of the mourners paid any attention to the meaning but, on the whole, they liked the noise. Some even managed a sob or two, or choked around the second verse of psalm or hymn.

The British, reflected Jones, used to be rather good at dignity in death. Now they were increasingly inclined to Latin self-indulgence, spurred on in this feel-good self-flagellation by leaders both secular and clerical.

Jones spent much of the rest of the day mulling over the occasion. In middle age he was becoming an expert on funerals and memorial services. Being a natural pessimist he much preferred them to weddings or even christenings. There might be a lot of hypocrisy in the last rites, but there was no false optimism, at least not about life on *this* earth. The trouble with the church services which celebrated events at the beginning of life was that they raised hopes which one lived to see dashed. The promise of life after death might be an empty one but at least no one in the congregation would be aware of the fact until they too had passed that particular threshold. He wrote in the diary that night:

The British do hypocrisy brilliantly and Fleet Street most of all. Everyone suspected that at best Stan Morris was a very ordinary little man and that at worst he was a pretty nasty piece of work. Yet he was celebrated with beautiful music and ancient words, and pure humbug from that odious Eddie White.

There is something comforting in the knowledge that even the most miserable sinner is sent on his way with tunes of glory, tinkling cymbals and all that jazz. I don't have much time for the C of E in the normal course of events but they do funerals better than the Romans. A full Requiem is just too heavy on smells and bells. As for those atheist and agnostic meetings where the world and his wife feel entitled to say a few words about the dear departed, they are just dire. Oh well, RIP Stan.

On the whole the notion that he was bumped off by some Ulster Volunteer hit squad seems to have proved perfectly acceptable. Extraordinary how this generation of journalists pride themselves on their forensic antennae and investigative know-how, and yet time and again they're rolled over on occasions like this. They don't even ask questions, let alone get answers.

Still, you only have to watch Eddie White being sanctimonious to realise what a *deuxième*-rate lot they are. Likewise the politicians. I have a feeling the whole shooting-match is about to come apart at the seams, though I'm not entirely sure how. I suppose we may just go on gurgling gently down the plug-hole but I have a hunch there's going to be a bang not a whimper.

That seemed a sensible place to end for the night, but just as he closed the book the phone shrilled. "Jones," he said. He always answered like that. Force of habit. And the name was so nondescript it gave very little away.

"Chris, Gordon here. I wonder if you could possibly take a shufti round here at about eleven hundred hours. We've hooked you-know-who and I'd be grateful if you could sit in and see fair play."

"Can do," said Jones. "Is this on the record or 'sources close to' ...?"

"The real McCoy."

"And you just want me to observe?"

"If you wouldn't mind. I think our man would find your ... er ... gravitas ... reassuring."

Jones grimaced. "So whose name goes on the piece?"

From a younger, less secure man this might have sounded like a whinge. But the last thing Jones wanted was publicity. Besides, he had a nasty feeling that this would turn out to be an exercise in whitewash. Number Ten were obviously using the circulation war between the *Intelligence* group and Chinese Ken's lot to their advantage. Jones very much doubted whether anything substantive would emerge from a formal interview. It would be like the infamous "interrogation" of the traitor, Sir Anthony Blunt, by a complaisant *Times* all those years ago. All white wine and smoked-salmon sandwiches. If you wanted pay-dirt you had to pan for it. At least that was Jones's view.

"Me and a very bright new girl called ..." The Major paused, knowing that on this occasion "Thingy" simply wasn't good enough. "Er ... Felicity ... I think. I felt we wanted some sort of, um, cross-generational input."

Gordon had obviously been talking to someone from the advertising agency, thought Jones. Or perhaps, thinking the unthinkable, they had finally succumbed to the lure of a media and marketing consultant.

It wouldn't have happened in Beatrice's day.

"I'll be there," he said laconically.

16

CONSENTING ADULT ENTERTAINMENT

"Jolly good party!"

Colin was smashed. So was Sharon.

He was consoling her, unexpectedly, having bumped into her, literally, at the wake.

"*In vino veritas*," he hiccuped.

"No, *El* Vino not *In* Vino," she slurred back. "I don't know about Very Tarse. Sounds charming. Yes please. Mine's a double. Double Very Tarse."

They had certainly pushed out the boat for Stan. No expense spared. Stan's tipple had been Veuve Clicquot with Courvoisier chasers. Or was it the other way round? Colin wasn't sure whether it was the long drink that chased the short one or vice versa. When he was sober he would find out from someone who would know. He'd phone Harry's Bar. It might make a paragraph for the diary.

Whether the champagne chased the brandy or the brandy chased the champagne, it was very much the sort of tipple you'd expect to get when celebrating a colleague brutally murdered by "the men of violence", whoever they might have been. And Stan had been "one of the great popular journalists of his or any other age". Those were the words of Chinese Ken himself. They were not true but they were what one said at times like this and they were what one believed, especially when one had consumed as much alcohol as Colin. He did not know how he had got here, to this flat with this woman, nor what he was doing. Sharon didn't know either. But she was in grief.

Oddly enough, no mention had been made of Stan's reporting from the front line of sexual behaviour. No one had paid tribute to those hours of painstaking research with Sharon, of his way with the *double entendre*, of his knowledge of novel coital positions and his frank advice on "how to get the best out of your woman". The assumption had been that this side of his career was best not mentioned in church. Or even in public. The circumstances of Stan's passing demanded dignity. The minute of silence in the House of Commons and in the General Assembly of the United Nations was understandable as a tribute to a life laid down in the cause of freedom of speech. Reference to the dead man's interest in musical condoms would have muddied the waters and diluted the respect. In death, Stan had assumed a gravitas and bottom which was denied to him in life.

Sharon did not recognise this grave, stately, respectable Stan. *Her* Stan was warm, drunk as often as sober, loud-mouthed, generous, greedy but above all, sexy. Good-looking? No, you couldn't say that. Indeed, an impartial observer would have said that Stan teetered on the brink of being physically repellent. Other men in particular were perplexed by his success with women, for they saw him simply as someone seedy and smelly, and slightly down-at-heel.

However, Stan oozed sex in a way which was incomprehensible to most other men. He was unusual, particularly among Englishmen, in that he actually enjoyed women and was curious about them, as well as being unalarmed. He enjoyed their company and he adored making love with them. "With" not "to". This was important. For Stan, sex was a team game and Sharon and others sensed this at once and were seduced by it. Stan was not bothered by concepts of "conquest" or "control" but of giving and taking sexual pleasure in equal measure. He was "good at sex" not because of any advanced technique, but because of enthusiasm and generosity of spirit. He was as keen on his partner's orgasm as his own and Sharon had always appreciated it. She smiled wistfully. It was curious to think that such an ordinary bloke could have been such a tiger in bed and given her so much fun. They had made good copy together. Good music, better copy.

Since his death she had declined the many offers of human consolation. In her professional sex correspondent's capacity she had acquired a large collection of sex aids in assorted colours and sizes, but none of them measured up to Stan. "Measuring up" wasn't actually what she meant, for Stan had never been spectacularly well endowed in that department. On the other hand her view, shared by others of her sex with whom she had discussed it, was that the size of the male organ was of concern mainly to men. She had always heard that the Japanese tended to be frustratingly small but had never been disposed to find out. Once, briefly, she had had a fling with a Finn who boasted a massive member. She had found sex with him uncomfortable at best and painful at worst. She had written about it, as a result of which there had been a formal complaint from the Finnish embassy. No, Stan had been just right in that respect. They were a good fit.

"Fancy a drink?" Sharon asked Colin, though she was just sober enough to know that a drink was the last thing either of them needed.

"Don't mind if I do. Don't mind if I do." Colin was trying to light a cigarette and not making a very successful fist of it. At the third attempt he achieved combustion. "I think I may be pissed," he said.

Sharon thought so too. "Would you rather have a coffee?" she asked, meaning to be kind.

He was affronted. "I'm not *that* pissed," he said. "I'd love a gin. Do you have any Angostura?"

"Yes, as a matter of fact."

She and Stan used to make cheap champagne cocktails: sugar, angostura, Cyprus brandy, Spanish champagne. Heavy on the sugar and the pink, and you could be drinking vintage Widow and VSOP. There was champagne in her fridge left over from life with Stan but she wasn't going to fix cocktails now. Not with Stan only a few days dead. "You want a pink gin?" she asked.

A drunk's drink, she thought to herself, just like crème de menthe was a tart's drink, sticky and emerald and vulgar. Pink gin was so, how could she put it? – so extraordinarily alcoholic. Most mixed drinks were designed to disguise the alcohol. But the pink in a pink gin emphasised it. She would have a G and T like the ones she and Stan used to drink when they weren't doing the cheap champagne cocktails. They'd knocked back G and Ts all over the place, on freebies everywhere under the sun, just as they'd had sex practically everywhere under the sun too. And in the pouring rain at least once. A lot of the experts were inclined to say that booze wasn't good for the sex but it hadn't worked like that with her and Stan. *Au contraire*. Brewer's Droop, they called it, but despite the booze Stan never wilted. Those brilliant booze-fuelled couplings. The time they'd joined the mile high club under a first-class blanket on a half-empty flight to Singapore when she just knew the stewardess could see what was going on. She'd half thought of asking her to join them but her nerve failed. And that night under the stars in Barbados; and on the Orient Express, crossing the Alps and looking at the mountains and she came noisily and deliciously just as they got to the Italian frontier. She could feel him now, thrusting deep and rhythmically, while his hands ... She must write a book about their sex life together. A memorial volume dedicated to him with profits donated to the Stan Fund and the permanent Stan Memorial. She just knew *Noise* readers would lap it up and those readers, those wonderful, wonderful readers ... they would want to share in her grief and perpetuate Stan's memory for ever, so that he really would be like Eddie White had said not dead but just waiting in the next room ...

"Penny for them?" slurred Colin from the sofa.

"Sorry," she said, "I was miles away."

"I could see that," said Colin. "If you ask me, you're almost as pissed as I am."

She smiled. "Pissed maybe, but not as pissed as that. I'll get those gins."

The bottles were on the sideboard in the dining area. She rinsed a tumbler with the bitters, poured a generous helping of Gordon's, then a similar measure for herself, went to the kitchen, added water to the one and tonic to the other, returned, gave the pink one to Colin, raised her glass in a mocking and mildly unsteady salutation and said, "Chin, chin!"

She and Stan had always said "chin, chin!".

Colin raised his glass, paused for a second, and said, "Absolutely!" "Chin, chin!" was not part of his vocabulary and, for a moment, Sharon felt as if she had been caught using the wrong fork at a banquet.

She crossed her legs and looked hard at him. He was an awful mess – that suit for instance. He must surely have slept in it. And for several nights running.

"So where were you?" he wanted to know.

"In the kitchen," she said.

"Don't be daft. I *know* your body was in the kitchen. But where was your soul? Where were you in your head? When I said 'Penny for them'."

"I was just thinking."

"About what?"

"How do you mean, 'what'?"

"You know, 'what?' – as in, 'what were you thinking?' " He giggled.

"Oh, nothing." She smiled at him in a lop-sided not particularly amused way, which she often used professionally and which usually seemed to work in the sense that even quite famous men with long experience of saying nothing remotely meaningful to newspaper interviewers often opened their hearts and minds to her in a remarkable way. She tended not to have sex with interviewees, mainly because people were such filthy gossips and being an easy lay for the celebrity of the week wasn't a reputation after which she much hankered.

There had been the occasional exception. Hotel bedrooms and an incredible hunk could be quite a turn-on. They'd never amounted to anything more than an hour or so of uncomplicated physical fun. One or two of her conquests had sent flowers or phoned, but she had always discouraged any attempts at a second helping. Once, on such occasions, was enough. She never told Stan about these celebrity quickies nor he her about his – if they existed. Sharon's view, rightly or wrongly, was that lady celebrities were not as likely to take their clothes off for Stan of the *Noise* as their male counterparts for herself. For a male reporter, too, the risks were incomparably greater. She might be known as a bit of a tart but she was hardly going to be had up for sexual harassment or rape. A wrong play by Stan could have been a disaster.

"I don't believe you," said Colin suddenly, with a vehemence that jolted her out of these sexual reveries.

"That's your privilege," she said and wondered why this pathetic and mildly creepy drunk was sitting in her flat late at night, getting even drunker on *her* gin. They both ought to be in bed, but definitely, very definitely, not together. Yet at the same time she dreaded her empty bed and was desperate for a body with which to share it. Perhaps there was something invitingly crumpled and vulnerable about the youngest of the Majors, poor disinherited fellow that he was. No, perhaps, on reflection, not. He was really rather revolting.

On the other hand ...

"You didn't say whether anyone had ever told you how pretty you are?"

"Pretty?" Sharon pouted. "How pretty am I?"

"Pretty as ... pretty as a peach ... er, pretty as poetry, as pottery ... pretty as pie ... pretty as a parakeet."

"A parakeet?! Please!"

"Pretty as perfume, pretty as paradise, pina colada, pineapple, pan bagna, pretty as a panama hat."

"You're pissed."

"Pretty pissed," he agreed.

"It's complimentary, my friend." A waiter had said that to her once. In a taverna in Camden Town on presenting her with coffee and brandy after a lunch which was solitary for reasons she could not now recall. She had spent the afternoon in bed with him and though she remembered little of the experience the remark had stuck in her memory, falling out of it at the oddest moments. As now.

Colin looked at her, pissed and nonplussed.

"You do say the oddest things," he said.

17

A BRIEF CHAPTER
OF ERRORS

Perryman's driver, the disturbingly well-informed and erudite Trumper, dropped him off at the *Noise* and *Conscience* compound with a word of advice, bolstered by what sounded like inside knowledge. "Don't take any bullshit," he said. "Ken Lee's not a happy man. He's giving White a hard time. White's giving it back. They're split up the middle."

"How do you know?" Perryman asked innocently.

Trumper grinned. "Driver-talk," he said succinctly.

Perryman knew exactly what he meant. All the top drivers came from the same background; same regiment, same agency. They worked out in the same gym, played golf at the same courses, belonged to the same Mafia.

"My dear Lee," said Perryman a few moments later, fingering his signet ring and using the form of address most calculated to annoy Chinese Ken, "of course it was a fucking cock-up as you so colourfully put it, but it was rather more your cock-up than ours. If you are going to play silly buggers and send *Noise* reporters and photographers into the Prime Minister's country residence using such a crass subterfuge as a laundry van then I can only say that you'll have to live by the consequences."

"My man died by the consequences," said Ken.

"Don't let's split hairs," said Perryman smoothly. "Our patrol came across two trespassers at a time of national crisis. It was unfortunate that one of our men opened fire and that your man got in the way of the bullet, but these things happen. It was, if I may say so," he continued, "outrageous behaviour and I trust you'll deal severely with whoever was behind it."

"You just killed one of my men," said Ken. "One of my best men. And you tell me I'm outrageous. Jesus Christ, man. It's you lot who've perpetrated the fucking outrage."

"Don't be silly." Perryman gazed at the Proprietor long and hard in his best head-of-school manner. "You're in bad enough odour already with your scandalous allegations about the Prime Minister and Mr Sanderson-Wright. That matter, as I'm sure you will have guessed, is in the hands of the solicitors from whom you will be hearing shortly. I think you'll find it's been an extremely expensive mistake."

"You know we've got proof," said Ken. "You've seen it."

"Our advice is that we have a cast-iron, copper-bottomed, twenty-four-carat case," said Boy, "but we'll see about that in court. Meanwhile there is the delicate matter of your deceased employee, Mr, er, Morris."

"We shall tell the truth."

"Which is?"

"That one of Fleet Street's finest was gunned down in cold blood by our own side. Friendly fire of the most wanton and despicable kind."

Boy Perryman rubbed the palms of his hands together so that they made a rasping noise like two sheets of sandpaper scraping against each other. "You're being silly again," he said.

"I don't think so." Ken did not sound wholly convinced.

"First of all, while I concede that your readers may like to read the scandals unearthed by your so-called 'reporters' they don't – as you well know – approve of their methods. Provided they don't know they don't care, but if they think you've been smuggling people into the PM's back garden just when he's at his most vulnerable they're not going to like it. And if you then accuse our boys of shooting your man in the back they're not going to like that either."

Ken had to acknowledge, inwardly, that there was some truth in what the man was saying. His were "people's papers" and the boys in our armed forces were people's people.

18

PRIME SUSPECT

Meanwhile, in another part of the city the heavy mahogany sideboard in the *Intelligence* boardroom groaned – loaded sideboards always "groan" in newspaper speak – under a dish of smoked-salmon sandwiches made with crustless brown bread, and two bottles of Chablis cooling in ice buckets. They were evidently to be served a little later when coffee was over. Coffee was Colombian in a gilt-edged cafetière. The cups were Royal Worcester. The sugar came in caramel-coloured cubes. The milk was warm.

When Jones arrived, ushered in by the butler, Gordon and "the new girl", Felicity, were already ensconced. Jones had seen several Felicitys come and go during his semi-detached time with the *Intelligence*. They usually lasted about two years before they or the Majors grew bored. Some left to marry; some crossed the road to a rival; some were frozen out – straightforward firing not being *Intelligence* style; some melted into a side-show like the letters column or the crossword.

This Felicity looked fairly typical. Skinny, blonde, petite, gamine, goodish legs, short skirt, white silk shirt, gold chain with crucifix, a scent of something crisp and flowery which he guessed was more Floris than Dior.

She gave Jones a cool, appraising look from icy blue eyes. "Not stupid," he thought approvingly. Her smile gave away no more than his own. "Brilliant to meet you," she said. "I've been a fan since I was so high."

Jones felt his age which was, he sensed, the real purpose of her remark. He noticed that one of her upper front teeth was slightly out of sync, the rest being almost Californianly even.

"Good of you to come," said Gordon, beaming tweedily. He always made remarks like that to his grand contributors, trying to con them into thinking that their relationship was on a higher plane than the commercial, that turning up to meetings such as this, as and when required, was not part of the deal. He knew, just as Jones knew and as Felicity knew, that it was not particularly good of him to come. Nevertheless, Major Gordon was mindful of those luncheons at Bretts and the Savoy Grill. His stars could be induced to jump ship, perhaps particularly so now that Lady Beatrice was no longer at the helm. It was to her, not him, that many of the old stagers owed their allegiance. Hence it was that he always remembered to express his gratitude and invariably to ask, never to command. Thus: "I say, Christopher, I wonder if you'd awfully mind . . ." Or, "Christopher, old boy, I know it's a fearful imposition but . . ." And, today, following the remark about Jones's goodness in turning up, an ingratiating, "How do you take it? Milk? Sugar?"

Jones said he took it just as it came, black, no sugar and thought, irritably, that after two decades of drinking Gordon's coffee the bloody man really ought to know that he didn't take milk or sugar. "So the PM's broken cover," he said. "What in God's name has he been playing at?"

"Doing much what the *Noise* story said, if you ask me," said Gordon, squeezing a driblet of coffee from a corner of his moustache with his finger and thumb. "Having it off with that beastly Sanderson-Wright."

"Which", said Jones judiciously, "is not what he's about to say to us today."

Gordon looked shifty. "I think not," he said.

"Then what, exactly?"

"He'll deny everything."

"I presume this is one of Boy Perryman's damage-limitation ploys?"

Gordon coloured. "Boy and I have been talking," he said.

Jones shrugged. "Not my business," he said, "but I take it

you're not about to submit Her Majesty's first minister to the third degree."

"He wants to make a statement," said Gordon, "and he wants to make it to us."

"No money's changing hands?"

"Certainly not." Gordon managed to look genuinely shocked. "The *Intelligence* has never indulged in cheque-book journalism. It goes against all Mummy's principles."

Jones allowed himself to be side-tracked. "And how *is* your mother? I'd rather hoped she'd be here today."

Once more Gordon turned a little pinker. "There have been one or two changes," he said. "Mummy's taking a back seat from now on. Her idea. She's finally beginning to feel her age."

"That'll be the day." Jones allowed both his eyebrows to levitate in genuine scepticism. "I'd heard, of course, but I'll be interested to see how it shakes down."

"It'll shake down just fine. Just fine. You see, things move on. New blood and all that. It's important that we bring in bright young graduates like ... er ... Fi ...'

"Felicity," said Felicity, *sotto voce*, staring into her coffee and taking her turn to colour up. She wore very little make-up.

"Felicity," said Gordon. "Quite."

Noises off interrupted this awkwardness and presently the door was opened and the butler said, in B-movie butlerese, "The Prime Minister and Mr Perryman, sir, madam."

Jones had witnessed similar entrances so many times before that he no longer found them amusing or even odd. He noticed, however, that the new girl had to bite her lip.

Time was [wrote Jones in his diary, when he had transcribed his notes and reflected on what had taken place] when I would have been impressed, awestruck even by the title "Prime Minister". Not any more. World events have so diminished our status that it would have been difficult even for a Churchill to cut much of a dash. Recent incumbents, however, have been so far off Churchillian status that the title has become as empty as that of Warden of the Cinque Ports or Poet Laureate. Even Tony Blair turned out all piss and wind after the honeymoon.

The Prime Minister was upstaged by his Press Secretary. Which is fair enough. The Press Secretary carries more clout these days. Spin doctor and patient. Much like organ-grinder and monkey. Interesting that we, the paper people, gave every appearance of being more confident than our visitors. I know the circumstances were difficult for Sutton and Perryman, but even so it's a symptom of the times. Editors and senior hacks *do* feel more confident than politicos. And they *are* more powerful.

I thought Sutton seemed ill. He'd lost weight and had an etiolated look, grey and slug-like. Couldn't help feeling sorry for him. Perryman looked cockily defensive.

No one else was sure that Jones was keeping a diary but his constant scribbling had not escaped notice. There was talk. Nevertheless, there had been no evidence of indiscretion yet. Gordon frowned at him and for a moment Jones laid down his pencil.

"Do you have a statement, Prime Minister?" asked Gordon.

"The Prime Minister does have a statement, yes." Boy Perryman was at his most orotund. "I thought the form should be that we read this to you and following our discussion here we'll put it out through the P A. The statement therefore will be a matter of public record. However, what the Prime Minister says in response to your questions is exclusive to you. Does that meet with your agreement?"

Gordon acknowledged a more or less perfunctory nod from his colleagues and said, "Sounds fine, Boy, old boy."

"Good," said Perryman. "Then, with your permission, Prime Minister, I'll read it through quickly and we can proceed to the interview."

The Prime Minister, wan and trembly, managed a feeble smile and said, "Yes, Boy, you do that."

So Boy began to read.

The Prime Minister, Bryan Sutton, and his Parliamentary Private Secretary, Kim Sanderson-Wright, have had their attention drawn to serious allegations made in recent editions of certain national newspapers.

After consulting the law officers and his own personal solicitors, the Prime Minister has decided not to take legal action nor to seek the punitive damages which he is advised he would most certainly be awarded were the matter to come to trial. Instead, he will take the course which he believes most appropriate and which has recently been made possible by legislation instigated by Her Majesty's

Government in order to curb excesses by the media and to protect the rights of the individual.

He will accordingly be presenting his case to the Journalistic Ombudsman for the Printed Word. Subject to the Ombudsman's decision, representation will be made to the Fair Play Commission.

As is well known, Her Majesty's Government does not believe that the courts are a proper place for the resolution of malicious libels such as the one recently committed. The Prime Minister is, however, aware that failure to seek legal redress may, in certain quarters, be construed as an admission that there is some foundation in the aforementioned libel.

The Prime Minister wishes to make it clear that nothing could be further from the case. It is his belief that every citizen should have the right to counter public libels, falsehoods and other matters of this kind, no matter what their financial position. It was to this end that the Fair Play Commission was established. The Prime Minister places the greatest possible faith both in the JOPW and in the FPC, and hopes that by setting an example in following the procedures appertaining to both institutions their value and importance will be universally recognised and his example followed.

In accordance with legislation any repetition of the allegations pertaining to the Prime Minister and Mr Sanderson-Wright before the adjudication of the JOPW and, if appropriate, thereafter of the FPC, will result in the suspension of the newspaper or other journal perpetrating the falsehood and the automatic imprisonment of the Editor and the writer responsible for doing so.

Perryman coughed and pushed his half-moons down towards the end of his nose. "That's it," he said.

There was a pause. A pregnant one except that no one seemed inclined to give birth.

"Yes," said Gordon eventually. "Well."

This got no one anywhere.

Jones's brief was to say as little as possible, so he kept his counsel but jotted down some thoughts. He wondered, in his notes, what stunted camel of a committee had drafted such an execrable example of English prose. That word "matter", for instance. Who had given birth to that word, he wondered. "Grey matter" was the only "matter" that mattered and no one with any pretensions to grey matter could have drafted that. Still, his job was merely to lend silent gravitas to the proceedings, so he sat looking grave and said nothing.

"May I ask a question?" This, of course, was Felicity.

"Shall we go on the record?" This from Gordon.

Perryman repeated the question silently to his boss by raising an eyebrow to which the PM replied with an almost imperceptible nod. Jones reflected on the language of signs and searched for the sub-text in this body language. In his book he wrote what was blindingly obvious to all of them: "Perryman in charge and Prime Minister not happy."

Gordon did complicated things with switches, buttons and knobs to an ancient tape-recorder which looked as old as his mother. Jones was amused by this Reithian technology but said nothing.

"Testing . . . testing . . . testing," said Gordon and did some more twiddling until his voice came back loud and more or less clear.

At the same time Perryman produced a tiny black object which looked like an electric razor. "I'd like to have our own copy," he said. "Just in case. If you know what I mean."

Gordon glared at Perryman's toy as if it were a video-nasty. "Will that thing pick it all up?" he asked sceptically.

"Of course," said Perryman.

Gordon evidently did not believe him. "Righty-ho," he said. "From now on everything is on the record unless otherwise made clear, in which case I shall stop the tape." He nodded at Felicity rather as the conductor does at the leader of an orchestra at the beginning of the overture.

"May I ask the Prime Minister where he's been for the last forty-eight hours or so?" Her voice was modern Oxford, much nearer classless than the Oxford of an earlier generation, that nasal toffee, overlaid by a hint of flat northern vowels and a suggestion of glottal stop.

"He's been recharging his batteries," answered Perryman quickly. "As you're aware, this has been a particularly stressful few weeks, with a number of overseas visits including a difficult Commonwealth Prime Ministers' Conference. The Metropolitan Police strike also took its toll. I'm sure you'll agree that even the Prime Minister is entitled to a break from time to time."

"But wouldn't it be more normal to spend that sort of holiday with his family?" Felicity was beginning to lose inhibition and warm to her task.

Sutton managed a wan smile. "My dear," he said. "You're obviously much too young to have teenage children of your own, but if you did have three children in their early teens you would know that much though you may love them they aren't always restful. I'm absolutely devoted to my family but there are times, I think, when all of us need to get away even from those we most love."

Felicity obviously didn't like being "my deared". "So when you felt you had to 'get away', as you put it, you preferred to be with Mr Sanderson-Wright rather than with your wife?"

Boy Perryman wasn't having this. "With respect, Gordon," he said, "that's the sort of question I'd expect from one of Ken Lee's people at the *Noise*. It's not the kind of line one associates with a quality paper like the *Intelligence*. If that's going to be the line I'm afraid I'll have to ask you to turn that thing off while we think again and draw up some more acceptable rules of engagement."

"I only . . ." Felicity began, but Gordon had already thrown the crucial switch.

Jones felt this was the situation for which he had been summoned. "With respect," he echoed, "I think what Felicity . . . Miss Windsor . . . is trying to get at is whether or not the Prime Minister actually spent this time with Mr Sanderson-Wright. As Mr Sanderson-Wright is the Prime Minister's PPS it would be perfectly normal and proper. No one in this building is in the business of perpetuating the sort of scandalous gossip that's appeared elsewhere. Nevertheless, I do think it's important that we know the truth."

These emollient words did not fall on altogether stony ground. Nevertheless, the tape recorder remained off.

"Off the record," said Sutton, sounding unhappy, "I did spend much of the time I was allegedly 'missing' with Kim, but so bloody what I should like to know. I mean, as Chris said, he's my PPS dammit and if a prime minister can't spend a couple of days with his PPS what can he do? I mean the idea that we were up to anything, anything, er, untoward, is absolute balderdash."

"So where exactly were you?" This was from Gordon.

"At Chequers."

"Then why all the secrecy?"

"What bloody secrecy?!"

Boy Perryman came in with an unctuous oil-pouring interruption. "The Prime Minister has a point, Gordon. There was never any secrecy. The Prime Minister was at his official country home working on papers with his PPS. There's nothing secret about that."

"But" – Felicity was cross – "your people said they didn't know where he was."

"I never said such a thing."

"Well, maybe not you personally, but someone at Number Ten said they didn't know where he was."

"Even the PM's entitled to some sort of privacy, for heaven's sake." Perryman beamed round the table. He obviously felt he had scored a clincher of a debating point.

Jones decided an intervention from him was in order if the meeting was not to disintegrate. "Wouldn't it be possible", he enquired softly, "for the Prime Minister to say, on the record, that he and Mr Sanderson Wright spent the relevant period working on papers together at Chequers, where they did not wish to be disturbed?"

Everyone looked at everyone else. No one could see any objection, anodyne though this statement might seem. Jones noted: "I don't think the new girl is going to last much longer at the *Intelligence*. She's far too sensible to go to bed with Gordon or Ronald and her journalistic style's much too abrasive for them."

Gordon turned on the machine again and the Prime Minister spoke. "During the period in question," he said, "I was at Chequers working on papers with my staff and colleagues including my Parliamentary Private Secretary, Kim Sanderson-Wright."

"But ..." began Felicity, but Gordon had turned the machine off again. Felicity did not look amused.

"You can't say fairer than that," said Perryman.

"Well, I think you can, actually," said Felicity. "I mean there are serious and apparently corroborated allegations that the Prime Minister has ... I'm sorry but there's no point in beating about the bush ... been having it off with his PPS and all we're getting is anodyne crap about how the two of them have been blamelessly toiling away at Chequers. It won't wash. It really won't."

The others seemed considerably discomfited by this fearless display of plain speaking.

"I think perhaps it's time we had a drink," said Gordon, picking a bottle from its bucket and heading towards the Screw-pull.

"If you don't mind, I'd prefer something a little stronger," said the Prime Minister, not only an alarmingly pale colour but perspiring heavily. He dabbed at his forehead and smiled. A wan effort. "A Scotch, if you have such a thing."

Gordon poured him a Famous Grouse, large and neat, was about to offer ice or water but didn't do so when he saw Sutton take a drowning man's gulp at the unadulterated hooch and look visibly relieved. He didn't even cough. Gordon set down the bottle of Grouse alongside his blotter and dealt with the wine.

Jones, watching him pour the wine steadily and evenly into the four glasses, was reminded of a croupier rolling out the cards. He supposed that Gordon was a bridge player rather than a poker one. He, partnered by Felicity; the PM by Perryman. Jones to referee. "May I make a suggestion?" he enquired smoothly and the others nodded. Perryman, he sensed, was suspicious of him. The rest trusted him. More or less. "I propose that we talk through the various questions we want to discuss, off the record; then, when we've arrived at some sort of consensus, we go on the record. And once that's happened the words can't be altered or tampered with without everyone's agreement."

No one looked very happy about this, but all seemed to recognise that it was the best compromise.

"I don't see how we can evade the main issue," said Felicity, threatening to destroy confidence even before it was established.

In his little book Christopher Jones wrote: "New girl definitely won't last out week. Too clever by half."

He smiled at her with complicity but she did not smile back.

19

FOREIGN BODY

The Prime Minister and the press were absorbed by the unfolding drama in which they were playing such leading roles but not everyone, even in the media, was completely taken up in the circus.

An out-of-work spear carrier such as Fisher took a passing interest in the front-page headlines, but they could not deflect him from the construction of a new life. While the Majors and Ken Lee, White and Pool played high-profile games with the Prime Minister and Boy Perryman, Fisher beavered away on his mid-life crisis and his new identity. Fisher had a letterhead designed with a flash company logo. He bought a new suit. And he began to network.

Fisher had always said that a journalist was only as good as his contact book. Fisher's contact book was a lifetime of business cards presented at cocktail parties and publication parties, embassy lunches and art gallery dinners. He had been dutiful and conscientious with his favours, his thank-yous, his well-placed puffs for those most likely to be useful later. He didn't think of himself as corrupt but merely prudent; hedging his bets against a rainy day. Now the rains had come and he was raking in his chips.

It was often uphill work. Hardly anyone seemed to have a secretary any longer. Ninety per cent of his letters went unacknowledged. No secretaries meant that the phone was seldom answered by a human. All executives above the most junior level sheltered behind an answering machine. Fisher grew to hate Mozart and Haydn, punctuated by a tinny voice advising him that he was held in a queue. When the same voice advised him to punch "1", "2", "3" or "*", depending on what he wanted, he simply became irritated and confused. E-mail was little better. "Message sent" said his computer. Yet he only had the machine's word for it. "Sent where?" It might as well have been outer space for all the response he got.

After a wall of silence which lasted several weeks Fisher began to despair. But then, at last, a letter came back from the void. Many many years earlier, as a young diarist, he had attended a reception at the embassy of a virtually unknown country celebrating its national day. He was the only British journalist present and his hosts appreciated it. His warm thank-you letter was rewarded with inclusion on the embassy's mailing list, so that he received regular press releases (binned with matching regularity), a card every Christmas and even the occasional invitation. Now the years of politeness – some described it as fawning creepiness – paid a dividend.

Fisher's first appointment as a would-be media consultant was therefore with the Ambassador of the People's Republic of Surago.

Surago, which Fisher had had to look up in his atlas, was, as every schoolboy knows, the former Belgian Honduras, an archipelago off the Central American coast, which relied for its dubious prosperity on sugar, tourism and latterly – and more satisfactorily – oil. After a flaky banana republic start under a coalition of white Belgian settlers and indigenous Uncle Tom figures there had been a left-wing coup led by General Methuselah Foom, the bastard son of a Belgian missionary and a Suragan nun. General Foom's emissary in London was His Excellency Dr Xavier Simenon, LL D (Liège), BA (Ghent), a dapper figure on the London cocktail-party circuit. Fisher had gained access to Dr Simenon (known to his friends, for obvious reasons, as Georges), thanks to the good offices of a friend and colleague who was just about hanging in as the last known diplomatic correspondent. In the old days every paper had at least one diplomatic correspondent whose main job was to write spy stories. Thanks to Glasnost, IT dumbing down and downsizing they had been virtually eliminated.

Certainly General Foom's regime was badly in need of some media consultancy. An extremely sketchy record on human rights had alerted Amnesty International and International PEN, who together carried on a sporadic campaign for the release of various of the General's opponents, a surprising number of whom claimed to be poets. The previous year there had been an unfortunate incident when two British tourists had been shot dead outside the central Casino. Also, a British Voluntary Aid worker had been raped, almost certainly while in police custody. The subsequent cover-up was ill conceived. To suggest, as the government's spokesman seemed to, that any Western female under the age of twenty-five who set foot on Suragan shores was "simply asking for it" was not, on the whole, what the world wanted to hear. Tourism plummeted. Luckily the international oil companies were not so squeamish. Indeed they rather preferred dealing with totalitarian regimes (there was no legal opposition in Surago) on the grounds that it made life so much simpler. Unfortunately the great oil companies of the world enjoyed a popular reputation which was little more enviable than the General's. Their support was certainly lucrative, but it did not play in the opinion polls.

To counteract this unfortunate image General Foom took to describing himself as the "People's Friend". His government also bought a full page in the *International Herald Tribune*. This was devoted to extolling the General's friendliness as well as many other qualities, not always evident in his rule so far: all-round philanthropy, kindness to animals, dedication to environmental protection, the arts – even poetry, which was a claim calculated to elicit hollow laughter from the Central Prison in Port-du-Soleil, the nation's fly-blown little capital.

Dr Simenon's embassy, small but elegant, like the Ambassador himself, was a three-storey house in Belgravia. The Doctor kept Fisher waiting in a comfortable ante-room for an acceptable ten minutes, which nevertheless served to make the point that the Ambassador was a busy and important man, whereas Fisher was not. He was, however, served with a cup of excellent coffee by an English butler (was another point being made? Fisher wondered) and, after entering the ambassadorial presence, with champagne in a cut-glass flute. Fisher, who had been trained to be curious about such matters, was unable to read the label on the bottle.

So, Mr Fisher," said HE, raising his glass with a trim grin and a simpered "*Santé*", "you believe that perhaps we may be of mutual benefit to each other."

Fisher was about to be side-tracked on the matter of whether this was a tautology when he remembered that his career was at stake and that if he blew the opportunity of a first account on a question of correct English usage he would be in trouble on the home front. "Yes," he said.

Dr Simenon raised a mildly interlocutory eyebrow and sipped from his glass. He was a dapper figure in a three-piece suit with a starchy white shirt and an imitation Brigade of Guards tie. Black, almost, as your proverbial hat, but with just a suspicion of pinko-grey, which hinted that he, like the General, might have a trace of Belgian blood in his ancestry, though not, almost certainly, from the conventional side of the blanket. "General Foom is my very good friend," he said. "We were brothers in Belgium in the 1960s during the struggle for independence. I was at the university and he was at the Military Academy. We were as one. What is being alleged in the Western press about my dear friend and our great President is very shocking."

"Very shocking," said Fisher. "I've been very shocked by it. And saddened."

"We are great believers, the General and I, in the English 'Fair Play'," said Dr Simenon, "the 'Stiff Upper Lip'. When the umpire says you are out you must walk to the pavilion *sans question*. And so on and so forth. We in Surago believe that we are not being given an entirely fair crack of the whip. It is the opponents of the Fair Play who are cracking the whip and it is time for a change of hands. Do you not agree?"

"Absolutely," said Fisher. "I'm a great believer in 'Fair Play' on a level playing field and with equal goal posts. As far as my company is concerned that's the name of the game. And it is my aim, and that of my colleagues, to ensure that our clients benefit from these core beliefs which are at the heart of our strategy."

Dr Simenon smiled encouragingly. "*D'accord*," he said. "Chin, chin." And, leaning forward, he clinked his glass against Fisher's, causing a decorous "ping" and the death, according to Fisher's superstitious upbringing, of at least one fisherman at sea.

"And so" – Dr Simenon smiled – "what exactly is it that you propose?"

Fisher had prepared for this moment but he was not happy with it. A proposal such as this – demi-fraudulent, soft-at-the-edges, all structure and no substance – was not, he felt, what he was about. One of the reasons he had chosen journalism was that it involved telling the truth. Politicians, diplomats and lawyers had no obligation to truth. Indeed they made a virtue of not telling it. The lawyer became possibly priggish about how his personal opinions and beliefs must not in any circumstances interfere with his professional brief. It didn't matter how criminally guilty he (or she) believed the client to be, he (or she) still had to behave as if his (or her) belief was absolute. ("Privately, m'lord, I think he dunnit, but publicly it is my solemn duty to persuade the jury otherwise.") It had always amazed Fisher how many professions were dedicated to telling falsehoods in the interests of expediency. ("We all know such and such, old boy, but we can't rock the boat, can we, so we'll all agree to say so and so instead. OK?") Time was when journalism had seemed an honourable exception. They were the awkward squad whose duty was to call foul whenever the Great and the Good fell out of line. Now, however, the hacks had their snouts in the trough along with the rest of them. "Well," he said, with a judicious pause and ponder, worthy of the most oleaginous QC, "I can't help feeling that first-hand knowledge is what is at issue here ... the problem is that many of those who pontificate about the state of affairs in Surago simply don't know the facts. They don't understand the other side of the story. You have allowed your opponents to gain the upper hand because, quite reasonably, you regard their arguments as beneath contempt."

Fisher didn't like this one little bit. He didn't believe a word of the garbage he was spouting. He knew perfectly well that Surago was a tin-pot dictatorship ruled by a corrupt self-styled General, who was on the take and whose preferred methods of debate were imprisonment without trial, if not torture, rape and murder. He was also pretty certain that the little Doctor who was even now smarmily refilling his glass was of similar kidney to the boss. If, as sometimes happened, Fisher's true self were to leave his body and hover a few feet above this miserable performance he would disapprove quite vehemently of what was going on below. But life was life and his true self remained rooted within his feeble frame.

"So what do you propose, Mr Fisher?" Dr Simenon's smile suggested that he *was* hovering somewhere above the scene, could see right into Fisher's head, and was perfectly aware that his words were just so much cant and hypocrisy. Nevertheless, he knew that for the sake of cordial relations with the "People's Friend" something had to be done. Or at least seen to be done. He had no illusions that hiring a "Media Consultant" would make any difference to the way in which the world perceived the Suragan government. On the other hand it would look good in his next dispatch home. "Ah," they would say at External Affairs, "old Georges Simenon is cooking something up in London. Old Georges has a plan. You wait and see."

And General Foom, on being told of this in Cabinet, would smirk and say, "He's a good man, Georgie. We are like brothers he and I. He is my very good friend."

So Fisher really had no need to deliver this preposterous little speech for actually the account was his before he even entered the room.

Nevertheless, even the emissary of the People's Republic of Surago felt obliged to conform to certain conventions. The game must still be played.

"Well, sir, as I understand it, you have absolutely nothing to hide. The problem, as I see it, is that so very few opinion formers understand the Suragan situation at first hand."

Dr Simenon nodded encouragingly from the far side of his enormous desk. His glass stood in front of him and his hands rested on his chest, the points of the fingers forming an "A-frame" of appraisal. Presently he took a cigarette from a silver box on the desk top, inserted it into an ivory holder, lit the end and drew deeply.

"I think, in the first instance," said Fisher, duly encouraged, "that a visit should be arranged. Not exactly a press trip but not quite a parliamentary delegation. A mixture. I think we should be sure that we have one or two public figures, such as Members of Parliament, who are likely to be well disposed; and some superior journalists, writers with bottom – Martin Amis, Salman Rushdie, that sort of thing."

"Perhaps not those two gentlemen," said Dr Simenon gently, "although General Foom is extremely keen on the *oeuvre* of Lord Archer of Weston-super-Mare. He is also my very good friend."

Fisher gulped. He had never thought of Jeffrey Archer's books as constituting an *oeuvre*, but it was a nice thought. "Quite," he said.

Dr Simenon blew an almost perfect smoke ring. It hung between them, a grey-blue halo, little bigger than a man's hand.

"In principle, however, your idea has merit. How many people would you envisage on this visit?"

"Oh, quite small. Probably not more than about half a dozen. Ten at the absolute outside."

"In that case", said the Doctor, "there should be no problem in arranging the best available travel with Suragair and accommodation either in the Government Guest Houses or the Marx-Lenin Plaza. Before the revolution it was the Hilton International. I understand that under the new regime it has improved out of all recognition, but I have yet to stay there so I cannot speak from first-hand experience."

"Good," said Fisher. "So we're in business?"

"Oh yes, Mr Fisher." The Ambassador laughed. "We're in business, Mr Fisher. Indubitably."

"So how exactly should we, er, proceed . . .?"

For a moment Dr Simenon seemed taken by surprise. Then he laughed again. "You mean terms, Mr Fisher . . . contracts . . . money?"

"Well, yes, actually. My company's rates are extremely competitive but . . ."

"Naturally, naturally," Simenon waved the implied vulgarity aside. "I'm sure that will present no problem at all, Mr Fisher. No problem at all . . . but now" – and here he pulled out a gold fob watch from a waistcoat pocket and gave a startled frown – "but now I am afraid I am running late and I have a vital appointment in connection with affairs of state. Forgive me please. Martha will show you out."

Even as he spoke the door opened and an attractive secretarial-seeming figure came in and stood, hovering and smiling.

Fisher could take a hint. The Ambassador presumably had a bell-push under his desk for summoning Martha. Either that, or she had been instructed to enter the office at a pre-set time. It didn't really matter. He seemed to have won his first piece of business and it was as easy as pie. The money side seemed a bit vague but he'd send in an invoice and even though he was disinclined to trust Dr Simenon any more than Amnesty International would trust him, he knew enough about business to accept that at moments such as this risks had to be taken. And why should the People's Republic not pay his bills? They needed him at least as much as he needed them. Besides, it could be a good trip. He wondered whom he was going to invite.

20

CHINESE WHISPERS

Chinese Ken had once had a passage in a book drawn to his attention. Ken was not what one would call a reader. That is to say he could cope with words as conveyers of information or makers of money, but not with the word as a medium of improvement or enjoyment. He had never in his life read a novel and certainly wasn't going to start now. However, he could see that in a sense he lived by words and he had been quite taken with a paragraph shown to him by a member of staff many years ago. It was from a novel called *The Paper Palace* by someone called Robert Harling, himself evidently a newspaper man, though not, as far as Ken could see, a proprietor. Harling had created a newspaper owner called the "Baron" and he had written of him, "Nothing mattered so long as words were in movement and more movement meant more argument and that was what he wanted, and the more pointed and personal the argument the better for the Baron."

In a quirky and uncharacteristic way Ken had the paragraph inserted in a small silver frame, which he kept on his desk and from time to time he would read it through slowly and consider it.

Owning newspapers was, he supposed, about power. Or influence. He had trouble telling the difference. As a press baron he liked to think that he set the agenda for the nation, perhaps even for the world. The blank mind at breakfast was filled and programmed by the thick black type at the top of Ken's front pages. If he wanted to abolish the monarchy he said so in enormous capital letters. (On the whole, he was in favour of the monarchy provided it did as it was told, preferably by him.) If he felt the government should go he told his editors to lead with something along the lines of "IN GOD'S NAME GO!" or "OUT, OUT, OUT!" or even " F*** OFF!"

Ken and his editors believed that an opinion poll was useful in bolstering such invocations. They added authority and gave him and his minions a more plausible excuse for speaking on behalf of "the People" Unfortunately, opinion polls tended to be expensive. Plans were well advanced, however, for the organisation to "acquire" or possibly invent its own polling agency. Since this would do minimal actual polling but rely (like his newspapers) on the in-house inventiveness of his staff, considerable economies could be effected. Failing that, some long quotations would do, preferably labelled "Exclusive" or even "World Exclusive". Neither meant anything but they looked good and they gulled the gullible. Ken paid two former prime ministers a fat retainer just so that their names could be taken in vain. Not too often. But just once in a while: "In an exclusive interview with the *Daily Noise* last night, former premier Jim Bishop lashed out at his ex-colleagues. 'We've been betrayed,' said Bishop, speaking from his Surrey home ..." And so on. He preferred the "Exclusive Interview" to "The Former Prime Minister Writes Exclusively in the *Noise*". Although such articles were, naturally, ghosted by a *Noise* staffer the old politicians tended to take more interest in "their" written articles than in their spoken interviews.

Such exclusives were usually bolstered with a pithy leader saying something along the lines of "These Guilty Men". His political editors had a serviceable all-purpose leader explaining in fiery three-word paragraphs precisely why there should be an immediate general election. None of this had any serious political effect, but it created enormous *Sturm und Drang* on Breakfast TV and it made him feel almost sexually pleased with himself as he chomped through his wholewheat Munchie-Munchies and watched half-baked pundits breathing hot air at one another between the commercial breaks.

He had always enjoyed making trouble. And he had always harboured a preternatural greed. To be able to cause grief and make money at the same time was therefore doubly satisfying. As a child he had been a perpetual menace – the sort of boy who poured green ink over his sister's hair, wrote anonymous poison-pen letters to his best friend and betrayed parental confidences. "Mother thinks you drink too much." "Dad's Secretary came round while you were out at bridge." He would have been a success in the Hitler Youth or Chairman Mao's Red Guards. Other people's tears were an endless source of satisfaction. *Schadenfreude*. He had always torn the wings off butterflies but for preference the wings of butterflies he knew and loved.

To do so in print was a habit he had acquired at boarding-school aged twelve, when he had produced a sort of samizdat publication called *Sneak*. It spilled the beans on bed-wetting, mutual masturbation, staff sex and secrets of every kind. In the end it had led to his expulsion and he had not looked back. In a sense the rest of his life had been a revenge. And a satisfying one at that.

The circulation war he waged against the *Intelligence*, Lady Beatrice and the Majors was, he told himself and his staff, a fact of commercial life. Once, in the bad old days, one of the great national newspapers was forced off the street by industrial action. It was the printers, as usual, defending their "old Spanish customs" and, for once, a proprietor had had enough and dug in his tiny toes. In the sane commercial world which came into being after Mrs Thatcher's accession, rival newspapers would have capitalised on their enemies' misfortunes.

Not then. Instead of going for the jugular, the editor and proprietor of the strike-bound paper's greatest rival agreed that it would be unsporting to take an "unfair" advantage. Queensberry Rules applied. Business was carried on as if it were cricket. A handshake was as good as – arguably better than – a contract. It was a world in which Chinese Ken had been educated but it was not one with which he had any sympathy. If Ken had been in such a situation he would have been shameless. His paper would have used every conceivable device to win readers away from the stricken foe. By the time the other paper was back on the street they wouldn't have had any readers left. It would have been like starting again from scratch. "So your favourite newspaper has let you down," Ken would have shouted to the nation. "Don't worry. You can read it all in the *Noise* instead. The *Noise* will never let you down. We never close. Letters to the editor? Obituaries? You name it, the *Noise* does it best. More important, the *Noise* does it. The *Noise* gets on with the job. There's no shirking at the *Noise*."

And so on.

Just sound business sense, Ken would have said.

This would have been true as far as it went but with the *Intelligence* it went much further, for the *Intelligence* and the Majors represented everything that Ken detested. They stood for beatings and cold baths, decency and common sense, discipline and deference. When he was a child Ken had, for a time, to be governed by men and by values similar to those of the *Intelligence*. Now that he was not a child he was getting his own back. This deeply personal revenge was not something he often admitted, even to himself, but it was none the less real for that.

So when he glanced, as he often did, at the quotation from *The Paper Palace*, the words "the more pointed and personal the argument the better" had a deeply felt meaning. He relished the pointed, personal argument in which he was engaged with "Ancient Britain" because he hated the sort of people who belonged to it. He loathed snobs and toffs and privileges and old money and titles and people with pink faces and pink coats who rode to hounds, and most of all he detested the Majors, with their faded gentility and their patronising smiles and their pervasive condescending sense that he was just a common little man on the make, whereas they represented the blue blood of Old England.

Or something like that. The very thought of nature's school prefects made him so savage he became inarticulate. Which contributed to the incandescence of his rage when he heard that the Prime Minister had come in from the cold and was spilling some sort of beans at the *Intelligence*. The tip-off was reliable, for the *Noise* had a long-established mole at the *Intelligence*. He was only a messenger but messengers had the advantage that, particularly in organisations like the *Intelligence*, they are virtually invisible. If Major Gordon was reduced to calling even his senior staff "Thingy" he was unlikely to consider a mere messenger as a human being capable of intelligent thought, let alone espionage. At the *Intelligence* the man was ill-considered and ill-paid. Ken Lee paid him double and in cash, and made him feel appreciated. No one at the *Intelligence* questioned the fact that one of their messengers habitually took his holidays in the Caribbean. They didn't even notice.

Ken's first instinct on receiving the messenger's phone call was to kick his waste-paper bin round the office for a minute or so. Then he buzzed for Pool, who promised to come immediately. He would, thought Ken. Little Pool had his uses but that didn't mean he had to like him, let alone respect him. He had, grudgingly, to admit that this was not the case with Eddie White. Insofar as Ken liked anyone he liked White. The same went for respect. Respect wasn't part of Ken's vocabulary but if it had been he would have accorded it to Sir Edward White. He knew that if he buzzed White then White would *not* come running.

His fingers hovered over the intercom for a few uncharacteristically indecisive moments. He had only just demoted him. Or promoted Pool. Had the old rascal suffered sufficiently? Did it matter? Was Pool man enough to cope with a situation such as this? Did Ken *need* White?

He buzzed him.

"Bit tied up at the moment, boss," said Sir Edward. "Can't Mr Pool deal with it?" He laid particular stress on the "mister". He knew his own title was ridiculous and corrupt, but he also knew that Pool and, for that matter, his Proprietor would dearly like handles to their names.

Chinese Ken said he wanted to see Sir Edward absolutely pronto, which was to say like yesterday, and was privately quite pleased when his minion said he'd see what he could do but he couldn't be everywhere at once and, in case he hadn't noticed, he had a newspaper to get out.

Pool arrived just as this conversation ended. This meant an embarrassing few moments. Ken was not going to tell Pool what was going on until White was also there. Waste of time. He would have to repeat himself and he was a believer in economy of effort.

Pool told him everything was going very well, which was less than the truth.

Ken supposed that everyone needed his Pools. Pool belonged to that class of unremarkable players known as "a safe pair of hands". They were nature's number twos – always on time, always spelt correctly, never a risk, nor an original thought, nor a word out of turn. It sometimes seemed to Ken that they had inherited the earth and become life's top bananas, but whenever he found himself thinking this he reflected that whatever else he might be no one could describe him as a natural subordinate. Nor indeed a "safe pair of hands". Which was precisely why he needed men like Pool.

Even so, it irked and unsettled the Proprietor to have to spend time alone in his company. Pool's self-satisfaction had a smugness which made Ken feel like an unrepentant sinner trapped in the sights of a particularly unctuous and long-winded lay preacher. He was a little man in every sense. Etiolated as well. He didn't look as if he saw much fresh air. "When did you last have a holiday?" Ken asked absent-mindedly. "You're looking peeky."

"Oh, I don't really believe in holidays," said Pool. "If your work is as fulfilling as mine there's really no need for them. I don't like being away from the shop."

"Mmm." Ken sipped. "How do you unwind, William?"

"Unwind?" The concept was clearly alien. If Pool unwound he'd stop ticking. A tight spring and a balanced pendulum was what kept Pool moving. No nonsense about flesh and blood. He was a small clockwork toy, not a human being in the accepted sense.

Chinese Ken sighed.

HIDDEN AGENDA

The Prime Minister's interview was not going well.

In itself, this was unsurprising. Bryan Sutton's position was not strong. He had been caught out, or appeared to have been caught out, in a homosexual relationship with his PPS. Even if he had not been happily married with young(ish) children this would have provoked comment. As he *was* supposed to be happily married, with dependent children, the comment was almost bound to be unfavourable. The fact that he appeared to have reacted to the public revelation of these matters by doing, not to put too fine a point on it, a bunk, made matters worse. The death of a reporter from the *Daily Noise* while investigating the allegations put an additional stain on a far from gilded lily. The PM was in deep do-do. It was difficult to see what else could hit the fan, though in situations such as this that was what people always said. Faced with disaster, victims are inclined to whistle in the dark, but as Noël Coward put it "there are bad times just around the corner". And, in this instance, the bad times were likely to get worse.

These were the thoughts of everyone in the *Intelligence* boardroom and yet it was in all their interests to try to save the situation. At least, that was the premise. The Prime Minister had spent his whole life aspiring and perspiring to office. He was not about to abandon all that hope without a struggle. Those buckets of sweat were not to be lightly betrayed. He would cling to power like kitchen film to Tupperware. A bigger man, thought Jones, would have resigned with the best grace possible, but the Prime Minister was not a Big Man. In Jones's experience prime ministers seldom were. The nearest he had known to a "Big Man" prime minister was Mrs Thatcher. Their relationship had always been frosty, but he couldn't deny that she was exactly that.

Boy Perryman's colours were firmly nailed to the Prime Minister's mast. He could have ratted but despite his chameleon past his options had expired and his chances of preferment under any likely alternative were minimal. He was – genuinely – almost as keen as his boss to find some way of wriggling off the hook.

As for the *Intelligence*, their reaction had nothing really to do with the matter in hand, let alone anything as pretentious as "the national interest" (which was what they pleaded in Dr Clancy's eccentrically argued and thunderous editorials). All they cared about *really* was the opposition. If Chinese Ken, the *Noise* and the *Conscience* were *for* something then the Majors and the *Intelligence* were *against* it. And vice versa. It was as simple as that.

Press commentators like the archly lugubrious Sebastian Cobbler (a freelance "media expert" who contrived improbably to write for both the *Intelligence* and the *Conscience*, as well as a multitude of weekly magazines) pontificated in pseudo-academic terms about the "right-wing press" and "newspapers of the Left" but the distinctions were ill-founded. At least, that was what Jones believed. Jones was not at all keen on Cobbler. The antipathy was actually profoundly personal but both men pretended it was academic. Jones's view was that Conservatives were conservative when it suited them. Radicals likewise. It was no more meaningful, in his opinion, than dividing papers into "broadsheets" and "tabloids". The idea that the former were serious and responsible and the latter vulgar and feckless was not entirely true. A broadsheet such as the *Conscience* might disguise its smutty prurience under a layer of prim disapproval, but it could be as salacious and intrusive as the tabloid *Noise*. Indeed, if anything, the *Conscience*'s sanctimoniousness made it worse. This was Jones's considered opinion. It was, he felt, why Chinese Ken disliked Pool more than White. At least White was an honest rogue. Pool reminded him of a shifty vicar or a pederast. Cobbler, however, seemed to take Pool at his own estimation: a cross between Einstein and Mother Teresa with just a suspicion of Machiavelli.

In this case Gordon White-Lewis and the *Intelligence* held no particular brief for Bryan Sutton nor for the party he led. In normal circumstances he could take or leave both. These circumstances, however, were not normal because they were determined by the attitude of the enemy. Chinese Ken and his troops had first indulged in a vindictive pastiche of "investigative journalism", then used the result to pillory the victim. They were now *against* the Prime Minister. Which meant that the *Intelligence* was *for* him. Ideology didn't come into it.

As a relative newcomer, Felicity was less happy with this reactive stance than her boss, but despite her coltish bolshiness she knew that, for the time being at least, she would have to live with it. Jones, as always, kept his true opinions to himself, appeared to sit four-square on the fence but was probably as committed to the majority view as the majority. There was an old Chinese saying to the effect that the only live fish was the one who swam against the tide. Like most ancient Chinese adages this sounded more profound than it actually was. Jones's apparent lack of emotion sometimes made him seem like a cold fish to his enemies, but even though he often appeared to swim with the tide the waters in which he actually performed were deep enough to be still. No one really knew in which direction Jones was swimming and this was the way he liked it. Sometimes, as now, he might appear to be drifting but, as those lizard-like eyes suggested, he was always drifting to a purpose.

"With respect," he said, "time is against us. We need to resolve this to catch the first edition. And I take it, Gordon, that you're thinking of a front-page lead with a fuller version on the inside between the letters and the leaders?"

"Something along those lines," agreed Gordon, briefly distracted by Thingy the F-girl's legs, which she had just crossed. Her skirt had ridden up another six inches. Major Gordon was a sucker for young legs.

Boy Perryman nodded. "I hope you understand the extraordinary confidence we're putting in you," he said. "We're not going to any other newspaper; we're not going to TV; we're just putting out the briefest of statements to the Press Association. Apart from that this is exclusive to you because, frankly, you're the only people we can really trust. It's a sad comment on the state of the modern media but one simply can't rely on anyone else – even the BBC – to put the interests of the nation before their own."

'Bullshit,' thought Gordon, which was more or less what everyone, including Perryman, was thinking. Especially Christopher Jones. And even more especially Felicity-Fiona.

"Not even the BBC?" she asked, with false naïvety.

"Especially not the BBC."

The inflection in Perryman's voice was obviously intended to suggest that he considered the BBC a subversive threat to the national security. In fact, it was perfectly clear that the PM had to be kept off the television screen if he were to have the slightest chance of political survival. He was not a pretty sight. Had you seen him in the street you might even have put him down as a mental patient on day-release. Indeed, looking at him, Gordon felt a pang of guilt. It passed speedily. His allegiance was to the paper and this was a brilliant coup provided they could pull it off. And one in the eye for Ken Lee. How dare the little runt think he could bounce the country's leader out of office. This wreck of a man before them now might not inspire confidence, but at least he was the elected leader. Gordon was a believer in democracy. His definition of the term might not meet with universal approval but at times like this he felt a duty to stand up and be counted on behalf of one man and one vote.

"Righty-ho!" he said. "I think that the inside pages should begin with a brief introduction to the effect that the Prime Minister, aware of disgraceful and unsubstantiated allegations in certain quarters, felt it necessary to reassure the nation on a number of matters."

"Though", Boy Perryman interjected suavely, "since these disgraceful allegations are likely to be the subject of legal proceedings he is unable to comment further, save to say that the entire matter is in the hands of solicitors."

"The law officers of the Crown actually," said the PM. His voice sounded querulous yet husky. He coughed, apologetically. "It is for the Attorney-General and the Solicitor-General to take action in the courts. This is not a private matter. It is an attack on the very concept of elected government. As Stanley Baldwin so truly said, these are the actions of the harlot. If we allow ourselves to be led down this primrose path we really will end up on the everlasting bonfire. You mark my words."

This outburst was met with an embarrassed silence. It was clear that Prime Minister Sutton was not himself. Gordon found himself wondering at what point not being oneself made one unfit for office. At the very least the Premier needed a holiday. Perhaps that was the answer. He could make a statesmanlike statement of defiance in tomorrow's *Intelligence*, then take a proper holiday, preferably with his wife. "Is Mrs Sutton standing by you, Prime Minister?" he asked.

"I think we should leave Mrs Sutton out of this, Gordon," said Boy Perryman. "She's been pretty upset. As you can imagine."

"I'm afraid there's no way Mrs Sutton can be left out of this," said Felicity. "She's in it whether she likes it or not. Even if we do the 'decent' thing and pretend she doesn't exist there's no way anyone else will do the same. We'll just look ridiculous."

Jones was emollient. "Someone has to take a lead," he said. "Just because no one follows suit doesn't mean to say it isn't worth doing. One wants to demonstrate that the *Intelligence* occupies the high moral ground, even if everyone else persists in sticking in the swamps and bogs. But I'm sure we can compromise. We can make a reference to Mrs Sutton without hounding her and the children. There's no need for that. It should be possible to be a paper of record without resorting to yellow journalism."

"I think this is all a bit of a red herring," said Gordon. "Let's try to tackle the interview, then argue about the bits and bobs."

"I'd rather you didn't refer to my wife and children as 'bits' and 'bobs'." The Premier was piqued and over-emotional. It was looking as if this story would have to be concocted without his active participation in all but a very literal sense. Mr Sutton was here but he was not here.

"Right," said Perryman. "Let's try."

Gordon ran a finger round the inside of his collar, grimaced, switched on the machine and, in a stilted, actorish voice quite unlike the one he employed in everyday usage, said: "Prime Minister, it's good to see you back and in such fine fettle, after the allegations that have been made against you in another paper. Do you have any comment to make on what has been written elsewhere?"

"Yes," said the PM. "That is to say, 'no'."

"What the Prime Minister means", said Boy Perryman hastily, "is that were he free to comment on these disgraceful and unsubstantiated suggestions he would dismiss them out of hand. There is not a scintilla, not a scintilla of evidence, for anything that has been alleged. However, as these matters are now the subject of legal action at the very highest possible level he is unable to refute them as he would wish. He is, though, able to say that he is deeply saddened by the way in which some sections of the media have gone about their work."

"But", said Felicity, "what about the letters and the pictures? You can't say there's not a scintilla of evidence. There are scores of scintillas. An absolute bonfire of them."

"I'm sorry." Perryman smiled. "The Prime Minister has already said more than he should. Everything will be rigorously examined and investigated in the proper way, but the proper way will be determined by the authorities after due consultation. The proper way is not to make wild and unsubstantiated allegations to the press."

"Well." Felicity looked righteously indignant. "In that case what's he doing here?"

Gordon shook his head. "Dear, really . . . I don't think that line is going to get us anywhere."

"What the Prime Minister is doing here", said Perryman icily, "is putting the record straight. As the first minister of the Crown this is something that he is not only entitled but obliged to do."

The Prime Minister poured more whisky into his glass, not very accurately, and made a noise half-way between a cough and a belch. "Nothing wild and unsubstantiated here," he said, and grinned.

"Are we talking about a 'statement' or an 'interview'?" Gordon sounded nervous.

Boy Perryman and Christopher Jones exchanged glances and a barely perceptible flicker of eyebrows.

Perryman pulled a closely typed sheet of paper from his breast pocket, unfolded it and laid it out on the table in front of him, making a performance of smoothing out the creases and then of adjusting his spectacles. "I've made one or two notes," he said, "to clarify matters."

That word "matters", thought Felicity with distaste. Why couldn't politicians say "things". It was like saying "monies" when you meant "money". Just a pathetic attempt to convince your audience that you knew what you were talking about.

"If, for a moment, I could address the ridiculous stories that have been doing the rounds," Perryman continued. "I cannot enough emphasise that this business about the PM going 'missing' is, not to put too fine a point on it, absolute tripe. All of us, from time to time, need periods of peace and quiet, and this was one of those moments. The Prime Minister has an extremely busy and highly pressured life and he needed to get away from the day-to-day demands of office and have a brief moment of reflection. The fact that he chose to do so in the company of his closest political aide is entirely right and proper."

"But there has" – Gordon spoke slowly, picking his way through the words like a man crossing a stream on slippery stepping stones – "been, and I don't want to seem to be indelicate ... there has been a suggestion that the relationship between Mr Sutton and Mr Sanderson-Wright" (he had done well, he thought to remember the PPS's difficult double-barrelled name) "... was not all that it might have been. Well, no, that it was rather *more* than it might have been."

"Kimmy and I were at Trinity together," said the Prime Minister. He beamed.

Off with the fairies, thought Gordon.

"I don't think we want to get into all that," said Boy. "It's damaging to the office of Prime Minister and First Lord of the Admiralty. One must distinguish between the individual and the position he holds in society. If we indulge in this sort of muck-raking we diminish the highest elected office of state and in so doing put democracy itself at risk. Enough damage has been done already. We all suffer if we go into this squalid accusation. It demeans us all."

"With respect," said Felicity, glaring, "it's already been gone into. It's too late to not go into it."

"We shouldn't forget the vocabulary of negotiation," said Jones. "Honour among thieves and so on. We're here to get a result and time is not on our side."

"As I see it," said Gordon with ill-concealed desperation, not to mention incomprehension, "we only have one course of action, which is, more or less, to dump on the *Noise* story from an extremely great height. They're going to run another piece which says that the PM and his PPS have been behaving scandalously and must resign. Our only course, therefore, is to say the opposite."

"Even if it's not true?" ventured Felicity. Despite her charm and intelligence the – comparatively – old men around the table were becoming progressively more irritated. It was mutual, though. She was at least as upset by them as they were by her.

"Truth doesn't come into it," said Boy Perryman. " 'Truth' in politics is never cut and dried. As you will discover yourself when you've been around as long as the rest of us."

"Hear, hear!" said the Prime Minister who appeared to have been asleep. He closed his eyes and yawned.

"'It's business as usual,' said a buoyant Prime Minister in an exclusive interview late last night. Sweeping aside recent rumours and innuendoes as 'a tissue of lies got up by those who would happily see this great country of ours slip ingloriously beneath the waves which once Britannia ruled'." Gordon was reading from a prepared script, the draft, presumably, of tomorrow's lead story.

He dabbed at his left eye with the index finger of his right hand – a characteristic gesture of his when wishing to seem visibly moved.

> For longer than most of us care to remember [he continued] "respect" has been a dirty word. Yet lack of respect has cost this country dear. Bryan Sutton is Prime Minister of this great country of ours. As Bryan Sutton, private individual, he may or may not command respect. That is not a matter with which this newspaper is concerned. But as Prime Minister of Great Britain he commands, indeed demands, respect. For without conferring our respect on the Prime Minister we deny respect to our monarch, to our country and ultimately to ourselves. Without that respect we are nothing. It is the view of this newspaper that it is time, in the national interest, to cry out that enough is enough, that the time for disrespect is long passed and that now, if we wish to succeed in an ever more threatening world beyond these shores we must, in the words of our most famous team song, "Swing, swing together, steady from stroke to bow". For if we do not, then assuredly we shall swing, swing together in another more sinister sense. The choice is a stark one: on the one hand lie the gallows; on the other "a tall ship and a star to steer her by". The Prime Minister is *our* Prime Minister and he is at the helm. We owe it to him and to every last one of us to swing together, steady from stroke to bow. The only alternative is disaster.

He paused to dab again.

The ensuing moment of silence, stunned if not stirred, was punctuated after a second by the snore of the Prime Minister.

For the bright new girl on the block this really was the final snore. Felicity shut her eyes and counted to ten slowly, swore silently and vividly, then picked up her notes and left without a word.

22

THE HARLOT'S PREROGATIVE

Fisher found it hard to understand how or why he should apparently be unemployable and yet consultable. No one was going to give him a "job" with all the concomitant paraphernalia of office space, contributory pension scheme, paid holidays, sick benefit, apparent (though illusory) financial security and access to the staff canteen. And yet, inspired and tutored by Jeannie, he seemed to be taken seriously when he presented himself in an altogether more pretentious guise as someone offering advice rather than seeking employment. In relative terms he came cheaper as a "media consultant" than a staff hack but surely, he argued to himself, there was more to it than that. The interview with the Suragan embassy was the first of several. They did not all lead anywhere but even so . . .

His stationery was passing clever. The actual paper was of higher than average quality and coloured "barley white" to distinguish it from the boring conventional "white white" which was the norm. In a crowded in-tray it immediately stood out from the competition. "Fisher Cadogan Fisher" had an authoritative neutrality and suggested age without fustiness. Putting "London, Rome, Hong Kong, New York" at the bottom of the page was an almost total con. He himself was the London office and he had friends in the other three places who were prepared to offer him a pro tem poste restante in return for bed, board, drinks or other services when they were next in London. That was all. Yet no one seemed disposed to call his bluff.

Not having an address which was smart or "prestigious" (he hated that misused word and yet it seemed to be compulsory media-speak for "smart") he decided to dispense with it. His writing paper gave no clue as to his real and unfashionable postal address. Instead he gave a phone number; a fax number; and an e-mail number. In the old days such codes readily revealed where a person lived. He was mature enough to remember lettered London telephone exchanges such as FLAxman or JUNiper which were code for addresses in Chelsea and West Kensington respectively. They were long gone. However, even after the change to all-digit numbers there was still a world of difference between, for example, acceptable 0171 for inner London and the social and commercial death of 0181 for outer or suburban London. Latterly, telephone numbering had become so complex that it was impossible for all but the phone equivalent of a train-spotter to tell whether a number was based in Taiwan or Timbuctoo. Let alone Land's End or John o'Groats. This meant that there was no way of knowing whether Fisher was operating from a small terrace house in a grotty south-of-the-river inner suburb (true) or a Park Lane penthouse (false).

Jeannie persuaded a friend in the art department to design a discreet logo involving entwined "F"s. This was incorporated into his business cards as well as his letterheads. Together she and Fisher worded letters, proposals and curricula vitae in a style calculated to dazzle potential clients without giving them too much information. Not that there was much information to give.

She also helped him choose an adequately fitting off-the-peg dark suit, shirts, ties and shoes, and made him have his hair cut by a proper barber. When this had been done Fisher was afraid he looked as if he were an art dealer or second-hand car salesman. *Superior* works of art and *superior* second-hand cars, but second-hand all the same. What's more, if he had been a potential customer he wouldn't have bought one from him. Looking at himself in the mirror of life he didn't regard himself as entirely kosher. But then a hack's natural suspicions and antipathies died (moderately) hard.

As a "media consultant" Fisher envisaged giving advice on the inside and out. If someone on the outside, such as Dr Simenon, wanted to get in then Fisher was his man. If, on the other hand, a newspaper or other organ was having problems in communicating with Joe Public then Fisher was the organ's man too. He was not simply a poacher turned gamekeeper – he was both at once. Or so he hoped.

Thus it was that he found himself called to pitch for business with the *Intelligence*.

The opening came through Colin White-Lewis. As fellow literary editors the two had been acquaintances, bumping into each other at book launches where they would nibble canapés together in corners while griping about their host's parsimony, particularly with regard to smoked salmon and alcohol at parties such as this. What they really had in common was that they knew they both had oxymoronic jobs, though most of the time they had to pretend otherwise. The fact that they were in similar boats meant that with each other the need for bluster was reduced.

After he lost his job, which was before Colin ran into troubles of his own, Fisher sent him a letter on his smart new writing paper. He had taken the precaution of telephoning him first to warn that he was newly converted to, ahem, consultancy. Colin, being fundamentally a good, if slightly curate's, egg replied that there was not a lot he could do himself but that if Fisher were to write formally he would pass the letter on to his mother and brothers with an appropriate endorsement.

The result was broadly typical of the way in which things were still done at the *Intelligence*.

The day after Fisher's letter was on-passed by Colin, Major Gordon and Major Ronald found themselves in adjacent pews at the directors' urinal.

"Did you get Colin's bumf about some consultant chappie?" asked Gordon.

"Yah," said Ronald, using the drawled Germanic affirmative peculiar to his class and generation.

"What think?"

"Can't do any harm to have the bugger in." Ronald zipped himself up and walked over to the hand basins. "I'm not averse to a spot of consultancy. Not a lot anyone can teach *us* about running a newspaper but no one can accuse me of not keeping an open mind. I understand he used to work for the *Conscience*. He might have some inside information."

"I'll fix it. What do we give him? Half an hour before conference?"

"Half an hour's ample." Ronald grinned. "He can have one and a half cups of proper coffee but he has to be out of the building on the dot."

And so it was that Fisher came to be confronting the two Majors in the boardroom of the *Intelligence*. The men were, of course, engulfed in crises: the crisis of their mother and younger brother; the crisis involving the Prime Minister; the ever present crisis of falling circulation and dying readers. But it was essential to their particular interpretation of "Englishness" that no matter how dire life really was, one carried on as if nothing were the matter. It was the state of mind that kept the band playing even as the *Titanic* was slipping under the waves and made a cricket match out of every blood-curdling skirmish in Queen Victoria's little wars. It was not much in evidence in post-Thatcherite Britain, though the Majors firmly believed that the reintroduction of National Service would put it right in no time. That and the introduction of corporal punishment. Capital too!

Anyway, there was no way the Majors would rearrange the meeting with Fisher just because all about them was in disarray. On the contrary. To have done so would have been interpreted as a sign of weakness.

There were three of them to one of Fisher. The Majors, or more precisely Major Gordon, had asked Felicity/Fiona/Thingy to "sit in" on the meeting. Yet again. But this was a last-chance saloon for everyone. Her presence was explained briefly and vaguely to Fisher in the introductions. Fisher wasn't stupid. It was obvious that the girl was someone's protégée and that, whatever her talent and qualifications, this was a casting-couch situation. It didn't look to him as if it was working out.

"I'm afraid we're on a pretty tight schedule," Gordon began, "so I have to ask you to be brief. Our next appointment is at 11.13 sharp. Time waits for no man, especially in newspapers. We are at the mercy of events. That's the nature of the beast."

"Well, actually," said Fisher deriving a hitherto unexpected confidence from his new stationery, clothing and success with Dr Simenon, "that's what my colleagues and I are in the business of trying to change. We aim to make time stand still. Or, better, I want time to wait for *us*."

The two Majors exchanged a raised eyebrow. Felicity scribbled on a pad and did not look up.

"Meaning?" enquired Gordon, a touch testily.

"Meaning that the received wisdom has traditionally been that newspapers are reactive. But increasingly we have seen proprietors and editors becoming more and more pro-active."

"Surely", said Ronald, "the point about a newspaper is that your job is to report what's happening. Take a football match. If England lose to Germany 2–0, we have to report it. We can't pretend there was any other result."

"With respect," said Fisher, "that sort of thinking is already way out of date. Sport's a very good example. Half your competitors are devoting as much space to 'Fantasy' games and sports as they are to the so-called 'real thing'. It's far more cost-effective because you don't have to send a member of staff to report it or even watch it on television. You make it up. And making it up means that you can be positive and up-beat. If you make it up England always beats Germany."

"I'm sorry," said Gordon, "but we at the *Intelligence* take some pride in the fact that we are a *news*paper." He stressed the first syllable so strongly that his moustache seemed to flutter in an alarmingly surreal fashion, like a painting by Salvador Dali.

"Well, I'm sorry too," said Fisher, "but the whole idea of the *news*paper really went out with Beaverbrook and the ark. No one's believed in it since the sixties. People have paid lip-service to it but it's not true. No names, no packdrill, as you'd say but there were so-called campaigning journalists even in the seventies who made amazing reputations by *not* reporting the facts. They invented them. Or, if they had scruples, they selected the ones that made for the best entertainment. It kept costs down and it meant they could stay on top of the situation. This 'reporting' stuff is hopelessly expensive and very restricting. You can't possibly make sensible plans if you're always worrying that something will 'happen' which makes you have to react to it.

"All this Prime Minister stuff, for instance. I'm afraid your paper's hopelessly out of touch. You seem to be trying to establish what *actually* happened. People aren't interested in that. Not unless it's fascinating. There's no virtue in telling the truth if it's screamingly dull. People won't read it. They won't even *believe* it these days. You probably think that reporting so-called facts makes people believe you. Absolutely not. Today's market won't accept what you call 'reality' because it's too dull. We know that truth is stranger than fiction but try telling them that. It makes one wonder if you're interested in selling your product at all. If the press says the Prime Minister had an affair with his PPS, then as far as 'the people' are concerned he did, whether in so-called reality, he did or didn't."

Jeannie had been coaching him very thoroughly over the last few weeks. He was beginning to get the hang of this devil's advocacy. Indeed he almost believed it.

"That's a very cynical way of looking at life," said Gordon.

His brother nodded. "Frightfully cynical."

"Oh, come on," said Fisher. "You're in the entertainment business. Truth and entertainment aren't compatible. Even proper newspapers in the so-called 'good old days' distorted the news. Claiming to report 'the truth' was always a hypocrisy. Nowadays other newspaper proprietors have the decency to admit it. They don't pretend. They're in the fine tradition of the *Beano*, the *Dandy* and the *National Enquirer*. All that crap about a 'newspaper of record' is complete eyewash."

The Majors seemed genuinely aghast.

Fisher realised that his new self-confidence had got the better of him. He decided to go for broke. "Look," he said, "one of your opponents has just appointed a Travel Editor whose main claim is that she has never been abroad. Not even on a day trip to Boulogne. They think that's funny. Rather smart. What's more, the readers agree. Another has just fired the Books Editor and appointed a 'spoiler editor' whose only job is to gut review copies of books and rewrite them as 'news stories'." (He spoke here from the bitterness of all-too-recent personal experience.) "Ignorance and invention. Those are what sell papers today. Get real! And get greedy! Join the club!"

"That may be true elsewhere," said Gordon, "but not here. At least the *Intelligence* still has integrity."

"Integrity doesn't pay the bills," said Fisher. "You're losing money hand over fist."

"We're not in the newspaper business to make money," said Ronald defensively.

"But you're not in it to lose money. How much longer can you afford to go on? Sooner or later you just won't be able to pay the bills."

"We run a pretty tight ship here," said Gordon. "Tighter than perhaps you imagine."

"OK," said Fisher, recognising a cul-de-sac when he came to one. "What about the cover price?"

"What about it?" Both Majors were becoming hostile as well as defensive. Fisher recognised the need to back off or at least to soften his attack. "What if there's another price-cutting war?"

There was, at the time, an uneasy truce in these cut-throat and seemingly suicidal hostilities. For a period nearly all the so-called "quality" newspapers had reduced their cover price to the point where they were effectively giving themselves away. Indeed they often *were* giving newspapers away. Passengers on trains such as The Cambrian Coast Express or The Flying Liverpudlian were given them in first class; guests in Jolly Trencherman Hotels got them if they ordered a full English breakfast; one marketing whiz-kid at Fisher's former office had even proposed giving them away with every Barbara Cartland novel sold. This had been vetoed after someone said that there had once been a plan to give away free Barbara Cartland novels with every copy of the paper. Evidently it had ended in tears. The consensus of the meeting was that the new notion might prove similarly sad. But it just showed what could happen when marketing men were allowed to run amok. Fisher's view was that sooner or later papers would pay people to buy them. The circulation war could be that intense.

Those days were in abeyance, though most of those involved thought the lull in the fighting would be over by Christmas.

"We shall do exactly as we did before," said Gordon.

"Which was nothing," said Fisher. "Masterly inactivity."

For the first time since Fisher had started speaking Major Gordon allowed a whisper of a smile to part his lips. It was barely noticeable, scarcely elevating the whiskers or revealing a glimpse of the discoloured ivories, but it was a concession of a kind and Fisher felt relieved. "Precisely," he said. "Since the days of the Founder we have always taken the view here that it is often better to do nothing than to do, er . . . something."

"I quite agree," said Fisher, feeling that the phrase was essential if he were to have the slightest chance of salvaging anything from this uncomfortable half-hour. "Far better to do nothing than to do something silly. On the other hand, far better to do something sensible than to do nothing."

For the first time the girl spoke. "Confucius he say," she said. And grinned.

The Majors looked blank. Fisher flushed but managed a smile of self-deprecating agreement. "Having said that," he struggled on, "one must be prepared for the fact that your competitors are going to go back to price-cutting. They'll be giving their papers away and indeed, if my intelligence is correct – and I think it is – they'll actually be paying people to take them."

"I beg your pardon," said Ronald, "people are going to be paid for getting a paper?"

"It may be presented slightly differently, but if you stop to think about it that's what half of your competitors are doing already. All those coupons for cut-price weekends and discounted restaurant meals. It's just another way of saying, 'Take the *Daily Bugle* and get paid for doing so.' So I think that before the year is out you'll find one or other of the big groups offering cash incentives for taking their paper."

"But that's ridiculous," said Gordon.

"Not if it forces you or someone else out of business. The advertisers won't mind."

The Majors looked at each other in what they would like to have thought was disbelief.

"So papers will be paying their readers to boost circulation."

"I believe so."

"Who in particular?" asked Ronald.

"That I can't say," Fisher beamed. "But my sources are impeccable."

As it happened he was making it up. But it could perfectly well be true.

The Majors looked at their watches.

"It's been most interesting, Mr Fisher," said Gordon, never short of a cliché. "Don't call us – we'll call you."

He talks like his newspaper, thought Fisher, but out loud he said, "Thank you so much for sparing your time. I'm most grateful."

The men nodded.

"Fe ... um ... Fi ... er ... Thingy here will show you out," said Gordon. And the two men collected their papers and what was left of their wits before leaving for their next and, they managed to imply, vastly more important meeting.

When they were alone the girl smiled at him. "I don't suppose you're doing anything for lunch?" she enquired, her inflexion making it very plain that if he did have plans he would be a fool not to change them.

23

LEGENDARY LUNCH(EON)

T he meal to which Fisher then entertained her was conspiratorial and conducted almost entirely to their mutual
satisfaction. They ate in a dark corner of an ancient Italian
restaurant: penne putanesco – the pasta of the Genoese prostitutes
which seemed appropriate to them both – accompanied by a bottle
of Montepulciano. To seal their accord, a grappa apiece and two
double espressos and Effie insisted on paying. She had decided for
Fisher's benefit to abandon the deliberate ambiguity of Felicity/
Fiona with this new "f" nomenclature. "It's very kind of you," she
said, "but I think this should be my shout. I can put it down to
'entertaining contact'."

"Can you still do that?" asked Fisher, impressed. "I haven't
been able to do it since the late seventies. Those sods in accounts
want names and phone numbers for everything. And they ring up
to check. Bloody cheek. How on earth can you maintain a discreet
contact if some wanker in a suit rings up to ask if it's true you had
lunch at the Savoy with me last week and did you have the sole
and the Chablis."

"They don't do that at the *Intelligence*," said Effie. "A
gentleman's word is his bond. If you say you had sole and Chablis
at the Savoy with an important contact from the Department of
the Environment they believe you."

"Even when it's not true."

"Especially when it's not true." She laughed. "They're incredibly naïve. It's quite sweet, really." She frowned. "Well, sometimes. Not often, actually."

"You're not happy in your work?"

A waiter greased over to their table with a wine bottle and showed it to Fisher with an oleaginous smile.

Fisher waved it away. "Show it to madam," he said. "She's paying."

"The Majors are paying," she said, "and I'm sure the wine's fine. Just pour it."

The waiter looked affronted but did as he was told.

"It must be bloody not having a proper expense account."

"No one has an expense account these days. Not unless they're on the board. And I can claim some things against tax."

"I know about being self-employed," she said. "There's a distressing amount of it in my family. I think it's genetic. Economic haemophilia. And nowadays you can't claim anything against tax unless you've got a receipt in quadruplicate. Everyone hates the self-employed. They think you're all skiving."

"Oh, I don't know." Fisher swilled a mouthful of wine, puckered his lips and tried to look expert.

Effie appeared not to notice. "Well I do," she said. "People in offices and big corporate organisations think they're the only ones who understand the meaning of work. Small business and self-employed people think the same. I've seen both sides. I know. Trust me."

"And ...?"

"And what?"

"The two sides," said Fisher. "Whose side are you on?"

She shrugged. "I'm not sure it's a question of sides," she answered. "But I've had the *Intelligence* up to here." She put a hand to her throat and Fisher noticed an engagement ring. "I haven't been happy for a while but this whole Prime Minister thing is just yuk."

"Yes," said Fisher uncertainly.

"Also, I have a feeling it could be much more fun telling other people how to do their job rather than actually doing it."

"That's your definition of consultancy?"

"Yes, actually. No offence. It's the way of the world. Those who can, do; those who can't, consult."

"Except that in newspapers those who can, can't. If you see what I mean."

The pasta arrived.

"They've made it with anchovies," said Effie. "It's supposed to be pilchards. They think it doesn't matter, that we won't notice the difference. It's just like newspapers. It's not that they can't do it, it's just that they don't see the point. They think modern readers are too dumb to tell the difference between the real thing and complete crap. On balance, they're probably right."

"Surely", said Fisher, "the point is that modern 'readers', to use a patently obsolete word, actually prefer crap to the real thing. The real thing is difficult. You know – long words, complicated ideas, all that old-fashioned stuff."

She smiled. "I think we may be going to get along," she said, "but I'm not entirely clear what you're going to advise newspapers to do. Why should they pay you to tell them what they know already?"

"Good question, but everyone does nowadays, so why not me? You need bullshit and high gloss. Some of the new computerspeak comes in handy. Words like 'Cascade' and 'Tile', 'Digital', 'Analogue' ... loads of graphics ... tell them they've got to have websites for everything. The real point is that they'll take it from an outsider in a suit called 'Fisher Cadogan Fisher' but not from the same person if he's on the payroll. That person is an insubordinate nerd. I know. I have been he."

"Him," said Effie, "him not he."

"That sort of distinction is meaningless in modern communications," said Fisher. "Think 'brand', think 'image', think 'consumer loyalty'."

"Do you believe that?"

He chewed on his penne. "I'd rather not," he said after a moment's thought, "but I don't see any other explanation. Do you?"

"No," she said. "You know, some of my contemporaries from Oxford are actually in charge of things on some papers. There's a girl called Cassandra Phillips who's the Features Editor on the *Post* and a really really dim bloke from Trinity who's supposed to be running obits on the *Noise*."

"But they don't have obits on the *Noise*."

"No," she said, "I suppose not. He was always a terrible liar. Anyway, the *Intelligence* is hopelessly old-fashioned about age.

They're all ancient. I'd have to wait for ever before I was allowed actually to run anything. So I think maybe I should give consultancy a try and see if I can run things that way."

"I see," said Fisher. "Do you feel you have the qualifications?"

"Give me a break." She smiled. "Since when did 'qualifications' have anything to do with it?"

Fisher smiled back. "Such cynicism in one so young," he said. "So OK. Tell me about yourself and precisely what contribution you think you can make to this great organisation of mine."

So she did. And although Fisher wasn't really taking much of it in he was impressed by the noise she made and also by the visual effect which accompanied it. If, as he was inclined to believe, the world of newspapers was really operating in a post-literate society then words themselves no longer mattered. Which was how, more or less, he came to propose the grappa and to take on Effie as his very first member of staff. She was going to have great pleasure in giving in her notice at the *Intelligence* that very afternoon.

But not before nipping into accounts and claiming for today's lunch.

24

CLEANSING
THE PALATE

B ack at the *Intelligence*, the Majors' minds also turned to the matter of food, though not exactly lunch.

"I'm sacking the cook." A great newspaper, as Lady Beatrice so frequently told her sons, was more than its front page. An editor had to keep all his balls in the air and never take his eye off them. This was one of her ladyship's most famous and characteristic mixed metaphors. In practice what she meant was that if things are going wrong in important areas an editor can always cheer himself up by making a huge song and dance in some other less important area, especially one where no one will dream of answering him back.

Major Gordon's moustache was at the quiver and his cheeks were a dangerous purple. "Cynthia did her guinea fowl with rhubarb on Sunday and it was a complete bloody disaster. A complete bloody disaster. Every single one of her recipes seems to consist of ramming sticks of rhubarb up every conceivable orifice of the bird in question. If it moves, stick a stick of rhubarb up its bum. That's not my idea of *haute cuisine*."

Major Ronald frowned. "That's a little harsh," he said. He had always rather fancied the cook and had himself been responsible for tempting her away from one of the glossy magazines some years before. She was not as young as she had been and, like others in her line of business, she had become a little broad in the beam and choleric in complexion. But then who hadn't? Major Ron still had a soft spot for the old girl.

"She's well past her sell-by date and you know it." Ronald wondered who his brother had been talking to. This "mad-axeman" mood was usually provoked by someone else putting him up to it – usually the wife. Truth be told, there was a sense in which Major Gordon was all froth and no beer. He would occasionally rampage round the office threatening mass redundancy to all and sundry, but the mood usually passed. The staff called him "the man with the rubber hatchet."

"She has a very loyal readership," said Ronald. "She's trusted. Her recipes work."

"No," said Gordon. "My mind is made up. The cook's time has come. Remember what President Truman said: 'If you can't stand the heat, you must get out of the oven.' "

"I think the word was 'kitchen'," said Ronald, "not 'oven'. But be that as it may, I feel that the cook is perfectly able to withstand the heat of either."

"Let's not argue about it. This is an editorial decision. Nothing to do with management. But even if it were a management decision I'd still make it. We need to downsize if we're to remain competitive."

"I beg your pardon!"

"Granted. You heard what I said. We need to shed some fat. We have to become a lean machine. Profit. We have to think profit. To make profit we must downsize."

"And so you're firing the cook."

"Correct. The cook must go. I'm faxing her."

"I've never heard you talk about 'downsizing' before." Major Ronald suddenly had a thought – not something that often troubled him. "Good grief!" he said. "You've been talking to that 'consultant' chappie."

His brother turned a pinker shade of pink. He hadn't talked to anyone, but he had been thinking. Always dangerous in his case. "Up to a point," he said. "But that's by the way. The cook's going. In fact she's gone. I've dictated a fax."

"I'd have fired the chef before the cook," said Ronald.

The chef was the man, Charles, who prepared the meals for the directors' dining-room. He was the fourth in succession and his real name was not Charles. However, all chefs at the *Intelligence* directors' dining-room were called Charles, on the same principle as Major Gordon calling everyone whose name he could not remember "Thingy". It saved no end of trouble and the chefs rather liked it. They tended to have been christened "Fred", "Bert" or, latterly, "Gary" or "Elton". Charles was, on the whole, an improvement.

"Don't be silly," said Gordon. "You know perfectly well that Charles is to the *Intelligence* what the apes are to Gibraltar. He's a symbol of permanence and prosperity. Getting rid of Charles would be like sacking the butler. You might just as well go on the nine o'clock news and read out a statement saying we're broke."

"Well, I'm not so sure," said Ronald. "I don't think Enid's half as bad as you make out. She gets a terrific postbag."

"So she says. We've only got her word for it. No, my mind's made up. The cook's out."

His brother shrugged. Perhaps Gordon was right and it was none of his business. All the same, he didn't care for the petulant tone of voice nor the truculent body language. He was unaccustomed to them. Up until now the only person who had thrown her weight about was their mother.

The cookery column in the *Intelligence* had actually been invented by Lady Beatrice herself during the Blitz when, she was fond of saying, she was "a mere chit of a girl". The idea was said to have come from Churchill, or at least from Lord Woolton, the Food Minister and inventor of an eponymous and disgusting pie. The wartime recipe columns were designed to educate a strictly rationed nation in ways of making ends meat. Literally. The infamous Woolton pie was an all-vegetable affair pretending to be as succulent as steak and kidney. It wasn't.

The early *Intelligence* recipes grappled with the grisly problem of turning swede and snoek into *haute cuisine*. It was an uphill task. The column was published once a week, on Thursday, and was unsigned. It did not even have the words "our own correspondent" or "a special correspondent" in the stylishly self-effacing fashion of the day. The recipes simply appeared. There were rumours that they were the work of Beatrice herself, but this was unlikely since she had never been able even to boil an egg. Not that this would have been much use since, officially, the British were limited to an egg a fortnight. Or thereabouts.

Try as the anonymous author might, the wartime columns made depressing reading. The passage of time made them more depressing yet. Trawling through those crumbly-dry, yellowy-brown pages in the *Intelligence* library half a century after the event was more depressing still. In a world of ostrich breast steamed with lemon-grass and chanterelles on a coulis of mangosteens and tayberries it was worse than salutary to read about how, in 1942, you could make an almost recognisable faggot from whalemeat.

After the war, rationing became even more severe and the cookery columns reflected the gastronomic frustrations of the day. Britain had won, for heaven's sake, and yet there were unlimited chocolate bars in Austria and barely a mint with a hole in it in the whole of Britain. The *Intelligence* ploughed dourly on with little homilies about nettle soup and dandelions and, in 1947, "Swede Denis Compton", followed soon afterwards by "Cream Stanley Matthews" based largely on cornflower and "Camp" coffee.

Early in the 1950s the column began to change, accurately reflecting the climate of the times as the *Intelligence* in those days always did, with an eerie aplomb. At last rationing disappeared and the redoubtable Elizabeth David, almost single-handedly, transformed the cooking and eating habits of the English middle classes. Indeed, her earliest books, on Mediterranean and French Country cooking, were written and published "when food rationing was still in full force, and [they] of necessity contained suggestions as to what ingredients might be substituted for quantities of bacon, cream, eggs, meat stock and so on. A list of stores to keep handy and where to buy them was also included, and a few recipes for dealing with tinned foods."

Triumphantly, Mrs David then went on: "Such advice no longer seems necessary, so these chapters have been eliminated." The *Intelligence* joined in the hurrahs and took on a new cook who signed his column "Gastronome" in a deliberate echo of the rival "Bon Viveur". "Bon Viveur" was, in reality, a husband-and-wife couple who enjoyed some fame, if not notoriety. "Gastronome" was also a couple, but they remained effectively anonymous. They were in fact a pair of homosexual men, the elder a distinguished diplomat – part of the Blunt, Burgess, Maclean *galère*, though almost certainly not a spy – and the other a much younger photographer. Like Elizabeth David herself, they were devout francophiles and much given to foreign holidays. Suddenly the *Intelligence* began to offer potato dishes from the Savoie, peasant soups from the Auvergne, Breton ways with mussels and Norman treatment of tripe. There was a certain amount of dissent from the retired military of the Tunbridge Wells–Cheltenham axis but, on the whole, such readers did not concern themselves with the cookery columns which appeared, in the fashion of the times, on the "Women's Pages" which featured all the obvious unmasculine topics such as knitting, fashion, children as well as food, though not yet drink. The day of the wine correspondent was still to come.

"Gastronome" carried on into the sixties, when the senior half of the team died in mildly suspicious circumstances after a dubious evening with friends in Tangier. There followed a succession of not entirely successful experiments mainly, and uncharacteristically, involving "celebrity" cooks, some of whom had appeared on what Lady Beatrice called "the television" (she always preceded the machine with the definite article). The present cook, Enid Kitchener-Clarke, was taken on in the seventies. Enid came on the national food-writing scene at the same time as her colleagues Fay Maschler and Delia Smith. If anything, she made even more of an initial impact than the other two. With her thigh-length boots, black Harley-Davidson, Havana cigars and pet parakeet, she was a striking figure. Her cooking was erratic, inventive but always *sounded* entertaining. She was the sort of teacher who inspired rather than indoctrinated. She was not meant to be taken too literally. When Major Gordon complained that she was forever sticking rhubarb up birds' bottoms he was correct, but she would have been horrified to think that her readers were doing exactly as she told them. She wanted them to go away and think about it, make up their minds and probably compromise. She would expect readers to substitute a carrot or celery stick for the rhubarb or, if using rhubarb, to mix it with ginger and mouli it into a coulis. "You've got to use your imagination for Chrissake," she would say. "I use mine, now you use yours. Picasso never did painting by numbers, so don't expect to be a decent bloody chef by cooking by numbers."

Unfairly, what, in one's twenties, is tolerated as charming eccentricity can be seen, in middle or old age, as batty peevishness. And Enid, like the Majors, would never see fifty again.

"I'm thinking of reviving 'Gastronome'," said Major Gordon.

"But we haven't had 'Gastronome' for a quarter of a century," protested Ronald. "It's fearfully old hat. You've got to have a cook with a real name and a photograph at the top of the column."

"Well, I think we could set a trend with this one," said Gordon.

"I think the market's ready for it. Nostalgia coupled with the thrust of an ... er ... cutting edge. You can't stand still when it comes to cooking. We have to be seen to be pushing out the end of the envelope."

"You *have* to have been talking to that consultant chappie," said Ronald. "What on earth do you mean by 'pushing out the end of the envelope'?"

"Oh Ronnie," said Gordon, looking arch but embarrassed, "you do sometimes sound like a high court judge. Pushing out the edge of the envelope means advancing into the twenty-first century in the full blast of the white heat of technology."

"That doesn't sound like us. The *Intelligence* has always got where it was by resisting that sort of mumbo-jumbo. We stand still when all about us is a Gadarene stampede of headless chickens." He gulped slightly at having perpetrated this mixed farmyard metaphor. "If you see what I mean."

"Not really," said the senior Major, "but the decision has been taken. 'The return of Gastronome' has rather a good ring to it. It'll be written in-house so we'll save Enid's salary."

"But you'll have to pay her off and give her a decent pension."

"Yes, well, maybe. That's your pigeon. Nothing to do with *me*. That *is* a management decision. Your baby entirely."

"And who, pray, is going to be the new 'Gastronome'?"

"Well, I rather thought", Gordon smiled wolfishly, "that as the last 'Gastronome' contributors were chaps who helped out at tea parties, we should repeat the experiment."

"Meaning?"

"Well, I thought" – Gordon shuffled some papers on his desk and looked shifty – "that we'd have a left-handed trio: Dr Clancy, Trotter and Stomper-Watson."

"For a start," said Ronald, "I don't think you're right about their sexuality. I happen to know that Brendan Clancy has a child in County Cork. I have to pay the maintenance through the office."

"Why on earth?"

"I can't divulge very much," said Ronald a shade prissily. "Clancy was on some foreign assignment in the dim and distant when he knocked up this girl. We said we'd do the decent thing and pay the bills. The *Intelligence* was like that. Still is. At least that's what I like to think. Chaps behave like gentlemen."

"You never told me that before."

"You never asked. I think the experience had a salutary effect. I doubt whether the Doctor has let a woman past his lips since then. You know what the Irish are like. I don't think anyone had told him where babies came from. If they had, they'd got it wrong. Said nothing would happen if you did it with the lights out or your fingers crossed. Clancy's always been gullible. On the other hand you're probably right about Trotter. In fact, almost certainly right, though I'd say he was passive when it comes to sex. Not interested in male, female or even neuter come to that. But Stomper-Watson's a dark horse. I should say he bats and bowls. An all-rounder."

"Not more than club standard," Gordon put in sniffily.

"I wouldn't know," said Ronald. "You're probably right. Middle-order batsman and second-change bowler, but keenish."

"Well, whatever." Gordon had obviously had enough gossip. "I'm making them 'Gastronome' with a clear instruction to get rid of the *rhubarbe en orifice* style of cuisine. I want the sort of food you used to get at the Revellers: toad-in-the-hole, bubble and squeak, spotted dick. Our readers want the cooking nanny gave them in the nursery, the sort of food you associate with leather armchairs. Savouries. Plenty of offal and stodge."

"But", protested Ronald, "I thought you wanted a gay 'Gastronome'."

"Precisely," said Gordon. "That's the sort of food poofters do best. It's a well-known fact. And while we're on the subject of sacking people, there are one or two provincial cricket correspondents who I think should be given the old heave-ho."

Ronald looked at his brother curiously. Their mother's self-elevation seemed to have gone to his head.

25

FREEDOM OF
THE PRESS

How infinitely less complicated, thought Ken, to run one's newspapers without constraints involving such bourgeois abstracts as "facts", "truth" and "accuracy". Lee and Eddie White might, in an old-fashioned former world, have felt resentful that the Prime Minister was granting an exclusive interview to an opposition paper. The PM might have said something "interesting" to the *Intelligence* and they would then have been forced either to use his "interesting" quotation with a humiliating reference to the fact that the remark had been made to someone else, or to find something more boring from elsewhere. An attributable source was the enemy of invention; a real-life interviewee was the death-knell of creativity.

Now, mercifully, the conventions had changed. The poor hacks at the *Intelligence* were hamstrung by their constraining proximity to their gift horse's mouth. Ken's papers, however, far from employing any genuine source material, could invent whatever suited them. They could fly like a bird in a cloudless sky or an airliner without flight controllers. This indeed was the freedom of the press.

"Sutton's singing to the *Intelligence*," said the Proprietor as Eddie White finally entered his office, managing to convey the insolent deference of one who has been inconveniently summoned from matters of far greater import.

Had he not been at the beck and call of Chinese Ken he would not have come. But he was making it clear that he came at his own pace. This was definitely not a run. He nodded at Ken. "Evening, boss," he said, then inclined his head at Pool but said nothing.

Ken motioned towards the chair alongside Pool's and White sat.

"What's Sutton saying?"

"Your guest is as good as mine," said Ken.

"My guess is pretty good," said White. "Yours too, or I'm a Virgin Mary. What does sweet William think?" He swivelled to face his fellow Editor and nominal superior. It was not difficult to see who wore the trousers in this situation.

"I presume the Prime Minister is offering a defence. If so, it will have to be a defence of the indefensible."

"What makes you say that?" Ken had produced a nine-inch Monte Cristo cigar, the phallic trademark of the B-movie mogul through the ages. There was a bullying edge to his voice which was given extra menace by this new prop. He clearly wished his audience to believe that the cigar had been personally rolled between the thighs of his woman in Havana. Ken was seriously into the pursuit of power, with a peppery coda of sex to give it added excitement. He wanted some sport with little Pool.

"So who's setting the agenda Mr Pool? Eh? Who's setting the agenda? That's what we have to be sure about." And he lunged at Pool like a duellist with a smoking épée. "It's the press that set the agenda, isn't that right? Even the politicians say so. 'Whinge, whinge, whinge. Who's running the bloody country. It shouldn't be the journalists.' That's what I hear from the back-benches. Front-benches too. Know what a senior government minister said to me only this morning? No names, I'm not revealing my sources. He said the press are in the driving seat because they've created a 'democracy of information'. Those were his very words. 'Democracy of information'! 'Sounds good, doesn't it? 'Democracy of information' my arse! He thinks the reason the press are running the country is because we're giving them information. You can tell he's not reading the *Noise*. If he was he'd know it was all game shows and gossip, sex and shopping. We're the generation that took the 'news' out of 'newspapers'. That's why people buy the product."

He blew a cloud of blue smoke towards the ceiling as if to indicate exactly what he thought about 'democracy of information'. "I don't give a monkey's jockstrap for 'democracy' or for 'information' and as for the two of them lumped together . . . Tell you what, though, this bloke believed what he was saying."

"The theory being that information used to be confined to a small ruling class," said Pool, "thus effectively excluding the majority of the population from the decision-making process. Knowledge equals power. For example, in 1938 only the British Establishment knew about Edward VIII and Mrs Simpson. Under the modern system that would be impossible."

The other two regarded him with distaste and disbelief.

"Meaning that nowadays everyone knows who's sucking the Royal toes," said Sir Edward.

Pool shifted uneasily in his seat. Unlike the other two he had a degree – rather a good one. He was cleverer than them and had letters after his name to prove it. Yet when he said something which demonstrated this superiority the others managed to make him feel stupid. It should have been the other way round but, try as he might, he could not make it so. It was annoying, very. He should have been a don. Universities respected brains like his. He had only become a journalist because he believed he had a mission to inform and because he was passionately addicted to the beauty of the written word. His life in newspapers had been something of an unlearning curve. "You *could* put it like that," he said, aware that he was sounding wet.

"Only you'd prefer not to."

"Well, I *am* supposed to be editing a serious newspaper."

Ken Lee favoured him with a long smiling look which conveyed neither warmth nor humour – only menace and distaste. "A *serious* newspaper," he said, "a *serious* newspaper. Isn't that what one calls an oxymoron?"

Little Pool felt even smaller. It was an insulting remark, but what made it worse was that "oxymoron" was the sort of word that he was supposed to use and which Chinese Ken wasn't meant to know. It was deliberate, of course. Sometimes Pool felt that the only reason Ken employed him was for the purpose of humiliation. He was the token intellectual, a demonstration that uneducated, self-improved, homespun Chinese Ken had really hacked it. Ken could click his fingers and Fellows of All Souls would grovel. Forget intellect or knowledge, it was power that rated. Ken's power may not have come from the barrel of a gun but it was naked, unashamed, ruthless and flamboyant. Hong Kong Chinese entrepreneurs enjoyed hiring Western vice-presidents as lapdog trophies. Thus with Chinese Ken and little Pool. Ken was the master now, no matter what sort of spoon had been thrust into Pool's mouth at birth.

"The *Conscience* will be a 'serious newspaper' when it starts making money."

This was a lie for all sorts of reasons. One of the reasons Ken owned the *Conscience* was that it was not a tabloid and could therefore be described as a "quality" paper. In real life Ken, and most people engaged in the inky trade, knew that the distinction was meaningless. The broadsheets were a different shape, but that didn't mean that they couldn't be just as mucky. They too used paparazzi pictures. They intruded into private grief. They too could be salacious. It was also generally accepted that the *Conscience* lost money but creative accounting could produce any result Ken wanted. It suited him to have the world believe that he was subsidising the *Conscience* out of his own pocket but the truth was that the *Conscience* advertising revenue was quite respectable and the paper now cost virtually nothing to produce, since there was hardly anyone but Pool left on the staff.

That was a slight exaggeration. In the provinces, Ken had one or two weekly papers staffed solely by an editor with two part-time assistants. Even he, however, recognised that, although desirable, this level of staffing was impossible on a national daily. Nevertheless, impressive economies had been achieved. Foreign correspondents and bureaux had been axed; secretaries replaced by computers and answering machines; those few remaining reporters virtually chained to their desks (just as those ancient manual typewriters had been in the days of the old technology); and, of course, the whole archaic apparatus surrounding old-fashioned hot-metal printing had vanished without trace.

In the old Fleet Street world one of the main tasks of an editor was to brief members of his own staff. This was less and less true. It was cheaper and more economic to rely on stories from agencies and other papers. The editor's main function now was to select them from his screen or VDU and transfer them into the printing operation. Ken also encouraged the hiring of younger and younger "journalists" on the public grounds that they were uncontaminated by ancient corrupt customs but on the private principle that they were immeasurably cheaper than their more experienced elders.

The paradox was that although the staff employed by Ken had

shrunk beyond recognition the size of his papers had increased in apparently direct proportion. Around a quarter the number of people were producing four times as many words as in the past. Ken described this as a triumph for efficiency, though not everyone agreed.

Pool determined that silence was the better part of valour and after looking at him expectantly for a few moments the others decided that he wasn't worth the sport. It was as if they thought he was an undersized fish to be thrown back in the water.

"So," said Ken waving his cigar like an orchestral conductor, "what's our line?"

"Assuming", said Sir Edward, all mandarin smirk, "that the *Intelligence* are going to whitewash the PM we have to do the opposite. So we continue the attack, take the credit for flushing the little bugger out of the rough and demand his resignation in the national interest. We could run a readership poll saying that ninety-six per cent of *Noise* readers think he should go." He chortled. "Three per cent undecided and only one per cent in favour of him staying. That's our gay readers."

"I didn't think you had any gay readers after your line on AIDS," said Pool sharply.

"There is such a thing as a neo-fascist poof," responded Eddie, smiling infuriatingly. "And we've always felt a responsibility for minority groups. Owners of Staffordshire bull terriers have rights too."

"I'm not sure we have to do a direct opposition job," said the Proprietor. "That's what they'll be expecting. You can bet your life there'll be a lot of pompous crap about 'irresponsible voices elsewhere demanding resignation' and so on. Surprise, surprise. We must provide an element of surprise."

"We can't agree with them," said Pool. "That would be suicidal."

"I was rather hoping we'd overthrow the government," said Sir Edward. "That *was Noise* policy."

"Policy shmolicy," said Ken. "If you did a *real* readership poll how many people would have a clue what the paper's policy was on anything except tits and bums? You've got more gay readers than people who know what the *Noise*'s political policy is. I own it, for God's sake, and I don't know what your policy is. I don't suppose you do either."

"That's not entirely fair," said White.

"Now you're sounding like Pool," said Ken, "and I don't pay you to do that."

"Well, what's *your* idea then?" White was riled.

Ken sucked on the Havana. It looked like a khaki carrot and had about as much life in it. It seemed to have gone out but after a few Herculean sucks a feeble glow appeared at the end and Ken removed it, inspected the embers and appeared satisfied. "First of all," he said, "we take all the credit, as Eddie says. That's right and proper. It also happens to be the truth, though that's neither here nor there. Then we deplore the fact that he chose to give an interview to just the one paper. We might point out here that there is a disturbing precedent with the way that that left-handed art-historian Anthony something, friend of Her Majesty, behaved when he was exposed as a traitor in *The Times*."

"Blunt," said Pool.

"That's the name," said Ken. "They interviewed him in the boardroom – all kid gloves and smoked salmon sarnies. That's what those poncy majors will be doing with Bryan Sutton even as we speak." He put on a pretend-Catering Corps major voice. "I'm terribly sorry to have to ask you such an embarrassing question, Prime Minister, but may I, with your permission, enquire whether you are, actually, the head of government in the United Kingdom? And is your name Bryan?"

He grinned round his cigar.

"That's easy," said White. "But after that ... what then?"

"Like I said before, I am not happy about losing Mr Sutton after all the work I put in on him. But business is business, life is life, politics is politics and a week is a long time in all three. Personally I think Sutton is dead in the water. But we need to stay flexible. You never know. Lazarus came back from the dead, so why not the Prime Minister. I'm not happy about the way things have been handled here, but there's no use crying over spilt milk. It's all water under the bridge. Any case, blood is thicker than either."

Neither Editor had much of a clue what their Proprietor was going on about, but they both nodded none the less.

"We support the Prime Minister," said Ken, "up to a point. No witch-hunt. No victimisation. He's come out and made a statement, even if it's in the wrong place and to the wrong people. But, OK, fair dos, mote and beam, let him who is without fault cast the first whatsit and all that stuff. We're going to give the guy a break. 'Break' being the operative word. What we say is that a man's private life is his own affair and he's come out and owned up. He's the elected first minister, blah blah, democracy, one man one vote, not part of press role to interfere in due process of this and that. On the other hand, notwithstanding all this garbage, never before has the pressure on those in public life been such as it is now and we owe it to the Prime Minister, as to all who seek to serve our great and glorious nation, to take a holiday now and then and what he should do now is take leave – if necessary extended. Meanwhile number two stands in pro tem."

"Isn't that a bit limp?" Coming from Pool this was a severe case of pots calling kettles black.

"Not if it's properly written," said Ken, thereby deftly delegating any possible blame and identifying his scapegoat with his customary precision. If this ploy didn't work it would not be Ken's fault for making a wrong decision, it would be his Editors', for not expressing it properly. White and Pool would do their best to pass blame on in their turn, but they knew unpleasantly well that in reality the buck stopped here, with them.

"So," said White, "you want us to say that the Prime Minister is a good thing but that he's overdone it and needs a rest."

"Yup," said Ken.

"And", continued Eddie, "because he is presently not himself nobody should pay the slightest attention to anything he may say in any other place."

"That's about it," said the Proprietor. "I want sympathy, compassion, understanding but firmness. Oh, and a sideswipe at those who seek to exploit a sick man for their own sordid commercial advantage might not come amiss. 'It beggars belief that a responsible organ should trick the nation's leader into making statements when he is so manifestly incapable of making them.' Or words to that effect. That's your problem. I'm only the boss around here. The words are your problem. OK? Any questions?"

Little Pool looked rueful but recognised that there was no point in saying anything. It would only be construed as insubordination and treated accordingly. He had no wish to be squashed any further. Particularly in front of his rival Editor. Privately he was wondering what had happened to the notion that he was now supposed to be the senior of the two. The Proprietor had said, hadn't he, that in future Sir Edward would be responsible to him,

Pool. Had he forgotten? Or had he not meant it? Was it another of the great man's whims? Or had he died and gone to hell?

No matter. He would simply shuffle off and do as he was told. It was ever thus. He would take it out on one or two of the secretaries or a leader writer or two. That would make him feel better, if only marginally. Never mind, he would be setting the agenda.

The fact that it was the Proprietor's agenda and not his own was depressing, but it was par for the course.

The two Editors took their leave. As the door shut behind them Ken blew a stream of bluish smoke in their direction and swore casually and for no particular reason.

26

A FOREIGN AFFAIR

"The Fleet Street 'Freebie' is a strange affair," said Fisher. Effie nodded. Fisher was enjoying his new role as tutor in journalism. The girl was a model pupil. "Recipients of the freebie tend to call them 'trips'," he continued. "This has a marginally less pejorative ring to it. 'I'm off on a freebie to Bermuda' carries as much guilt as a dirty weekend in Brighton. 'Got a trip to Barbados' is felt by hacks and PR ladies to be at least verging on the legitimate. If a journalist were to admit that he had got a 'trip to Barbados' the universal response would be 'you jammy bugger' but it would be regarded as marginally acceptable even though speaker and audience would know that what was actually meant was a 'freebie'."

Effie smiled.

" 'Trip' ", he continued, "leaves open the possibility that the venture is being paid for by the newspaper. In the days before 'new technology', newspapers were quite munificent in such matters, sending staff to all parts of the globe so that they could find out what was going on in foreign parts. Then they reported this to their supposedly avid readers."

"It sounds rather sweet," she said, "the age of innocence."

"Well maybe . . . the modern generation of thrusting, acquisitive proprietors and editors saw at once that this was a hopelessly expensive operation and of only marginal interest to a very few old-fashioned, élitist readers whom, frankly, they were better off without. Your modern Brit, they argued persuasively, was not interested in abroad except as a place for cheap, sexy holidays. There was always a little mileage for xenophobic stories about loony bureaucrats in Brussels trying to destroy the British way of life, but there was absolutely no need to send someone to Brussels in order to write them. Quite the reverse. You could write much more lurid and therefore circulation-enhancing stories in the sanctuary of the office far away from foreign influences."

"Is this true?" she asked. "Or are you just being middle-aged?"

"Don't interrupt," he answered, "I'm just getting into my swing. As part of the cost-cutting the new brooms abolished the so-called 'foreign bureaux', which even quite populist newspapers maintained. These offices in such desirable cities as Paris, Rome and New York were well known as havens for has-been free-loaders living the life of Riley on massive expense accounts. The new brooms also let it be known that revolution, fire, pestilence, civil strife, famine and all the other pretexts on which hacks had hitherto expended the fruits of their boss's unremitting toil and self-sacrifice would in future be covered from London with, if necessary, help from news agencies or the occasional local journalist paid at the rate prevailing in the country concerned. Since, almost by definition, the countries where these events took place were nearly always in the third world, such rates were satisfactorily low. Very occasionally indeed a paper would send one of its journalists to a foreign part, either to do an exclusive interview with a major world leader or to report on some particularly harrowing human disaster. This tokenism was often more or less secretly subsidised or capable of substantial reim-bursement by the Inland Revenue."

"You're reading this," she said. "You've written it all out."

"Yes," he said, a touch shiftly. "I thought a set-piece speech might come in useful." She laughed and he continued. "This parochial approach appealed, on the whole, to the natural paranoia of the British people but it did not altogether appeal to foreigners, especially to those who felt the need to get some sort of message across to the British. For such people the answer was simple. If British newspapers were suddenly too mean or too broke to afford abroad, then abroad would have to pay. Hence the 'freebie'. Foreign tourist boards did it; foreign airlines did it; foreign intelligence agencies did it.

"Some newspapers, more old-fashioned or, you could say, hypocritical than their rivals, said that they would have nothing to do with such bribes. On the whole they were not believed. Even if, for instance, a paper resolutely set its face against the 'freebie' and refused to allow members of its staff to accept them, they had no control over the freelances who supplied their apparently insatiable demands. Some of these people were even referred to as 'contributing editors'. Technically they were not 'on staff'. This meant that they could accept hand-outs because – of course – they were doing so in their capacity as private individuals. The fact that an article by them might suddenly appear in the publication to which they habitually contributed was entirely coincidental. OK?" he asked.

"I need time to think about it," she said.

Over the past few weeks Fisher had conducted a self-taught crash course in this sophisticated double-talking world. Now, after much negotiation, and more nudging and winking than he could ever remember, he had the bones of an interesting press trip to the People's Republic of Surago and was beginning to put serious flesh on them. Dr Simenon had been emollient, charming and, as far as he could see, remarkably effective. The tickets had arrived from Suragair. Being a "People's Republic" Suragair naturally only had one class ("People's") but, as so often in such cases, Orwellian standards prevailed and Fisher was given to understand (much winking and nudging here) that some classes were more equal than others and that only the best would do for "our very good British friends".

Dr Simenon had delegated (he was a delegator of assurance and aplomb) much of the itinerary fixing to someone called Gabrielle Casson of the Ministry of Public and Personal Affairs in Port-du-Soleil. He wasn't entirely certain what Gabrielle's title was, but she was in charge of the Suragan end of things and she certainly seemed to have influence. She had even arranged for the group to have a luncheon at the Presidential Palace, at which General Foom himself would be host. It was to be understood that the General's remarks on this occasion would be off the record but she intimated that he might be prepared to grant an on-the-record interview on some other occasion. That, however, would have to be confirmed at a later date. It would, Fisher was given to understand, depend on how the lunch went. If General Foom was favourably impressed then such an interview would take place. If, however, he took a dislike to any or all members of the party, then it would not. Mr Fisher must realise that while the President was a good friend to the British people he was not keen on the forces of Western Imperialism and the lackeys of the fascist United States of America.

Fisher told Mlle Casson that he understood perfectly and wondered to himself whether she enjoyed more than the President's ear. He was reputed to be a man of many mistresses.

The itinerary did strike him as being mildly eccentric. There was, for example, a visit to the national fish cannery and to the national sugar refinery, as well as an evening of music and dance by La Troupe Folklorique de Surago. A whole day had been set aside for official briefings at the Ministry of Culture, the Ministry of Tourism, the Ministry of Trade and the Foreign Ministry. There was a boat trip to the holiday island of Sainte Bernadotte to inspect progress on the new International Airport and the Resort Village and Casino. At Fisher's request some time had been set aside for "leisure" and "own arrangements", though Gabrielle had made it very clear that members of the party would be accompanied by a guide and/or interpreter at all times. This, she explained, was entirely for the benefit and assistance of the visitors, but Fisher, not born yesterday, assumed that these people would be "minders" from the Ministry of State Security.

Ah well, his not to reason why.

Picking a suitable team was more of a problem. He and Effie – he was no more clear than Gordon about whether she was really Fiona or Felicity but "Effie" seemed much preferable to "Thingy" – had agonised over this.

The final selection was not, on the whole, their first choice. One would have thought, at least Fisher and Effie would have thought, that ten days all found in a sub-tropical paradise would be to die for. Evidently that was not the universally received wisdom and their invitation was spurned by so many, both organs and individuals, that they began to suspect conspiracy.

" 'Surago not to die for – shock verdict of British Movers and Shakers,' " said Effie, crossing yet another name off the A-list.

"It's 'no go to Surago' from Britain's Great and Good," agreed Fisher, putting the phone down on a recent Booker Prize Winner who had been nobbled by the Society of Authors.

Men and women whom they knew to be not in the least busy pleaded "pressure of work"; papers and magazines that they *knew* relied on free hand-outs for half their articles regretted that they never accepted such offers; one or two cited previous engagements – weddings, book launches, libel hearings – that they were sure were bogus.

They were due to convene in a week's time. Meanwhile Fisher shut his mind to the potential for disaster and concentrated on getting their press kits together. Everybody must have a biographical sketch of President Foom with a colour picture of him meeting Mrs Thatcher many years earlier; also the official history of Surago; the Suragan five-year economic plan; two complimentary swizzle-sticks from the Marx-Lenin Plaza Hotel; an artist's impression of the new International Airport; a sheet of "Essential phrases in Suragan" (things like "Excuse me, what is the clock thank you" which caused Fisher no end of grief); a miniature of "Coq-au-ron"; a set of picture postcards depicting the fish cannery, the sugar refinery and other monuments to the revolution; and a map of the island with the street names rendered, inexplicably, in Chinese (Fisher faxed Gabrielle about this and she promised to have English-language versions with her when she met their flight). All this was packed into glossy folders covered in pictures of smiling Suragans cavorting on a beach under palm trees, which in turn was put in a Suragair plastic overnight bag, which each member of the group would be presented with at the VIP lounge immediately before departure.

Fisher sighed. This was what "media consultancy" was all about. He had not expected, when commissioning his smart stationery or buying the executive suit, to have to spend so much time on his hands and knees stapling together pages of gobbledegook which his guests would shortly be jettisoning unread and unlamented. It was what the client required, however, and, as he was beginning to realise, the client was always right. The client would not be pleased if, despite state-of-the-art press packs and a tickety-boo itinerary, no hacks showed up. Yet despite all the blandishments deployed by Fisher and his staff Surago was proving distressingly difficult to sell. Freeloading seemed to have gone out of fashion.

27

AN EDITOR WRITES

The Martian tourist, that notional ignoramus, traditionally summoned to demonstrate the absurdity of life on earth, would have been baffled by the press coverage following the Prime Minister's reappearance. But you wouldn't have to be a Martian tourist to be baffled. The Man on the Clapham Omnibus would have been just as confused.

In the *Intelligence* Major Gordon had abandoned the first golden rule of editorship ("An editor who writes for his own paper has a fool for a contributor" – Anon) and allowed himself a column with the single word "Comment" at the top. At the bottom it said "The Editor". How this differed from the unsigned editorial columns which appeared next to the letters was not immediately clear to Martians or general readers. To those in the know, however, it meant that Gordon wanted a clear run at writing his own words without having to endure discordant yapping from the Chief Leader Writer, Dr Clancy, and his henchmen, Trotter and Stomper-Watson, of "Words" and "Obituaries". As an editor with a proprietorial interest Gordon was in a strong position on the paper, but he did not get his own way without a struggle.

It was in the nature of the *Intelligence* that it contained a much higher proportion of old sweats than its rivals at the cutting edge of the new technology such as the *Noise*. The callow employees there did, on the whole, as they were told. If not, they could easily be dismissed with little or no compensation. Men like Clancy and his gang, on the other hand, were fully paid-up members of the awkward squad. Sacking them was likely, even in a virtually union-free climate, to be time consuming and expensive.

At moments such as this Gordon, therefore, preferred to step outside the minefield of the leader columns and head for his own goal. "Own goal" being the right expression. If he got it wrong in a column signed by "The Editor" he would have only himself to blame. There would be no refuge in "collective responsibility".

In this personal, though quasi-anonymous, article Gordon wrote, "The Prime Minister, though clearly irritated by recent criticisms, was in fine form. If ever a man was 'up for it', this was he."

Over at the *Conscience* the leader, written by Pool, but unsigned, took a very different view. "The Prime Minister", said the *Conscience*, "is clearly unwell. In the east few months his performance in the House of Commons and elsewhere has been lacklustre. His recent, sudden and unexplained disappearance was the behaviour of one who, if not exactly deranged, is not, for the time being at least, 'himself'. To put it plainly, in the football idiom of our times, the Prime Minister is no longer 'up for it'."

This "up for it" phrase was ubiquitous. It seemed to cross many barriers including those between the tabloids and the broadsheets.

"Come on, Bryan!" said the *Noise*. "You're not up for it."

Over breakfast in semi-detached semi-suburbia Fisher ground his teeth through muesli and Greek yoghurt, trying to read between the morning's lines.

"The *Intelligence* had an exclusive and Chinese Ken is trying to trump it," he said to himself (Jeannie having long since left for the agency), "but very few people care."

The *Noise* also boasted a page-three photograph of a naked, rangy black girl with pert breasts and bottom, and a free Eurostar weekend in Paris for anyone who clipped five coupons from the paper. It carried, too, a story about a TV soap star allegedly caught having oral sex in the back of a taxi in Piccadilly, and a sperm bank in Paraguay which was supposed to contain the frozen semen of the entire Nazi High Command.

"Why pretend?" muttered Fisher, himself preoccupied with arranging his press trip to Surago. It seemed much more important than this front-page silliness. "Does the Prime Minister matter? Do the readers believe the Prime Minister matters? Does the Prime Minister sell newspapers? Does the Prime Minister sell newspapers if he's caught *in flagrante* with his PPS? Answers to the first three; definitely "no", answer to four; "maybe". The conclusion being that sex was the bottom line. The Prime Minister without sex did not sell newspapers; with sex he might sell newspapers; but fewer newspapers than sex plus soap stars. Sex plus Prime Minister plus soap was the goal to which modern newspapers aspired. The more Fisher thought about it the less convinced he was that newspapers should go on dealing with politics at all except in the most perfunctory manner. They had long ago stopped reporting abroad except for major earthquakes (provided Britons were involved), hijacks and kidnappings (British victims also a prerequisite), sporting encounters (yet more British victims required) and very spectacular drug busts, rapes and murders (Britons again, though not necessarily as victims). Perhaps he should prepare a position paper on removing politics from newspapers. The economies would be significant and it would also put politicians even more firmly in their place. Starve them of the oxygen of publicity and they would wither and die. Or at least resume their proper place in the order of things – servants of the people who did as they were told, kept the drains unblocked and made the trains run on time.

"Yes, I'd drop politics," said Fisher, spitting out a piece of grit which had somehow found its way into a segment of dried banana. "Mug's game. Nothing in it for the consumer. Just takes away space from sex and shopping and sport."

A few miles nearer the centre of town, and the centre of power, Boy Perryman gently pushed down on the plunger of his cafetière and thought much the same, though from a different perspective. Politics had, in the past, been described as "far too important to be left to politicians". Perryman had a modicum of sympathy with this, but if politics really was too important for politicians then it was certainly too much for mere journalists. His own view, typical of a government press spokesman, was that journalism itself was much much too important to be left to journalists. He had an old-fashioned view of journalism but an up-to-date one of journalists. They needed to be regulated and policed, a job which inevitably had to be performed by politicians acting in co-operation with the law. Journalists were certainly not fit to be involved in politics except as onlookers and chroniclers. The modern fad of thinking that hacks were players on the political scene was, most emphatically, not one that he personally countenanced. Unfortunately, he reflected, he was not always his own master in this matter. If he were, he would have dealt entirely in prepared statements and "no comments". He certainly wouldn't have demeaned himself by answering questions from the press, much less break bread with them. He would have called press conferences when he wanted them, not when the media snapped their fingers. He would not have wimped out.

But needs and his masters must.

He couldn't honestly fault the *Intelligence*'s coverage. They had done what they said they would and perjured themselves on behalf of the boss. In doing so they made him sound *compos mentis*, which he wasn't, and fit to lead the government, which he *definitely* wasn't. Theirs was the authorised version, for they had actually spoken to the man in person. The fact that the man had responded by making the wrong noises was tiresome. It meant that the *Intelligence* was forced into telling deliberate lies. Necessary lies, lies for the national good, good, wholesome lies acceptable in the eyes of God, but lies none the less.

The paradox was that the rest of the press, the *Conscience* and the *Noise* foremost among them, had got the story more "right" than the *Intelligence*. They had done this without access to the tiresome "facts", which so often got in the way of a good story, and they had reaped the benefits.

They said the PM was in poor shape. This was true. They said he had done nothing which merited resignation, but that he should take a holiday. This, in Perryman's book, was fair.

His book might seem, to opponents, to be biased but he would contest that. In the words of one of his most celebrated predecessors, Sir Bernard Ingham: "We bring a certain – and necessary – detachment to the job." Not many on the other side of the fence on which Perryman liked to think he was sitting would have agreed that he was in the least "detached". He, however, believed that he was, as he put it, "above the fray". That did not prevent him being loyal to his boss. Fiercely so. As old Ingham put it a "pukka press officer" has a duty to "protect his institution and its leaders".

He never thought he would find himself allowing the *Conscience* or the *Noise* to set his own agenda. He had always prided himself on doing his own thing with only passing reference to outside events or persons. But that didn't mean he wasn't receptive to sensible ideas wherever they came from. Most of what these two papers wrote was, he thought, the usual drivel. The former was expressed in the style of the back-benches of a dim senior common room in a not quite first-rate university, while the second was couched in a bastard polemic by barrow boy out of Speaker's Corner. But the holiday idea was sound enough.

He wondered if it might be the moment to call in the services of the party's latest benefactor-on-the-make. He did not care for Spiros Plastiras, a descendant of the Greek General so snubbingly mispronounced by Winston Churchill as "Plaster-arse", but he had just given the party several million, handed over personally to the PM at Number Ten. He did say then that if ever Bryan wanted to avail himself of his yacht or one of his mansions around the world he had only to ask.

This might be such a time. He poured himself another strong black coffee and frowned at the shrill headline in the *Noise*. A carefully worded statement from the Premier's doctor; the absolute necessity for a short period of absolute rest and total privacy; the certain prospect of a complete recovery; a brief regency in the safe and unthreatening hands of the Deputy Prime Minister; a message of sympathy from the monarch (nice one, Boy); and a general public-relations gush of "steady as she goes".

The story would go away very fast if it was handled right. Stories nearly always did. They were like buses or sexual partners. If you were patient and waited in the queue another one would always turn up. Life moved on. Boy Perryman smiled to himself. He would never, in a million years, have allowed himself to be described as a "spin doctor" but he knew a thing or two about public relations. There had been far too much headless-chicken behaviour over the last few days. It was time for a spot of masterly inactivity. He would do as the *Conscience* suggested and defer, for once, to the volume of the *Noise*.

28

UNBEATABLE VALUE

Greenspace Airport, or, to give it the official name, London Greenspace, was a confidence trick. The public was being asked to believe that it was the "new London airport" but it was over a hundred miles from the capital and the much vaunted "Hi-Speed" rail link was little more than a glimmer in a planner's eye. Its inaccessibility didn't bother the copywriters or the marketing men, but their glitzy campaigns on behalf of the new airport fooled nobody worth fooling. The result was that London Greenspace was a magnet for the losers of the world. The only travellers were Mecca-bound Muslim pilgrims; basement bucket-shop back-packers; victims of "bargain" packages to cut-price costas; business people embarking on deals in countries of which only they and the occasional Doctor of Geography could possibly have heard. The aircraft which carried these unfortunates were dilapidated pieces of ironmongery passed down from the first to the third world like old clothes to the Oxfam shop. They carried all the essential certificates of airworthiness but they did not inspire confidence. Suragair was one of the airlines consigned to London Greenspace and its single decrepit Jumbo, *Princess of Surago*, was typical of the aeroplanes which limped in and out of this plate-glass white elephant in the middle of nowhere.

By a sleight of hand which would have shamed a three-card trickster in Oxford Street, the same hucksters who persuaded the poor and the gullible that London Greenspace really was a state-of-the-art main door into the metropolis had also conducted a successful assault on the coffers of the European Union. In the early days of "Europe" there had been "butter mountains" and "wine lakes" but these seemed to have been eaten and drunk. Latterly they had been replaced by vaults of money. To qualify for the fruits of these coffers one had to demonstrate need. If you could prove that yours was a "deprived area" then the European bureaucrats so reviled by the British press (with Chinese Ken and the Majors displaying rare solidarity) shovelled the stuff out in millions. Greenspace was just such a place: industry had clanked to a close, the mines had dried up; those able-bodied males who had failed to get on their bikes and find somewhere more prosperous milled around street corners, beat up their wives and girl-friends and were regularly scrutinised by Ph.D. students and documentary film-makers for glum theses on the plight of the terminally unemployed in a post-industrial society.

So Greenspace got grant money for being a basket-case while at one and the same time pretending to be at the white-hot cutting edge of the new technology. It made very little sense. It was to this strange symbol of the pre-millennium malaise that the members of Fisher's Suragan press party made their way one grey morning. Fisher had originally considered a minibus from central London but managed to do a deal on rail tickets with Mister Speedy, the newly privatised company which was supposed to be running the rail link with London Greenspace. Mister Speedy was a consortium whose leading figures were an ice-cream entrepreneur from Stoke and a Belgian ferry company, and Fisher was negotiating for a consultancy to advise on the setting up of a new in-house magazine. Things were not looking good for Mister Speedy, which was being attacked by the feminist lobby for male chauvinism and by rail consumer groups under the Trade Descriptions Act. The latter maintained that an average speed of just over forty miles per hour could not properly be described as "Speedy". The company had become the butt of newspaper cartoonists and diarists, and the Belgians were starting to get restive.

In the circumstances the company had been only too happy to issue first-class tickets and complimentary drinks vouchers for Fisher's little party. An executive coach would meet them at the station and convey them to the Suragair VIP Lounge, where there would be more free drinks. Fisher was old-fashioned enough to believe that free drink, champagne for preference, would dull most hacks' sensibilities sufficiently to blind them to the imperfections of all other arrangements. He was usually right although, he had to concede morosely, not as infallibly right as he had used to be.

He and Effie were standing at the barrier to Platform Five well before the appointed time. They were apprehensive. Fisher remembered an Irish short story (could it have been a Somerville and Ross?) in which an old lady decided to give one last ball in her crumbling mansion, made elaborate preparations for the event but forgot to send out the invitations so that no one came and she was left alone amid the candelabra, the lobsters and the champagne. Fisher felt disturbingly like the little old lady in the story.

He told Effie about it. "Don't worry," she said briskly. "*Someone* will turn up. And provided it's a bum on a seat, anyone will do. I'm almost sure Miles Popplewell from *Suave* will be here. He sounded really keen."

"And he's the Travel Editor?"

"Travel and Leisure, I think. I've never met him but he's supposed to be very good, even if he's a bit of a fogey. Gay, of course, although he pretends not to be. And *Suave*'s really high-profile these days. You must have seen Miles on the *Witching Hour*. He often does the 'Endpiece'. Quite witty in a slightly *passé* mid-nineties sort of a way."

"Past my bedtime," said Fisher rattily. He was not enjoying the idea of Miles Popplewell. He looked at his watch and wondered if this was going to be a disaster.

"Excuse me," said a self-consciously breathy female voice, "are you the Fisher Cadogan Fisher party for Surago?"

Fisher looked up and saw a vision in mauve. At least it was what Fisher called mauve although he knew instinctively as he took in the mauve Ascot hat, the mauve artificially shoulder-padded jacket, the mauve mini, the mauve stockings and, God help him, the mauve slingback shoes, that in fashionspeak the name of the colour would be something altogether more high-flying – the sort of word one might find on a pretentious wine list to describe the latest Chilean Cabernet Sauvignon. Perhaps, he mused, the woman was wearing claret or burgundy, or indeed Chilean Cabernet Sauvignon. From Armani, possibly. Fashion was not within his ambit. "Yes," he said with an equivocal intonation which suggested that he reserved the right to change his mind.

"Lesley d'Harcourt," she said. "From *Suave* magazine." She extended a limp hand, which Fisher shook reluctantly. He was mesmerised by the impossibly long finger-nails which were as mauve as the rest of her.

"I understood Miles Popplewell was representing *Suave*," said Effie frostily. She and Ms d'Harcourt did not shake hands.

"Miles couldn't do it after all. Something cropped up. You know how it is. I shouldn't really be here either. I can't stand press trips usually. But I thought there might be a paragraph or two in it for my pages."

"Your pages?" Fisher raised an interrogatory eyebrow.

"The Style section," she said. "I'm the Style Editor. So I do all the Style pages."

"Oh," said Fisher and was about to make something of it when he felt a clap on the shoulder and turned to see a red-faced man in a shiny black suit with a grubby red tie.

"You must be Fisher," said the man in a north-country accent mellowed by nicotine, alcohol and – Fisher guessed – many years of living in exile south of the Trent. He seemed vaguely familiar and Fisher thought he recognised Eric Glenn, the Old Labour Member of Parliament for Thistlethwaite. Fisher had seen him often on various TV shows, though he looked different without make-up.

"Glenn," said Glenn. "President of the Anglo-Suragan Friend-ship Society. Old Simenon at the embassy gave me the details, so here I am. I tried getting hold of you but you're very elusive."

This was a lie. Fisher had e-mail, a mobile and a British Telecom answering service. Not to mention Effie. He regarded himself, with some reason, as the least elusive man in London.

"I'm awfully sorry," said Effie, "but Dr Simenon didn't tell us."

"Didn't he?" said Glenn. "Oh well, not to worry. It's Glenn. G–L–E–N–N. I'll probably knock off a little something for the *Staggers*. I'm well known in Surago if I say so myself. Old Foom and I are like that." He crossed a couple of fingers to indicate male bonding.

"Oh," said Lesley d'Harcourt, "of course. President Foom. I think I interviewed him once at Claridge's. He tried to get me into bed. He was rather a sweety, though. If you fancy dictators."

"He's not actually a dictator," said Glenn. "In fact, Suragan elections are based on an extraordinary sophisticated variant on the Hare Clark System of Proportional Representation. It's unique. No doubt young Fisher here will have explained it all in one of his press releases." And he chortled knowingly.

"I hate to disagree," said a languid latter-day Bloomsbury voice, "but it's not exactly one man one vote. Fisher, old fruit, lovely to see you. I don't think you know my friend Sharon from the *Noise*."

"Colin!" exclaimed Fisher, eyeing the crumbly corduroy figure of his former Literary Editor sparring partner Colin White-Lewis with a mixture of relief and annoyance. "You didn't say you were coming."

"I left a message on your machine," said Colin. He had gone a little pink.

Fisher turned to Effie. "Did we get a message to say Mr White-Lewis was coming?"

Effie made a pretence of consulting the notes attached to her clipboard (black leather with Fisher Cadogan Fisher embossed in gold).

"Oh yes", she said, "I've got you down as 'freelance'. I hope that's right. And, of course, Sharon from the *Noise*. Your Mr van Blanco told us you were coming."

This last was only very loosely true. There *had* been a phone call from a Mr van Blanco who purported to be from the *Noise*, but it had been virtually impossible to understand what he was saying. He kept going on about sex. Effie had put the phone down on him and then rung the *Noise* to see if they had someone called van Blanco on the staff. By way of response the switchboard had put her through to the same drunken idiot who rambled on as unintelligibly as before, mainly about sex, though now that she came to think about it the name Sharon *had* been mentioned.

Effie thought she was doing rather well.

So did Fisher. He was proud of her.

Between them they performed introductions. Rumpled, crumpled Eric Glenn shook hands with rumpled, crumpled Colin White-Lewis. Tarty Sharon shook hands with tarty Lesley. The men's crumply rumpleness was similar, though far from identical, and the same could be said of the women's tartiness. Sharon, for instance, oozed *Noise* just as Lesley dripped *Suave*. Sharon was, in a word – Lesley's word – common. Her style was unashamedly "come-hither-what-you-see-is-what-you-get". What you got was a ludicrously short black skirt and a tight crimson top. These accentuated tapering legs and a bum and boobs (her words) which would have been described in her newspaper as "pert". Indeed everything about her was "pert". For once, the definitions of *Noise* and *Intelligence* etymologists such as Stomper-Watson and Dr Clancy coincided: "Saucy or impudent in speech or conduct; (of clothes etc.) neat and suggestive of jauntiness." Sharon Taylor was all these things.

Colin, by contrast, was as far away from "pert" as it was possible to be. His shabbiness was a Bohemian carelessness, as opposed to Glenn's counter-jumping proletarian scruff. He was wearing bottle-green corduroy trousers and a brown tweed jacket with padded elbows of a sort once favoured by assistant masters in dim preparatory schools. His shirt was woolly and so was his tie. Presumably he had not realised that the climatic conditions in Surago were likely to resemble a Turkish bath. His wire-wool pepper-and-salt hair stood up in spikes like Struwwelpeter's and he gave off an odour of mustiness like a dog just in from the rain. All in all, he looked as if he had been assembled at speed in a shop for cast-off body parts as well as clothing and yet, Fisher reckoned, as much thought and care had gone into his lack of grooming as into Lesley d'Harcourt's ensemble. He was central casting's idea of the Warden of All Souls, and wardrobe and make-up had let themselves rip.

"Odd," murmured Fisher to Effie, once they had completed the introductions, "but four more than I expected. Not that I suppose we'll get a word out of any of them."

"You can take a horse to water but you can't make it drink," said Effie. "Like you said, it's bums on seats that count. But you're going to have fun keeping them in order. I almost wish I were coming with you."

"Hmm," said Fisher, "it's not too late." Then he took Colin to one side. "Who's the floosie?" he asked. "She doesn't seem quite your type."

Colin flushed. "She's rather nice, actually," he said, "and surprisingly bright. In an uneducated, animal sort of way."

"Is that what you call it?" asked Fisher, looking arch. "By the way, I don't think we've heard from your mother. Do you know if she's coming?"

"My mother!!" Colin did not exactly shout the words but they came out much louder than intended and with a vehemence which momentarily silenced the entire group. "You haven't asked my bloody mother?"

"And why shouldn't he ask your bloody mother?" Lady Beatrice arrived, as so often, dead on cue. She was at her most imperiously *grande dame* in an electric-blue suit and a matching velvet hat with a wide brim and a bandana, the sort of headgear a maverick lady gaucho might have worn on an Argentinian *estancia* at the turn of the century. Her face, under a pancake of powder, was a ghostly white; her eyes were mascaraed to panda proportions. Somehow she managed to convey the impression that this whole adventure was in a mysterious way below her, indeed was virtually an assault on her dignity. She clearly believed that her presence alone gave it a touch of class, which would otherwise be wholly lacking.

She obviously did not expect nor want an answer from her son, so instead shook hands with Fisher saying, as she did, "Mr Fisher, I presume. Beatrice White-Lewis. So good of you to ask me."

Fisher gave her a weak, wan smile and murmured something unintelligible but non-committal. Good PRspeak.

"Did you get an acceptance from the old bat?" he asked Effie *sotto voce*.

"Of course not," she hissed back at him. "She wouldn't deign to actually reply to an invitation. Still I'm surprised she's here. I thought she'd left the paper."

"In which case she's bored. Nothing better to do."

He glanced at his watch. They would have to board the train in ten minutes. He knew this was a bad moment. Every member of the party would be having second thoughts about the wisdom of joining the trip, especially now that they had seen their fellow travellers. Nevertheless, Fisher was exultant. Five people. Lady Beatrice herself. *Suave* magazine. The *Noise*. This would impress the officials in Surago.

"I'm so sorry, I do hope I haven't kept you waiting."

Fisher turned and recognised Christopher Jones. Jones had been a semi-legendary presence throughout his journalistic career. Part of Fisher resented Jones enormously, but part aspired to his condition.

"I'm so sorry I didn't let you know whether I could make it," said Jones. "One simply doesn't know until the very last moment if something is going to crop up. But I'm glad to say that in this instance nothing did." He nodded in the direction of Glenn. "Morning Eric." Then kissed Lady Beatrice on both cheeks with a rather presumptuous "Beatrice, how unexpected and how wonderful", which she nevertheless seemed to enjoy. It was not quite clear whether or not he knew Colin, so Fisher introduced them and

Jones said, "Yes, yes, of course, we know each other well." Colin did not look so sure. Jones had obviously not met Lesley or Sharon and gave no hint of whether he was pleased to see them or not.

"Too smooth by half," thought Fisher. He was now feeling so confused that he honestly could not remember whether he had invited Jones or not. Or whether Effie had asked him. Or if so whether she had told him. Jones was in one of those light-tan lightweight tropical-style suits which imply world-weary worldly wisdom as effectively as an antique cabin trunk festooned with sepia labels from long ago scrapped mailboats. Cream silk shirt, monogrammed cuff-links, paisley tie, a complexion of light teak and a hint of Bay Rum smoothing the sleek, slightly too long silver locks confirmed the impression created by the suit and added a whiff of caddishness confirmed by the hooded grey supercilious eyes and the sensuous mouth, which was just a tad too fleshy. You would not have been surprised to learn that he had once been a major in the SAS, nor to find him in a transvestite brothel in Caracas. How much of this was a tried and tested disguise was a difficult question. Jones's stock in trade was mystery. On the whole he succeeded well.

He was quintessentially difficult to place.

So there they stood, surrounded by baggage which reflected their personae as accurately as their faces, their clothing and their body language. They were a motley crew, but no more so than the hundreds of similar groups who set off for exotic destinations every year. In the months after their return an astute student of the national press might have remarked on the sudden eruption of puffs for the plainly unappealing Republic of Surago, but as these favourable mentions would be surrounded by armies of similarly uncritical articles about other countries who had the nous to arrange "press trips" such as this, the astute student might not have noticed.

Fisher beamed at his charges. "Time to board!" he called out, employing an arch, not to say archaic turn of phrase intended to disguise the prosaic style of their departure, and the press party obediently shuffled on to the platform and into the train. Thank God, thought Fisher, that he had persuaded Dr Simenon to stump up a couple of magnums of champagne. He did not recognise the name on the label, but it claimed to come from Epernay. He had only plastic beakers. And the bubbly might be lukewarm. But what the hell? They were off for a week in a sub-tropical paradise with not a care in the world. It beat work.

Or so they all supposed.

29

DOING THEIR
DUTY-FREE

The Prime Minister had intended travelling to Casa Plastiras, his benefactor's hide-out, in the magnate's private aeroplane. Unfortunately this had been diverted to Hong Kong and Macau to pick up some newly influential Chinese apparatchiks judged likely to facilitate the future development of various Plastiras enterprises involving narcotics, gambling and prostitution. All of these were considered crucial growth areas in the new Beijing-dominated world out there. The British had always been hopelessly naïve about such matters in Plastiras's estimation. They had never had the courage of their own corruption. Unlike Plastiras. "To believe," he liked to say, "one has only to believe." What one chose to believe in was immaterial, although Plastiras's own belief was in himself. "Self-belief" worked best for him. Others might bestow their beliefs further from home. That need not be a handicap, provided it burnt sufficiently strongly. Plastiras believed with a passion. Had he invested this belief in, say, Christ, Buddha or Karl Marx, it would, he considered, have been fatally diluted. It would probably have got him by, but not as efficiently.

The Plastiras people had apologised for the inconvenience and arranged for a section of the weekly Suragair flight to be set aside for the PM's own personal use. It would be entirely private, he was assured, no one else would know he was on the flight; he would board after the common herd and alight before them. General Foom, a good friend of Plastiras as well as of "the people" and of the United Kingdom, was sending one of the state Cadillacs.

As it turned out, his embarkation was not as private as he would have wished. It is a journalist's job to be nosy so that although the members of Fisher's little party had made serious inroads into the champagne – some more so than others, Eric Glenn being the worst offender – their antennae began to twitch the moment Captain Travers came on the tannoy to announce an unavoidable delay to flight SUR101 to Surago International.

"I'm glad we've got Travers," said Fisher to Lesley d'Harcourt who was sitting next to him in Club (though Suragair called it "Flying Fish Class" – the claim that Suragair was classless was apparently, without foundation), "Travers is their best man. He's been with Suragair since they were founded. He's flown everywhere. Tremendous experience. Most of his career was with Cathay Pacific, though I think he was one of the first Concorde Test pilots. Him and Trubshaw. Travers and Trubshaw. They were quite a double act I believe. He cut his teeth on Lancasters during World War Two."

"Wouldn't that make him rather old?" asked Lesley. She was a nervous passenger at the best of times.

"I suppose it would," admitted Fisher, "though the story is that he lied about his age when he enlisted."

"Even so ..." The buckle on Lesley's seat-belt had been extraordinarily difficult to fasten and there was a strong smell of cigar smoke in the cabin. Also, the public address system was faulty, unless Captain Travers's voice was always accompanied by crackling and a high-pitched whine. If he really had flown Lancasters in World War Two it was perfectly possible. She was not sure she could recommend readers of *Suave* to fly Suragair on the evidence so far.

"Ladies and Gentlemen," said the voice, "this is your Captain, Captain Travers speaking. I apologise on behalf of Suragair for this slight delay in our take-off. The Johnnies in the Control Tower tell me they hope to have us up, up and away before too terribly long, so I hope you'll bear with me for a while. I do heartily recommend our in-flight magazine, which you'll find in the pocket in front of your seat together with various bits of bumf about emergency exits and fire drill, which you might like to take a quick decko at without getting unduly agitated, only I am required to draw your attention to it under some sort of ruling from Brussels or what have you. Incidentally, football lovers among you may be interested to know that the latest score we have from Wembley is England Two, Moldava Nil. And on the subject of football, may I say how very pleased we are to have the British Lionesses rugby team on board this flight. On behalf of myself and the crew I'd like to wish you ladies a successful trip to Surago and may the best man, that is to say best 'person', win. We should, incidentally, be able to make up this slight delay over the Atlantic as we have some unexpectedly favourable following winds. The weather in Surago is normal for the time of year and I understand there was an inch or two of rain in the night although at the moment it's just mildly overcast, with north-easterly breezes rising to, well, let's just say rising . . . er . . . so I'll sign off for now and be back just as soon as we get news from the tower."

"Rain!" hissed Lesley d'Harcourt. "No one said anything about rain."

"Oh," said Fisher, "it's not rain in the accepted sense. Not rain as we know it."

"The only rain I know", she said, "is wet. Isn't Suragan rain wet?"

"Well yes," said Fisher nervously. "But it tends to fall at convenient times. Under cover of darkness, for instance." He gave a brittle little laugh. "And even when you get caught in it, Suragan rain tends to be quite a dry rain."

"Like wine, you mean?" It was not entirely clear whether or not Lesley was being serious. "Suragan rain is Chablis, whereas British is Sauternes?" she continued.

Fisher shifted uncomfortably in his already uncomfortable seat. "Suragan rain is like Irish rain," he said, remembering a phrase of Dr Simenon. "Warm and friendly – like the natives. Being caught in a Suragan rain storm is like having an agreeable shower in one's own bathroom. It's a pleasurable experience."

"Bullshit," said Lesley unexpectedly. "I thought you used to be a journalist. You seem to have taken to public relations with remarkable ease."

Fisher said nothing. From behind the bright-orange curtain which separated "Flying Fish" from "Grapefruit" class came the noise of song. It sounded like the British women's rugby team's male-voice choir and they were singing "Oh why are we waiting?" to the traditional tune of "Oh come all ye faithful."

"Extraordinarily unfeminine, rugby football," said Colin, sitting next, naturally, to Sharon.

"Sexist pig," said Sharon pertly. "Why shouldn't girls do it? If I was younger I'd have a go. You get coached by all those hunky rugger bugger blokes." It was funny, she thought to herself: in theory hunky rugger bugger blokes were what she fancied but in real life she found herself with Stan and now Colin. Two less hunky people were impossible to imagine.

"It's not blokes they're interested in," said Colin. "They're interested in each other. Just listen. That's lesbian singing."

Sharon was about to repeat that he was a sexist pig when the women's rugby team switched from "Oh why are we waiting?" to another song whose chorus carried all too clearly through the curtain:

'Cos we're all queers together
Excuse us while we go upstairs,
Yes, we're all queers together
Excuse us while we say our prayers.

"See what I mean?" said Colin. "All queers together!"

And then, before, she could reply, a remarkably fine and loud soprano came in with the solo verse:

My name is Cecil,
I live in Leicester Square,
I wear open-toed sandals
And rosebuds in my hair.

"Good Grief!" Colin exclaimed, "I haven't heard that in years. At least they know the words. I'll say that for them."

An enormous steward with a smile like a melon slice hurried through the cabin attempting, without much success, to frown. As he disappeared through the curtain a second chorus came belting out, appreciably louder than the first.

"So you used to sing it yourself?" Sharon asked, pertness triumphant.

"A very very long time ago."

"But you're not gay?"

"I might have been," he said. "I don't think I knew much about girls. One didn't in those days."

"That doesn't make you gay – just ignorant. Anyway, I bet you half those rugby women are raving heteros. Ooh, that's a thought!

I bet Eddie White and van Blanco would like something on sex and women's rugby."

"You reckon?" Colin had only the foggiest fix on the thinking, if that was the word, behind the *Noise*.

"Do you think they'd talk about it?" she asked.

"Why bother?" he wanted to know. "I thought you always made everything up."

"Not *everything*," she said. "You've got to have a bit of truth at the bottom of the story. Then you sauce it up."

"Oh," he said, not understanding, "I thought real life was supposed to be stranger than fiction."

"It might be," she said, "if you could ever find out what was really real. If you see what I mean."

He didn't understand, but it didn't matter.

Behind them the singing had ceased. The enormous steward emerged triumphantly.

"How do you reckon he managed that?" asked Colin.

"Probably offered them free membership of the mile-high club," she replied. "He's gorgeous. Bet he's hung like a gorilla."

Of course in real life Sharon attached little or no importance to the size of male genitalia. It was what men did with what they were given which mattered. Or so she always said. Stan had not been over-endowed. Far from it. But he was a prodigious worker. In her fantasies, however, Sharon had to admit that sometimes she did let the idea of size run away with her. Readers liked it from time to time as well. And men, of course, were obsessed by it.

"I read somewhere", said Colin, "that the sexual organs of the gorilla were among the smallest of all known primates."

"I didn't know bishops had big balls."

"That's not what I said. I just said gorillas had small ones."

"That's not what the *Noise* says." She grinned. "Do you think Fisher realises I'm doing a series on 'Sex in Surago'?"

"He's mad if he doesn't," he said. "Are you going to make that up?"

She grinned again. "Most of it," she said. "But I think there'll have to be a *little* research." And without warning she made a quick lunge at his trousers, giving his own testicles a more than playful squeeze, which caused him to let out a high-pitched yelp and made his mother, across the aisle and a row in front, turn round and fix him with one of her most imperious and disapproving stares.

Lady Beatrice and Christopher Jones were having an altogether more chaste and up-market discussion.

"I'm delighted you're on the trip," said Jones unctuously. "When I heard you'd retired I was afraid it was true."

"Ah," said the old girl, almost coquettishly, "you should have known better than that."

She was fond of Jones. He flattered her and told her jokes and gossip – not something that many people did.

He might have been fond of *her* as well, if he had not effectively eliminated fondness from his repertoire. It could interfere with professionalism and objectivity. Lady B was, he thought, more than ever like a bothery parrot, impossibly wrinkled under the pancake and with a "stuff-you" attitude to everything and everybody, which expressed itself in deflating squawks and cackles. "I'm not entirely clear what *has* happened," he said.

"Nor's anyone else," said Lady B, "but it would be a dull old world if we were clear what was going on. Fog's rather fun, don't you think? One thing you can be sure of, though, is that I'm not stepping down to spend more time with my family." She cackled. "Do you suppose we could get a gin? One can have too many bubbles and they do play havoc with the digestion."

"I'm sure that even on Suragair they carry gin," said Jones. He pressed the steward summons without optimism. "Have you noticed", he said, "how the size of the stereo equipment carried by the male airline passenger under, say, forty years old, varies in inverse proportion to the prosperity of the host country?"

The anecdotal evidence of the day certainly supported him. Surago was one of the world's poorest nations and yet its citizens on this flight nearly all had with them tape decks, loudspeakers and amplifying kit which would have carried the tones of the three tenors over the whole of the Home Counties. They tended to wear baseball caps, frequently back to front, fluorescent shirts, track-suit bottoms and flip-flops. The women, who were not, generally, encumbered with hi-fi's, did not wear hats but secured their lustrous black, mainly straightened hair, with bandeaux which matched their bright low-cut blouses. Their gazelle legs were accentuated by white or silver sling-back stilettos and tight imitation designer jeans, which also drew attention to their extraordinarily high-slung bottoms, which made even Sharon Taylor's tight, muscular buttocks look droopy-drawed. You could balance a champagne glass on the top shelf of a Suragan female bottom. Some did, though most Suragan males did it with glasses of rum punch or cans of Pink Star, the national beer, brewed under licence from North Korea.

The steward-summoning system was obviously kaput.

"Why do you imagine we're waiting?" asked Lady B.

"I don't suppose the electrics work," said Jones. "They certainly don't give the impression of servicing the no-smoking signs. I'll find someone in a second. There's probably an unattended bottle of Gordon's in the galley."

"I didn't mean the gin, Christopher," she said. "I was referring to our take-off. All that piffle from Flying-Officer Kite about the control tower. Either the electrics really *have* failed and the wings won't flap, or we're waiting for someone." She fluttered eyelashes as caterpillared as Dame Barbara Cartland's. "But, darling, if you *did* fancy speaking to the steward I'd like my drink straight up with a twist and just a smidgen of martini." Saying which, she suddenly leant forward, peered out of the window and made a satisfied parrot noise. "Just as I thought," she said. "I think this might turn into a more amusing excursion than I had dared imagine." She patted Christopher Jones's tropical-trousered thigh. "Do look! And then run and get us both a properly dry martini. There's a dear boy!"

Jones too craned his neck and saw a heavily built black automobile pulled up alongside a set of landing steps. A handful of flunkeys and minions stood around in attitudes of semi-ceremonial respect. Hands were shaken, sadly, almost as if being wrung and the Prime Minister, the Rt. Hon. Bryan Sutton, diminished, hunched and grey, though unmistakable, walked slowly upstairs, with the winsome figure of his Parliamentary Private Secretary, Kim Sanderson-Wright, discreetly holding on to his elbow to cushion a fall and assist in upward mobility.

"Ah," said Jones, raising an eyebrow, "I should have thought of that. That Greek spiv friend of Sutton's has a five-star fortress in Surago. Our little love-birds will be holing up with him, don't you think?"

"Absolutely," said Lady Beatrice. "And what are you going to do about it?"

"Respect their privacy," said Jones, laughing. "I'm not some tabloid hack. In any case he's not going to say or do anything he hasn't said or done already. I shall sit back and enjoy the flight." Still, privately he was pleased to see that the PM was on board and to know that apart from Lady Beatrice none of the other members of the press party were in on the picture. It was a position he always enjoyed.

"Quite right, dear boy. And don't forget the dry martini. Very dry. Just a whisper of Vermouth."

Lady Beatrice's pulse was racing to a pocketa-pocketa Walter Mitty beat. Jones was the only other member of the press party sitting on the side of the plane which afforded a view of the Premier and "Catamite Kim", as she referred to him in her mind's notebook. That meant there were only two journalists on the flight who realised they were within a few feet of a scoop. In her youth Lady Beatrice had been a considerable correspondent. There had long been a prejudice against women in front-line journalism, but for a while she had belonged, along with such famous women as Clare Hollingworth, Evelyn Irons, Audrey Whiting and Ann Sharpley, to that small group of reporteuses categorised by stuffy chauvinist organisations such as the State Department, the Quai d'Orsay and (worst of all) the British Ministry of Defence and the Foreign and Commonwealth Office as "not women in the accepted sense". In a relentlessly masculine world she and they had defied conventional categorisation and become honorary men.

"Rat-like cunning," she murmured to herself ... "plausible manner". What would she have done if they were in a Dakota, she a mere chit of a girl and the Prime Minister in question Major Attlee. She would have got the story, that was for sure. She would have phoned it over from the luggage hall while the rest of the press were waiting for their bags. And she would have smirked horribly when the cables started raining in on her colleagues in the middle of the night: "INTELLIGENCE LEAD ATTLEE LOVEFLIGHT STOP WHYNOSTORY QUERY FILE SOONEST STOP PROPRIETOR UNAMUSED"

"Exclusive: PM flees. Drama of Late-Night Escape. 'Let he who is without sin cast stone,' says Attlee." And so on. There would have been a large photograph of her. The alluring one of her looking butch and windblown. It had appeared over her deathless prose for decades. Underneath there would be no reference to her family involvement with the paper. It would simply say "B.F. White-Lewis of the *Intelligence*", or "The *Intelligence*'s B.F. White-Lewis". A few years earlier it would have been simply, "By a Special Correspondent". Then management had decided that it was time for reporters to come out from behind the cloak of anonymity. It had seemed bold and prudent at the time, but in retrospect Lady Beatrice thought that perhaps it had been the first step on the slippery path towards "personality journalism".

She smiled. Just because she was an old bat left over from a previous reign was no reason why she shouldn't show a modern generation how it was done. Even smugly suave Jones at her side. He who had been everywhere, done everything, seen everyone but was so often so smooth and sophisticated he didn't deign to share his knowledge with the readers. Oh yes, there was life in the old girl yet. "On second thoughts", she said, "don't worry. I'll get the drinks. I need a pee anyway."

Jones glanced at her, looking mildly scandalised.

"Sorry," she said, almost flirtatiously, "I mean I need to powder my nose."

"My housemaster used to ask if anyone wanted to turn their bicycle round when enquiring about calls of nature," said Jones.

Lady Beatrice stared at him uncomprehendingly. "Do you want Vermouth in your gin?" she asked.

"Not a lot," he answered.

"Very well," she said, undoing her belt and levering herself out of the seat. She was not entirely clear what she was going to do but she had invariably found "natural authority" a workable substitute for "plausible manner". No matter where or with whom she was, Lady Beatrice always managed to convey the impression that she was in charge. Walk briskly and purposefully; avoid eye contact wherever possible; and carry your handbag as if it were a truncheon which you would not hesitate to use. Thus, on this occasion, she stood to attention, inhaled deeply, counted to five and then set off in the direction of the women's rugby team like an All Black flanker entering a ruck. It was a curious characteristic of Suragair that Club Class was at the back of the aeroplane. First Class, which in this instance meant Bryan Sutton and Kim Sanderson-Wright, was up in the nose cone. This had nothing to do with comfort but everything to do with safety. In the all too likely event of a crash, Suragan air safety statistics suggested that the people in the middle of the craft were at the greatest risk. Therefore the airline put the higher payers at either end. So Lady Beatrice had to get through steerage, which included nearly all the native Suragans as well as the British Lionesses.

It was an impressive attempt. She shot through the curtains to find the aisle full of female rugby players in song. She did not flinch. A couple of neat sidesteps, a skilful dummy, two threatened hand-offs with her bag, an adroit change of direction which took her across a row of empty seats into the parallel aisle and she was there at the curtain which – she assumed – separated her quarry from the vulgar herd. A deft pluck at the cloth, a swift shimmy, a pull back on the curtain now behind her and she was in the Prime Minister's escape capsule.

And her instincts had not failed her. The Queen's first minister was unattended save by his Private Secretary. There was no sign of any Suragair crew. The old lady of Fleet Street had the fugitives all to herself.

The only problem was that Bryan Sutton seemed to be out for the count. His seat was reclining as far as it possibly could, which meant that it had virtually turned into a bed, and he was snoring lightly with a Suragair face mask over his eyes. Beside him the ferrety Kim Sanderson-Wright was idly turning the pages of what looked to Lady Beatrice like some sort of post-modernist *Boy's Own Paper*: a *Boy's Own* glossy magazine, complete with centre-folds, pubic hair and flaccid organs. He seemed oblivious to the scribe's entry, assuming, she presumed, that it was a flight attendant with a scented flannel with which to mop his fevered brow.

"Mr Wright," she said, in the "Doctor Livingstone, I presume" tone of voice which had induced fear and trembling in unwilling interviewees since the days of Lord Haw-Haw and some of the most spectacular murderers ever to go down at the Old Bailey. "Mr Wright," she repeated, "I'm afraid I'm from the *Daily Intelligence*. And I'd like a word."

She had forgotten that she was not, any longer, from the *Daily Intelligence*, but old habits died hard. Besides, she had been having a number of second thoughts in that direction.

Sanderson-Wright dropped his magazine with a startled gasp, which Lady Beatrice found reassuring as well as gratifying. "Good Lord," he said. "It's Lady Beatrice White-Miller, isn't it? I thought you were dead. What brings you here?" He seemed uncertain about whether or not to stand.

"Never mind that," she said. "There are a number of things that would interest my readers. I need to speak to the country's leader. The people have a right to know what's really going on."

"Oh bugger the people!" said Sanderson-Wright. "It's people like you, drivelling on about the bloody people, that have got us into this mess. Nobody gives a nun's fart for the bloody people and you know it as well as I do."

"May I quote you on that?" enquired Lady Beatrice with dowagerly menace.

"Of course you can't quote me. And you can't quote Bryan either. He's out for the count. The chief steward's given him a shot of something spectacularly sleep inducing. He's going to be comatose until we arrive in Surago. And now if I'm not mistaken we're on the verge of taking off. I think you'd better return to your seat before the captain insists." He smiled as if he thought he held the upper hand. "I think I should remind you", he said, "that our friend Mr Plastiras effectively owns this airline. He also effectively owns the country to which we are about to fly. As you probably know, Mr Plastiras doesn't care much for journalists. Nor does the Prime Minister. And nor do I. So for the foreseeable future we can forget all that cant about the rights of you and your so-called readers and I can say eff off and no bloody comment. No bloody comment whatsoever."

"You're going to regret this," said Lady Beatrice, feeling uncharacteristically stymied, but adding with venom, "little man!"

Sanderson-Wright grinned and looked as if he was on the point of saying something impertinent when from afar there came a voice which, on an aeroplane, was as good as the voice of God himself.

"This is your captain speaking", said the fruity voice from the pulpit of the flight deck. "I'm happy to say that the control tower Johnnies have given us clearance and I shall be starting the engines in a moment or two prior to take-off. Your cabin crew, under the direction of the Chief Steward, Dr Lafayette McTavish, will be giving a demonstration of life-jacket drill, emergency procedures and that kind of thing and, well, that's it. As I said before, everything's absolutely tickety-boo. Thank you for flying Suragair and I'll be on the blower again just as soon as we're over the coast and well and truly heading for paradise."

Christopher Jones smoothed his way into the galley while this announcement was being made and came upon the enormous steward who appeared to be engaged in a gentle frolic with a female member of his crew. "Dr McTavish?" he enquired in the style of an Imperial explorer and, on receiving the expected "Yes Man!" response, announced that he and Lady Beatrice would like two proper gin martini cocktails, to which the Chief Steward replied that if he and her ladyship would care to buckle their seat-belts, Fabiola would be right along with the drinks and would they like the peanuts or the taco chips?

Jones duly returned to his seat, closely followed by the drinks, which though on the warm side, consisted of tumblers of virtually neat gin with slivers of lemon. As he raised his glass, the elderly *Princess of Surago* taxied down the tarmac of London Greenspace preparatory to take-off.

From behind the curtain the soprano was back on song:

Now this is number one
And aren't we having fun?

Then there was a pause. Captain Travers revved his engine and the plane began to wallow along the runway. The crew sat down hastily; the doors of several luggage compartments flew open; Fisher's press party closed their eyes and pressed their fingers into the arms of their seats and/or the hands of their companions all except for the Member for the Crag Division of Scarpington who was asleep.

As the ancient Jumbo staggered into the air its wheels retracted with a juddering thud and the ladies' rugby team broke into a rambunctious chorus:

Roll me over,
In the clover,
Roll me over, lay me down and do it again.

They had lift-off.

30

PASS THE SICK BAG

For those on the press trip to Surago the centre of the universe moved, more or less, with them. This was partly because they were naturally self-centred people but also because journalists are prone to the delusion that the news or opinions which they have to impart are, *ipso facto*, more significant than those offered by anyone else. Self-importance, despite what the training manuals said, was the single most essential qualification for journalism. "Rat-like cunning, a plausible manner and a little literary ability" (Tomalin's laws of journalism) came later.

The members of the British Lionesses' rugby squad also suffered from "centre-of-universeism", though to a lesser degree. Lady rugby players were not generally as self-important as hacks. Despite their athleticism and addiction to physical contact they were often defensive and deferential, at least off the field. They suffered constantly from the male prejudices of men such as Colin White-Lewis and particularly from the patronising quips of male sportswriters, who based entire match reports on feeble jokes about handbags. When, however, they were together as a unit they did develop a certain mutual self-absorption and defiance. It was not so much that they thought of themselves as being at the centre of the universe, more that they blocked out the rest of the universe, thus creating their own. Like Lady Beatrice, they really didn't *care* what anyone else thought of them nor even *whether* anyone thought of them at all. For them, nothing outside their team had much reality. And for very few of them was there much of a world outside that of women's rugby. "Oggy, oggy, oggy!" as they chanted in their communal bath and, indeed, in their Suragair "Grapefruit class" seats, "Oggy, oggy, oggy! Who's afraid of Virginia Woolf, Virginia Woolf, Virginia Woolf? Oi, Oi, Oi!"

The Prime Minister, even of a nation as diminished as the United Kingdom, might be forgiven for thinking himself at or near the centre of the universe, but for all his faults, Bryan Sutton never suffered from serious conceit. Rather the reverse. A sickly, ill-favoured individual even from childhood, he had always, with reason, considered himself out on a limb – a rotten limb at that, a far from golden bough, liable to collapse at any moment and send him plunging still further from where it, whatever "it" was, was at. Whereas most politicians were driven by an overwhelming sense of those qualities so spectacularly possessed by his benefactor, Mr Plastiras, Sutton's ambition was fuelled, in a bizarre way, by his inferiority complex. Shyness made him bold, mediocrity spurred his competitiveness. Born to be second-rate, he was lucky to find himself in a world dominated by those of like calibre. Until this uncharacteristically flamboyant episode he had been the ultimate grey man. However, he had just enough intelligence to be surprised by his traceless rise to the premiership and, curiously, as the *Princess of Surago* jolted through the clouds he felt more peripheral than the hacks, the lady rugby players or the Suragan citizens with their outsize stereos and bum-hugger denims. He knew that he was surplus to requirement, that there was virtually no virtue in him, that once removed from office he would be as forgotten as he was previously unknown. He had got where he was because no one, not even he himself, had thought of himself as a threat to anyone. The whole thing was a hideous mistake and he was the first to admit it.

He was right. In Ten Downing Street he was, well, he was in Ten Downing Street, with all that this implied. Once gone he was gone. Without the king's clothes he was no longer king. Such self-knowledge was probably his sole redeeming feature though power, sex, alcohol and middle age had all conspired recently to impair it. As Prime Minister he had come as near as ever to being high spirited. Now he was at his lowest ebb in years.

Nevertheless it was he who, however briefly, left the gap. Of course the press group and the ladies' rugby team left behind friends and relations who "missed" them. There were those who noticed their absence with regret and felt the want of them. Some of these "missing" sensations were deeply felt but they were the private emotions of private people and not significant in the "real" world portrayed by newspapers and television. These private and public worlds collided from time to time so that, for instance, Major Ronald and Major Gordon privately "missed" their mother and their brother because they were kith and kin, but also in a more professional sense because they were, in a minor way, people with a public persona. Even Colin would qualify for a paragraph or two of obituary, at least in the *Intelligence*. Lady Beatrice might get as much as half a page on a quiet day. Neither Major missed members of his family very much, for it was not in their nature and they were busy men. They tended to take those around them for granted.

"Missing" the Prime Minister was a different matter altogether. There were people – his apparently deserted wife and children, his elderly mother in Minehead – who missed him as a human being but, as the Majors, Eddie White, Albert van Blanco and even little Pool knew only too well, this was just the sentimental gilt on the pragmatic gingerbread. "Missing Prime Minister" was a major news story. Or could be for a short while. The attention span of the average newspaper "reader" was an ever decreasing item. Even so, you could run with "Missing Prime Minister" for a day or two, particularly if you could eke it out with an exclusive interview with Minehead Mum. A rigged opinion poll might give it an extra fillip, although polls were over-expensive and no longer sexy. Almost as far past their sell-by date as Bryan Sutton.

"I think", said Ronald to Gordon, on the day of the *Princess of Surago*'s departure, "that the Prime Minister story is losing its legs."

Gordon shrugged. "He's a dull little fellow. Or was, until this latest hooshmi-bangmi. You think he's past history?"

"Don't *you*?"

"Well." Gordon picked absent-mindedly at a piece of lunch stuck between his front teeth. "It's up to us, don't you think? If we say he's past history, then past history he is. That's the power of the press. And so on and so forth. If we decide he's still the burning issue of the day then he'll be a burning issue. Personally I think he's a bit dull for a burning issue. I don't think he's going to do wonders for the circulation. Not now that we've got the sex thing out of the way."

"There's nothing more to come on that front I suppose?" asked Ronald fretfully.

"No. And it's all pretty sordid, to be brutally frank." (Gordon had never been brutally frank in his life and was not about to begin now.) "I think we should give the temporary regime a couple of weeks and see how they get on. Then, depending on their performance, we can either demand for it to be made permanent, or insist on the real PM's reinstatement, or tell them to go to the country and hold a general election."

"Demand", "insist" and "tell" were all words which macho editors employed in the modern world. There was no longer any of that old-fashioned mealy-mouthed stuff about "respectfully suggesting" or "would it not be in the best interests of those concerned if . . .".

Chinese Ken's people were even more robust.

"The Question is . . .", said Ken to Eddie White and William Pool. "The Question is, do we move heaven and earth to find out where the little poofter's got to and then get the pickies to prove it, preferably with him sucking a couple of male toes and cavorting by the side of the pool in some exotic foreign paradise? Or do we leave him alone and find someone else to play with?"

"He's yesterday's news," said White, "*and* he's a politician. We don't want too much politics in the *Noise*. Readers don't like it."

"*My* readers want politics on the front page," said Pool. "Though the way the *Noise* dealt with it, this hasn't been a political story anyway. It's just another sex scandal."

"Excuse me, sunshine," said Eddie. "If we weren't able to serve up 'just another sex scandal', as you so snottily call it, our circulation would be through the effing floor and our share values with it. 'Just another sex scandal' sells bloody newspapers and sex scandals don't grow on trees. You've got to rake your muck and monger your scandal. You need real expert creative journalists."

"I don't give a monkey's whether it's a sex story or a political story," said Ken. "I only care about whether or not it's going to make any money. My hunch is he's gone skiving off somewhere which would cost us a fortune to get to. And it'll be some millionaire's hide-out which'll make Chequers security look like something out of Enid Blyton. It'll probably be in a country where they have an old-fashioned secret police force like the Securitate or the Tontons Macoutes. I don't want any more dead hacks on my hands. I don't want to pay out stacks of expenses so that a bunch of paparazzi can eat lobster and guzzle rum punches, so thanks but no thanks."

"Talking of dead hacks," said Eddie White, "little Sharon's off on some junket in a foreign paradise. Belgian Honduras. Only it's got some crappy new name no one can remember. All initials. Or was it Belgian Barbados? Maybe she'll end up in the same foreign paradise as our great Prime Minister."

"Who's paying for that?" asked Ken sharply. He could, of course, have paid several times over for Sharon to swan off to Surago but he was damned if he would, even if he had been responsible for the death of her man, Stan. He wasn't running a charity, as he kept reminding those who worked for him. The old days of Spanish customs and fictitious expense claims would not be coming back. There was a widespread belief that it was the print unions who had crippled Fleet Street in those dire days before Margaret Thatcher and Rupert Murdoch restored a proper "boss culture", where money talked and the workers bloody well did as they were told. But as far as Ken and most of the other bosses were concerned it wasn't just the printers who were in the conspiracy but the journalists as well. It was a well-known fact, in the boardroom, that your average hack was a skiving drunken leftie with the morals of a diseased killer rabbit. Ken couldn't have become Ken in the days of SOGAT, NATSOPA and yes, the National Union of Journalists, of beer, sandwiches and skittles at Ten Downing Street and Jack's as good as his master. Well, Jack wasn't as good as his master and nor was Jill, so he was buggered if he was going to have little Sharon taking him for a ride even if she was still in mourning. Which frankly he doubted as she was a tough little tart, otherwise he wouldn't be paying her.

These thoughts passed through the Proprietor's mind in no more time than it would have taken to shout "Hold the front page!" or "You're fired!".

"Don't worry. It's a freebie," said Eddie White. "The PR company's taking care of everything down to the airport tax and the hotel minibar. And she's doing a series on sex in the sun and sand among the amazingly inventive and promiscuous natives of the ganja-crazed Central Americas. Virgin priestesses pleasuring the local vicar; child prostitutes in illicit trading with package sex tourists from Japan; circumcision rituals; penis gourds; you name it, Sharon will have it and be sharing it with readers of the *Noise*."

Little Pool was looking white around the gills. This was not what he had joined up for. And whatever the other two thought or said he would jolly well lead the paper tomorrow on the International Monetary Fund meeting in Helsinki or on Global Warming. That would show them.

Meanwhile far out across the Atlantic, the *Princess of Surago* provided a ramshackle cocoon for the principal object of these deliberations. Both Bryan Sutton and Kim Sanderson-Wright slumbered fitfully in their VIP area, as did every member of the press party except for Christopher Jones. Jones was reading the galley proofs of an autobiography by a dim former diplomat called Haddock which he was reviewing for the journal of the Institute of International Affairs. It was a miserably self-serving little memoir, but Jones felt obliged not to say so since he and Haddock were members of the same club. He would have to think of something anodyne instead.

From behind the curtain some of the women's rugby party were singing "Eskimo Nell". The Chief Steward loped past and favoured Jones with a smile. Jones smiled back and returned to his Haddock.

"Good morning Ladies and Gentlemen, Girls and Boys, British Lionesses!"

Christopher Jones, half asleep over the Haddock memoirs, could have sworn that Captain Travers actually said "Good Morrow" but was awake enough to realise that even he wouldn't have done such a thing, not, at least, on Suragair. It must have been a combination of his own drowsiness and the fruity bonhomie of Captain Travers. He sounded more like the landlord of a newly "themed" pub in the Thames Valley than a pilot. Though come to think of it, reflected Jones, that's what pilots did sound like. Perhaps they all retired to become mine host, sporting handlebar moustaches and canary-yellow cardigans. The cabin crew were snapping back the window blinds and dispensing warm orange juice, cool croissants and wide grins. The atmosphere inside the aircraft was foetid with sleep. Outside, dawn lit up the clouds like Shiaparelli's shocking pink lipstick daubing fairground candy floss. The effect was so garish that Jones thought it seemed artificial, almost as if it was a special welcome effect laid on by the Tourist Board.

Captain Travers continued to crackle over the tannoy. "We'll shortly be commencing our descent into Surago International," he said. "Unfortunately we will be a few minutes behind schedule because, er, for technical reasons, we weren't able to make up the time lost on the ground at London Greenspace. However, we will be on the deck at around ten thirty in the morning local time and I'm happy to tell you that the weather in Surago seems to have perked up quite a bit. The rain has ceased and in parts of the island we have sun. I hope you've enjoyed a comfortable flight with Suragair. In a few minutes I'll be asking you to extinguish your cigarettes and fasten your seat-belts as we begin our descent. I anticipate normal landing but in the event of any problem with the landing gear the crew will be demonstrating the safety position which you will be asked to assume. Should it be necessary to evacuate the aeroplane at speed there will be special shutes for you to slide down at all the exits. Actually, they're jolly reliable and rather fun. My grandchildren said it was just like playing on the Bouncy Castle when they tried it but, aha, that's by the by. Oh, and for those who are interested the final score at Wembley was England Two, Moldova Two, so the English boys held on for the draw."

As it happened this second-half collapse had caused the *Noise*'s chief football correspondent considerable grief, expressed in a furious tirade against the England manager and all who played under him. This appeared under the not entirely successful headline "Moled-ova!". The language was appreciably more doom-laden than that which had been used to report the scandals surrounding the Prime Minister. Phrases such as "night of shame", "day of disgrace" and even "national humiliation". (This last caught the mood of the article but was edited out of the final editions on the grounds that it was over-long for the average *Noise* reader – "five effing syllables for Chrissake," complained the Night Sports Editor.)

"What does he mean, 'anticipate normal landing?'" asked Lesley d'Harcourt sharply. "I'm not dressed for an *ab*normal landing. You're not catching me sliding down a shute in *this* skirt."

"Oh," said Fisher, "I don't think he means to be alarmist. He said he 'anticipates normal landing' so I think we should do the same. On the other hand he's bound, under international regulations, to warn us how to behave in the event that the anticipated normal landing does not take place."

"You certainly *have* taken to PR," she said, "and when do you imagine his grandchildren were bouncing down the escape shutes?"

"I should think", said Fisher, disconcerted by the *Suave* woman's sharpness over breakfast and hoping that it would not be sustained, "it was either some sort of routine practice drill or the staff day out. They have an annual garden party at the airport for the Suragair staff and their families. Rather a charming practice."

"My readers anticipate normal landings," she said, "and so do I. I'm not going to be able to recommend an airline which doesn't land normally. And why don't the seat-belt and cigarette signs work?"

"Technical fault," said Fisher. "Just one of those things. Could happen to anyone. It'll be rectified as soon as we get into Surago International."

As he said this the aeroplane suddenly plummeted, causing several orange juices to capsize. At the same time the engines roared as if the clutch had slipped. The manoeuvre only lasted a few seconds but the sense of collective fear was tangible. No one had liked Captain Travers's remark about the normal landing.

Once more, his voice crackled out from the flight-deck. "We've begun our descent, everybody," he said, "so I must ask you to do the necessary with your seat-belts and cigarettes. We may experience a spot of turbulence as we come down through the cloud belt, but there is absolutely no cause for concern. No cause for concern whatsoever."

"I can't say", said Lady Beatrice, dabbing at spilt orange with a paper napkin, "that this pilot inspires confidence. Nor his aeroplane. And the breakfast is perfectly putrid. The sort of thing one used to get in Romania under Ceauşescu."

"Funny you should say that," said Jones. "My information is that Suragair bought the plane off Tarom a couple of years ago. It's one of the oldest Jumbos still in the air. As is Captain Travers. But neither of them has a particularly evil track record. They're by no means as bad as some third world airlines."

"Hmm." She glanced at his reading. "How's the Haddock?"

"Pretty much what you'd expect."

She said "Hmm" again and they both smiled, knowing exactly what the murmur conveyed. It was a very old British method of communication, but effective if you knew the code.

Now the cabin crew emerged and, standing at the ends of the various compartments, did a mime show while Lafayette McTavish conducted an almost entirely unintelligible commentary through a hand-held mike which connected, up to a point, with the sound system.

"It was the life-jacket demo I liked best when I was a hostess," said Sharon. "You could make it ever so sexy. Almost like a strip. We used to have a competition to see who could get the most applause."

"Five hundred words on the Chief Steward," said Colin, who had not known that Sharon once worked for an airline. "For a start, whatever sort of doctor do you imagine he is?"

"Probably a brain surgeon," Sharon replied.

"No, brain surgeons are all misters," said Colin. "My guess is that he's a Doctor of Law. Belgian Law, I assume. How about LL D, Lumumbaville?"

"That sounds racist to me."

"It's not meant to," said Colin. "I should imagine Chief Steward on the Surago/UK flight is a higher-caste job than practising law. From what little I've heard there isn't any law practised in Surago. Not in the sense that we understand it. Law in Surago is what General Foom says it is."

"OK," said Sharon. "So he's a lawyer who's better off working as an airline steward. What about those ludicrous names?"

"He's named Lafayette after a half-Belgian ancestor who was a hero of the great slaves' uprising."

"What slaves' uprising?"

"I'm not sure, but they're bound to have had one. It was standard practice in this part of the world. Or he may not have been an ancestor. He may just have been a national hero whom people get named after. McTavish was either an explorer who took a wrong turning, or a missionary who had an illicit liaison with a local girl, or a mercenary general who commanded a division in the war of independence against the Belgians, or the name is a corruption of something native originating in Africa. Not 'Mc' but 'M', or 'Em apostrophe'. 'Tavish' would have been something full of glottal stops and grunts, the sort of thing Sir Laurens van der Post specialised in."

Sharon giggled. "Which do you think are the right answers?"

Colin chewed thoughtfully on a piece of limp and faintly rancid croissant. "It'll be in the press kit."

"Surely the Chief Steward won't get into the press kit?"

"In Surago it's perfectly possible. I have a feeling everything in Surago is perfectly possible."

"I thought Fisher would have given us press kits at the airport."

"Didn't you hear?" said Colin. "Technical fault. Or technical hitch. There are going to be a great many before this trip is out, just you wait and see. Have you noticed how 'spokesmen' always explain mistakes by saying they're 'technical'. It's PRspeak for saying 'It's not *our* fault'. It's another way of saying 'Act of God'. It's an all-purpose, blanket way of saying 'leaves on the line'."

"Leaves on the line, sweetie?" Sharon was examining her face in a hand-mirror. In a moment she would be applying lipstick and mascara. On a smarter flight she would have risked the loo, but Captain Travers seemed to be having trouble controlling his charge and she did not want to break a leg. Besides, the smell up there was something dreadful. The flush mechanism had given up somewhere in the Bermuda triangle.

"You know. The classic British Rail excuse. Every time a train was cancelled or late they said there were leaves on the line. That was a sort of 'technical' failure. It's what you say when you know perfectly well that you've screwed up and everyone else knows you've screwed up but you're damned if you're going to admit it. The sort of behaviour you expect from an agriculture minister confronted by a mad cow. And then there was 'the wrong kind of snow'."

"I remember the wrong kind of snow," said Sharon. "Bit like having a headache or 'I'm not in the mood'."

"Not in the mood?" Colin didn't quite follow.

"Not in the mood for a bonk, stupid. You, know, 'fancy a quickie, darling?' or 'Your place or mine, baby?' and if the bloke can't get it up he says, 'Not in the mood, thanks awfully' or 'I've got a headache'. Men never say 'I can't get it up'. Silly, really."

"Don't you ever think of anything else?"

"Anything else what?" she wanted to know, pouting on to a stick of peachy pink cosmetic.

"Except sex?"

"Not a lot," she said. "It's what I get paid for. And it's fun. And I'm good at it. And my Editor thinks it's great for circulation. So what else is there to think about? Will you have it off with some of the rugby team? For my sake?"

"Oh really, Sharon." He was quite shocked, although uncertain whether she was serious. The plane gave another yet more stomach-churning lurch and on the other side of the aisle Eric Glenn, achingly hung-over, was noisily sick mainly, though not exclusively, into the sturdy brown paper bag which Suragair had provided for such a contingency. The sick bags were almost the only thing on the plane which would have scored more than half marks. Glenn mopped himself down, not expecting, nor getting any help from the cabin crew. It was just as well the seat alongside him was unoccupied. He placed his bag as far away as possible and looked away, thus trying to disown responsibility, much in the same way that Captain Travers and his ilk might hide behind the smoke-screen of the technical fault.

"Had a bit of an accident, Eric?"

"Er, no, Madam Speaker, merely a technical fault."

He wondered if he had been wise to accept this trip. He had assumed it would be preferable to his poky little flat in Victoria – more of a bed-sit to be honest. It would mean he could get out of his loathsome weekend constituency "surgeries" in Scarpington where he had to pretend to listen with sympathy to all the cranks, outcasts and derelicts who came whingeing to him for comfort, support and whatever else the local MP was supposed to provide in this God-forsaken nanny state. It was made worse by his occasional journalism. His bloody constituents had a vile habit of reading his columns and quoting them back at him.

"Oh, but Mr Glenn, you said in the *News of the World* the other day that you should love your neighbour" or, "Oh, Mr Glenn, you said on the radio that everybody had a right to a fair day's pay for a fair day's work."

And he longed to be able to say, "Balls! Balls! I don't believe a word of that garbage. I only do it for the money."

But, of course, he couldn't do that. Instead he put his head on one side, puffed on his pipe and looked immensely wise and sympathetic, and said something which was just as much balls as he had said in the paper or on the radio, but which kept the buggers happy or at least ensured their vote in the next election. Well, even throwing up on a grotty flight on a sardine tin of a

Caribbean Jumbo was preferable to that, and once they got wherever they were going there'd be a drink or two and free meals, and nothing much to do except listen to tour guides and interpreters, and look appreciative and concerned. He was good at that. And all he had to do in return was to write some pretentious rot about the emerging economies of the former banana republics, Britain's obligations to aid countries less sophisticated than their own. And so on ...

He retched again as Captain Travers turned sharp left and did something noisy to his wing flaps. He had heard the odd word through the fog of his hangover about descents and landings, and wondered if it had something to do with the lissom physical jerks the Suragair girls had been performing. Probably not. More likely to be a traditional native dance of welcome. Charming custom.

Peering out through the window he saw that they had come through the clouds. They appeared to be travelling through spiky green mountains, dangerously close. Then they were past them and the terrain flattened into an ochre-brown plateau. They were quite close to the earth's surface and Eric was aware of what looked like tin shacks and trucks on a muddy road. Before he was quite ready for it, there was a bump and a thud. Then the plane seemed to become airborne again, before descending with a second bone-jarring encounter with terra firma. As was obviously the custom on Suragair, a number of overhead lockers burst open, though without any very harmful effect.

Seconds later Captain Travers came on air again. "OK chaps!" he announced. "Welcome to Surago International. As anticipated, we have normal landing. Thank you for flying Suragair and may I ask all passengers to remain in their seats until ..."

But his voice was drowned out by enthusiastic cheering and clapping from the Suragan passengers who had already seized their hi-fi equipment and other personal baggage and were scrummaging their way towards the exit. From Grapefruit class the voices of the ladies' rugby team came loud and clear chanting, "Oggy! Oggy! Oggy! Oi! Oi! Oi!"

As the plane finally shuddered to a halt the Prime Minister and Kim Sanderson-Wright were pleased to see that a venerable pink Cadillac, flying a vibrantly multicoloured flag from its bonnet, was easing slowly towards it.

Fisher was just as gratified to observe a tall, statuesque Suragan woman standing with a large placard saying "Welcome British

Journalists!". He turned to Lesley d'Harcourt. "See!" he said. "Normal landing as anticipated and not a technical hitch in sight." He gestured towards the girl with the placard. "That'll be Gabrielle. She's from the Ministry. From now on, she's in charge."

Lesley d'Harcourt glanced at him frostily, raised an eyebrow, but said absolutely nothing.

31

SLOW NEWS DAY – NOTHING TO REPORT

B ack home, minding the shop, Effie had the time and the inclination for reflection. She wondered, unconvincingly, if she should have been a banker instead. Or a diplomat. She could have been either. But despite its shortcomings the world of communication had an irresistible allure.

For the journalists left behind in London these were dog-dull days. This often happened in the aftermath of high drama. The sexual shenanigans of the Queen's first minister and his subsequent abdication – temporary or not – created a hiatus. For those who believed in the significance of "public life" it was difficult to pick up the threads. Because no one was sure whether Sutton had gone for good his departure was not even the end of a chapter, let alone a book. You couldn't draw a line under him. He might be back.

Beyond and behind the front page, life in Britain bumbled along. The *Intelligence* cook remained sacked but took it badly, despite some belated magisterial emollience, consulted lawyers and took her case to an industrial tribunal. The new cooking team was not a success. Crosswords were compiled; cross words exchanged. Football club managers were dismissed with a regularity and ruthlessness which made newspaper cooks seem pampered; various national teams were excoriated for losing to foreigners at games that the English invented. The chauvinist paranoia of the press was compounded when the winning foreigners were amateurs, particularly if they were of British stock, and most particularly of all if their ancestors had been sent abroad as convicted criminals. The idea that a squad of English professionals should be out-cricketed by a team of chicken farmers and post-office workers, whose great-grandfathers had once been found guilty of tickling salmon or doing unmentionable things to sheep, galvanised pure-blooded Brits such as Chinese Ken and Albert van Blanco into frothy frenzies of indignant xenophobia.

For Britons not much interested in "public life" everyday existence was as various as usual. Those given to slumbering behind life's net-curtains sleep-walked their way through their allotted span exactly as they would no matter whether the world outside was basking in the light of paradise or burning in the fires of hell. Those who racketed about on a helter-skelter of emotional highs and lows, dicing with life, death and the pursuit of happiness, continued to do so just as they would if the end of the world were nigh or indefinitely postponed.

Journalists were different because they believed in "public life". They had to be for it was their livelihood. For some of them life was easy because they were part of a newspaper pattern which reflected certain inexorable daily events. For example there was in all the so-called "quality" newspapers such as the *Intelligence* and the *Conscience* a paragraph devoted to "Birthdays". These were culled from such sources as *Who's Who* and even a "Birthday Book" containing the names and birth dates of those luminaries whose birthdays were thought worth recording in the "quality" newspapers. New technology rendered this a wonderfully easy exercise. The birthdays of the allegedly Great and Good were all on disk and duly appeared on the relevant day. Once upon a time the *Intelligence* had boasted a Birthday Correspondent with two spinster secretaries to assist him. Latterly, the job was just one of Stomper-Watson's many duties.

Quite why this item appeared and what on earth it had to do with "quality" no one seemed to know. There had been a time when such newspapers did not record birthdays but did list the names of distinguished people who were ill, as well as, when appropriate, the nature of the illness and the place of confinement. Thus, as it were, "The Hon. Marcus Tregorrick, Treliske Hospital, Measles". This allowed people to send the Hon. Marcus get-well cards, flowers and grapes, as well as explaining his absence from the social round. Rather useful. Possibly even "news". But fiendishly labour-intensive and therefore expensive. In the great "rationalisation", therefore, illnesses were dropped. Birthdays, being cheaper, were an acceptable substitute subject, even though, as they only appeared on the actual day concerned, they were generally too late to be of any use. Rather the reverse, for a principal effect was to tell people something they had forgotten. Thus, the breakfaster or commuter was always being made to realise that he had failed to buy a birthday present or card for someone supposedly near and dear, and that it was too late to retrieve the situation.

Many other parts of the "quality" press had a similar quality. Obituaries were easy because not a day went by without someone or other toppling off the perch and it was never too difficult to cobble together a valedictory essay of some kind, even though these had latterly grown more revealing, not to say scurrilous. Thus "he was unmarried" was now replaced by "he was notoriously fond of small boys", "did not suffer fools gladly" was now "stuffy, pompous, deaf and short-tempered" and "convivial", "liked a drink".

Other such areas included most of sport (although the reporting of all but the most important matches had been phased out because, like illnesses, they were too expensive); the weather; the court circular; stories based on the previous evening's TV programmes (a complete no-go area in the days of Lady Beatrice's prime). Other "soft" topics such as food, travel and the problematic cookery, and most features, had nothing to do with news. There was a time when some of them were topical but this was long gone, except for a few very obvious exceptions such as the absolute obligation to run recipes for "Christmas Fayre" half-way through December.

Book reviews were more of a problem than they might have seemed for whereas the number of race meetings or tolerably distinguished deaths remained more or less constant, publishing was irritatingly seasonal. There was a huge glut of "distinguished" fiction in September and October, but virtually no books in January or August. This was explained away as "marketing" but like most things to do with "marketing" was the gut reaction of suits who had never read anything in their lives except for a diploma in the subject conducted by other suits whose experience of a world beyond "marketing" was limited in the extreme.

A paper such as the *Noise* contained fewer words, had no aspirations to "quality" and not even a residual desire to be a "paper of record". (This last phrase, long forgotten, was used by editors, especially of *The Times*, to justify such arcane items as Hansard, verbatim court reports and schools' rugby results.) This meant greater variety, though there were some regular features such as the daily naked lady. The naked lady was not "news" in any meaningful sense although there was a caption detailing her age, dimensions, occupation, domicile and a quotation (made up by a *Noise* reporter) giving some more or less fatuous aspiration to do with travelling, jobs or boy-friends. The girls were nearly all professionals and the pictures came from agencies. You had to have a different girl every day (though the same ones often appeared several times in the course of a year, sometimes with wigs and new details in the captions). It was a peculiar form of journalism but as reliable and formulaic as the obituaries in the "serious" newspapers.

The real difficulties came in two main areas: "News" and "Promotion". As far as "news" was concerned the difference between the Majors and Chinese Ken was fundamental. The former still clung to the antediluvian idea that a newspaper's job was to report on what was happening in Britain and the rest of the world. This was probably an impossible task but, as far as "news" was concerned the Majors were "reactive" and "descriptive". Ken, conversely, was "pro-active" and "prescriptive". Ken took the initiative and set the agenda. The Majors played "catch-up" and paid lip-service, at least, to something they quaintly called the truth. Ken couldn't give a stuff for the truth; didn't believe in it; and wouldn't have subscribed to it even if he had.

The Majors' view of "news" was unashamedly old-fashioned. A long-gone lunch-time legend, Rene MacColl of the *Daily Express*, a giant by-line in his Beaverbrook heyday, expressed the Majors' motto as well as anyone. "Essentially," wrote MacColl, "my job is to watch what goes on in the world and ask men and women what they are about and why they behave as they do." This, incredibly, involved being away from his desk for weeks on end. He added, with an ingenuousness unrecognisable to a later generation. "This I find fascinating." In the ultimate heresy old MacColl, in his final piece of advice, wrote that "one of the best rules of all is 'news, not views'." Even the Majors accepted that this was out of date. "News without views is not news at all," said Gordon. "Just facts,

facts, facts. Bones without flesh. People are too stupid nowadays to deal with 'news' without interpretation. It's not enough to tell them the story. You have to tell them what to make of it." There had been a broadcaster once, a grim, colourless apparatchik whose name Gordon could no longer remember, who had campaigned (though without conviction) on the basis of "a mission to explain". Neither Major had the vision to be described as "a man with a mission" but had they been compelled to adopt one they might have gone for "explaining". Certainly their belief in the stupidity of their fellow man was absolute. This being so they would be failing in their duty if they didn't help their readers to make sense of the stories they were being told.

This was not Ken's view, because Ken believed he had a "mission to entertain" and none whatever to inform or explain. Besides which, Ken did not believe that "news" could ever be dictated by, well, "news". He and his staff decided what was "news" and what wasn't. Quite apart from the loss of control, to do otherwise would be cripplingly expensive. A "reporter" like Rene MacColl must have cost Beaverbrook a fortune, constantly flying off to the far corners of the globe and for what? No one in Britain gave a monkey's for what happened abroad unless a British team was playing or a Briton was killed. Or kidnapped. Kidnapping was not a bad story. Nowadays, anyway, everybody could get that stuff off Sky TV or the Internet. Which was what he encouraged his staff to do. Why go to the trouble and expense of interviewing some two-bit politician when you could nick it all off David Frost or one of the Dimblebores on TV.

Thus Ken mused as, across the globe, the *Princess of Surago* came down to earth. Or would have mused if he were given to musing. Left entirely to his own devices, he would have dispensed with journalists in the old-fashioned sense altogether. On the *Noise* this had almost been accomplished. His perfect newspaper was naked ladies, football and bar-room style "columns" by taxi-drivers and topless waitresses.

"Promotion" was another matter. Ken enjoyed "promotion". Sometimes it was comparatively subtle. For example, when he took over the *Conscience*, Ken's first act had been to insert a one-line inscription on the front page immediately under the title. Now instead of simply "The *Conscience*. Est. 1873" the potential reader was assaulted with "The *Conscience*. Est 1873. The World's Greatest Quality Newspaper". This was, of course, an almost completely meaningless claim, but Ken's marketing department said it had increased circulation by 9.27 per cent. This impressively detailed figure was said to be produced by "research" though, like practically everything to do with Ken's newspapers, it was more or less made up. Pressed, Ken might have claimed that it was an "educated guess" although there was, in truth, nothing educated about it whatever.

The furore over "PM in Gay Sex Romp" had deflected Ken from things promotional. "Big danger of taking the eye off the ball," he said to Eddie White. "How many readers do you think we put on with that story?"

White said he didn't know.

"We're practically giving the *Noise* away, aren't we?"

White agreed.

"And our circulation increase has slowed down to practically nothing."

This also was true and White nodded again.

"So we can't reduce the price any further?"

"I don't see how."

"Mmm." Ken chewed on his burnt-out Havana.

"So the logical next step is to pay people to buy the paper."

Eddie gave his Proprietor a more than usually sharp look. "Isn't that a bit of a tautology?" he asked.

"Don't get smart with me, Edward. Speak English. You wouldn't put a word like that in the paper."

It was, as always, a bad sign when Ken called Eddie Edward.

"What I mean", said the Editor, "is that if you pay someone to buy something then they're not buying it."

"That doesn't follow," said Ken. "If I'm a greengrocer and I pay you to come into the shop and sell you a carrot, I've still sold you the carrot."

"But" – Eddie was beginning to feel out of his depth – "if you pay me ten pence to come into your shop and I then spend five pence on the carrot you're minus five pence."

"But you've still bought the carrot."

"I'm sorry," said Eddie, "but I don't see what this has got to do with newspapers."

"Tell you what," said Ken, whose thought process was gathering speed. "What about running a lottery?"

"What about running a lottery?"

"Each copy of the *Noise* would be a ticket. You'd have a

different number on each copy, then have a draw once a week and the winning copy gets a million nicker."

White went white. "A different number for each copy," he said. "That's a logistical nightmare. Besides, there are laws against that kind of thing."

"It's a brilliant idea," said Ken. "That'll really really get up Murdoch's and the Majors' noses. Check it out."

Such were the preoccupations of the men with their hands on the tillers of the national press. In these circumstances they could hardly be expected to give much thought to the intrepid little band of hacks about to try to get to grips with the island fiefdom of General Methuselah Foom. The hacks, the Prime Minister and the ladies' rugby team were in a far-away land of which Chinese Ken and the Majors knew nothing. There was a circulation war to be fought in the centre of the universe which, as far as they were concerned, lay somewhere between the Isle of Dogs and Kensington High Street. Some might sneer at the new press barons, call them Little Englanders and Eurosceptics, ask what did they know of Wapping who only Wapping knew. But this did not deflect men like Chinese Ken from their Grand Design.

Forward, forward let us range.
Let the great world spin for ever down the ringing grooves of change.

That was the philosophy of the great men who controlled the Fourth Estate. Well, up to a point.

32

DANCING IN THE STREET(S)

The band played "Colonel Bogey".

Bands did, thought Jones, on occasions such as this. The tune suited a primitive military ensemble with its emphasis on the thwack of drum and blare of brass. Even the Central Band of the Surago National Guard could manage a recognisable rendition.

"Hitler", he couldn't help murmuring to himself, "has only got one ball ... Göring has two but they are small and Himmler ... has something sim'lar ... but poor old Goebbels ... has ... no balls ... at all."

He smiled. He wondered if there were similar words in honour of Methuselah Foom though neither his four-syllable christian name nor his single-syllable surname would fit the scansion. Useful that so many of the Nazi leaders had such names.

He assumed that Borman and others also featured in the original but he couldn't remember. He thought of asking Lady Beatrice but decided not.

The band wore tight white patrols with black riding-boots, sky-blue jackets with scrambled-egg frogging and scarlet shakos. The uniforms, though flamboyant, were unmended and unclean, looking like hand-me-downs from the Ruritanian Army. In military terms the soldiers were a shower, but despite their shoddy turn-out and slovenly drill, they played with zest.

"I'm told they've got the best jazz section in Central America," confided Fisher to Lesley d'Harcourt.

"That's just the sort of thing *Suave* readers would like to know," she said, unclenching her lips just long enough to let the sentence escape. In the unlikely event of her enjoying a single moment of her visit she was clearly going to be damned if she showed it.

Out of the corners of their eyes the members of the press group observed (even if they did not recognise) their Prime Minister and his PPS being bundled into the pink Cadillac by two bulky men in dark suits and darker glasses, heavy and enveloping as goggles. Then the car spun away, its balding tyres skidding with menace on the damp tarmac. The ladies' rugby team, not apparently accorded VIP status, were trudging towards the squat, square, barely functional terminal building. The rusting sign on the flat roof had several letters missing but was trying to say "Surago International Airport". Jostling around it among a profusion of hoardings that advertised cigarettes, alcohol, soap-powder and the President himself were a throng of Suragan citizens waving flags, cameras and what appeared to be brightly coloured rags.

Gabrielle regarded her British visitors with something well in excess of depression and not far short of shock. As a child she had been educated to believe that the British possessed a number of impressive if dissonant attributes such as "*le* fair play", jingoistic Imperialism sang-froid and immaculate, if anachronistic kit. What she saw on the runway at Surago International looked shifty, defeatist, soggy lipped and as dishevelled as the band of the National Guard. She was destined to spend the whole of the next week shepherding this crew about her native land. She had been led to believe, by her upbringing and by the bland encomia of Dr Simenon, that she would be dealing with truth's messengers, the representatives of the free-est, finest press in the whole of the civilised world. Perhaps so, but she was not confident.

Fisher thrust out a hand. "You must be Gabrielle," he said. "I'm Fisher. We've spoken on the telephone."

"Yes of course." She smiled, showing deep double dimples. "How nice to meet you at last." Two could play at clichés.

Fisher introduced his team, all of whom, even Glenn, managed a more-or-less firm handshake and level, if red-eyed, stare.

"I am sorry," she said, "the bus must park by the terminus. It is not allowed to come to the runway. We will walk. It is not far.

Then we will go to the hotel and there is a chance to freshen up before the briefing. The Director is anxious to greet the British press and to explain the programme himself."

"Are the press kits ready?" Fisher sounded anxious. He was keen to minimise hitches, technical or not.

"Oh yes, we have the press kits prepared," she said, as if the matter had never been in doubt. "They are in the hotel rooms. There is everything you need to know. Also some very exclusive information on the new fast transit railway system, also the hydro-electric plant and the dam, although some of this is classified."

The group fell into step behind its leaders. Their dressing and general co-ordination was much like the band's.

"Do you enjoy the theatre?" Gabrielle asked conversationally but of no one in particular.

Colin, who had privately decided that one of his functions was to act as the party's principal intellectual and aesthete, answered for his colleagues. "I think we'd be fascinated by anything theatrical," he said. "What's on?"

"We are very lucky," said Gabrielle. "The National Theatre are about to celebrate the first night of *My Fair Lady* by Harold Pinter."

"Did you say 'Pinter'?" asked Colin nervously. "I didn't think *My Fair Lady* was one of his things. He's not known for his music."

"No, no." One of Gabrielle's stilettos snagged an emerging pot-hole in the tarmac; she stumbled slightly but stifled the ensuing curse. "The musical version is based on the original which is by Pinter."

Colin frowned. He had sensed before this trip began that it would be a voyage into Wonderland. A world in which Pinter wrote *Pygmalion* was just such a place. Under the control tower the band was playing "Seventy-six Trombones". Gabrielle probably thought it was by Sir Edward Elgar.

"Aren't you confusing Harold Pinter with George Bernard Shaw?"

"No, no." Gabrielle smiled like a teacher spelling out a fact of life to a backward child. "This is a well-known fact. Do you not know the work of Pinter? In Surago every schoolchild knows this work. In Surago he is the most famous playwright except for President Foom. And your William Shakespeare. Many musicals have been adapted from unmusical work: *My Fair Lady, Oklahoma, West Side Story, Cats*. *Your* version of *Cats* is based on the poems of T. S. Eliot but the true *Cats* is from the ancient Suragan *Histoire du Chat*, which dates from the fifteenth century. It is very *folklorique*. The cat is very important in our culture."

Colin decided it was time to change the subject. "Have you always lived in Surago?" he wanted to know.

She looked mildly put out at such a peremptory guillotine of intellectual conversation. "No," she said. "I spent two years working as an au pair in Islington and I did a Masters in Central American Feminist Novellas at the University of East Anglia."

"Oh," said Colin, and shut up.

"Here", she said a few moments later, "is our bus."

The bus was a surprise. They had all been expecting a jalopy – the vehicular equivalent of the *Princess of Surago*, cast off by London Transport around the time of the General Strike, covered in graffiti and psychedelics. The Routemaster lives. But not here. The press bus was a brand-new twenty-five-seat Mercedes with a WC, a bar, air-conditioning and tinted windows.

The mood of the party brightened perceptibly and they climbed in. Gabrielle took hold of a microphone. To further journalistic surprise the machine functioned. Her husky voice was efficiently amplified with not a hint of a whine or a crackle as she introduced their driver, Gaston, a giant in impenetrable Ray-Bans who looked as if he had escaped from Suragair cabin crew.

"Ladies and gentlemen," she continued, "now we drive to our hotel. The journey will last approximately one half-hour. We will commence by travelling down the magnificent Avenue Methuselah Foom. Then we pass through the suburbs of the city before entering Rue Fidel Castro. The hotel is on the Place de la Revolution opposite the Parc des Martyrs. On the other side is the Presidential Palace, residence of the President for Life, although he also has a country palace, La Retraite, at Le Petit Choufleur overlooking the sea. Now I will not disturb you until we arrive because I know you are all tired. So just sit back and enjoy the ride."

She smiled winsomely and gave a soft, throaty half-laugh. "God she's sexy!" thought every one of the men. "Tarty little cow!" thought the women.

Gaston engaged gear and the bus purred smoothly towards the airport exit. At least it *would* have purred smoothly had the tarmacadam surface of the road matched the sophistication of the press transport. So it bumped and jolted, although the bumping and jolting was vastly reduced by state-of-the-art German technology.

The ladies and gentlemen of the press had, in a manner of speaking, all been here before. A certain world-weary cynicism was a stock-in-trade of Fleet Street hacks, particularly among those of advanced or advancing years. They'd all, even Sharon and Lesley d'Harcourt, visited underdeveloped countries and tin-pot dictatorships. They knew what to expect.

As the Mercedes turned into the Avenue Methuselah Foom they were confronted by lines of oleander and bougainvillaea. On either side of the road there were snappy street lights with portraits of the President hanging from them (uncomfortably reminiscent of corpses swinging from gallows or, more specifically, Mussolini and mistress suspended from the lamp-posts of half a century before). The road surface was immaculate but apparently underused. Apart from the bus there was a handful of pink Volkswagen beetles with taxi signs on them, an occasional elderly *camion*, one Leyland double-decker of much the style they had been expecting to travel in themselves. They also passed two horse-driven vehicles – the horses emaciated, the carts primitive contraptions which seemed to have been hastily cobbled together from wooden planks and old bath-tubs. There were also police in large numbers. They travelled in emerald-green Harley-Davidsons with side-cars. They had side-arms attached to their webbing belts and some sort of rifled machine-gun strapped to their torsos. The man in the side-car even had another gun mounted on the chassis immediately in front of him. It all seemed slightly excessive.

This grand but underpopulated highway was not more than about five miles long. When it ceased it did so with a suddenness which was almost shocking. The Mercedes moved from showcase to slum with not a whiff of transition. The sterile near emptiness of the avenue debouched on to a road which was little more than a gravelled track with ruts and holes everywhere. In some cases the pavements had perfunctory kerbs, but elsewhere the road continued right to the front door of the people's dwellings. These were, in apparently random alternation, either rudimentary tower blocks or shanty-town shacks of corrugated iron. Women squatting by discarded oil cans washed clothes and small children; market stalls displayed exotic fruit and stringy meat, soap-powder, bright pink sweetmeats, cans of spam, girlie magazines and bicycle parts. The near desertion of the Avenue Methuselah Foom was succeeded by an almost impassable gridlock of rickshaws, tractors, motorised tricycles, pedestrians and livestock.

"Reminds me of Kathmandu," said Jones to Lady Beatrice.

"Ever so like Tiranha," said Sharon to Colin.

"I was in Bangladesh once," said Lesley d'Harcourt to Fisher. "I promised myself *and* my readers I would never go again. Now look at me."

"Jesus," said Eric Glenn to no one in particular. "Just like the bloody constituency on a Friday night. I should have stayed home."

It is one of the conditions of travel writing that every scribe should be able to produce an instant comparison. The jaded nature of their trade means that every such writer's first reaction to each new place was that it was just like somewhere else. In real life, of course, the point was that nowhere was really quite like anywhere else. In this respect, and perhaps this alone, Surago was entirely typical. In truth, it was not quite like anywhere else although, naturally, when the journalists' accounts finally appeared in Britain they would have taken on an identikit identity which might as well have been done with writing by numbers.

Staring through the tinted windows of their air-conditioned bus, the ladies and gentlemen of the British press did not see reality, only somewhere else they had been already and not much liked. They had done this before and they would do it again.

33

NOT UP FOR IT

The hotel was the Bristol, named after the Marquess of that ilk whose eponymous hostelries littered the globe. There were more modern hotels in Surago but they were run-of-the-mill middle-executive links in mediocre international chains. There were more luxurious ones as well, but they were "beach resorts" and not appropriate for the first, serious, fact-finding part of the journalists' mission. There would be a final weekend of frivolity by the seaside but the big smoke had to come first.

Jones had a suite with a balcony overlooking the gardens. The rooms had a faded grandeur he found agreeable and familiar. His drawing-room was lit by a vast *fin de siècle* chandelier; the antimacassared chesterfield would have been at home in the Victoria and Albert Museum. So would the bathroom fittings, which were by Heath Robinson out of Tinguely. The pictures were sepia prints full of crinolines and parasols, spats, titfers, waxed moustaches, stove-pipe hats and cheroots deployed on verandas and balconies ornamented with enormous plants in pots.

On entering this mildewed splendour Jones smiled softly and began an inspection, pacing slowly along the walls and examining the pictures, kneeling down to look under the bed, where he was pleased to find a blue-and-white chamber-pot, slightly chipped. He tried the taps, which coughed rheumily before hacking up a staccato torrent of Limpopo effluence, all grey-green and greasy. He sat on the bed and bounced up and down a couple of times. If it had been a cricket wicket he would have put the other side in first. It was lively and unpredictable, with one or two rough patches which would, sooner or later, take spin.

There were French windows, hung with yellowing net curtains, leading to his balcony which was narrow and, Jones judged, capable of collapsing at any moment. He tried the handle gingerly at first and then, as it did not budge, exerted more pressure until it suddenly gave way and the window sprang open almost taking him with it. His rooms, though not air-conditioned, were, he realised, surprisingly cool. The outside atmosphere was damply hot, like a sauna immediately after someone's put water on the coals in the bucket. It was also smelly, an all-embracing aroma-therapy, but although Jones thought he detected lilac and orange blossom and exotic scents whose names he could not speak, there were other more nose-wrinkling pongs which suggested dung, automobile exhaust and household refuse. The noise was a similarly rich compound of unsilenced motor-scooter, horse's hoof, human imprecation, police car siren and, in the distance, tantalisingly unclear, coming and going in the sluggish breeze, music which could have been from a live band or a loudspeaker system amplifying the latest Suragan hits.

Jones leaned over the balustrade and sniffed.

What he smelt was trouble.

All through his career he had played on his journalistic reputation as a "trouble-shooter" and yet that was less than the half of it. Any fool could "shoot" trouble but it took an expert to sniff it out. Once upon a time in journalism, the ultimate prize had been something called a "scoop", a word which was defined by all the dictionaries in an arid form which failed even to hint at its excitement and mystery. In dictionary terms a "scoop" was a piece of news published in one newspaper ahead of the others. In recent years the term had become extinct, or so debased that it was meaningless. Thus a broken embargo or a total fabrication could be dignified with the traditional announcement accorded to "scoops". The usual was "Exclusive" which not only sought to convey the idea that it was peculiar to the claimant but also smart.

In the old days the adjective was merited. Jones's "scoops" were not just based on reporting, describing and analysing, but also on having the nous to be in the right place at the right time. Jones somehow contrived to be at the volcano *before* the eruption. He had a nose for disasters of every kind and therefore he anticipated them. He was like a great batsman. He saw the ball early.

Now, gazing out over the municipal gardens and the city beyond, he smelt scoop. Precisely how or why he could not have said. Of course, tyrants such as General Methuselah Foom toppled in time and Jones would not have required unique prescience to sense that Foom's time would come. On the other hand there was no particular reason for thinking it was up just yet. Such dictators seldom if ever died in bed. Naturally there were exceptions. Mediaeval monarchs were great survivors and even in this century Generalissimo Franco and Chairman Mao had emulated them. Even regular tin-pots such as Mobutu of Zaïre and Idi Amin of Uganda had managed to escape and Gaddafi and Castro in Libya and Cuba had exceeded almost every expectation. Jones had reported on them all and interviewed several. These were good of their kind. He was an observant reporter, an acute interrogator and he wrote well. But that wasn't the point. A number of his rivals could have managed at least as well, had they managed to be in the same place at the same time. They hadn't. That was the secret of Jones's success. Call it rat-like cunning; call it luck. Whatever it was, he had it in spades and no one else did.

There had been too many armed police on the way in from the airport. The place felt ramshackle. If he were being rational he would have linked the two and made a logical connection, but there were plenty of impoverished, ill-housed, unproductive, basket-case countries where the proletariat were effectively contained by a ruthless application of what was sick-jokingly called "internal security". Some of them went up in smoke; some didn't. The conjunction was commonplace.

No, there was something else here. Something in the air.

Jones took a monogrammed silver cigarette case from his pocket, tapped a politically incorrect unfiltered red Marlboro three times against the lid and lit it from his lucky talisman ex-Russian Army surplus Zippo. On the pavement below there was an ancient hurdy-gurdy predominantly green but decorated Romany style like a gypsy caravan or canal narrow-boat. The organ-grinder was a slight, fine-featured man of not more than five foot. He wore denim dungarees and a straw sombrero. On one shoulder he had a small monkey. As the man cranked his machine it played a wistful honky-tonk version of "Auld Lang Syne". One of the organ-grinder's legs was wooden, skilfully turned and varnished, so that it resembled a piece of Victorian furniture.

Jones wondered idly if it had been looted from the Belgian governor's palace in the aftermath of the revolution. It was not such a fanciful notion. Or perhaps it had been lawfully acquired in a sale. Lot Thirty-something. Property of a gentleman returning to Europe. Jones exhaled a thin stream of blue smoke from each nostril and watched it eddy into the sulphurous mainstream of the Suragan ether. This place felt like Teheran just before the Shah left town. Or Prague in sixty-eight the night before the Russians crushed Dubček and his fragile, false spring promise. Jones remembered both, alas, too well.

"Should auld acquaintance be forgot," he mouthed quietly, along with the street music. Time was when he would have been in a place like this with a serious, hard-bitten corps of foreign correspondents all fighting each other for exclusives of one sort or another but all meeting up together in the bar for late nights of yarning and carousing, before becoming the best of enemies again some time around dawn. Those men, and some women, were professionals, craftsmen, backed up by a Fleet Street foreign desk of equally consummate skill. Jones sighed. Now he was here with a rag-bag of PR people, sex correspondents, fly-blown MPs and superannuated proprietresses. "Jones on a junket." He laughed and flicked his cigarette butt over the parapet. He watched it do a couple of neat somersaults before going into free fall like an Olympic diver off the high board. It fell, still smouldering, on the pavement a few feet from the organ-grinder, but neither he nor his monkey gave it a glance.

Behind him on the far horizon of his gloomy drawing-room there came a knocking sound.

He assumed at first that it was faulty plumbing, then wondered if it was rats behind the skirting. Either would have tallied with his first impressions of the Hotel Bristol, Surago. Gradually, however, the sound increased in volume and its regular beat suggested human origins. It was probably, he thought, room service with a welcome bowl of flowers, bottle or, most likely, press kit. On trips such as this the press kits fell like confetti. Almost the greatest challenge was finding ways of disposing of them without upsetting one's hosts and their public relations officials. On one famous occasion a press party in Buenos Aires had made their press kits into paper aeroplanes and released them from the twentysomethingth floor of their hotel. Several had fallen on the glass roof of the *porte-cochère* where, embarrassingly, they had stuck.

"Come," he said irritably and was surprised, but rather pleased, when the door opened to reveal the undeniably sexy figure of their government hostess, Gabrielle. He ushered her into his parlour and motioned her to a *chaise longue*, where she sat criss-crossing her legs in a manner at once nervous and seductive. Jones recognised a *femme fatale* when he saw one and though experienced was not immune.

"I am sorry to intrude," she said, "but I see that you are an *homme du monde* and I understand that you have connections."

She smiled coquettishly and would, Jones felt, have tapped the side of her nose and winked had these been Suragan customs. She came to him with a gift of complicity and inside knowledge. Maybe more.

"Please don't apologise." He proffered a cigarette and she took it, allowing him to light it, then drawing deeply and exhaling through sensuously dilated nostrils.

Jones reflected that he had been right about trouble. If ever there was a harbinger of dangerous times it was Gabrielle Casson. Still, he was bound to admit that even if she was a trifle exaggerated she was a class act.

He smiled, in what he hoped was a well-connected manner. "How can I help?" he asked.

"I wish to defect," she said. "I am asking you to arrange for my political asylum."

She drew deeply again on the cigarette and ran her spare hand through raven hair. "I feel sure that you can arrange it," she said. "I have been thorough in my researches. And now that I have met you I am confident that I am not mistaken."

This was trouble all right.

"Forgive me," said Jones, "but why do you want asylum in Britain and what makes you think I can arrange it? After all, there's a British ambassador here. He's in charge of that sort of thing. Usually you go through normal channels."

She smiled, showing even white teeth which were so perfect that he wondered, for an unchivalrous moment, whether they were false. "You and I, Mr Jones, are not the sort of people who believe in 'normal channels'." He made a mental note about her use of "you and I". It was effortlessly inclusive and exclusive, putting the two of them instantly into a cocoon of mutual understanding.

"And I want asylum because I am frightened," she continued. "I do not want to be the mistress of the President for Life. I do not wish to be a slave. And if there is to be a revolution I do not wish to be in the firing line. It's simple." She glanced at her watch. "I am sorry. We should be in the lobby. We have to be at the Ministry for the briefing."

"Of course." Jones was familiar with press briefings, though the word "briefing" was a serious misnomer. Such lectures were many things to many men but they were never "brief".

"So may I count on you?" she asked huskily.

"Well, my dear girl," he began, "this is a little sudden and I hardly know you. It's highly irregular."

"My spies inform me, Mr Jones, that you yourself are 'highly irregular'. If I did not believe you to be 'highly irregular' I would not be entrusting you with my little secret. In fact, I am trusting you with my life. I hope you will take care of it."

Saying which, she kissed him lightly on the lips and was gone.

Jones smiled slowly and swore softly. His sense of smell seldom failed. There was going to be trouble all right.

BRIEF ENCOUNTER

T he Ministry was definitively drab, inside and out. The exterior was a sludge-grey rectangle of concrete blocks stained by the elements in various streaks of excremental pastels; the interior was hospital green. If the British press group had been told that it was the headquarters of the Secret Police they would have been unsurprised. The room to which they were led, along interminable uncarpeted corridors, was furnished with a plastic-topped table and a dozen or so uncomfortable chairs, which looked as if they were cast-offs from a village hall in the Outer Hebrides. There was a portrait of the President for Life on one wall and two barred windows with a view of rooftops and washing lines. As they were five stories up it was unclear what the bars were for. Jones wondered if they were expecting abseiling terrorists.

On a side table were a water dispenser and two chipped thermoses containing a thin brew of instant coffee, which bore only a passing relationship to the real thing. As this was coffee-producing country the sad parody seemed extraordinary. And in a land where citrus fruits grew like weeds there was no sign of orange, lemon or grapefruit, only a jug containing diluted condensed milk and paper cups in plastic holders. There was no air-conditioning but a single propeller fan at least dispersed the humid stale-nicotine-scented air.

The mood among Fleet Street's finest was jet-lagged and sour.

Even Fisher, smiling professionally and murmuring boosterish platitudes, was ill at ease. The bed in his room had not been made, the sheets were soiled and there was newly shaved stubble encrusting the already stained basin. Most of the others had enjoyed similar experiences. Jones was an exception.

The briefing was conducted by the Deputy Director for Tourism, who was responsible to the Director (who extended his apologies for being unavoidably engaged elsewhere but hoped to have the pleasure of meeting the group at lunch during their trip). The Director was responsible to the Minister for Tourism who was a relatively junior member of the government but reported directly to Orlando Foom, the President's twenty-six-year-old son. The Secretary of State was responsible for Culture, Tourism, the Family, Energy, Youth and Development – an impressive portfolio even if it sometimes lacked precision. In fact, this ambiguity was deliberate for Orlando was widely preceived as the second most important man in the country. He could almost have been called Minister for Life, though this would have been too conscious and deliberate. His title might not have made it clear but he was, for instance, responsible for censorship of all kinds and particularly for the State Broadcasting System. He was, *de facto*, Proprietor and Editor-in-chief of the government newspapers *La Vérité* and *La Nation*.

All members of the British party with the possible exception of Eric Glenn retained enough of the scepticism essential to their profession to know that any paper called *Truth* would be full of lies and any paper called the *Nation* would certainly not speak in the national interest. That portmanteau-portfolio also suggested that an important part of young Orlando's role was to be the Goebbels of his father's government. He was Minister for Make-Believe, for convincing people that things were not what they seemed. This, after all, was the purpose of this visit.

The Deputy Director was a thin, middle-aged man in a shapeless suit made from some sort of pale-blue canvas. On entering the room he circled the table, dishing out business cards to his visitors. These flimsy and muddily printed objects confirmed his title and said that his name was Jack Rouge-Thomas. "I am sorry", he said, sitting down and smiling forlornly at his guests, "that we have so little time. Normally an introduction such as this should naturally take the whole day, but Gabrielle tells me that you have a very full schedule and we will have to be finished within two hours."

His audience responded with a collective gasp of disbelief.

"I have here" – he gestured at an alarming pile of paper – "press kits for everyone, which will provide much of the information you require." He coughed and sipped from a glass of water. "So. Welcome to the People's Republic of Surago. The People's Republic of Surago is a democracy based on a parliamentary system of government. After Surago's independence from Imperialist colonialist oppression the electorate ratified in a national referendum to confer the office of Presidency for Life on the Person of His Excellency Professor General Methuselah Foom KGCS, D. Litt., etc. etc. The constitution is based on the Roman Law allied to modern democratic practices. Under the leadership of the President for Life this consists of an Executive, a Legislative and a Judiciary, duly elected and constituted."

Some of the group were old hands at this sort of monologue. Eric Glenn's fellow travelling had involved many years as a member of Anglo-Bulgarian Friendship Committees and back-bench parliamentary committees concerned with Nicolae Ceauşescu's Romania and Erich Honecker's East Germany in the old days before the wall came down. A large part of Glenn privately regretted the demise of Eastern European Communism. Those discredited regimes had been a pleasurable source of food, drink, travel and even sex.

Jones, Lady Beatrice and even Colin were experienced enough to have become inured to such bromides. On the whole they switched off and day-dreamed, while keeping just enough of an antenna alert for a gap in the fog of disinformation. For Sharon Taylor and Lesley d'Harcourt it was more of an eye-opener – or "eye-shutter". Sharon and Lesley had not come to Surago to learn that "Education is divided into primary, secondary and superior levels", nor that "goat accounts for almost ten per cent of Surago's agricultural exports" and least of all that the National Anthem was "All Hail Most Glorious Cradle of Our Forefathers". This was not going to cut ice with the Editors of the *Noise* or of *Suave* magazine.

M. Rouge-Thomas seemed oblivious to his listeners' boredom. On and on he droned, reading out statistics and statements in a flat, expressionless, nasal whine with never enough of a break to allow interruption or question. It was a curious exercise, for he must have realised that what he was saying was of little or no interest to his audience. Not one of them even did him the courtesy of taking a note. Fisher, realising that every sentence was another nail in the coffin of Surago's PR image, was squirming. Yet there was nothing he could do. The man was uninterruptable. He touched on everything: housing ... sewage ... defence ... mineral production ... the hydro-electric development ... the proposed nuclear power station ... the new airport ... the possible subway system ... forestry ... conservation ... All human life was there.

Expressed in this dry-as-dust, passionless monologue, all human life was a pretty dull do. And yet the Deputy Director was not lying. He was not even being particularly economical with the truth. He was simply being a crashing bore for, as every journalist knew, "news" was, almost by definition, "bad". Jack Rouge-Thomas was giving the good, or worse still the worthy side of his country's story. That might have been the truth but it wasn't "news". It wasn't even interesting.

When, after about an hour and a half, he finally drew breath, he was asked a question which had nothing to do with anything about which he had talked.

"Sex," said Sharon. "What about sex?"

There was a shuffle of interest from the somnolent group. The Deputy Director of Tourism ran a grubby finger round the inside of his collar, which was at least one size too big for him. It too was grubby, as was his neck.

"Sex?" he said. He seemed apprehensive. "Sex?" he repeated and looked nervously at Gabrielle.

She smiled at him but said nothing. She didn't have to since she exuded sex from every pore. This wasn't helpful, however.

"Sex," said Sharon. "My readers want to know about the Suragan way of sex. Do Suragans believe in sex outside marriage? How many Suragans are virgins at, say, sixteen? What are the figures on AIDS? What's the deal on prostitution? Are your brothels legal?"

"There are no brothels in Surago," said M. Rouge-Thomas.

"That's not my information." This was Colin White-Lewis. "I understand you have some of the best little whorehouses in Central America. They're on the Internet."

His mother gave him a distinctly old-fashioned look. "Colin!" she said.

Sharon tittered.

"Bed and bordello," said Eric Glenn. "That was what the place was famous for in the old Belgian days. White-Lewis is right. I recall George Brown one night in Annie's bar telling the most amazing story about local ladies of the night and ping-pong balls. I seem to remember rum, bottles and razor blades came into it. Your girls were famous."

"There is no prostitution in Surago." M. Rouge-Thomas was tight-lipped and obviously unused to dealing with fearless representatives of the free press. He glanced frantically at Gabrielle. "Under the laws of the Republic it is not permitted," he said.

"It's not permitted under our laws either," said Sharon. "Doesn't make a sod's bit of difference."

"I'm not sure it's altogether fair to submit Mr Rouge-Thomas to this sort of questioning," said Jones silkily. "We are, after all, guests in his country and he's had some fascinating things to say about life here and how his government is coping with the various problems they face."

"Oh, tit and bum," said Sharon tetchily. "My readers aren't interested in how many kilos of goat this place is producing per capita, they want bonking. What about the women's rugby team?"

M. Rouge-Thomas sensed a respite and smiled weakly. "We are very privileged to have the Great Britain ladies' rugby football team visiting our country," he said. "Surago is very new to rugby football but we hope to take our place on the world stage. Ninety-seven per cent of all schoolchildren in the Republic are playing ball games for at least one hour per week."

"You know that British women rugby players are all sex-crazed," said Sharon.

M. Rouge-Thomas seemed to interpret this as a statement rather than a question and said nothing.

"Can you tell us something about the Suragan fashion industry?" asked Lesley d'Harcourt, yawning.

The Deputy Director shuffled papers frantically and then, adjusting his spectacles, read: "Fashion accounts for only a small percentage of Surago's total exports. The national dress is particularly colourful. Suragan fabrics are of the highest quality. The Avenue of the 17th March is the equivalent of London's Savile Row and has many skilled tailors and garment manufacturers. The country's couturiers have an international reputation and collections have been demonstrated in London, Paris, Milan etc. etc." He looked up like a student who has just read out his essay and is seeking approval, though knowing in his heart of hearts that it won't actually quite do.

Lesley yawned again, more obviously this time. "I'd be interested to meet some of your" – she paused just long enough to indicate scepticism – "to meet some of your ... couturiers."

"I'm sure that will be possible," he said, looking at Gabrielle with an expression which clearly said that this was girl's stuff and nothing to do with him.

"I'm not entirely clear about the political set-up here, Mr Thomas." This was Beatrice White-Lewis. She pronounced "Thomas" as if the Deputy Director were Welsh. The old girl was still political to her finger-tips. "Perhaps you could enlighten us."

"As I have explained," he said, as if repeating himself to a child, "Surago is a parliamentary democracy."

"So there's an opposition?"

"Not at the moment. There is no need."

"You mean that opposition is banned?"

"No. There is no opposition because there is no need for opposition. All the people are united."

Lady Beatrice's son took up the cudgels. Despite their recent hostilities there must have been something lurking in the genes. "You're telling us that the President has a hundred per cent approval rating?"

The Deputy Director was perspiring. Nothing in his career had prepared him for this sort of question. His philosophy had always been that if you didn't want to hear lies then you kept silent. The job of the journalist in Suragan society was to report what he was told. This sort of rude hectoring was alien to the local culture. "Yes, absolutely."

"How do you know? Do you have opinion polls?" Colin White-Lewis appeared to scent blood.

M. Rouge-Thomas was floundering. "There is no need for opinion polls. The people are one hundred per cent behind the President. This is obvious. He is the people's President. Why should the people oppose him?"

Lady Beatrice was also enjoying the chase. Her nostrils flared. She was momentarily rejuvenated as if reliving the ghosts of interrogations past. "I understand", she said, "that internal security is partly in the hands of a secret police force called, I believe, the FSI: the Force Sanitaire d'Intérieur."

The Deputy Director looked despairingly at Gabrielle, who

showed every sign of enjoying his discomfiture. She gave a little moue of sympathy and a shoulder shrug, which absolved herself of any responsibility for this unexpected turn of events.

"There is no secret police force in Surago," said Rouge-Thomas. "All police and security is, as you would say, above the board. This is a free country. Very happy. All are smiling all the time. You will see. That is why we are anxious to attract more tourism from your country. So that you may share in our happiness."

"Do you cater for sex tourists?" This, naturally, was from Sharon, who had been impatient with the prissy questioning of the White-Thomases, which seemed to her to be getting dangerously close to an expression of concern on human rights.

Fisher had finally had enough. "I think", he said, "that lunch beckons."

He was learning fast. All public relations people knew that, no matter what, lunch takes precedence. It trumps all other cards.

35

NOT MANY DEAD

The revolution began after the ceviche but before the rat. The group had proceeded, without the severely discomfited Jack Rouge-Thomas, to the "Writers' House", a moth-eaten mansion built by a Belgian governor for a favourite mistress at the turn of the century and now a meeting place for the Suragan intelligentsia, or at least those involved, even loosely, with the written word. It was a place of chipped chandelier, peeling plaster and ancient antimacassar, not unlike the Hotel Bristol. Gabrielle invoked the names of Hemingway, Somerset Maugham and Lord Archer of Weston-super-Mare, but her charges placed as much credence on these claims as they did on her insistence that Harold Pinter wrote *My Fair Lady*. They were more inclined to believe that Wilson duPré and Nathalie Pavlova hung out here. They had heard of neither but Gabrielle said they were the grand old people of Suragan letters. Or possibly the *enfants terribles*. She did not seem sure.

In any case they were not present at lunch, which was hosted by the President of the Surago Society of Authors, a man whose name no one quite caught. He had written a novella in Creole, an epic poem on the history of sugar and the definitive life of President Foom. Also present were a large, jolly woman introduced as "The Agatha Christie of Surago" and a young, reptilian man described by Gabrielle as "our answer to Martin Amis".

The meal, contrary to expectations, promised well. Before

sitting down the journalists were given a "very typical" cocktail consisting almost entirely of very sweet rum. It was apparently called a Boum-Boum Belge in honour of a particularly lethal hand grenade which was a feature of colonial rule.

The first course was a ceviche of conch and tonsil-fish in a marinade of lime, lemon and coriander, accompanied by an unexpected Pouilly-Fumé. The main course of rat was apparently a national delicacy and came roasted in its own juices together with local herbs and some sort of indigenous yam. It was not really "rat", but "school of rat", being a nocturnal carnivorous rodent of rabbit-like proportions which lived in the mountains. It was said to taste like guinea fowl only stronger.

Alas, it had not even been brought to table when they heard the first explosion.

It was a big bang. Later, those who heard it, especially those who had a way with words, would conjure up any number of vivid and convincing metaphors and similes to describe it. All were more or less fanciful. At the moment itself the sound was quite simply a big bang. No more and no less. It was followed by a moment of eerily artificial silence during which the lunchers at the Writers' Union stared rigidly at nothing in particular.

Then there was noise. Everyone spoke at once.

"*Merde!*"

"Good Grief!"

"What in God's name was that?"

"Everybody keep absolutely calm."

"Was that a bomb?"

"Nobody told me there were earthquakes in Surago!"

"Hold the front page!"

It was a big enough bang to cause genuine alarm and therefore brought out a wide range of reactions – all more or less characteristic. Jones and Lady Beatrice not only seemed calm but also exhibited leadership qualities. They both appeared keen to take charge, though Lady Beatrice a touch more stridently than Jones, who was possibly stronger and certainly more silent. But definitely officer class. Colin White-Lewis disguised his alarm with facetiousness, as did Sharon. Lesley d'Harcourt was quite prepared to admit that she was frightened but was also put out by the inconvenience. It was as if she thought the explosion – if that was what it was – had been aimed specifically at her. Eric Glenn was almost totally passive and apparently prepared to go with the flow and do as he was told to an extent that was practically bovine. Fisher, who should, of course, have been in control, clearly wasn't.

Gabrielle, predictably, was the most practical. "Don't you have an English phrase about 'jumping the gun'?" she asked Jones. "Well, if I'm correct then some idiot has just jumped it. I shall telephone." And she left the room.

Somehow no one was now in the mood for roast rat.

Outside there was a sound of sirens. They could have been attached to ambulances, police cars or fire-engines. They could have been old-fashioned air-raid alarms.

"Sounds as if the balloon's gone up," said Eric Glenn, helping himself to more wine.

A new sound cut across the sirens. It was a flat yackety-yack like someone hitting typewriter keys, only louder and more explosive.

"If we were proper journalists", said Colin White-Lewis, "we'd be out there with our notebooks, dodging the bullets and recording whatever's going on. Scoopy-doopy!"

"Don't be so childish," said his mother. "Knowing you, you'd only get shot, which would be exceedingly tiresome for all concerned and most of all for you."

"No, seriously, there's clearly some sort of excitement going on. That's small-arms fire unless I'm very much mistaken. We've walked into a civil war. We should be filing soonest."

"If you think any editor in the United Kingdom would be remotely interested in a revolution or civil war in some two-bit banana republic then you must be even wetter behind the ears than I thought," said Lady Beatrice. "Even when I was in charge of the *Intelligence* I wouldn't have given this more than a down-page par in the Foreign Round-up. 'Revolution in Surago' isn't a story. In fact, 'No revolution in Surago' has more chance of getting in the papers. Most people assume that places like this have revolutions on a daily basis."

"I don't," said Lesley d'Harcourt. "I believed what I was told, which was that it was a tropical paradise with nothing but sun, sand and exotic culture. Instead of which we've got this. I could have been in Portofino this week."

"Revolutionaries can be really really sexy," said Sharon. "I really really fancy Che Guevara."

"I think," said Fisher, who had not bargained for this any more than anyone else, "the place to be in a situation like this is the

British embassy." He had a vague recollection of milling crowds on the roofs of Western embassies in Saigon as the Vietminh closed in for the kill.

"I agree that this is probably *not* the best place to be," said Jones evenly, hinting at a lifetime's experience of disorders such as this.

The automatic gunfire, if that was what it was, seemed to be getting closer.

Gabrielle came back into the room. She appeared cross and agitated, though her adrenalin level was obviously still well below panic stations.

"I apologise," she said. "The revolution was not supposed to begin until next month. It was agreed that it would be best to coincide with the rainy season. Unfortunately someone has crossed a wire. It is most inconvenient. I regret that our schedule will have to be reorganised. I cannot guarantee our safety in the city. It may be sensible to proceed immediately to the Bougainvillaea Beach Resort. It is quite remote. We should be safe there."

"I would have thought", said Lady Beatrice, assuming her most *grande dame*like expression, "that some luxurious seaside hotel was the last place on earth to go. If I were a self-respecting revolutionary I should be down there raping and pillaging as soon as the first shot was fired."

The rest of the group looked startled. Lady B had conjured up some alarming images.

"Drinking the minibars dry and screwing the capitalist scum," said Eric Glenn with the air of a man who would like to join in. After all, he was "Old Labour".

"I do wonder", said Jones judiciously, "if perhaps the British embassy might not be the better option. The Ambassador's an old acquaintance. Percy Finnan. He's an olive short of the full martini but he *is* the British Ambassador and taking care of people like us in a situation like this is what British ambassadors are for."

"Are you telling me that you knew there was going to be a revolution?" asked Fisher, scandalised. "And Dr Simenon. Did he know about it?"

"The revolution is designed to get rid of people like Dr Simenon so no, of course he did not know. I did not know that the revolution was going to begin so early. The timetable was supposed to be entirely different. It is most unprofessional."

"I really think I should have been told," said Fisher.

"Talking of minibars," said Eric Glenn, "we seem to have

finished that very decent Pouilly Fumé. Do you think we could conjure up another bottle? Or, in the context of the moment, would that be construed as looting?"

He clearly thought he had cracked a joke and laughed quite heartily until he realised that no one else thought it funny.

"Why don't we phone the embassy first?" asked Sharon. "They might be closed."

"The telephone is not reliable," said Gabrielle. "Besides, we do not know who might be listening to the telephone conversations. Especially during a revolution."

"You don't think we'd be safe at the Hotel Bristol?" It wasn't quite clear whether Lesley d'Harcourt was asking Gabrielle or Jones but she *was* clearly asking one or the other. She obviously reckoned they were the only two competent to answer.

"Ninety-nine times out of a hundred, yes, of course," said Jones. "But we'd be safer still at the embassy."

"They might target the embassy," she said, "like Peru."

"I think Mr Jones is probably correct. I think you will be safest at the embassy." Gabrielle had obviously cast her lot with Jones.

"Well, that's settled then," said Fisher. "Is the bus outside?"

Gabrielle said she thought so but would go and check.

The British were at bay. It should have brought out the best in them. Perhaps it would. But they were also journalists. Sort of. The common characteristics of journalists were not the same as the common characteristics of the British. Or were they? Journalists at bay might be a different matter altogether. They might coalesce or they might diverge.

The Suragan writers, the hosts, had, effectively unnoticed, vanished. One could hardly blame them. Who knew which side they were on? In any event it would not be sensible for them to be found consorting with a cohort of foreign journalists. This was almost certainly a domestic argument and in household disputes it was axiomatic that outsiders were the ultimate enemy. No matter how fierce the participants in an internecine matter such as this, they would abandon their antipathy if some bloody foreigner seemed to be muscling in on their turf. And if those outsiders were journalists so much the worse. Foreign press intruded, pontificated, patronised and caused resentment. The Foomists and the revolutionaries might hate each other, but they hated Johnny Foreigner still more. Fisher's press party knew this.

"This could be a slightly dodgy situation," said Jones. "Queensberry Rules don't apply."

He looked round at the group and was rewarded with a silent acquiescence. Nobody spoke. Outside, the firework noises showed no sign of diminishing. They were getting closer. Once or twice the chandeliers shook.

"What about our things?" Lesley d'Harcourt was the sort of person who would go berserk if separated from her "things". "My lap-top's at the Bristol," she said, plaintively, "and my pearls."

"Don't worry," said Fisher, sounding worried. "Wherever we end up we'll make sure that our lap-tops and pearls are in the same place."

No one believed him.

For a moment or so they were silent again, embarrassed and embarrassing. The quiet was disturbed by Gabrielle. "Your chariot awaits," she said, unexpectedly. "The bus is outside. The revolution is approaching. We should hurry."

And hurry they did.

It was an orderly embarkation, back through those benighted, soulless corridors, ducking unexpectedly through a drain-like subterranean tube, to a side entrance where the still surprisingly smart bus was waiting. The engine was running. The driver, somehow, had acquired a flak-jacket. Whose side, they all wondered, was he on? Only Sharon, scribbling as she ran, was taking a note.

The bus was an escapist's capsule, a purring cocoon of Western technology, a metaphor for the great divide between the first and third worlds. Once inside, the hacks felt safe. It was a bogus safety, no proof at all against the bomb, the mortar, the land-mine or even the sniper's bullet or random pistol shot. Rationally they knew that their shield was wafer-thin, but emotionally they felt quite secure.

This was as well for the world outside looked both fragile and threatening. The streets, so crowded an hour or two earlier were now almost deserted. Doorways were barricaded; windows shuttered; curtains drawn. They passed a blind beggar shuffling along an empty alley; stray dogs. Then suddenly, around a corner, they came upon a patrol of youths in combat fatigues strung out across the road and, in the middle, waving a pistol like a conductor's baton, a section commander swaggering with street-wise authority.

The bus slowed and stopped. Gabrielle walked to the open door and spoke to the soldier in Suragan patois. The conversation was incomprehensible to the rest of the party. It began confrontationally but veered towards the friendly and even flirtatious. Eventually the commander gave a sharp laugh, blew a kiss with his left hand and waved the bus through with his pistol-toting right.

"Whose side was he on?" asked Colin White-Lewis, as the door slid shut and Gabrielle sashayed back down the aisle.

"He doesn't know." She smiled. "He was Presidential Guard this morning. By this evening he may be People's Liberation Army. But right now he doesn't know. He's a 'wait and see'."

"Pretty, innit?" said Sharon, gesticulating vaguely at the colonial townscape, run down but replete with wrought-iron porches and balconies. They seemed to be skirting the city centre. The embassy was in a salubrious diplomatic quarter, leafy, quiet, boring, safe and they came on it suddenly and unexpectedly. Heavy iron gates, a coat of arms, Union flag, mown lawns, a porticoed mansion that looked as if it had been flown in *en bloc* from New Orleans. A Rolls-Royce ostentation representing a Ford Escort reality. There was a guard in a sentry box, native, bored, surly, apparently unaware of any disturbance elsewhere. He was locally recruited, a Suragan. He did not look as if he was entirely at home with the English language.

Fisher assumed the role of leader, though without conviction. "Hello!" he said, leaving the bus and standing toe to toe with the guard, though separated by the bars of the embassy gate.

The guard said nothing but looked impassive. He was chewing but not gum. Fisher wondered if it was some exotic substance but assumed, from the treacle-brown stains on the guard's teeth, that it was tobacco. "Hello!" he said again. "We've come to get away from the revolution. We're British passport holders."

The guard continued chewing, said nothing, but extended a hand. "Passport," he said then.

Fisher felt in his pocket and realised that all their passports had been handed in to the reception desk at the Hotel Bristol. "Sorry," he said and lapsed into the pidgin English so many English people adopt when confronted by people who do not speak their language. "No have passports. Passports in hotel. Have ... er ... American Express, Barclaycard, Driver's Licence."

"Don't get smart with me," said the guard unexpectedly. "I'll get the duty officer." And he retreated into his box and spoke into an ancient field telephone. Fisher turned to the bus and made apologetic gestures extending the palms of his hands, rolling his eyes and giving a dumb smile. From behind, and not very far, there came a crackle of gunfire and a couple of bangs.

After what seemed like an interminable delay a young man came crunching across the gravel. He was wearing dark-blue trousers and a starchy white open-necked shirt with blotches of sweat under the arms. He looked irritated, as if his siesta had been interrupted. "Yes?" he said.

"We want to come in," said Fisher.

"Well, you can't. The embassy's closed. Come back on Monday morning."

"I don't think you quite understand," said Fisher. "I have a VIP press party from the UK and there's a revolution going on. We've come here for protection."

"If it's press then you need to speak to Fanshaw. He deals with all that kind of stuff. He'll be here on Monday."

"Now look." Fisher felt a bit of bluster was called for. "This is a very important group. For instance, I have Lady Beatrice White-Lewis with me and a Member of Parliament."

"No, you look," said the man. "The embassy's closed till Monday. Come back then and have a word with Fanshaw. He'll sort you out."

"We're friends of the Ambassador," said Fisher. "Kindly tell him we're here."

"I'm afraid that's not possible. The Ambassador's not here either. He'll be back on Monday."

"Well telephone him."

"I'm afraid that's not possible."

"Well who's in charge here?"

"I am," said the insufferable man.

"And who are you?"

"Pigott. Second Secretary Economics. And now, if you'll excuse me I have work to do." Saying which he turned away and crunched back across the gravel, leaving a group of British passport holders saying very unkind things about the Foreign Office.

36

SICK AS PARROTS

F isher had not bargained for this.

Public relations people had a lot to put up with. Having been on the opposite side of the fence most of his adult life, he knew how journalists despised them and tried to take advantage of them at every opportunity. PR people had to deal with drunken journalists, sex-obsessed journalists and rude journalists who insulted their hosts by not dressing properly and nicking ashtrays, books, bottles of champagne and anything else they could conceal about their persons. PR people also had to grovel to their clients, few if any of whom understood even the basics of public relations. Clients seemed to assume that one could always whistle up any number of hacks who would do exactly as they were told, which meant, in effect, enthusing about the "product" over a full-colour spread in a national paper or magazine. In real life, however, hacks took whatever was offered in the way of bribes and hospitality, then bit the hand that fed them.

All this was understood. But being landed with a busload of reptiles in the middle of an armed revolution was something else. And being turned away by the British embassy was something else again. He had heard of deaths on press trips but these were almost always the result of coronaries brought on by extreme over-indulgence. Journalists got killed in wars. He knew that, too. But the sort of journalist who got killed in such circumstances was a hard-bitten, world-weary old pro who knew exactly what the risks were and who thrived on them. The only person on this trip who even came near this category was Christopher Jones. Sex correspondents and Style correspondents simply didn't qualify. Press trips were low-risk enterprises. Indigestion, hangover and perhaps unwanted pregnancy or social disease were usually the worst that could happen.

"Well," he said, "I suppose we'd better go back to the hotel."

"No." Gabrielle was adamant. "Definitely not the hotel. It will not be safe. The city centre is not the place to be. Look!" She pointed in the direction from which most of the noise was coming. Black smoke was pushing into the sky in two or three spiralling plumes. And even as they looked they could see the dragonfly specks of helicopters approaching from the north.

"I think Gabrielle is probably right," said Jones. "If there *is* fighting, and it very much looks as if there is quite serious fighting, then it will be around the town centre. It's likely to be chaotic. I mean look. If those helicopters do what I think they're going to do then we're better off out of it."

Even as he was speaking there was a sequence of firecracker reports from the sky in the distance and they could see puffs of smoke and flashes of tracer. They watched in silence as the squadron of some half a dozen helicopters made a low pass over the tallish downtown buildings, firing as they went. It was not all one-way traffic. There was also gunfire from the ground. Suddenly someone scored a direct hit. A small glowing blip appeared on the side of one of the helicopters and, in seconds, exploded into a gold and scarlet fireball which fell in slow motion to the ground. It was, in a gruesome, pyrotechnic way, rather beautiful. Like animal lovers at the bullfight, the watching Brits were enthralled and yet ashamed.

"I have an idea," said Gabrielle. "Let us see if Aristotle Plastiras will take us."

"What?" said Fisher. "Plastiras the plutocrat?"

"He is very rich," she said, "the richest man in Surago. And he is my good friend."

"And", said Jones, "he's a serious Anglophile. A sight more pro-British than the Foreign Office."

"I profiled him for *Suave*," said Lesley d'Harcourt. "He's rather a dish in a tacky taverna waiter sort of a way. I'd forgotten one of his places was out here. He's got so many. Rather like a one-man Club Med. Club Aeg in his case. He has his own private army too, doesn't he? Like the Duke of Atholl. Only his people aren't just theme-park warriors. They're ex-SAS. And he's got amazing state-of-the-art kit. He could nuke Cuba if he felt like it."

"Castro Fidels while Havana burns," said Colin facetiously. "That's a cigar metaphor."

"Not a very good one," said Sharon. "If you're talking cigars. Castro would be burning."

"Oh, shut up children!" said Lady Beatrice. "I think Gabrielle's is the best idea. Actually, it's the *only* idea. How far is Plastiras's place?"

"About an hour and a half by bus," said Gabrielle. "The road is very poor."

Fisher clapped his hands unnecessarily. "Right," he said. "The proposal is that we should go to the estate of Aristotle Plastiras and seek refuge with him. Does anybody disagree?"

Nobody disagreed. The decision had already been taken. Group dynamics were curious. Most groups had an opportunity to meet and possibly train together before being put to any test. The ladies' rugby team for instance. But not this one. Fisher's Surago party had to make up the rules as they went along.

The bus had a state-of-the-art stereo system. Gabrielle, mindful of her PR duties, put on a cassette of traditional native melodies sung by the Surago Singers. They had a hypnotic, melancholy quality which was curiously soothing, part Negro Spiritual part Roman Catholic mass. There was a strong sense of the slave plantation about them, of exile and dislocation. As the bus left the suburbs of the city and passed into open countryside they seemed to slip back in time too. In the handkerchief-size fields men stripped to the waist were hacking at banana and sugar cane or at the ground itself. They wielded hoes and machetes and scythes. Occasionally they loped along behind emaciated mules, oxen or horses. Once or twice, in hamlets of shacks and shanties, the Mercedes passed women swathed in bright, tent-like garments doing laundry by the village pump. Occasionally they saw an ancient truck, or bus, or a motorised three-wheeler van, but essentially this was an unmechanised society. It was poor but it was beautiful and the ancient music complemented it perfectly. Sitting in their ample armchairs, air-conditioned against the humidity and insulated against smells and sounds, Fisher's party might almost have been watching a movie in a West End cinema.

They weren't, however. The sense of security into which they were lulled was illusory. On the other side of the tinted windows there was true menace. One trigger-happy revolutionary with a bazooka and they'd all be dead. A land-mine would do just as well. The pitted, pock-marked track could well be studded with the things.

For half an hour the road zigzagged up an ever steeper hillside stepped with terraces of crop and vegetation. Then they were up on a *mesa*like plateau with panoramic views of the plains and foothills down below. Away in the middle a thick black pall of smoke lay over the city. They were, they realised, well out of it and yet here in the middle of nothing very much they were horribly vulnerable. Still, with luck everybody would be tied up in the city.

They stuttered on. The road was flatter up here on the plateau but it was only a dirt surface and not just ridged but littered with flinty stones, rocks and even boulders. They proceeded slowly and with caution. There seemed to be no humans around but there were enormous numbers of goats. This was also the land of the edible rat, but none of these was to be seen. Half-way across they heard a light drone from the sky and a single helicopter appeared. It seemed interested, for it hovered above them for a full five minutes, but it remained high up, well out of range of rocket or anti-aircraft fire from the ground. It showed no inclination to strafe the foreign press and presently turned and headed home.

The land was scrubby here, dotted with juniper bushes, dwarf oak trees and a robust form of sub-tropical gorse. It seemed to go on for ever, but eventually they reached the far rim of the saucer and another view looking out over another plain to another sea of azure blue.

"Shades of stout Cortez," said Colin. "Thalassa, thalassa!"

The others were beginning to find him irritating. Even Sharon.

"We are almost at the ranch," said Gabrielle into her microphone, jerking several of her charges out of a fitful sleep. The road started to descend in sharp, bumpy hairpins. Then suddenly there was on the left an adobe wall. It must have been ten foot tall and looked newly constructed. There was a wire of some kind running along the top. It managed to seem at one and the same time aesthetically attractive and defensively secure. It was the first structure they had seen in Surago which came anywhere near either. It seemed to go on for ever.

"Mr Plastiras owns many thousands of hectares," said Gabrielle. "All is surrounded by this barrier."

The road had improved. It had a tarmac surface. The wall sprouted arc-lights. Then sleeping policemen and even, a little further on, automatic tank-trap contraptions, designed to trap a vehicle in a clamp full of lethal tyre-puncturing teeth. There were no closed-circuit cameras to be seen but you could sense their presence. They rounded a bend and came to a sudden halt. In front of them was a camouflage-khaki Land Rover with a heavy machine-gun mounted on top. Fanned out on either side of the vehicle with automatic rifles raised was a platoon of small men in shorts, boots, immaculate webbing and Australian-style slouch bush-hats. Lesley d'Harcourt had not been quite right about the SAS. Aristotle Plastiras's private army was recruited from an even more alarming source. These looked like Gurkhas from Nepal.

An officer with a loudhailer stood up in the passenger seat of the Land Rover. "Would everyone please leave the bus. Hands on heads, please. There is no need for alarm provided you co-operate."

The accent and the self-assurance suggested Sandhurst training. Provided they did keep their hands above their heads the journalists were probably in safe-keeping. These did not seem to be trigger-happy revolutionaries.

The hot, sticky outside air hit them like a wall of damp loofah. The officer had a major's crowns on his epaulettes. His uniform was starchy clean and creased. He gave no indication of feeling the heat or humidity. He jumped down from his vehicle and walked towards the journalists. He carried a swagger stick, which he flexed as he walked. "This is private property," he said. "You must move on."

"We've come to see your boss." Gabrielle was taking the lead. She was taller than the Major.

"The boss isn't seeing anyone."

"Tell him Gabrielle is here. With a very important, very influential group of British journalists." She gave him one of her smiles and he proved as susceptible as everyone else.

"I'll call the Doctor," he said. "But he has guests; he's tied up; and there's trouble downtown. He's in the mood for keeping himself to himself."

"Just tell him it's Gaby and she needs help." She smiled again and he half melted.

"OK," said the Major. "You're a friend of his? Right?"

"Right," said Gabrielle.

This exercise in walkie-talkie was more encouraging than the one at the British embassy. Both were chain conversations, prone to the misunderstandings of all Chinese whispers, but the links this time were more robust, the speech less sibilant.

"He says you can come in." The Major was obviously surprised. "Get back in and follow me. And don't try anything silly. We've had problems with journalists before, but we know how to solve them. No photographs; no videos; no tape recordings. Understood? This is a secure area. So let's keep it that way."

Odd how even grown-up, fearless hacks become like putty when confronted by a tough-talking major with a swagger stick.

They drove, in silence, through massive automatic gates, over a moat filled with God-knows-what and across a state-of-the-art cattle-grid. It had a sleek, duplicitous appearance like a James Bond special effect.

Once past this security screen, the scenery became a park, safe, idyllic, green, sylvan, hedged, peacocked and springboked to a ha-ha, which separated this sub-tropical Capability Brownland from lawns lush and emerald under the watery caress of an ecologically nightmarish sprinkler system. There were hoops set out for croquet and a lawn-tennis court. Behind it was a building whose dimensions were somewhere between a palace and a small village. Its style was a sort of derivative hotchpotch, with slightly skewed genuflections in any number of not always synchronised directions – a Belgian colonial colonnade, turrets of Highland Gothick, Decimus Burton orangeries, Paxton conservatories, Roman fountains, a touch of Corbusier here, of Frank Lloyd Wright there, not to mention a Vanbrugh dome, a stable block in the manner of Goodwood House and a swimming pool from the school of Cecil B. de Mille.

A number of people were disporting themselves in the pool. In fact, it looked like an all-female water polo game. By the side on the marble terrace three older men were sitting under a couple of off-white Tuscan umbrellas.

One of these, a portly, silver-haired person in a purple towelling robe with gold trim, rose and ambled towards the convoy of jeep and bus. "My dear," said Aristotle Plastiras, removing the Monte

Cristo from his mouth just long enough to plant a smackingly decadent kiss on Gabrielle's butterfly lips, "how unexpected. But how delightful."

37

GOOD FRIENDS SHARE A JOKE

Aristotle Plastiras was not keen on the press. He rarely gave interviews. He was pathologically litigious, employed the most expensive lawyers and always won his libel actions, carefully paying his winnings into the Plastiras Foundation, which was famous for its world-wide good works.

Nevertheless he was very keen on Gabrielle; was impressed by English titles and therefore, by association, impressed by Lady Beatrice; and, of course, like everyone who was anyone he had, in the past, had "dealings" with Jones. Something to do with arms "dealing", which was one of his many interests. Lesley d'Harcourt seemed vaguely familiar to him but he had forgotten the *Suave* interview. It had only been done to publicise his new cancer research unit, had been conducted in his London office and had taken just fifteen minutes. She also looked potentially beddable, as did the pert blonde who, Gabrielle told him, was a reporter from the *Noise*. This was important to Plastiras, who had a very high testosterone count.

Gabrielle introduced everybody individually as they alighted. The ones who found least favour with the Greek plutocrat were Fisher, Colin White-Lewis and Eric Glenn. Plastiras's distaste was, as they say, "evident". Especially when confronted with Glenn. Grubby, free-loading and socialist. All three were anathema. Plastiras was scrubbed, soaped and scented; self-supporting, and crypto-fascist.

"*Mi casa es su casa* Gaby," he said, caressing her bottom with his cigar-free hand. "There are plenty of rooms in the cottages even with the Prime Minister and the rugby team. My niece, Emma, is their captain. She says she is the hooker." He sucked on his Havana and shrugged. "She says she is not a lesbian and I believe her. But some of her team ..." He raised his eyebrows and gazed ruminatively at a small blue cloud of smoke from his cigar.

The girls were still playing water polo but the Prime Minister and Kim Sanderson-Wright had beaten a retreat and vanished behind doors. The press group hovered uneasily, shifting from foot to foot, looking uninvited.

Plastiras did not wish to seem a less than gracious host even if he was an unwilling one. "Welcome to my humble abode!" he said expansively. "You must be exhausted. The staff will show you to your accommodation, then, when you're ready, come back to the pool and have a swim, some champagne, caviar, Suragoberries ... whatever."

The revolution seemed a long way away. So did reality. This was what a proper press trip was supposed to be like. The hacks shuffled off behind a brace of beaming Filipino lackies who had shimmied out through French windows to do their master's bidding. As they disappeared the PM and his aide emerged from hiding.

"This is a bit of a bugger," said Sutton. "I come here to get away from everything and within hours of arriving you've got an entire women's rugby team in the pool, a full-scale armed revolution and now half Fleet Street. It's not what I'd envisaged."

"That's life," said Plastiras.

"Not much of one." The events of the last few days had considerably diminished the Premier. He was like Cinderella after midnight: all pumpkin, no coach. The weakness around mouth and chin which power and accomplished make-up had concealed were now all too apparent. So too was a petulance which in the days of his pomp had looked like a sound no-nonsense refusal to accept no for an answer. He had become a little man again.

"I think one has to accept, Bry, that this one's not going to go away." Sanderson-Wright had always had a gift for stating the obvious in the most fawning manner imaginable. It was one of the characteristics that made him so attractive to the Prime Minister.

That and what, in moments of intimacy, Sanderson-Wright referred to as his "cute bum". "But Ari you're one of the ten richest men on earth. I thought this place was utterly utterly private. But look what's happened."

Mr Plastiras exhaled an exasperated cloud of smoke and put an only superficially affectionate hand on the Prime Minister's shoulder. Bryan Sutton had been useful to Plastiras for many years. He had eased the uneasy, made rough paths smooth and gone very close to legalising the illegal. Plastiras was a great believer in loyalty but it was not, in truth, his strong suit. Now, at last, he realised that little Sutton's usefulness was coming to an end. Which was going to mean a change in their relationship. "It's true", he said, "that we've been unlucky. The odds are against coincidences such as this. But these things happen. And if they happen here how much more likely are they to happen back home in Britain? I think you have to concede that it's going to be a difficult position to sustain."

"Ari, old friend. Do you think these newspaper horrors have come here by accident? It couldn't have been a tip-off?" The Prime Minister eyed his benefactor warily. "They couldn't have known, could they?"

"If there was a leak," said Plastiras, a note of steel entering his honey voice, "it certainly didn't come from here. But it's possible someone was informed. The British security services have always seemed to me about as secure as a *Private Eye* lunch. But that's not the point. Once your press have found a victim they are like a dog with a bone. They won't let it drop. They are like bullies in the playground. Forget right or wrong. They smell weakness as if they were hyenas. That is why I have always been careful to be strong. I am sorry to say this, but they see now that you are mortally wounded. I have to say, as an old friend, that I do not like to see you suffer. I think it is time for you to kiss the hands of Your Majesty and to go."

"I do have to say that I think Aristotle's got a point," said Sanderson-Wright. He had a pipsqueak voice, high-pitched and sibilant, even more so when he was attempting gravitas. "You could have a press conference, now the press are here. And they'll have to toe the line and do as they're told. Otherwise Ari's Gurkhas will deal with them. Hand them over to the people's revolution. I shudder to think what they'd do to the lackeys of the capitalist press."

"Why prolong the agony?" asked Plastiras. "And Kim's talking sense. For once in our lives we have a captive press corps. We can draft a statement, dress it up a bit so that it looks like a news report. The hacks can put their names to it and we'll send it out on the Internet."

"Do I have to speak to them?" Sutton sounded feebler by the second. "I do so hate press conferences. I had a session with those ghastly Majors at the *Intelligence*. It was an absolute nightmare."

"I think you'll have to join them for a drink," said Plastiras, "but we're in command. There's nothing they can do. We control all lines of communication. I'll make sure Major Ranjit impounds all lap-tops, mobiles and carrier pigeons." He laughed in a sickly pastiche of amusement. "And if any of them becomes impertinent we'll throw them to the rugby team." This time his laughter was a shade more convincing.

Luckily for all concerned, there was a coincidence of interest here. In ancient times the journalists would have been thinking furiously about how to outwit their rivals and colleagues. Not here and now in Surago. They were either not that sort of journalist, viz. Sharon and Lesley; or they were too grand like Lady Beatrice; or they were jaded and addled like Eric Glenn; or they were a poacher turned gamekeeper which meant Fisher; or they were practically all piss and wind, in other words Colin White-Lewis. But even if any of them *had* filed an old-fashioned foreign report full of exclusive revelations, quotations, the odd bomb and bullet, a spice of local colour and all the other racy staples of the old journalism, it was all Lombard Street to a China orange that no one in their London offices would have the first idea what to do with it.

This was the sub-text of the whispery meeting that was held in the sitting-room of Lady Beatrice's thatched, bougainvillaea-festooned, palm-fronded cottage on the far side of the croquet lawn with its five-star view of the pellucid azure ocean far below.

"We're in the middle of a serious revolution," said Colin, "and we've found ourselves holed up in the disgraced Prime Minister's secret hideaway. We're journalists. We have a duty to our readers."

"We have to be realistic," said Jones. "First of all, the Gurkhas have confiscated any means of communication. We can't file without their say-so. Which means Plastiras. Which means the

PM. Which means that until we get out we are in a *de facto* censorship situation. Second, we know practically nothing about the so-called revolution. London will be getting it live on CNN so they're in a much better position to write about it than we are. That's if they're interested. And as for the Prime Minister, well, so what? Everyone *knows* he's taking a 'holiday' and that he's almost certainly been screwing his PPS. What can we report that's new? Sweet FA."

"But we can't just sit here doing nothing," said Colin.

"You've done it throughout your career," said his mother. "Why break the habit of a lifetime?"

Colin went scarlet but said no more.

"Realistically," continued Jones, "the best we can hope for is that we will be able to send out one pool report under a communal byline. And we have to accept that Plastiras and the PM will read it and change it, or suppress it if they think fit."

No one spoke.

"So do we agree that this is what we ask for?"

"I think you're right," said Lady Beatrice. "It's not ideal, but we can't do better. I do think, however, that we should insist on little Bryan saying something or other, however anodyne it may be."

"We can but ask." Eric Glenn tried to look sage.

Jones looked round the room. "Agreed?" he asked. "Those in favour?"

Everybody raised a hand, albeit in a rather sheepish fashion.

And so it was arranged.

The press party trooped back to the swimming pool area where the Filipinos served Dom Perignon and canapés which did indeed include caviar. The lady rugby players had vanished, shooed away to another part of the grounds by their host.

After a few moments of very stilted conversation Plastiras pinged his crystal champagne flute with a mother-of-pearl spoon. "Friends," he said, "I am so very pleased that we are all gathered here together, even though it is a quite unexpected pleasure. Unfortunately revolutions make strange bedfellows. Perhaps if his little local difficulties become more serious we may even be welcoming my old friend President Foom before the day is out. Although for his sake we must hope not." He smiled. "Now, I appreciate how frustrating it must be for such a distinguished group of foreign correspondents to be removed from what your newspapers would probably refer to as the 'whiff of cordite'.

Nevertheless, it has happened and there it is. I know that you would all wish to report what is happening here and I would like to be able to make that possible."

He smiled again and looked at the ground in what was intended to seem a gesture of modesty though it came across as self-assured arrogance. "Of course, it will not be possible for you to give a blow-by-blow account of the fighting between government forces and the revolutionaries. However, we have an even more important story on our very own doorstep. As you will understand, it involves the Prime Minister of Great Britain, my honoured guest, and I hope that you and he will be able to come to an understanding about how best to present this quite momentous news.

"I know that he has an announcement to make to you and I hope that when he has made it all of us will be able to sit down and work out a form of communiqué which can be sent to London and which will serve all our interests equally."

Fat chance, thought every one of his audience, but no one spoke.

Bryan Sutton tried a smile and failed. Then he tried a joke with about as much success. "At least", he said, "I haven't excited quite the opposition stirred up by the President of Surago. You journalists are the only people who are really upset. It's not as if the streets of London are exactly running with blood. Not even Fleet Street."

He looked from one face to the next seeking sympathy but, finding none, stumbled on. "I'm giving up," he said. "For the sake of my country, my party, my friends, my colleagues and above all my family I wish to announce that as of this moment I am relinquishing the office of first minister of the Crown."

No one was very impressed by this, nor surprised, and in one or two cases, of course, not even interested. The hypocrisy was all too evident, especially the invocation of Sutton's hapless family!

Eventually Jones spoke. "I think, in the circumstances and with everyone else's permission, we should draft a communiqué. I propose that you and Mr Sanderson-Wright and myself and Lady White-Lewis should form an *ad hoc* committee to achieve this and that as soon as we have completed it this document should be communicated to London by the most effective means possible."

Mr Plastiras winked at Gabrielle. He never ceased to marvel at the ability of the English to abuse the language of Shakespeare and the King James Bible. On the other hand it was a wonderfully versatile tongue that could reduce a moment of such high drama to such bathos. "There are a table and chairs under the weeping avocado," he said. "The rest of us will amuse ourselves while you deal with affairs of state."

38

FILE SOONEST: COPY URGENTLY REQUIRED!!

The revolution in Surago was of virtually no interest to the British press. The only known British correspondent in the Republic was an elderly character who had wandered in to the National Press Club a decade or so earlier as if on the run from a Somerset Maugham short story. His name was Cecil Congreve, or so he said, and he claimed to be a stringer for Reuters, Agence France Presse, UPI, as well as a dozen or so of the leading national papers in the English-speaking world. The English-speaking world, however, had only his word for this. The claim was made on his business card, appearing along with some dodgy sounding academic qualifications, a *Légion d'honneur* and a Military Cross. There was no further evidence to support any of this.

Congreve put over a few lines about the fighting in between pink gins at the club and these, on arrival in London, were duly binned in favour of an abortion for a minor member of the Royal Family, a sex romp involving the cast of a TV soap opera in a Chelsea restaurant, the arrest on drugs charges of a famous footballer, a night-club brawl between two Test cricketers, a scare about beetroot causing breast cancer and all the usual stories for which front pages were regularly held. Marketing and Accounts were not keen on foreign revolutions. They did not build circulation and they involved inordinate expense. The new breed of proprietor now took a similar view.

The dispatch from Château Plastiras, however, had a quite

different effect. Suddenly Royal abortions, sexy starlets, delin-
quent sportsmen and health rumours seemed insignificant even to
Marketing and Accounts. In any case the story came effectively
free of charge. The airport in Surago was temporarily closed, so no
expensive visiting firemen could be dispatched from the UK or
anywhere else.

The basic story was couched in predictably anodyne prose, but
to the Majors at the *Intelligence*, to Chinese Ken, Eddie White and
William Pool at the *Noise* and the *Conscience* this hardly mattered.
If ever there was a case for creative editing this was it. The bones
of the story were there all right. It was now just a question of
putting flesh on them. And that was what modern editors and
proprietors employed "re-write men" for. (In the old days this job
was entrusted to "sub-editors" whose task was to fine-tune the
prose of reporters and correspondents so that they fitted the space
required in the most effective way possible. The job involved
correcting punctuation and grammar, shortening sentences, elimi-
nating gratuitous repetition and general polishing. It also involved
at least a residual respect for the raw "copy". "Rewrite men" were
quite different. They simply took one or two basic facts or ideas
from the article submitted and transmuted this base metal into
gold.)

Sometimes the final result was pure invention and bore no
relation whatever to the original. This was the alchemist's art taken
to perfection, but in the case of the Plastiras file the basic
ingredients were there in platinum spades with diamond knobs on.

"How are we going to play this?" Major Ronald asked Major
Gordon at the *Intelligence*.

"*Furioso*," said his brother who fancied himself as a music buff,
"*con multo* pulling out of stops."

"Pity that Mother and Colin are out there. Do we mention the
fact?"

"I think", said Gordon, "that we should say that they're there as
private guests of Plastiras. We'll put Christopher Jones's name on
the main piece as 'Chief Special Correspondent', then we'll
mention Mother as 'Proprietor Emeritus' and Colin as 'former
Literary Editor of the *Intelligence* who resigned recently on
grounds of ill-health."

" 'Ill health' or 'Personal reasons'?"

Gordon pursed his lips. "I prefer 'ill health'," he said. "It's not
entirely untrue. He'd been pretty seedy recently. Physically, I

mean. And mentally I'd say he was very nearly off his rocker, though I'd rather back-pedal on that. 'Personal reasons' could rebound on us. It suggests 'moral turpitude'. And I can just see one or two unscrupulous people saying that 'personal reasons' were just a euphemism for you and me."

"Mmm."

"Do we run the actual text of the file?"

"I'd rather not. It's frightfully dreary. We'll just lift the guts of it. Then I'll write the lead myself. Jones won't mind. I've done it often enough in the past." Ronald had always fancied himself as a writer and having no style of his own was happiest trying to ape other people's. "Then a massive leader about the country being at a crossroads; the importance of 'sleaze'; private morality and public performance; all that sort of thing. Then a feature on Surago. Profile of Plastiras. Profile of President Foom. Piece on Marxism/Leninism in Central America. One or two 'Why Oh Why?' pieces from Paul or Boris or Janet or Geoffrey. I suppose something on women's sports. That should do."

"Mmm."

The dialogue in Chinese Ken's penthouse was, naturally, more abrasive. He dealt with his editors separately. "Great story," he said to Eddie White, "and you've got sexy Sharon on the case?"

"Yup. Good eh?" agreed White. "Can't get through to her, which is probably just as well. I'm not convinced she'd make much sense in a situation like this."

"So who's going to write her copy?"

"Team effort," said White, "and we'll dig out one or two of her old pieces and rejig them. She's done a lot on sex in sport so we can work that up into a steamy piece about women's rugby. Also she did stuff on alfresco sex and sex in hot places. Then there's sex and politics, sex and power, sex and secretaries. What about sex and Plastiras?"

Ken suddenly seemed agitated. "Don't mess with Ari Plastiras," he said. "He's major league. I want him onside."

"Then I think we should run a *Noise* campaign to send in the SAS to rescue the rugby team. And the hacks as well. So we can have sex and the SAS. And sex and revolutions. It's good stuff. I'm going to get someone to run a piece on President Foom's girls."

"Who's President Foom, for God's sake?"

"He's the bloke in charge. Or who *was* in charge until this thing blew up."

"Did he have girls?" The proprietor seemed genuinely curious.

"Haven't a clue, boss," said White. "But I've told Sharon's assistant to do us eight hundred words on the presidential harem with a good dose of S and M. Some sort of hanky-panky in the state torture chamber. That always goes down well in Essex. And Melissa's good at that. She used to be on the staff at *Rubber Gear*. She did a brilliant piece on 'Dirty Deans and Kinky Canons in the Cathedral Close'. Magic."

"Didn't they sue?"

"Yeah. Brilliant."

"Great." Ken rubbed his hands. "It's good that Sharon's out there."

"Yup," said Sir Eddie. "I just had a little hunch when the press trip came up. Know what I mean? Something in the gut said to me, Eddie old son, this one's for Sharon. Long odds, but I sort of had a feeling something was about to blow up down there. And knowing what Plastiras has put into party funds *and* what he and Bryan Sutton have done for each other in the past, there was always a chance of the two getting together. So one way or another it seemed worth the risk, sending Sharon. Funny thing, instinct. You've either got it or you haven't."

This was all completely untrue. The whole thing was a fluke. But all the same Eddie White was the kind of man to whom luck adhered like glue. Or muck.

This was not, on the whole, true of William Pool. He himself scarcely believed in luck, let alone his own. He thought that whatever he had achieved was the result of ability in the abstract and hard graft. Others took the view that his rise to the editorship of the *Conscience* was a triumph of mediocrity over mind and matter and yet that hardly explained what had happened. Chinese Ken, who disliked him very much and yet was responsible for the promotion, recognised three qualities which were unusual in editors – though less so than in the past. First, Pool, unlike Eddie White, never came within a pack let alone an Ace of saying no or even boo to the Proprietor. Most editors sooner or later had delusions of grandeur. Pool had delusions, but they were limited to a narrow field. When it came to relations with Ken he was a walking affirmative, the ultimate yes-man. Second, he was very competent, in a way which other editors sooner or later found boring and beneath them. Pool was a hands-on editor and his hands were safe. He met his deadlines; he listened to lawyers; deferred to money-men, could even read a balance sheet. Third, in sublime contravention of the previous two qualities, he suffered from absolute self-belief. He honestly thought that he mattered; that he had a brain; and that when the *Conscience* spoke the world listened. There might have been a time when this was true and when a *Conscience* editorial toppled governments, caused a run on the pound or even disturbed a ministerial or episcopal breakfast. These days had long since gone and almost everyone knew it with the exception of Pool. Someone who really understood how far the paper had declined would have felt uncomfortable in the Editor's chair. Not Pool. He believed he was the continuation of a glorious past, whereas he was actually its ghost.

"And how will the *Conscience* be handling the news from Surago?" Ken asked him.

"Ah," said Pool. "We've actually got a bit of a scoop on our hands. I was dining at my old college the other day and one of the other guests was an awfully interesting man called Simenon. Dr Simenon, actually. He's no less than the Suragan Ambassador here although if, as seems likely, the Foomists are ousted I rather think he'll be seeking asylum. Anyway he's writing a leader-pager on the Suragan economy and the socio-political effects of disasters on the sugar harvest, together with the financial losses concomitant with a failure to channel essential investment into the infrastructure. Surago may seem just a far-away place of which we, ahem, know nothing, but it's actually of huge strategic importance because of the satellite tracking station. It's also, I feel, something of a paradigm for the third world in many of its contemporary shapes and forms."

"Have you not heard the news from Surago?" asked Ken menacingly.

"I most certainly have!" replied the truculent Editor, almost forgetting where he was and to whom he was talking. "Unlike some other papers I could mention not a million miles from here, we do actually maintain some sort of foreign representation and we have a man there by the name of Congreve. Quite a veteran, I'm told, though I've never actually met him. Anyway, he filed soonest. Couldn't say much because the situation's still confused, but I'm sure he'll be back with more before the first edition."

"When did you last check your e-mail?" the proprietor wanted to know.

"I'm not sure I entirely believe in e-mail as a matter of fact," said Pool. "Generally speaking, I leave that to others. Editing, I always believe, is essentially a cerebral activity. Technology's for technicians. Computers can do a lot but they can't write deathless prose."

Ken sighed. "God give me grace," he said. "The Prime Minister has resigned. He is in Surago holed up at one of the many fortresses Aristotle Plastiras maintains around the globe. He is there with Sanderson-Wright, the British women's rugby team and a minibus-load of journalists of various descriptions. Here . . ." He tossed across a printout of the Surago statement. "You'll see who the hacks are. Nobody from the *Conscience* I'm sorry to see. Unless the man Fisher is yours. You have a Fisher on staff, don't you?"

"Um." Pool went white. "It's a very common name," he said, "and this Fisher appears to be unattached. In any case I fired our Fisher some time ago."

The Proprietor's eyes narrowed to the slits from which his nickname derived. "Why did you do that?" he enquired with an equanimity which did not deceive even Pool.

The editor of the *Conscience* swallowed hard. "I didn't think he was very good at his job," he said.

His boss stared back at him, unblinking. "Ah," he said.

39

TRUNK CALLS

I t was the way the Gurkhas handled the lost luggage which upset everything.

The British press party was naturally at a loss without its bags. Journalists had come a long way since the 1930s when Evelyn Waugh and W. F. Deedes covered the Abyssinian campaign with enough trunks, cases, portmanteaux and valises to establish a small tented town. The modern hack rather prided him- or herself on "travelling light", although the term was relative. Several of Fisher's group had lap-tops, modems and portable telephones. The women, in particular, also had a considerable number of what they mysteriously referred as their "things". These were supposed by the men to consist mainly of incomprehensible feminine toiletries. Both Sharon and Lesley were certainly burdened with an enormous quantity of pantyhose and knickers. Lady Beatrice had a serious medicine chest with pills for purifying water, for combating diarrhoea and constipation, ointments for relieving snake and insect bites, cream for dealing with sunburn, footrot and and so on. She had a wariness about "abroad" honed over a lifetime of foreign travel. Some of this must have passed to her son. Colin had brought along what he described as "emergency rations". These resembled the tuck-box with which Lady Beatrice had once packed him off to boarding-school and included dried apricots, Kendal Mint Cake, a stick of thin American pepperoni, walnuts and several cans of self-heating cream of mushroom soup. One would have thought he was about to climb Mount Everest in the early 1950s. Eric Glenn, of course, carried alcohol, mainly vodka, to augment his duty-free.

And then there was Jones's diary.

Although it was only the latest volume of this compendious work, the current book already contained tens of thousands of words in Jones's small, neat hand. As he himself was – fairly – happy to admit, the work was a curate's egg of a production but the good bits were, if he said so himself, very good indeed. He was still not sure whether he would eventually attempt publication in edited but raw form as *The Jones Diaries* or whether he would make them the basis for his memoirs or autobiography (*A Life of Letters, Life at the Top, Stalking the Corridor, My Own Correspondent* – he enjoyed playing with titles, visualising book-jackets, counting his royalties before they were advanced). His diaries were his private pension plan. Their loss would have been a catastrophe. "Plastiras has very kindly agreed to let Major Chapati and some of his men go into town and collect our stuff from the hotel," he said to Lady Beatrice. He had taken a dislike to the Nepalese Major commanding Plastiras's private army and invented this derogatory nickname. He hotly denied being any sort of racist but nevertheless was pretty firmly of the opinion that the world would be a better place if left in the hands of the British officer class.

"Plastiras isn't such a bad sort if firmly handled," he added. "He's like a lot of foreigners, particularly rich ones. Give him the merest hint of weakness and he'll be all over you, but just remind him who's in charge and he's quite amenable."

Lady Beatrice had seen this point of view deployed in many parts of the globe in the crepuscular years of British power and influence, and she was sceptical. Despite appearances, her convict ancestry made her dubious about the British officer class and this inherent suspicion had, on the whole, been confirmed by the evidence of her own eyes. "Beware of Greeks bearing gifts," she said. They were sitting together in the shade of a luxuriantly weeping native tree. Gabrielle told them it was called "Rich man's folly".

Jones laughed. "I just hope the Suragans don't try any funny stuff. I saw Chapati and his chaps head off in a couple of jeeps and a five tonner, and they certainly put the fear of God into me. Armed to the teeth. All the latest gear. And every one of them itching to unsheath his kukri and cut throats. The most lethal collection of baggage handlers I've ever seen."

Lady Beatrice smiled and sipped from a glass of iced Earl Grey. From the distant pool the cries of the women's rugby team still rent the air. "Those girls seem remarkably high-spirited," she said. "Where's everyone else?"

"Siesta, I imagine." He leant back in his cane chair. "Are you happy with our pooled dispatch?"

"Oh," she said, "I'm past caring. Too old. Been there, done that. I wouldn't have agreed to the idea in my prime. But ... well ..."

Jones didn't believe a word of this. He felt certain that her ladyship's competitive journalistic edge was still undimmed. Nevertheless she *was* old. As he watched, the old girl put down her glass and settled in her chair. Her eyes closed and after a while her mouth fell open, though not wide, and she began to snore. Jones watched and day-dreamed. After a while he too must have fallen asleep because he suddenly jerked awake as half a dozen loud bangs sounded in the middle distance, followed by the noise of engines over-revved in low gear. Seconds later the small Gurkha convoy sped down the drive. Major Chapati sat in the lead vehicle, very stiff beside the driver. Seeing Jones awake in his chair he waved and smiled, teeth gleaming bright below his trim black toothbrush moustache.

He looked very pleased with himself.

Jones and Lady Beatrice dozed. The noise from the pool died away. Somewhere in the shrubbery a banana-tailed drongo sang its lonely song. The sun began to sink towards the sea. The sun was a vivid blood orange, the sea a pool of inky blue. In different circumstances the phrase or something very like it would have turned up in one of Fisher's press releases and been repeated by his guests with a few marginal tweaks to avoid charges of plagiarism. Thus the sun would become a tangerine, an exotic Suragan satsuma, a wounded orb, and so on and so forth. In travel-writing circles this was known as "creative writing". The sea would have undergone a similar metamorphosis.

But these were not normal circumstances, a fact of which Jones and Lady Beatrice were reminded a few minutes later, when Major Chapati hove in sight. On reaching their chairs he executed a smart salute which Jones thought bordered on the insolent. "My men have retrieved your party's luggage," said the Major, "and I have had it taken to your rooms. It will now ..." He smiled with what

Jones definitely interpreted as insolence. "So it will now be possible for you to change for dinner. Mr Plastiras expects everyone in the conservatory for drinks at nineteen hundred hours. Dinner is in the banqueting hall later." The Major bowed slightly, raised his swagger stick to his beret, turned crisply on his heel and sauntered away.

"Cheeky bugger," said Jones.

"A relief, though," said Lady Beatrice. "I never feel entirely comfortable without my things."

"Quite so," said Jones.

And the two of them retired.

On reaching his room Jones was relieved to see his case. His computer, however, was nowhere to be seen and on opening the case it was immediately obvious that someone else had been through it. His clothes, always immaculately packed, had been disturbed. Whoever had replaced them had done so neatly enough, but not with Jones's own fastidiousness. Seriously concerned, he unlocked the little padlock to the safe compartment in the lid where he kept the diary. There was nothing there. Someone had picked the lock. Jones swore. It was not a hugely secure lock but good enough to deter the average thief who, in any case, would not be interested in a mere notebook with handwritten scribbles. However, any half-decent soldier with British military training could have dealt with the device without any problem.

On the bedside table there was a list of phone numbers. There was one for Plastiras and another for something called "Orderly Room", which he took to be where the soldiers were. He dialled this number first.

When it answered Jones spoke authoritatively in his best Gurkhali. Seconds later Major Chapati came on the line sounding smug.

"I am missing my computer and a notebook," said Jones crossly. "Do you know anything about it?"

"Yes indeed, sir. We have the items here. They are quite safe."

"They may well be safe but I need them here."

"I'm afraid that is not possible, sir. Mister Plastiras's personal orders. There is an emergency. He has particularly asked that all electronic devices be kept safely here."

"My notebook isn't an electronic device."

"I am sorry, sir. I am obeying orders. We are concerned that it may contain sensitive material."

"Oh, for God's sake."

He put the phone down with a crash, thought about calling Plastiras, but decided against it. For a few moments he sat on the end of his bed, thinking. Then he began to smile. OK, everyone had played ball up until now, but if Plastiras was going to behave like this then they would have to retaliate. The time for politeness was past. He rose to his feet, straightened his tie and marched off to have words with Lady Beatrice. If she was onside, which he thought she would be, then there would have to be a council of war. He had an idea and he was fairly sure it was a good one.

His instinct was sound. Lady Beatrice's medical supplies had been confiscated. So had Colin's dried apricots and Kendal Mint Cake. Lesley was missing an item too delicate to mention. Sharon was not so delicate and was really really cross to think about Major Chapati and his men having a male-chauvinist giggle over her brand-new, five-speed, battery-operated Swiss doodah. Eric Glenn said he couldn't be sure but he was pretty positive that he was a couple of bottles of vodka short. And so on. Certainly all electrical devices from shavers to portable phones had gone missing. Even Fisher was cross, though as PR in charge he tried to inject a voice of sanity and restraint into the proceedings.

He was overruled.

"I propose", said Jones, after everyone had expressed their sense of shock-horror, mainly, of course, on behalf of their readers, their public and their right to freedom of expression – and not wounded *amour propre*, alcohol withdrawal symptoms and libido satisfaction deprivation, "that we promise the captain of the ladies' rugby team a slap-up dinner with as much alcohol and as many Chippendale full-Monty look-alikes as they can handle if they stage a diversion diverting enough for us to regain our stolen goods."

"Are you sure this is wise?" asked Fisher, thinking of the reputation of Fisher Cadogan Fisher.

"Probably not," said Lady Beatrice. "But there are moments when wisdom is a much over-rated commodity. This is one of them."

Sharon was dispatched to fetch the ladies' captain, Plastiras's niece, Emma.

Emma listened with gleeful incredulity.

"Let me get this straight," she said. "You want me and the girls to take Mr Plastiras, the Prime Minister and Mr Sanderson-Wright and debag them all and throw them in the swimming pool, and keep them in there while we sing rude songs."

"Yes." The press party was unanimous.

"And in return you buy us dinner?"

"Yes."

"With strippers?"

"Yes!"

"Not a problem," said Emma. "When do you want us to start?" Jones looked at his watch.

"How long do you need?"

"No time at all," said Emma. "Call it five minutes?"

"Make it ten," said Jones. "Good luck. Don't hurt them, just get their trousers off, throw them in and keep singing."

"You betcha," said Emma.

"OK," said Jones when she had left the room looking elated, "as soon as we hear them start we wait until Major Chapati and Co. go to the rescue, then we attack the orderly room and retrieve our gear, after which it's every man for himself. If you don't have your own means of communication use the phones, which I guess will still be working. Somebody ought to contact Congreve at the Press Club so he can cover any outlets we haven't thought of. And may I suggest, in the nicest possible way, that we ought to take this opportunity of giving a little publicity to Mr Pigott of the British embassy. I think the British public should be told how our diplomats treat British refugees during foreign revolutions."

It was just over ten minutes later that the group heard the first sounds of mayhem. Even from a distance the noise of thirty or so female rugby players baying for trousers was awesome, blood-curdling, almost primaeval. Fisher and Jones, Eric Glenn and Colin White-Lewis looked at each other and shuddered. This, they all felt, was feminism red in tooth and claw.

"Oggy, oggy, oggy . . . oi, oi, oi . . . oggy, oggy, oggy . . . oi, oi, oi!" The Prime Minister and Catemite Kim stood no chance. Plastiras might put up some resistance, but Jones doubted it. One British lady rugby player was worth a dozen male foreigners. As for the Gurkhas, well, had the rampaging sportspeople been male they would have skewered them in seconds, but Jones was banking on the chivalrous values of the British military bolstered by the ancient traditions of the mountain kingdom from which the Major's men all hailed. Johnny Gurkha would not lay a hand on a woman even under orders from the sinister Mr Plastiras.

From outside, a siren sounded, then military commands and the clatter of Army boots. The "oggy, oggy" chant grew louder, more menacing and, it seemed to the press party, triumphant.

"OK, chaps," said Jones. "Let's go for it. Just remember – you're Fleet Street's finest. Tell it to the world . . . the truth, the whole truth and nothing but the truth."

And out into the anarchic dusk charged the ladies and gentlemen of the press.

What followed was disciplined at first, then confused. As Jones had hoped, the alarmed soldiers had vacated the orderly room leaving the door open with only one young private soldier in nominal charge. Jones felled him with a single deft blow, which rather shocked the rest of the party but also had the effect of bolstering their confidence. On a table in the middle of the room, neatly arranged, were the portable phones, modems and lap-tops from the Hotel Bristol.

"Get your gear and scatter!" ordered Jones in passable imitation of an SAS commander.

And they did.

He calculated that they had as much as half an hour before Chapati and his men subdued the riot and realised the real reason for it. Only then would they come looking. He was, in fact, unduly cautious. It was almost an hour before the last member of the press was apprehended. This, unexpectedly, was Eric Glenn, who had found Plastiras's study and ensconced himself at Plastiras's desk, discovered a bottle of Napoleon brandy and a box of huge Suragan cigars and somehow managed to get through to Congreve, the clapped-out all-purpose Foreign Correspondent in the bar of the Press Club. Glenn's imagination, fuelled by the brandy and cigars, had run as colourfully amok as the ladies' rugby team. The line to downtown was crackly and Glenn's speech slurred, so that Congreve did not understand everything that the Member of Parliament told him. Besides, he too had drink taken. Nevertheless, he got the drift: "Orgy", "Swimming Pool", "Naked Prime Minister and Megamillionaire Philanthropist".

"Swimming Pool" was particularly good. It provoked the old hack's memories of Christine Keeler and Mandy Rice-Davies at Cliveden in the good old days. Congreve sharpened his pencil and prepared to wax lyrical.

Most of the others managed to get something through, although there were some communication problems. It was infuriating, as the minutes ticked away, to be told by one's flickering screen that one's "PPP negotiation" had been "timed out" or that there was an error with one's "windsock". Sharon, in particular, was unamused to be told by the *Noise* switchboard that Mr van Blanco was out to lunch and why didn't she call back in an hour's time.

"I'm in Central America and we're having a revolution," she wailed.

"That's your problem," said the operator and hung up.

This, of course, was a common reaction in London, but gradually the mood changed as executives like van Blanco drifted back from lunch (one or two of the more senior newspaper people did still indulge in this practice while banning it for their subordinates).

"What's this story about the Prime Minister being raped by women rugby players in a swimming pool in Central America?" asked Chinese Ken.

"The PM seems to have organised a putsch in Surago," said Major Gordon to Major Ronald. "The UN are going into special session. Perhaps he's been planning this all along."

"I don't know what to make of the stuff coming out of Surago," said little Pool. "Apparently the Prime Minister's taken command of a battalion of Gurkhas and is putting down a revolution. I didn't know we had troops there. And I'm told a second secretary at the embassy has massacred a whole lot of women rugby players."

"Sharon's filed," said van Blanco. "There's been an orgy all right."

"I want pictures," said Ken. "I don't care how or where or why or what, but I want pictures. Artists' impressions will do."

And so on. Next morning every paper led with the story. There were maps, all wildly inaccurate. There were photographs of all the known participants including several of naked ladies alleged to be the ladies' rugby team taking an early bath. There were rude drawings of Amazonian nudes having their wicked ways with the PM, his PPS and Plastiras.

There were headlines such as "SURAGO SEX SHOCK", "PM'S PLASTIRAS PASSION PLOT", "BRITISH RUGGER BUGGERS RUN RIOT IN HOLIDAY ISLE" and (in the *Intelligence*), "CONFUSION GROWS AS PRIME MINISTER DISAPPEARS IN WAR-TORN REPUBLIC".

Every paper had a completely different version of events but every editor and every proprietor finally agreed about one thing. "Great story!" they all said.

40

POST-MORTEM, AD ASTRA

The revolution in Surago was abortive and it was suppressed nastily and brutishly. The Presidential Guard remained loyal to Methuselah Foom, although there was a widespread feeling that next time he might not be so lucky. And there *would* almost certainly be a next time, probably not far off. Fighting of one sort or another went on for about a week, mainly in the capital although there were unconfirmed reports of rural massacres. Much of the killing had nothing to do with the so-called revolution. The insurrection was a good excuse for settling old scores and family feuds, as well as for looting, rape and indiscriminate mayhem. There were several lynchings and when the TV crews and photographers did finally arrive there were the usual almost obligatory pictures of maimed and rotting bodies in the streets, as well as one or two hanging from lamp-posts or palm trees. A number of these won prizes.

The fighting was unpleasant but despite William Pool's original opinion it was of no more than fleeting significance to the world beyond Surago. No one cared.

However, the Surago revolution did pass into the mythology of contemporary British history because of the peculiar British coincidences which accompanied it. Although the scandalous affair of their Prime Minister was already well known and almost universally believed, it had always been denied by those concerned and the Premier himself had clung on to power. It was only in

Surago that Bryan Sutton finally resigned and although he never actually admitted the affair the fact that his companion in his hideaway was Kim Sanderson-Wright suggested only one thing. It is traditional, of course, for the Prime Minister formally to surrender his office to the monarch but Sutton never did. Instead, he remained on Surago in a villa provided by the Foom government. Here he was said to be working on his memoirs, but although they were the subject of a fiercely contested literary auction it was rumoured that the former Prime Minister was, from the outset, suffering from a particularly severe form of writer's block.

The SAS did indeed swoop in to "rescue" Fisher's press party, including Gabrielle Casson and the ladies' rugby team. There were questions about this in the House of Commons and all the usual suspects wanted to know what it was costing the British taxpayer. The Armed Services Minister replied that the SAS had been on routine excercises in Belize and it had been useful for them to tackle a real-life emergency. The British press had been ferried by Chinook helicopter to a Royal Navy cruiser, which just happened to be on exercises off the Suragan coast. They were then dropped off in Mexico, whence they flew home with British Airways and not, to their intense relief, with Suragair.

The story was a brief sensation, but not one of any lasting significance. It filled the papers for a day or so, but then the papers and their readers became bored. And in all truth, there was nothing more to be wrung from it. The journalists had not even been in Surago long enough to write the features they had originally intended, though this did not prevent Lesley d'Harcourt from filling four pages of *Suave* magazine with a bizarre article about "Suragan Hi-Life" (sic). And, of course, Sharon managed Suragan sex-life with some highly questionable diagrams showing imaginative positions and some colourful but anatomically unlikely information regarding penis gourds.

Christopher Jones filed a number of classified reports for the benefit of various arms of the Intelligence Service and followed up with important lunches at the Athenaeum, the Travellers and the Rag.

There was something of a family rapprochement at the *Intelligence*. The story had given both Lady Beatrice and Colin a five-minute fame. Lady Beatrice made a number of television appearances from which she emerged as characterful and indomitable – so much so that she was offered her own chat show. Her two elder sons reasoned that on the one hand this would keep her fully occupied and therefore out of their hair and on the other that it was a sufficiently important forum to be a potential nuisance if used against them but, conversely, quite useful to have onside. Not that Lady Beatrice was easily placated.

"How sharper than a serpent's tooth it is to have a thankless child," she said acidly to her two elder sons.

To which Gordon, surprising himself with his erudition, responded: "No, no Mother – 'The oldest hath borne most: we that are young / shall never see so much, nor live so long.' "

After which the old lady felt morally obliged at least to go through the motions of forgiving and forgetting.

Colin, who had a terminal row with Sharon on the flight home, seemed crestfallen and saddened, and said that he wanted to retreat to Jura and write a novella. It was no hardship for the *Intelligence* to make this possible and to allow him to pen the occasional pretentious review for the paper's ever shrinking literary pages.

Eric Glenn returned to the back-benches, where he rumbled and gurgled like some small semi-extinct volcano whose eruptions became ever less rambunctious, until he resembled nothing more remarkable than a bubbling mud-flat in a permanent state of belching but unthreatening bother.

Gabrielle was accepted for a doctorate course in communications and culture at the University of Taunton (Minehead campus).

But the person who benefited most from the curious episode, as befitted the person who was most responsible for it, was Fisher.

Arriving back at Heathrow and not, mercifully, the appalling London Greenspace, he was standing in the queue for a cab when a chauffeur-driven Jaguar stopped alongside him. The back door opened and a familiar voice invited him in. It was little William Pool.

When the driver had put the luggage in the boot and Fisher had made himself comfortable, Pool said "Thank you, Trumper" and then, to Fisher, "How was Surago?"

"Suracome Surago," said Fisher fatuously. He had travelled Club class and had made free with the claret.

"I'm sorry I fired you," said Pool.

"You said you didn't. You said it was 'management'."

"Yes," said Pool awkwardly. "Well, I've persuaded them it was a mistake."

"It's taken long enough," said Fisher. "What changed their mind?"

"Well, actually . . ." The car emerged from the tunnel into the early morning grey of the M4 approaches. Pool ran a palm through thinning hair. "Well, as a matter of fact, the boss didn't realise that I, well, management, had got rid of you in the interests of, well, downsizing and all that. And when he realised that you had set up this whole extraordinary Surago story he was quite cross. In fact, the long and the short of it is that he wants you back."

"My old job?" Fisher thought for a moment. "I'm not sure I want it."

"Not necessarily," said Pool. "As far as I can see you can have any job you like. And name your price. But you'll find out soon enough. We're having breakfast with him. The Savoy Grill. You don't have to tell me *anything*. I'm only the Editor. Just Ken's messenger boy."

Fisher laughed.

There are many ways to be hired, he pondered: hands-on, hands-off; take-it-or-leave-it; name-your-price; you'll regret-it-if-you-don't; the Editor-in-the-back-of-the-limo; the Proprietor-at-breakfast-in-the-Savoy-Grill.

To himself, silently, he thought: the wheel is come full circle. Aloud he mused, "I shall need to bring my new colleague. And I'm not going back to that grotty shoe-box of an office." He smiled. "Meanwhile I shall have the kippers," he said, "and then we'll see."